FORGE BOOKS BY T. R. HENDRICKS
THE DEREK HARRINGTON SERIES

The Instructor

The Infiltrator

Praise for the Derek Harrington series

"Fast-moving, hard-hitting, and raw—a worthy follow-up to his acclaimed debut that will have military thriller fans ripping through the pages until the very end." —Taylor Moore, author of *Ricochet*

"Chock-full of nonstop combat and tactical scenes that will keep your pulse pounding. But at its most basic, *The Infiltrator* succeeds as a poignant story of a man fighting for his family."
—Steve Urszenyi, author of *Perfect Shot*

"Derek Harrington is the kind of hero you want to root for. He is defined by not only his determination and his unique skill set, but also his humanity."
—Lauren Nossett, author of *The Resemblance*

"Topical, relentlessly paced, and supercharged, T. R. Hendricks's writing barely gives you time to catch your breath. Fans of Hendricks will delight in his second thrill ride." —I. S. Berry, author of *The Peacock and the Sparrow*

"*The Instructor* was like the roaring of thunder, announcing a major talent in T. R. Hendricks. *The Infiltrator* is a lightning strike of a novel: electric, brutal, and brilliant. This sequel shocks in all the right ways." —Bill Schweigart, #1 Audible bestselling author of *The Guilty One*

"*The Instructor* is an unexpected pleasure, crackling with intensity, vivid with authenticity and emotion. T. R. Hendricks writes like a knife fight on a moonless night—fast, brutal, and bloody."

—Nick Petrie, bestselling author of *The Breaker* and other Peter Ash novels

THE INFILTRATOR

T. R. HENDRICKS

Tor Publishing Group
New York

NOTE: If you purchased this book without a cover, you should be aware that this book is stolen property. It was reported as "unsold and destroyed" to the publisher, and neither the author nor the publisher has received any payment for this "stripped book."

This is a work of fiction. All of the characters, organizations, and events portrayed in this novel are either products of the author's imagination or are used fictitiously.

THE INFILTRATOR

Copyright © 2024 by T. R. Hendricks

All rights reserved.

A Forge Book
Published by Tom Doherty Associates/Tor Publishing Group
120 Broadway
New York, NY 10271

www.torpublishinggroup.com

Forge® is a registered trademark of Macmillan Publishing Group, LLC.
EU Representative: Macmillan Publishers Ireland Ltd., 1st Floor, The Liffey Trust Centre, 117–126 Sheriff Street Upper, Dublin 1, DO1 YC43, Ireland.

ISBN 978-1-250-83297-9

The publisher of this book does not authorize the use or reproduction of any part of this book in any manner for the purpose of training artificial intelligence technologies or systems. The publisher of this book expressly reserves this book from the Text and Data Mining exception in accordance with Article 4(3) of the European Union Digital Single Market Directive 2019/790.

Our books may be purchased in bulk for specialty retail/wholesale, literacy, corporate/premium, educational, and subscription box use. Please contact MacmillanSpecialMarkets@macmillan.com.

First Edition: April 2024
First Mass Market Edition: June 2025

Printed in the United States of America

10 9 8 7 6 5 4 3 2 1

FOR MICHAELA AND CHARLOTTE

My KK and Charlie

Of all the things that I imagine, never could I have imagined the joy that you give me.

THE INFILTRATOR

1

The time had come to hit the hammer against the anvil, instead of just letting them feel the fire of the forge.

It's simple. They're not getting the picture. Not his words but they roll around inside his head all the same. Passed down from higher-ups, the sentiment preceded the new shift in strategy. A harder approach. Time for a pounding.

Easy to say when you're in a conference room back in D.C.

Derek Harrington, retired Marine Force Recon and wilderness survival expert, now press-ganged into service with the FBI, doesn't have that luxury. As point man in the effort against the domestic terrorist group Autumn's Tithe, not only does he have to watch the hammer fall, but he has to be the one to swing it.

Raising his binoculars, he scans the hilltop directly west of his position. He's in a good spot. Slightly lower than the hill across from him but the difference in elevation is negligible. Derek can still observe everything. The West Virginia trees and foliage provide ample cover as he lies in the prone position, glassing the enemy's camp.

A long, low saddle runs between the hills. Off to his left a two-track dirt road winds its way from west to east through the forest floor. Just enough of a break in the canopy allows him to see along its length. For his part, Derek only has to turn his head slightly and he can observe the entirety of the path as it weaves past his hill and continues on. The perfect vantage point for viewing comings and goings as well as the compound.

Across the way he can see their silhouettes moving through the trees. The larger shadows of cabins and workshops fill in the spaces between the pines and oaks. It's a clear morning and although the sun shines down, a mountain chill hangs in the air. Perhaps it's the air, or perhaps it's just him. Maybe he's getting soft in his old age. These people are trying to commit mass murder, after all, but still. Some of those shadows across the way are no bigger than his boy back home.

The thought intrudes despite Derek's operational disposition. Michael. His boy. His poor boy. A pang of heartache ripples through him. Will his son ever be the same after what happened? Michael seems to be a normal, happy kid so long as he can stay in his bed and play video games most of the time. Venturing out of his room, much less the house, could be a crapshoot with how he would respond. Getting him to school was difficult on the best of days and downright impossible on the worst. The only things that Michael regularly enjoys are playing baseball and fishing, no doubt reverting back to those activities for the comfort they brought to him before his kidnapping. Derek would need to keep easing him out there. Helping Michael to adjust to life outside the walls of the home.

They're not getting the picture. Send them a message.

The directive pulls Derek back to the mission at hand. The intel developed from the logging camp in upstate New York had given the FBI enough of a lead to put him into the field eight weeks later, this time in northwestern Pennsylvania near the Allegheny National Forest. It didn't take long for Derek to track down the second compound and call in the cavalry. The group there had received a lot of support staff from the first camp and had barely begun preparations for any sort of attack before HRT rolled them up without a shot being fired.

The subsequent interviews and plea deals divulged even more intel, which when processed and war-gamed by enough people in suits standing in rooms making themselves feel important, gave Derek his next foray. That time it was into a little no-man's-land where the southwestern tip of Pennsylvania meets the West Virginia border.

Word from the mastermind still at large had reached this cell ahead of him, despite what the Feds would discover later as an attempt to alter their tradecraft and forgo the use of electronic communications. The people there were well on the way to staging their attack, but in their haste they overlooked other logistics. When Derek called it in and the FBI arrived, the entire camp threw themselves at the feet of their apprehenders, begging for food, clothes, and an escape from the brutality of winter.

Still, the correlation was apparent. Not only was Autumn's Tithe growing more sophisticated, they were accelerating their operational timeline. Whereas that crazy old bastard, Marshal, had wanted each cell to carry out an attack every fall until he brought the United States government to its knees, it seemed Sarah—Hanna—was pushing the individual groups to launch against their targets as soon as possible. Maybe it was because of his interdiction that she felt the need to act quickly. Or maybe it's because she's a ruthless maniac bent on murder. Either way it didn't really matter. After the third camp was neutralized, the Feds had her and the group on the ropes.

Or at least so they thought. Derek had felt the same way until he came upon this compound, nestled in southwestern West Virginia. If he hadn't found it when he did it might have been too late. When word was sent back to higher-ups about the preparations being nearly complete, the reactions were furious. Hence the need.

Send them a message.

His radio earpiece crackles. "Hey, Slingshot." Derek cringes every time he hears the call sign. It had been given to him by Jason and Rob as some good-natured ribbing, but all things considered, Derek would rather have something a bit less obnoxious. "Can we get a SITREP?"

Derek takes one hand off his binoculars and keys the button attached to the front of his tactical vest. "Grizzly 6, nothing new. Developing the situation further. Will advise. Over," he whispers just loud enough to be heard on the other end.

"Roger that, Slingshot," Jason replies. "Hopefully we get some movement soon. The aviation boys are getting antsy. Said they don't think they can hold much longer."

Derek lowers his binos altogether and slips the cuff of his Marine woodland pattern camouflage blouse back enough to expose his watch. He keys up again, not bothering to hide the confusion in his voice. "Grizzly 6, Slingshot 6. My count has Reaper time on station for at least another seven hours. You mean the Apaches, over?"

"Bingo, Slingshot," Jason chimes back. "Flyboys getting nervous as usual." His own voice is laced with a modicum of exacerbation. Not surprising given his Airborne Ranger pedigree. The swagger of line troops almost always led to no small amount of eye rolling when it came to the concerns of other branches. This was especially true amongst the straight-leg infantry types of the world.

Marine Force Recon wasn't any different from the Army in that regard. Derek depresses his push-to-talk button. "If they're so nervous, get me Marines in Cobras instead of these National Guard wannabees next time. Devil Dogs will fly those things on spit and harsh language if they have to."

A few moments go by before the radio crackles again. Derek can make out the last vestiges of laughter dying out on the other end as Jason's voice comes through. "Wilco, Slingshot. Oorah!" the former Army noncom adds mockingly.

Derek smiles as he scoops up his binos and

resumes surveillance of the opposite hill. Despite their less than auspicious start together, a mutual respect and admiration had grown between the three former members of the military's elite. Derek found Jason and Rob to be seasoned professionals capable of proficient operational planning and execution the more time they worked together. Likewise, the duo had expressed to him on more than a few occasions their disbelief at Derek's survival skills, field acumen, and technical and tactical expertise.

The shared "mission first, people always" mindset set the stage for their successes. With each camp neutralized it was another notch on his handlers' belts, so much so that Derek was helping make their careers for them. Jason was now the leadership element's point man in the field, while Rob had been elevated to Assistant Special Agent in Charge of the entire task force. In return, they watched out for Derek, insulating him from the inevitable reach of FBI politics and logistical nonsense, while ensuring that he had every piece of state-of-the-art equipment, weaponry, and supplies at his disposal to make his time in the wilderness as smooth as possible.

Derek had to give it to the Feds on that front. His next-gen gear capabilities bordered on near-future science fiction at times. Not prototypes, mind you. Field-tested and certified equipment just waiting on budget appropriations for widespread distribution to the military. Billions will be spent fielding the gear en masse, but for a single individual the cost was negligible.

The concept for his loadout was all about combining multiple pieces of equipment into singular units to keep Derek light and mobile. His AN/PRC-177 multiband encrypted radio with satellite uplink gives him the ability to reach the forward command center, the helicopters holding so far out that their rotor blades can't be heard, and the drone pilot sitting in a trailer somewhere in the Arizona desert.

A specialized wrist-top computer, essentially a glorified, encrypted iPhone on steroids, sits in a camouflaged sleeve, reminiscent of what a quarterback wears to reference plays, on his left forearm. With it Derek can send and receive text messages with his command element, upload and download content like photographs or map overlays, mark his GPS position for satellite tracking, and passively transmit his vital signs. The computer even has a flora and fauna identification scanner, complete with a database of every known species indigenous to the United States.

A woodland camo boonie hat with a harness sewn into the interior lining supports an Enhanced Night Vision Goggle Monocular borrowed from the Army. Derek carries an M38 Designated Marksmanship Rifle, an upgraded version of the Marine Corps M27 Infantry Automatic Rifle, which has greater range, accuracy, and cycle rate of rounds than the standard M4 carbines that he was familiar with during his time in. A cutting-edge Leupold illuminated reticle scope combined IR beam, laser rangefinding, target designation, and live streaming capabilities into a singular optic. The enhanced rifle gives Derek the ability to see farther and shoot faster.

He only carries four magazines on the front of his vest in addition to the one already seated in the well of his rifle. The relatively low amount isn't ideal, but Derek accepts the trade-off for the alleviation in weight. He knows that if he ever gets into a major firefight his greatest weapon will be the radio on his back, not the rifle in his hands. Strapped in the dropdown holster attached to his right leg platform is a Sig Sauer M18 pistol should shit really hit the fan.

The remainder of Derek's tactical vest is outfitted with pouches containing the absolute essentials he needs should he become separated from his assault pack. A compass and maps. A trauma kit complete with hemostatic bandages and a combat tourniquet. A LifeStraw personal water filtration unit. One pocket contains tinder, lighters, and waterproof matches.

His assault pack, just a little bigger than a standard backpack, holds other items considered necessary but not essential. An insulated bivy sack to sleep in that can act as a VS-17 signaling panel if turned inside out. A larger field medical kit. A Katadyn water filtration pump to fill the integrated CamelBak reservoir. A solar recharging panel and spare batteries for his electronics. Four grenades: incendiary, smoke, fragmentation, and a flashbang. A suppressor attachment for the M38 rifle. Wire for setting snares. Tackle for fishing. Extra socks. Derek has a few emergency rations just in case, but he never starves while he is out, even in the dead of winter.

Rounding it all out is Derek's trusted StatGear Surviv-All survival knife strapped to his left leg platform. Matched with his survival skill set, the consolidated equipment further enhances his ability to travel quickly and quietly, allowing him to infiltrate and observe the enemy with lightning speed.

The loadout was proving itself so effective that the Marine Corps procurement guys were already getting hard-ons about fielding it to larger numbers, mainly Force Recon, Raiders, and snipers.

Trucks turning over heightens his attention. Derek forgets about the equipment and focuses his binoculars. Through the trees he can see the shadows of large vehicles moving. Derek punches the button to his radio. "Grizzly 6, we've got movement. Going to open channel."

He doesn't wait for a response. Rotating the housing ring around his push-to-talk button, Derek switches his radio to the frequency dedicated to coordinating the involved parties. "All task force elements, this is Slingshot 6. Report readiness condition, over."

"Slingshot 6, Saber 1. Redcon one."

"Cherokee 6, redcon one." The whir of the helicopters' rotors can be heard in the background of the pilot's transmission.

Jason's voice comes over again. "Grizzly 6. Redcon one."

"Roger," Derek replies, "all elements redcon one. We have vehicle movement inside camp. Stand by. Saber 1, you're on deck."

The pilot in Arizona keys back. "Roger over. Standing by."

Through the binoculars he can see the vehicles heading away from camp toward the west. Derek watches until the shadows and the decline of the hill swallow them from his sight but the sound of their engines never fades completely. He listens for the straining, sudden exertion of gears not meant for this mountainous terrain or navigating the steep twists and turns.

After a few moments the sounds of the engines

begin to increase. Derek shifts his gaze to the base of the hill, where the dirt tracks disappear into the tree line. Sure enough, three vehicles appear. A Chevy pickup in the lead, a U-Haul box truck in the middle, and a white panel van bringing up the rear. All three amble along, rocking back and forth as they move slowly over the uneven ground.

He keys his radio. "Saber 1, Slingshot 6. Type-three control, bomb on target. Advise when ready for 9 line."

The drone pilot crackles back. "Go ahead, Slingshot."

"Lines one through three, NA, break. Two eight niner eight feet. Civilian vehicles moving west to east. Grid mike lima eight four two, three niner seven, break. Slingshot laser, code one six eight eight. Northeast eight five zero meters. Acknowledge and advise when ready for remarks."

The vehicles continue toward him as the reply comes over his earpiece. "Roger, Slingshot, ready."

"Laser target line two three six. Final attack heading three three zero to zero three zero. Read back lines four, six, and restrictions."

"Slingshot 6, good copy. Two eight niner eight feet. Mike lima eight four two, three niner seven."

"Saber 1, good readback. Call in with heading."

"Copy Slingshot. Saber 1 in, heading three three zero," the drone pilot replies.

Derek lowers his binoculars and pulls his rifle over. Before looking through the scope he notices movement out of his peripherals. A quick glance shows the patrons of the camp coming out of the wood line to stand on the hill's edge. They wave to the vehicles as they bounce along the road, now a little less than halfway between the two hills. "Fuck," he mutters before acquiring the U-Haul in his scope.

"Slingshot 6, overhead. Ready for spot."

"Proceed south. Run in three thirty to one fifty. Laser target line two three six."

"Roger. Three thirty to one fifty for laser handoff. Ten seconds."

"Saber 1, roger. Ten seconds." Derek takes a deep breath.

"Slingshot 6, laser on."

Derek steadies his aim, keeping the red dot produced by his rifle-mounted laser on the side panel of the U-Haul. He tracks the truck as it moves from right to left in his field of vision. "Lazing."

After a few moments the pilot comes back. "Spot. Cease laser."

Derek switches off the laser but keeps his scope on the vehicles so that those in the forward command unit can watch the live feed. "Saber 1, do you have contact?"

"Slingshot 6, affirmative. Contact. Three vehicles moving west to east. Box truck is center mass."

His heart starts to thump in his chest. Despite the cool air, beads of sweat break out on his brow, and Derek can feel dampness in his armpits. "Correct, Saber, that's your target."

"Tally target," the drone pilot says, further acknowledging the acquisition.

Derek has the pilot call in the attack heading again. Upon receiving the appropriate response, he pauses momentarily. Derek swallows. "Cleared hot."

"Slingshot 6, Saber 1. Commencing engagement. Time on target, thirty seconds."

Derek squeezes his eyes shut. He waits a few moments, letting his years and experience dictate the length of his tactical pause. A couple of counts go by before he keys up again. "All Cherokee elements, proceed to incursion points, over."

The whir comes back through the radio. "Slingshot, Cherokee 6. Roger, inbound time now."

Derek's stomach gurgles. He spares a quick glance for the people watching on the hilltop. There is a steep and sudden *whoosh,* and then a flash. The concussive wave comes next followed by the erupting sound of an explosion.

The Hellfire missile detonates on impact when it hits the U-Haul. The contents inside, stacks of fertilizer laden with ball bearings and other forms of shrapnel, ignite immediately in a massive secondary explosion. The shrapnel and fireball produced burst through the windshield of the van trailing the box truck, engulfing it and the fully armed team riding in the back. The blast lifts the Chevy and throws it through the air like a Matchbox car, the vehicle crashing through the upper heights of the surrounding trees, severing limbs all the way back down to the ground.

Dirt and dust flies up in an all-encompassing cloud. Derek drops his head, one hand holding his boonie hat in place, the other pulling his rifle under his chest as the hot air rushes over him. A shower of shattered trees and rocks immediately follows the echo of the blast. Derek waits for the rain of debris to cease before conducting his battle-damage assessment.

"Saber 1, Slingshot 6. Mission successful. Three vehicles destroyed." He clears his throat, his mouth suddenly dry. "Estimate twelve casualties. Out."

Derek looks over to the camp. The entire landscape is awash in gray dust save for the flaming wreckage down below. For a few moments there is absolute silence. Then the screams come.

He can't see the families of those that were in the vehicles, but he hears their laments of shock and loss. It's a blessing that the hum of the rotor blades from the choppers comes a few seconds later and drowns them out.

The gray dust curls away as two Apache attack helicopters race in from the west and east. They flare up to halt their speed, the pilots briefly showing the underbelly of their aircraft before leveling out. As the aircraft dip back down, rockets, missiles, and 30mm cannons are menacingly brought to bear. A moment behind them, two UH-60 Black Hawks enter the airspace and form an outer perimeter. Ropes are dropped from both sides on each chopper and members of the FBI's elite Hostage Rescue Team begin fast-roping down to the deck.

They wear uniforms close to that of the Army. Fatigues in the operational camouflage pattern with olive drab plate carriers fastened over their chests and backs. Assault rifles and submachine guns dangle from their slings as the men zip down the lines. Once on the ground the individual teams get into wedge formations and race up the hilltop.

Derek glasses over the camp one more time. The group is in total disarray. Shock from the explosion. Staggered with their losses. Frozen by the sudden appearance of helicopters swarming all around them like a hornet's nest that's been kicked. As the members of HRT breach their perimeter the camp members fold, collapsing to the ground only to be put in the prone position, zip-tied, and searched. Already he can hear the sirens of the state police and fire departments making their way up the mountain road. Derek sighs.

Message sent.

2

Derek watches the aftermath unfold. Twenty minutes after the missile strike, surplus Mine Resistant Ambush Protected vehicles purchased from the military after the withdrawal from Iraq and the drawdown in Afghanistan come rumbling up the dirt track from the east. Painted midnight blue and emblazoned with the FBI seal on the doors, they lead a convoy of emergency vehicles. Stopping just before the flaming pickup, another platoon of the Hostage Rescue Team deploys out of the MRAPs.

They're dressed differently from the ones that air assaulted in, wearing olive drab flight suits with plate carriers and helmets matching the same. The agents provide cover as firefighters come up from the rear to start extinguishing the dozens of small fires before they can spread. Another detachment escorts a group of EMTs toward the camp.

Humvees and Jeeps pull out of the convoy and into the saddle between the two hills. From these more of the traditionally dressed agents emerge, wearing cargo pants and long-sleeve shirts covered by blue parkas with FBI stenciled across the back in thick yellow letters. They start pulling out pop-up tents and folding tables. Setting up generators, computers, and printers.

That would be the site exploitation teams then, waiting on clearance to enter camp.

Not long after that the helicopters peel off, and the squadron leader gives a congratulations to all on the ground for a "successful hunt." Derek resists the urge to key up. He'd love to tell the pilot to land his bird and say that again after listening to the kids crying as they watch the remains of their parents burning.

The exploitation teams start forward, the departure of the choppers signaling that the camp has been secured. More vehicles arrive with state police and local law enforcement. Before long the entire space between the hills is filled with all manner of stations and personnel.

A McDonnell Douglas helicopter passes overhead and hovers near the crater in the road. After a few of the MRAPs clear a space it touches down. Jason and two others jump out, all three sporting high and tight haircuts while wearing identical sunglasses. The top brass had arrived from the forward command center.

Derek waits for a while, in no hurry to go down and join the masses. After weeks of solitude traipsing through the woods to locate the camp, the sudden onslaught of so many people—numerous type-A personalities among them—could be a bit jarring. Instead he continues to lie prone, regulating his breathing and bringing himself to terms with what he just did.

He's not sure why it bothers him so much. He had called in air strikes before, albeit never on American soil. Moreover, he'd killed much more up close and personal, members of this group included. They were trying to commit mass murder. They had kidnapped his ex-wife and their son. Had tortured him. Tried to kill him and burn his family alive. He shouldn't be wrestling with this the way that he is, but it's happening all the same.

Perhaps it's because he had spent time with these people before. Heard their stories. Terrible, downtrodden tales from family after family. Or maybe it's the fact that the firefight in New York had been against the perpetrators of the group. Those in the camp, the ones that were there for support purposes, were long gone when Derek finally had it out with the men he had trained. They hadn't been on hand to witness their loved ones getting gunned down, sick fucks and deserving of such though they might have been.

Finally resigning himself to put it out of his mind for the time being, he pushes up from his position and pulls his bag out from behind a tree. The sooner he gets down there the sooner he can get debriefed. While rooting around inside Derek keys up his radio. "Grizzly 6, Slingshot 6."

Down below Jason raises a handheld radio up to his mouth. "Go ahead, Slingshot."

"Marking my position and proceeding to the assembly area. Do not engage to the east. I say again. Do not engage east."

"Roger, Slingshot. I'll spread the word. Come on down. Over."

"Roger, Grizzly. Slingshot out."

Pulling out the cylindrical smoke grenade, Derek clears a small area of leaves and then sets the ordnance onto the dirt patch. Pulling the pin, he steps away and shoulders his assault pack. A pop followed by a sizzle lets him know the grenade has gone off. He puts his left arm through the loop of his single-point sling and throws it over his shoulder, his rifle coming to rest muzzle down across his chest. By the time he begins negotiating the hillside orange smoke is wafting into the air above the trees.

He takes his time with the walk as well, having to weave around the backside of the hill to avoid a sheer face and find more suitable footing. Derek makes the turn back to the west, finally coming to level ground and proceeds toward the chaos. Emerging from the tree line and into the shin-high grass of the saddle he sees that a gut truck has made its way up the mountain road. The metal sides are already propped up and attendants are handing out coffee and donuts.

Walking through the clearing, he at first draws alarmed stares. To their credit, a few of the agents begin to reach for their sidearms or put a hand up to halt his progress but then they stop. His handler is there a moment later, a beaming smile on his face.

"There he is! Another camp taken down. How you feeling, big guy?"

Derek looks around at the way everyone is nonchalantly busying themselves, as if a missile hadn't detonated here an hour ago. Moreover, the weeks in the field are rapidly catching up to him now that the op is over and his adrenaline is wearing off. The two factors work in concert to deepen his rapidly souring mood. "Like I need a beer and a shower. In that order and as soon as possible."

The agent gives him a gracious nod and a smirk. "I can definitely help you with the first, and meet you halfway with the second. Hang on." Jason strides over to the gut truck and pushes his way to the front of the line. When he comes back he has two Budweisers clutched in his right hand, a wet towel in his left. "Best I can do on short notice."

Smiling slightly, Derek stifles a yawn. He drops his pack and leans his rifle on it while Jason pops the tabs on the beers. Handing one over, the two men share a silent toast. While Jason only takes a sip, Derek upends his can and drains it. Giving the empty to Jason, he takes the towel from his handler and wipes his face free of the camouflage face paint he's wearing.

"Anyway, I don't have to tell you, but great job as always, Chief." Derek had given up trying to correct the Army affinity for shortchanging the names of ranks. The other branches made about as much sense as a soup sandwich to him sometimes. "Stopped the bad guys again. Early word from the forensics team is that they had a shit ton of weapons up there. Some intel too. That combined with the amount of people this camp had and I think it's safe to say they were planning follow-on ops after their bombing."

"Yeah, well, I guess the interrogations will sort that part out."

"Sure will." Jason laughs. "Nothing like dangling a few years off in front of these podunks to see how quickly they sing. Especially the parents. It's like, hey, you wanna see your grandkids outside of visiting hours then you better start talking."

Derek attempts a smile, but his energy is bottoming out. He wants nothing more than to be done with this latest round. "Speaking of kids, can you get me out of here? I'd like to see my boy."

The other man pulls out his cell phone and starts

scrolling through it. "What? Oh, yeah, man. Sure. Of course. Let me just attend to this email right quick, and then I'll see about lining up some transpo. We'll need to debrief you first before letting you go, but that shouldn't be too long."

Derek sighs in response. "Never is."

Jason flashes one of his surfer smiles. "Come on, Chief, have a little faith. We've been doing this together a bit now. I won't let you down. A short hop over to Quantico and then a few hours max. Get you a shower and hot meal while we're at it."

He can already see the timeline. Quantico alone was at least two hours away by helicopter. From there it would be a bunch of hurry up and wait while the higher-ups all patted each other on the back. He'd be lucky to be on a plane before dark.

"Whatever you gotta do. Just so long as we're moving soon," Derek says as he turns away and looks across the field. The group coming out of the woods to the west toward him brings a genuine smile to his face, one which is returned by Chief Drysdale, leading their diamond formation. Even now it remains in place, a testament to the team leader's discipline and execution.

Turning back, Derek scoops up his gear and relieves Jason of his Budweiser. The man appears to prefer it that way, both of his hands now free to work his email response. "Hit me up on the net when that bird is ready," Derek says as he starts off to meet the team.

Jason glances up just long enough to see what is pulling his asset away and replies with a "You got it," before focusing his gaze back at his screen, thumbs flying over the digital keyboard.

Crossing the distance to meet them halfway, the four operatives comprise Derek's quick reaction force and extraction team, QRF-E for short. Originally the concept had been for the members of the QRF-E to accompany Derek during his long stints in the woods, but ultimately Derek's argument against it won out.

Citing that one man was much more likely to infiltrate the camp perimeters without detection, and the lack of survival skills training the members of the team would need to be out in the field for protracted periods of time, the leadership element reluctantly shifted the team mission to a support role. As much as he had come to care for the three men and one woman tasked with his immediate safety, Derek preferred the solitude. The simple fact of the matter is that he works best when alone.

Looking like someone carved him out of a piece of granite, Chief Petty Officer Eric Drysdale acts as the leadership element for the QRF-E. After thirteen and a half years on the teams he was recruited by the FBI to join the ranks of the HRT. Next in line for his own team, Drysdale jumped at the opportunity when approached about Derek's special support assignment.

Closing the distance to Derek, Chief Drysdale inclines his chin in quick acknowledgement. The two come together first shaking hands and then pulling each other into a bro hug. "Man, I've seen some sorry-ass Marines in my day, but you take the cake, Harrington," Drysdale says with a half-cocked smile.

"Yeah, well, let's see how good you look after a month in the suck," Derek replies.

"Shit, been there done that, brother. This is your rodeo, remember?"

"Think they would let me forget?" Derek replies with a nod over his shoulder to the FBI field operations underway.

"Not in their DNA," Drysdale returns with a shake of his head. He turns and spits behind him.

Stopping just to the right of the Chief is Brian Ortega, a tall and skinny Mexican-American from the Bronx. Also a Navy veteran, he did his time on Swift Boats, the operators designated to pick up SEALs from their extraction points on shores and rivers. Stripping his helmet off, Ortega runs a gloved hand through sweat-soaked waves of black hair. Afterward, he gestures with the helmet to the flaming wreckage down the road. "Damn, boss, you really fragged their asses huh? Barbecuing their nuts right on Broadway!"

He starts to laugh. Derek glances over at the younger man and his laughter falters. Drysdale recognizes the look on their principal's face and quickly steps in. "Stow that shit, sailor."

Brian looks from his team leader to Derek and then back again. He sets his jaw and clears his throat. "Roger that, Chief. My apologies, Derek."

Giving the younger man a nod, Derek smirks. "Don't worry about it, Ortega."

The Chief's eyes linger on his fellow Navy alum, giving him a look that conveys there will be further discussion later on. Normally flanking the team leader to his left of the diamond formation, Angelica Ortiz comes up behind Ortega and gives him a halfhearted slap on the back of his head.

"Leave the boss alone, pendejo," she says before turning her attention to Drysdale. "That goes for you too, Chief." Drysdale chuckles as Ortiz turns to

Derek. "Never mind them, mi amor. You look just fine to me." She finishes the statement with a wink.

Derek cracks a smile at the woman's simultaneous motherly, flirtatious, and one-of-the-boys demeanor. "Thanks, Angie."

A Puerto Rican native who saw significant combat in Afghanistan as an Army medic, Ortiz returned to Florida after getting out, working first as a paramedic, then Miami-Dade police, SWAT, and eventually the FBI. Ortiz had taken Ortega under her wing as a tactical little brother. Given their last names, the pair started being referred to as the James Bond traditional "Double O's."

Save for the H-S Precision .308 sniper rifle strapped to Aaron Gerbowski's pack, the fourth member of the QRF-E, the entire team is armed with the same 9mm pistol and weapons chambered in 5.56 so that they can match Derek and one another, giving them the ability to pass off either firearms or ammunition to him or between themselves. Drysdale and Gerbowski each carry a version of the rifle Derek does, modified with under-the-barrel M203 grenade launcher attachments.

Brian, acting as the team's machine gunner, is armed with a snub nose, collapsible stock M249 Squad Automatic Weapon. However, when Angelica saw that she was to be the only true rifleman, she sounded her fury and demanded to carry a SAW as well.

"We're only a four-man team, are we not?" she said, accosting Rob and Jason at the same time.

"Yes, but—"

"But what? If we have to pull him out of some shit, we're going to need all the firepower we can get, right?"

"The team billet calls for the medic to be a rifleman. There's too much gear to carry otherwise."

"Oh, for fuck's sake," Ortiz said with a toss of her hands and a roll of her eyes. "I'll still carry your precious M27 so you can call me what the billet requires," she replied, mumbling "assholes" under her breath afterward. The woman then strapped the rifle to her pack, scooped up an M249, and absolutely owned the qualification course while wearing her full combat load. So impressed was young Ortega that he too agreed to carry an M27 attached to his bag, so that either of them could be classified as a machine gunner or rifleman. Rob and Jason couldn't say shit after that.

Bringing up the rear of the diamond formation, Gerbowski is as straight laced and even keeled as they come. Derek had taken a particular liking to the younger man, instantly noting his potential when they first met. His cauliflower ears pop into view while rotating to check their six. A former collegiate wrestler, Gerbowski made a fledgling attempt at an MMA career post-graduation before joining the Bureau.

With a degree in accounting, he initially had no interest in tactical work and spent several years as a Special Agent tracking white-collar crime. But the discovery of Gerbowski's hidden skill set by his superiors during range qualifications set him on the path to Derek's support team. Honed on the Great Plains since he was old enough to hold a rifle, a place where thousand-yard shots were common enough, the career athlete and outdoorsman could group his shots within a dime's diameter. After that day and after being heavily recruited by the Denver FBI SWAT team, his career turned to the sniper's course and then, eventually, the QRF-E.

"Anyway, boss man," Drysdale begins, "they getting you outta here soon or what?"

"So they say, but not home. At least not right away."

"What? They're making you go back to Quantico?" Ortiz asks.

"Bingo," Derek replies. "Something about needing to debrief me there."

"Bet it's the new SAC," Gerbowski says from over his shoulder as he checks the rear yet again.

Derek furrows his eyebrows. Drysdale shakes his head and rolls his eyes. "Yeah, I wouldn't doubt it. Tedesco had emergency surgery shortly after you went in this time. He's fine and all, but gonna be out of the game for the foreseeable future. So the FBI appointed a new SAC to fill his shoes. Special Agent in Charge Samuel Liu. They didn't want to tell you mid-op since it really didn't affect anything in the field. One less thing to worry about, you know?"

"Yeah, I get it. But you think it's him calling me back now?"

"Wouldn't doubt it," Drysdale replies.

The man's tone keys Derek's intuition. "What? Is he some kind of moron or something?"

Gerbowski chuckles. "Liu? Nah, quite the opposite actually, but he's a real peach. Gonna win the war against Autumn's Tithe all on his own."

The seriousness on Drysdale's face lets Derek know that the assessment is spot-on. "Guy's a fobbit, Derek. Spent his entire career in intelligence functions one way or another. No field time to speak of. Rumor is that's the only thing holding him back from being bumped up the chain of command. You know what that means, brother."

"Yeah," Derek says, exhaling. "Just what we need, someone looking to make a splash."

The sound of rotors returning cuts the conversation short. "That's probably your ride," Drysdale offers, and then adds after a few moments, "Good luck over there, boss."

"Thanks, team, as always. Hey, Gerbs!" Derek yells over the increasing buzz of the approaching Black Hawk helicopter. "You've got the flask, right?"

"Never leave home without it, boss."

"Well, break that shit out. Can't close a successful op without our tradition."

Besides their weapons, the contents of the packs everyone on the team carries is the only other differentiator between members, each being filled in accordance with their particular skill sets and Derek's support needs. Drysdale carries extra ammunition and grenades. Ortega, the techie of the group, carries spare components for Derek's wrist-top computer, radio, and optics as well as extra batteries and solar cells. He also has a small UAV that he can quickly assemble and deploy should localized surveillance be required.

Ortiz carries the team's lifesaving equipment, to be applied to Derek as a priority. Gerbowski's squat, muscular frame allows him to shoulder additional ammo, while also carrying rations, water, purifier filters, fire starting equipment, rope, 550 cord, and a flask of WhistlePig whiskey.

Gerbowski unslings his rucksack. After a moment of digging into a side pocket he produces a flask embossed with the Force Recon emblem on the side. Aaron unscrews the top and hands it to Derek. He raises it up to them. "To going home. Not dead yet."

Instead of taking a swig, Derek hands the flask to Ortega. The younger man's eyebrows rise, but after seeing the sincerity on Derek's face, he accepts. "Not dead yet," Brian repeats before upending the flask. He starts coughing after swallowing down the whiskey.

He tries to hand it back but Derek gestures to Gerbowski. Aaron takes his swig and then hands it off to Angelica, each of them handling their shots with ease. Drysdale makes a quip about needing to carry Hennessy from now on and then takes his allotment. Derek is the last to go, tossing back the liquid and enjoying the sweet warmth it produces. Shaking the flask, he then hands it back to Brian.

"What? Again?"

"Consider it recompense."

Frowning, Ortega works his mouth open and closed, his tongue flicking out while his face contorts. "Seriously?"

Chief Drysdale chuckles. "You heard the boss. Time to man up!"

Taking the flask, Brian brings it halfway to his lips. "We need some tequila on these ops." Ortega upends the container and chugs until it is fully drained. Pulling it down, he immediately doubles over into a coughing fit that quickly devolves into dry heaving. The rest of the team laughs and pats him on the back as the chopper comes into view.

. . . . .

Off to the left orange smoke wafts up from a nearby hilltop. He shifts his rifle scope to cover the terrain in that direction. After a few minutes a man in Marine Corps camouflage walks out into the open at the base of the hill. Kellen places his crosshairs onto the man and starts tracking him as he makes his way across the field.

"Think that's him?" his spotter asks as he stares through his scope.

"Range," Kellen replies. He starts adjusting the knobs on his riflescope according to his own estimate. Once he gets the specifics he can fine tune from there.

The spotter picks his head up from his optic, his eyebrows furrowed. "You know we ain't cleared to engage. This is purely recon."

"Range," Kellen repeats. His voice is an even monotone.

"Did I not just say we can't shoot? Besides, I don't much feel like taking on the entire FBI and half the fucking cops in West Virginia."

"Are you not prepared to die for our cause?"

"Hey, fuck off, man," the spotter replies. He eases down his spotting scope and lifts a digital camera with a telephoto lens. The man snaps pictures as he continues. "I'm as dedicated as the next guy but there's a difference between fighting the good fight and throwing your life away with nothing to show for it."

Kellen sighs. He adjusts his cheek on the buttstock and flicks off his safety. The spotter reaches out and grabs onto the barrel, pulling the rifle down. Kellen's face flashes toward the man, his features a blank slate, his eyes devoid.

"The fuck is the matter with you?" The sniper says nothing. Eventually the spotter wilts under his gaze, as so many often do. Overhead a chopper can be heard on its way back to the scene. "Come on, man.

We best retrograde. Don't need to risk one of these birds seeing us on their return."

The spotter doesn't wait for a response. He lets go of the rifle and starts to inch his way back from their observation post. Kellen rights his rifle and looks through the attached optic. The man in the Marine camouflage is standing with a group of HRT members now. No clear shot. He reengages his safety.

3

Heavy boots pounding over the concrete slab outside her door pulls Sarah's attention away from the maps spread out before her. Hypervigilance snaps back into place and her hand instinctively drops to the pistol on her hip. Three regimented knocks bang on the metal door. She had appropriated the circuit room in the back of the tipple to serve as her office. It's a far cry from the space she used to occupy overlooking downtown Manhattan.

"Come in," Sarah calls from behind the folding table that serves as her desk. The door sticks and then shudders as it swings open.

Two forms, like upright walking bushes, step into the room. The ghillie suits the men wear are designed for woodland camouflage. Long tangles of green, brown, and black strings are matted together with other shapes like leaves and moss. If lying prone in a nest of brambles similar in color they would be nearly invisible to anyone walking by. You'd have to step on them to know they were there, and even then you might not notice.

The taller of the pair, Kellen Pugh, comes in first. He cradles his M24 sniper rifle across his chest, the military's version of the tried and true Remington bolt-action hunting rifle. It too is wrapped in a version of the ghillie camouflage. The man steps to the far corner as his spotter, Frank Neville, comes in behind him. While Frank lowers his hood, Sarah watches as Kellen slowly props his weapon against the wall. The motion reminds her of a mother placing her napping child into a crib.

"Fuck, it's good to get outta this shit," Frank says as he pulls off the top and slides his trousers down. Underneath he wears a set of Realtree hunting fatigues.

"It'll be better when you get a bath. The two of you reek."

"Yeah, well, you spend three weeks out in the boonies and see how you smell, sister," Frank returns as he scoops up a folding chair and sits down by the door. "And not for nothing, you don't smell much better than us."

The left side of Sarah's lip ticks up in a slight smirk. Frank is a colossal ball buster, but he's always straight with you. The man's squat frame being adorned with a face reminiscent of an elderly pug helps with the comic relief. To be honest, Sarah couldn't be mad at the man for anything, least of all a quip about her body odor. They tried to do the best they could for hygiene in the camp, but in reality you were lucky to bathe once every few days. If that.

"Seriously. It's really annoying to have to put this crap back on after taking it off. Why the hell you make us walk the last four miles is beyond me. No one's been out to this broken-down heap in a decade. We coulda driven right up."

Sarah shakes her head. "You willing to chance the camp's security on that? I'm not. Not the way we're getting picked off. Speaking of which . . ."

Kellen comes to stand next to Frank, the latter throwing a grimace at the statuesque man before turning back. As usual Kellen's face is unreadable. "It's gone, Captain," Frank says. "They were ahead of us again. Feds hit the place as the trucks were rolling out for the op. Blasted them to hell with a missile and then choppers swooped in and snatched everyone up. There wasn't anything anyone could do, they were so fast."

She clenches her fists. "What do you mean a missile? How did the camp not hear the choppers before they were able to target the trucks?"

"It wasn't the birds. It was a drone strike," Kellen replies flatly.

"A drone?" Sarah adds, looking up at the man. "They used a drone missile on American soil? Fucking bastards." The implications of that alone certainly raised the stakes. It also lent further credence to her suspicions. Even if you combined the surveillance assets of the nation's entire intelligence apparatus and removed all of the commitments of such from around the globe, the U.S. still didn't have the capacity to comb the entire continent.

Certainly the FBI didn't on its own, and while interagency collaboration was much more frequent and fluid in the post 9/11 era, even what could be spared wouldn't come close to what was actually needed. Someone was out there getting them in the neighborhood first. The Feds have a scout, and she's pretty certain she knows who her former colleagues got for the job. "Did you get what I asked for, then?"

"Yeah, hang on a sec," Frank returns. He pulls over his backpack from its spot on the floor and starts rummaging through it.

While he does so Sarah regards the sniper standing next to the chair. The man's eyes bore into her own. Kellen seems to never blink, and he barely ever speaks. Even while Frank fishes through his bag muttering curses under his breath, the man stands and stares.

Lanky and muscled, Kellen is built like a marathon runner. His fatigue pants are hiked up above his waist, giving the impression that his long arms and legs are disproportionate to the rest of his body. His face is mouselike, with a long protruding nose, ears sticking out to the sides, and large brown eyes. His hair is shaved short on the sides, lengthier now given the duo's weeks in the field, with a thicker patch high on his scalp. All of it is the color of deep rust.

Kellen's most prominent feature, however, is his tattoos. Starting in the space between his shoulder blades, two identical snakes twist over his shoulders and wrap around his arms, each ending with the head on the tops of his hands. The skin of the snakes is marbled vibrant orange alternating with patches of reddish brown.

The information relayed to her when discussing his file was that while Kellen was in sniper school with the Army, he emerged as top in his class at infiltration, despite his obvious length while lying on the ground. In conjunction with his red hair the instructors began calling him Copperhead. The name stuck, and the tattoos followed shortly after graduation.

Of course, Kellen came to be known by other names as well. His odd nature and antisocial behavior alienated him from everyone in the camp. Soon after learning his nickname from the service the others started teasing him, calling him the Viper Sniper and Corporal Pew Pew Pew.

The name that reigned over them all was Reboot. This came from the man's tendency to freeze whenever you asked him a question. Kellen would stand there, silent for minutes at a time, before finally giving you an answer. It got so bad that people started slipping behind him to mimic pushing a button on his back to "reboot the system." Supposedly a challenge existed in the camp to see who could get the highest number of reboots before Kellen noticed what everyone was up to.

"Here you go," Frank says as he powers on the camera. He stands up and hands it over.

Taking it from him, Sarah keys the arrow button and begins flipping through the images. Even with the remnants of camouflage face paint she can tell that it's Harrington. Tsk'ing with disgust, she sets the camera down and pushes it aside. Sarah flops back against her chair, rubbing her eyes.

"I take it that's him, then?" Frank asks.

"Yeah, it's him," Sarah groans in reply. "I was sure he wasn't working for them when we first met. Things were too . . . disjointed then. Now there's no doubt. The man is a master manipulator." The last she gives over begrudgingly. The sting remains long after the admission. She was no slouch when it came to dissecting a mind. To have had the wool pulled over her eyes for so long . . .

"All the more reason," Kellen growls.

"How's that?" she says looking up at the man, but he quickly retreats back into himself. When he doesn't answer, Sarah looks at Frank.

"Vasily Zaitsev here had him in his crosshairs," Frank returns, thumbing over at the man.

The speed with which Kellen whirls around is blinding. He slaps Frank's hand out of the way with his own and then crashes a ridgehand into the man's throat. Frank's eyes go wide as he thumps back down into the chair he was sitting in. The man clutches his neck, gasping for air even as Kellen drives his boot into Frank's chest.

Toppling over to the floor, Frank sits incapacitated as he struggles to breathe. His eyes go wide with terror as Kellen nonchalantly bends down and draws a Smith & Wesson knife from his boot. Holding the blade pointed to the floor, Kellen starts toward the man to finish the job.

"Put it away. Now."

Kellen slowly looks over his right shoulder. Sarah has her 9mm Glock drawn, her thumbs aligned one atop the other along the left side of the weapon. Her face is stern. Her hands don't waver. Kellen slides the knife back into the scabbard and then stands to face her.

"Grab your shit and get the hell out of here. I swear, Pugh, you so much as twitch the wrong way and I'll drop you."

The man's eyes remain vacant, his face a blank canvas. After a moment he turns and gathers his gear.

Cradling his rifle, Kellen strides out of the room, stepping over Frank without so much as a spare glance.

Once she is sure he has left the building, Sarah holsters her sidearm. She goes to her knees next to the downed man. "Try to lie still. I'm gonna grab Sage and a couple of others to get you over to the infirmary."

Frank makes the smallest of nods while continuing to wheeze. After they've taken him away she strides across the yard, the coal tipple structure looming behind her. The angled conveyor belts and chutes jut out of it like paralyzed limbs. Fog-laden hills surround the loose camp. Tall stands of brush and thin trees obscure the dozen or so tents and plywood buildings that the group uses for their housing and necessities. Piles of crushed stone covered with black coal dust still litter the ground, a constant reminder of when the mine was operational.

She throws the flap back and steps into Kellen's tent. The man is seated on his cot and facing the entrance. A cleaning kit lies open next to him. He looks up briefly but upon seeing her goes back to carefully working a bore snake through the barrel of his rifle.

"Care to tell me what the hell that was all about?"

Pugh shrugs. "The man lacks conviction."

Waiting for more, Sarah presses when he doesn't elaborate. "Conviction? He's out here, isn't he? He's lost everything and wants to see this through just as much as the rest of us."

"Wrong."

"What the . . . the hell did you just say?"

Slowly his head turns to her. He locks eyes and doesn't turn away. Long moments drag on before he finally answers. "Your friend. I had him. That man stopped me from taking the shot. We could have ended their pursuit but he was more concerned about his own skin."

"You had no orders to engage. This was purely a reconnaissance. And what is this 'friend' horseshit?"

He turns back to his rifle, picking up a cloth and rubbing it down. "This is the third camp he's neutralized in as many months. Four total if you add New York. I'm beginning to think this man means more to you alive than dead."

Sarah grinds her teeth, the muscle along the right side of her jaw pulsating. "Listen to me, Pugh. I won't have you questioning the convictions of others, me least of all. You've only joined us recently yourself. I knew those people in New York. In all of the camps. Don't presume to ever know what my intentions are. You're here to do a job. I'm the one that tells you what that job is. Understand?"

He gives a ghost of a nod. "Furthermore, you may not have noticed, but our resources are stretched pretty fucking thin. That includes personnel. We can't afford to have any of it wasted. The next time you take exception to something someone says, make sure you leave them serviceable."

"I won't go back out into the field with that man."

"Frank isn't going out into the field with anyone. You crushed his larynx and broke his sternum. Army-trained spotters don't grow on trees. It's going to take some doing to replace him."

"I'll work alone. I'm better that way anyhow."

Sarah shakes her head. "You're not hearing me, Pugh. There is no working alone. Not for what I have planned."

Kellen lets out a deep sigh and sets down his rifle. Turning to look at her again, he folds his hands in his lap. "They are wiping us out. If we don't act soon, there won't be anyone left for your plan."

"You don't get to devise strategy, get it? You certainly don't get to lecture me on it. You're a tool. An asset for me to deploy as I see fit. Nothing more. Those were your orders when you were sent to us and they haven't changed. If I say reconnaissance then that's all you do. I don't need a half-cocked, trigger-happy jerkoff upending years of planning and sacrifice just because he wants to see the pink mist. You disobey my orders again, and they'll never find your remains. Have I made myself perfectly clear?"

Kellen gives a single, emotionless nod. "Crystal."

"Good. Now grab your shit and get the hell out of my sight. When you learn to keep your goddamn hands to yourself maybe I'll allow you to stay with the rest of us. As it is, you just made a ton of extra work for me tonight having to settle down the others. Frank is pretty popular, and thanks to you I'm going to have to convince them not to hang your ass."

Standing, Kellen slings his rifle, grabs his assault pack, and then picks up his ghillie suit. If he is in any way annoyed with being banished from camp so soon after returning he doesn't show it. "When do you want me back, Captain?"

"Three days. I need to plan our next move and I don't want the distraction of your BS getting in the way of that."

Without another word Kellen brushes past her and steps out of the tent. Sarah follows, watching as the man heads for the tree line without so much as turning his head to survey the rest of the camp. If he had, he would've noticed the no small shortage of blistering stares leveled his way. When she figures enough distance has been put into place between everyone, she turns back to the tipple. Now that Pugh is no longer an issue for the next seventy-two hours, she can focus her attention where it's needed.

Before that happens, however, she needs to make a call.

4

The man picks up on the third ring. "Hello, this is Daniel. How may I assist you?" Each word drips with years of customer service–enriched falsehood. In the background a constant buzz floods the line. Voices echoing through open spaces. Italian leather shoes tapping their heels on marble floors.

"Go secure," Sarah says flatly into her satellite phone.

"Yes, of course. One moment while I connect you to her office," Daniel replies. A series of clicks comes back through the receiver while the buzz in the background fades slightly. Once the clicks have stopped Daniel's voice returns, this time deep, hushed, and devoid of any pleasantries. "Where the hell have you been?"

"Busy."

There's a pause before he answers. "Busy? Are you kidding me? Busy? That's all you have to say?"

"What do you want me to say? It's not like we have the best connectivity out here."

"Oh, please," Daniel replies, exasperated. "That's

the best military encrypted uplink money can buy you're talking through. You can reach out any time you want."

"You know what I mean. I'm just learning about the latest now. I called as soon as I could."

"Oh. That." He emphasizes the second word with pointed sarcasm. "You mean the latest disaster that you're supposed to be in charge of?"

Sarah swallows her indignation. For as much of an asshole as Dan can be, she needs him and the connections that he represents. Still, there are limits to her patience.

"I'm not happy about it either, but if anything this proves my point."

Another pause, longer than the last. "Excuse me? What did you just say?"

"I think you heard me just fine. When I spoke to you last time I told you this would happen. The old man's vision was filled with promise. The execution of it is stuck in the fifties. They're a step ahead of us at every turn and they're rolling us up one by one."

"And I believe we told you that you're not the only cog in this wheel. We have sources in all the agencies, and nothing has come through our channels. With our network I think we would know if they were on top of us that much."

Now it's her turn to pitch back the sarcasm. "I'm not sure why burning camps and dozens upon dozens of arrests aren't enough proof for you at this point, but I went out this time and secured my own. The man I told you about. He's working with them. Leading them right to the camps with pinpoint accuracy."

"I just told you. There's nothing—"

"Stop talking to me as if you understand my

job!" Sarah shouts into the phone. "You're a fucking secretary. Use your head. If there's nothing coming through your channels it's because they've got him off the books. Even with your connections you won't be able to get into everything that's compartmentalized."

Moments tick by as the man on the other end of the line digests the deluge. Sarah doesn't wait for him to finish doing so. "They've got the drop on us. A few more months of this and we'll be finished. We've got to turn the tide on them, and fast."

"Oh trust me, even this glorified secretary can see that. Between you and me you're skating on thin ice. She is not pleased. Not at all. So much so that we're developing other contingencies. Right now you're the golden child special investigator, but favorites can change. I think you can read between the lines what that means for you if those contingencies are successful where you were not."

Sarah feels a spasm ricochet through her body, simultaneous fear and fury coursing through her veins. Having this pompous ass lob thinly veiled threats is enough to get her hackles up, but she bites her tongue. Daniel is a braggart, but his conduit is a direct channel to very real power that can easily fulfill his promises.

Taking a deep breath to steady herself, Sarah presses on. "I'm not trying to be a backseat driver here, but that would be a mistake. The more eyes and ears that are brought into this thing the greater potential for it getting discovered."

"'Cause you're doing such a great job of keeping it hidden on your own?"

"The network, you prick," Sarah growls despite her best efforts not to. "Right now they think we're a bunch of backwoods revolutionaries with our noses in Bibles and worshiping portraits of David Koresh. They must certainly realize there is a larger backing but I doubt they know the extent, let alone who at this point. If she starts expanding things the potential for someone to overhear—or, worse, leak information—greatly increases."

"Your concern is duly noted," is Daniel's snarky reply.

This is getting nowhere fast. Sarah takes a tactical pause to steady herself before working to pivot the conversation. She softens her tone a touch. "Just listen for a minute. Please."

The man sighs. "Go ahead," he says with no shortage of exasperation in his tone.

"I have a plan, but to do it you have to loosen the reins. I can't keep this going with you two trying to run it from there. I certainly can't keep us afloat if you refuse to adapt to the situation and continue to force me to stick with the old man's manifesto."

Long moments tick by. Daniel's voice finally comes back, evenly and without the bite it held earlier. "All right. I'll play along for now. I'm not making any guarantees, but walk me through what you have in mind. If I think it has merit I'll bring it to her for consideration."

Sarah moves the phone away from her mouth and exhales. Her heart is thumping in her chest when she gets back on the line. "Okay, first and foremost we need to take advantage of these photos. They may have Derek sectioned off, but if we're lucky we can identify one of the other agents in the pictures and back our way into this."

Over the next several minutes she gives him the

quick overlay, touching on the broad strokes. She leaves out just enough operational detail to preserve the integrity of the plan so that they can't supplant her with someone else. When she finishes Sarah waits patiently for his response.

"That . . . just might work."

She exhales again, not even bothering to move the phone away. "If we're going to do this we've got to move quickly. That's no small amount of material that I'm going to need, and it'll take some time to get the personnel in place. On top of that there are the preparations at the site. We're talking several weeks at a minimum."

"I understand. Don't worry about the hardware. We've got that covered. You're right though, the transit is a bit of a concern. Airlift probably won't be an option for this."

"And the message to my guy on the inside? You'll be able to trigger that for me?"

Daniel actually chuckles. "That's the least of your worries. He'll definitely be in the system. We can get to any federal facility. And if he's in a hospital like you say he is, it'll be even easier than the prisons."

"They'll have to put him in one. The guy has late-stage leukemia. He'll need to be under constant care."

The man pauses before replying. "That's low, even for you."

Sarah shrugs despite the man not being able to see it. "I use what I have available to me. The man is dying. He doesn't want that to be for nothing. This is his way of ensuring payback."

"Well, not saying that you've got the go-ahead, but send me the pictures through the secure file exchange, and then start making what preparations you need to on your end. If she gives the green light I'll reach back out."

"I'll upload them as soon as we're done," Sarah agrees. "Remember though, go through a contractor. The facial recognition programs in the agencies could have flags or alerts built in."

"Appreciate you laying it all out for me, what with my being just a lowly civil servant and all." When Daniel speaks again his voice has returned to his office tone. "Thank you so much for your call today. I'll be sure to pass along your message just as soon as she's available."

Sarah recognizes the pattern for their closing. "Standing by," is all she replies with. A moment later the line goes dead. Sarah clears the call history per protocol, and then sticks the phone in her pocket. She makes her way back to the tipple to get the SD card out of Frank's camera and upload the files.

* * * * *

At Quantico, Derek tries to get out the door as quickly as possible, but the suits have other plans. After gearing down and scrubbing the weeks' worth of filth off of his body, he changes into cargo pants and a polo before heading upstairs, en route to one of a million identical conference rooms. Before he can get inside Jason stops him in the hall. "Hey, can you give it a minute, Chief? The new SAC is on his way and wants to meet you before we get started."

Stifling an exhale, Derek stands off to the side. "Yeah. Sure." Jason makes an attempt at small talk, filling him in on baseball news he wasn't privy to while out in the field. Derek makes his best attempt at remaining engaged, but as the minutes tick by he grits his teeth against his growing frustration. Checking his watch for the third time, a booming voice suddenly calls out from down the hall.

"This is him, isn't it?"

Derek takes note of the change in Jason's demeanor. The aloof California boy attitude gets dropped and is replaced with some old-fashioned soldier rigidity. When Derek turns he sees an Asian man in his mid-fifties striding toward them. The man's hair is skintight on the sides and ends in a perfectly level salt-and-pepper flattop. Tall with a lithe build, the man wears an impeccable pair of navy blue checkered slacks, shoes that probably cost more than Derek's paycheck, and a starched white button-down shirt. His sleeves are rolled halfway up his forearms and his top button is undone, his silk tie slightly loosened.

The quality of his attire and the way in which he wears it immediately registers as a contradiction to Derek. Trying to appear as one of the grunts while donning what is surely more than a thousand-dollar suit never works out as well as the perpetrator might think. The diminutive administrator trailing behind him carrying stacks of files and the man's matching jacket while the SAC's hands remain empty helps to solidify Derek's initial assessment. For whatever reason the thought of a spring coiled too tightly comes to mind.

When the man reaches the duo he extends his hand. Derek takes it and almost has his arm wrenched free as a result. "It's about goddamn time I got to meet you." A stream of agents, assistants, and analysts continue past them into the conference room, Rob is amongst them, all passing by save for the one carrying the SAC's possessions who stands patiently nearby.

Jason takes a small step to the side so that he is standing somewhat between the two of them. "Derek Harrington, this is our new task force commander, Special Agent in Charge Samuel Liu."

Liu waves a dismissive hand. "Let's leave all that SAC nonsense out of it between you and me, eh, Derek? After all, it's not like you're an agent or anything. No need for such formalities. Sam is just fine."

Derek returns the handshake with a pump of his own and a curt nod. "All right then, Sam."

Liu lets go and takes a step back. "I gotta tell you, I really admire how you handle yourself, Chief Warrant Officer. Very impressive from what I've reviewed of the previous assignments, and then it goes without saying for today's work. Of course, I shouldn't expect anything less from a DEVGRU and Force Recon veteran, right, Harrington?"

"Thanks," Derek replies flatly. "I don't mean to be impatient, but I've been out in the field for weeks and waiting here for some time now. I'd like to see my family. Could we get underway?"

The smile that Liu flashes seems genuine enough on the surface, if it wasn't for the fact that it doesn't match up with his eyes. In them Derek can see the indignation. Clearly this is a man used to setting the schedule according to his time and no one else's. The fact that he hides the reaction so well shows Derek that he's a practiced politician on top of everything else. It's a combination that he'll have to keep an eye on.

"Of course, Derek," Liu returns, gesturing to the open conference room doors behind them. "After you."

With another nod and a quick glance at Jason, the

four proceed inside. Everyone stands upon the SAC's entrance and he takes his time getting settled before allowing everyone to take their seats. Derek finds an empty chair halfway down the long table across from Jason and Rob. He and Rob share an acknowledging nod for the success of the operation. Afterward Rob turns back to Jason. They shuffle papers and files back and forth, leaning in to speak softly to one another. Derek slouches in his chair and rests an elbow on the table.

"All right, everyone. Let's begin," Liu announces to the room.

The new SAC proceeds to put Derek through the ringer. Liu, along with the cadre of analysts and administrators, have him walk them through the operation. Not just the actions at the camp resulting in the drone strike, but also the identified potential sites that he had scouted over the weeks leading up to the assault. Derek recounts each in painstaking detail, only to do so again and again as different departments are rotated in.

First it's the Counterterrorism Division and the Terrorist Screening Center. Then Counterintelligence. The Insider Threat Office needs a private session given that Sarah was once one of their own, and that there could still be infiltrators in the Bureau. After the Weapons of Mass Destruction Directorate receives their update, the briefings turn more bureaucratic than operational. The Office of Internal Auditing and the Office of Integrity and Compliance have a combined session. Derek languishes through the questions that the Office of Professional Responsibility raise.

Twice he passes on the meal they offer him, hoping to get out the door. When it becomes apparent the meetings are going to go on for a long while Derek interrupts them and asks for whatever the cafeteria can send up. Liu makes a grand show of having a subordinate sitting in the chairs against the wall retreat to get the food, not just for Derek but for him as well. He doesn't allow anyone else in the room to place an order.

Everything discussed is framed and presented in tempered code. It isn't lost on Derek that the entire process seems counterproductive to the supposed secrecy of their mission against Tithe. Granted, each office is represented by as few people as possible, and Rob had assured him that any of the Bureau's people present have the highest level clearances and were read-in on the operation, but still. The last SAC certainly didn't approach briefings this way. It was as if Liu was trying to reinvent the wheel after demonstrating that he was the one who came up with the design in the first place, and taking credit for it too.

Derek has reached his limit as the briefing for the Office of Professional Responsibility drags on. Liu sits back in his chair, reveling in Derek recounting the same information yet again. In response Derek stares at the senior agent as he delivers each word. The SAC's smug face doesn't change.

As he finishes talking through the missile strike yet again, Liu suddenly pitches forward and slaps the table. The action upsets what had been a previously docile set of mundane interactions. "This is some handiwork, Chief Warrant! I bet there's nothing like shoving a missile up the enemy's ass, am I right?"

Derek throws a sideways glance at Jason and Rob. The other men return his gaze with a pleading look in their eyes. It registers, and for the slightest moment he hesitates, knowing that they'll bear the brunt of any resulting shitstorm, but Derek can't go along with this any longer. His exhaustion and frustration takes over as he turns back to Liu. "You'll forgive me if I'm not overjoyed at having blown up a bunch of people this morning."

Liu recoils a bit at the remark. "I'm surprised to hear you say that. You just stopped a major terrorist attack with that drone strike. No need to be sore about it. These people have to learn that if you fuck with the bull, you get the horns. They keep this up and we'll go full shock and awe on them."

Derek sighs and shakes his head. He looks over at Jason. "Is my ride to the airport ready? I'm done here."

Liu looks at Jason with disbelief before turning his attention back to Derek. "Hey, Chief Warrant, you're not losing your resolve, are you? We need you in this fight. There's going to be a lot more triggers to pull before this is seen through to the end."

He can almost read his handlers' thoughts, both men willing him not to take it any further. Derek spares them a sympathetic glance before doing just the opposite. "I remember this one time a senator flew into theater, and the local two-star wanted to walk him through the AO. Me and a couple of my guys got sliced over to watch him, but the general had his own personal security detachment."

Liu folds his arms, a shit-eating grin locked on his face. Derek goes on. "We're walking through this neighborhood and school lets out. All the kids rush over. They're running around us. Shaking hands. Laughing. Talking in their broken English. Couldn't be happier to see us. My guys and I are joshing with them. Giving out candy, stuff like that, when a kid on the other side of our formation yells out.

"I look over and there's the general's PSD slamming their buttstocks into kids' heads. Kicking them. Pointing their muzzles at them. Needless to say the kids scattered, and the ones on my side followed suit."

"I'm not sure I see where you're going with this, Derek," Liu says.

"After we got back and handed the senator off I went over to the PSD team leader and asked him what he was doing with those kids. He told me he was 'neutralizing the threat' to his principal. That's when I told him he wasn't neutralizing a threat, he was creating thirty more."

"By slapping some kids around?"

"You see, that's the thing. Those kids are gonna grow up one day, and they're not gonna remember Americans as the great liberators who brought freedom and Burger King to Baghdad. They're gonna remember getting kicked and punched and buttstroked by a bunch of gorillas when it wasn't necessary. How do you think they're gonna act when they're ready to shoulder their own rifles?

"Marshal and the like, they can burn in hell for what they're trying to do. I know better than anyone how ruthless Tithe's true believers can be. I'm the first one to admit that they need to be stopped before they cause a bloodbath, and I'm not shying away from sending rounds downrange to do so. But we need to stop them in such a way that we're not fighting this same damn problem twenty years down the road. Also worth mentioning is the fact that I don't want to be looking over my shoulder when I'm seventy wondering if little Jimmy is all grown up and ready to get revenge."

Liu's grin is gone, replaced instead by a scowl. "This little Aesop fable your way of telling me you don't approve of my methods, Harrington?"

"Tell you what, Sam," Derek replies while standing up. "Next time, come out to the field and lay your eyes on those kids whose mothers and fathers we vaporize. Then you can tell me what I think of your methods." He spins to Jason and Rob. "Call me when you're ready to move again. I'm going home."

Stunned silence wraps the room as he exits. Derek is more than halfway down the hall when he hears Liu begin to rant at the agents still present.

5

An unmarked car is waiting for Derek outside the building. The agent behind the wheel starts the hour drive north to Ronald Reagan Washington National Airport.

At the outset of his working with the FBI it was decided, in particular by Derek himself, that for appearances he should travel commercially as much as possible so as to reinforce his cover story. It would be hard keeping that up if he took off and landed in private government jets everywhere he went. Anyone with enough brains to pay attention would immediately flag the behavior, and Derek already knows he's dealing with an adversary at the top of her class, even in light of the success they are having against her.

After clearing security it's another two hours before his flight boards, so Derek kills the time with drinks at the bar. Bourbon chased with beers. He gets just enough of a buzz to drown out the day's events before taking his seat. The wheels finally touch down in Indianapolis well after midnight. The shuttle takes forever getting him to his unassuming Ford Fusion in long-term parking. Climbing into the driver's seat he pulls out his cell after turning the car over.

At my car. Headed home, he texts.

The ellipsis flashes underneath his message and a few moments later the reply comes through. **Ok sweetheart. Drive safe.**

The term of endearment lets him know that Maureen is on duty tonight. Putting the car into gear, he eases out of the parking lot. From there it's a forty-minute drive as he circles Indianapolis to the east before turning north. It's close to two in the morning when he pulls into his subdivision nestled in Fishers, Indiana. Weaving through the connecting side streets brings him to the last ring of houses surrounding the pond at the center of the development.

The FBI-provided house is a two-story colonial painted maroon with cream shutters. Pulling into the drive, Derek throws the vehicle into park and takes out his cell.

Here. Is the front door open?

I just unlocked it, comes the reply.

The tradecraft exchange lets them both know they're not compromised. Derek shuts the car and makes his way inside. Stepping through the door reveals a staircase with a slender hallway to the left of it leading to the back of the house. To his right is his home office, to the left a formal dining room.

He walks through the hall into an expansive open concept space. Above him a loft walkway connects the upstairs bedrooms and overlooks the lower level. The family living room sits before him while off to the right is his bedroom and the garage. It had originally been labeled a guest room, but he gave up the master upstairs to accommodate the needs of his father. That, and he preferred being on the ground floor.

Off to the left is a kitchen lined with white cabinets, complete with a center island topped with blue-gray marble. Maureen stands behind it, her left hand stirring a cup of tea. Her right hand drops from behind her back down to the countertop a second later. To the untrained eye the movement would have resembled something akin to her scratching an itch, if it was noticed at all. Derek knows that in reality her hand was hovering over the .380 she keeps in her waistband. Even with the coded messages, she wasn't taking any chances until she had eyes on him.

A woman in her early sixties, she has black hair cut into a bob. Her features, and that of her husband, Al, are close enough to Kim's that no one would second-guess their being family. Tall and slender, the woman always seems to be cold. Even now she wears a gray Colts sweatshirt and blue jeans.

"Tough trip?" she says evenly.

Derek throws his duffel bag and suitcase onto the nearby couch. "Ran longer than expected."

"We noticed."

When Derek eyes her she holds his stare.

"Yeah, well, they don't exactly keep to normal schedules, now, do they?"

Maureen shrugs. "It is what it is. Al and I get it. Even Kim to a degree. Michael doesn't."

He rubs the back of his neck. Not wanting to get into it any further, he shifts to the opening she provided. "Speaking of, how is he?"

Before she replies, Maureen can't help but smile. "He's good. Such a good boy. He's reciting the states and their capitals constantly. Practically has them all committed to memory at this point. And there's a baseball game this Saturday. He's going to be ecstatic when he finds out you'll be there. You will be there, right?"

"Yes. It'll take some time to sift through everything that was uncovered. Probably have a few weeks at least."

"Well that's a start," she begins, and then after hesitating for a moment, Maureen adds, "I suppose."

Derek feels his annoyance welling up from inside. It had mostly dissipated with his drinks and resting on the plane, but was now inching its way back into place. Combined with the day's events, on top of the weeks spent on mission, Derek has had his fill. "Like you said. It is what it is, Maureen. You got this? I'd like to go see my boy now."

"I'm on it. Get some rest."

Taking the back staircase by the side door off the kitchen, Derek ascends to the second floor. He looks into the master, seeing his dad asleep, his ghostly form illuminated by the bluish-white light of the television mounted on the wall. The old man's prized possession, his over-under grouse hunting shotgun, hangs on two brackets above the bed.

He walks on, crossing past the bedroom door that sits between the master and Michael's room. Ever the mother and nurse, Kim had selected that bedroom so that she could always be equidistant from either of them if she was needed.

Derek approaches his boy's room at the end of the loft walkway. During the day he would use their specially arranged knock to let Michael know he is on the other side. Given the late hour, Derek gingerly rotates the doorknob to Michael's room and cracks the door open just enough to peek inside. Michael lies splayed out on his bed, his covers tossed askew. Derek steps in and eases the door closed, wincing at the almost imperceptible click the mechanism makes when shutting it. Turning back he takes in the walls adorned with Yankees posters and pennants, a holdover to his New York birthright.

Derek adjusts the blankets over him, then caresses Michael's hair. He spares a long look and smile for his son before turning to head for the door.

"Dad? Is that you?" comes the half-awake muttering from behind him. Derek spins around and crouches down.

"Hey, buddy, go back to sleep."

"Daddy. You're home," Michael mumbles, slightly more awake, his voice tinged with joy.

"I am, pal. Now go back to bed." Derek goes to stand but Michael grabs his hand.

"Don't go, Daddy. Stay with me. Please?"

Heart melting, Derek lets himself get pulled down. Easing his considerable bulk into the twin bed, he throws his arm over his son as the boy twists to nuzzle into him. "Okay, bud, but only for a few minutes." They're both asleep moments later.

Slipping out of bed early the next morning, Derek heads downstairs. Despite it being barely past six thirty, he finds Al working in front of the stove, scrambling eggs while bacon sizzles in a frying pan. As tall as Derek, the man is nearly as muscular even though he's in his sixties. A teal polo shirt is tucked into a pair of slate-gray khakis, framing his broad shoulders and slim waist. Silver hair rests at his temples while the rest of it is black and perfectly combed. A leather holster sporting a Smith & Wesson .40 caliber and a spare magazine sits on his right hip.

Looking up from cooking breakfast, his features explode into a wide smile, showing the wrinkles of age that weren't present mere moments ago. "There he is!" Al removes the dish towel from his shoulder and wipes his hands. He grips one of Derek's hands in both of his and shakes it vigorously. "Welcome home, Marine!"

"Good to see you, Al."

"And you as well. Coffee?"

"You read my mind."

Derek sits at a stool by the island while Al retrieves the coffee. He passes it over and Derek takes a long pull from the mug. "Ahhh."

The older man chuckles. "Not like that roofing tar they used to give us in the field, huh?"

"After so many weeks I'd even take that crap."

Al laughs again. "I hear ya," he says while turning back to his cooking. The man spent his years as an intelligence officer with the 3rd Infantry Division out of Fort Stewart, Georgia. Derek doesn't know the whole story, of course—those details would be classified—but Al apparently crossed paths with the CIA during Vietnam and was recruited shortly after. He met Maureen at the Farm.

Unlike the lukewarm relationship Derek had with her, he had immediately taken to Al. Their backgrounds in both the military and the intelligence community, along with their penchant for cigars and bourbon, basically ensured a match made in heaven. He had to tip his cap to the FBI for that one. Derek appreciated having two seasoned professionals watching over his family, but actually getting along with them made the cover that much easier.

"Another tough go of it?" Al asks while flipping the bacon.

"Yeah. You could say that."

"You've been at it a while now. Any hopes of it letting up soon?"

"There could be some light at the end of the tunnel."

Al nods and Derek smiles, appreciating the clandestine conversation for what it is. So much being said in so few words.

"Daddy!" Michael yells as he comes running into the kitchen. Derek scoops up his boy, who immediately throws his arms around his father's neck. "I knew it wasn't a dream!"

"Nope, I'm here, buddy," Derek says while squeezing his boy tight.

The older man smiles at them with a pair of plates in his hands. He puts the plates down in front of them. "Hey there, little man."

"Hey, Uncle Al." To Michael, Al was the youngest brother of Kim's father. Since both of her parents had passed on, it was the easiest story to sell. Having family in the area combined with Derek landing a job in Indianapolis made moving halfway across the country from Long Island that much more plausible. "Are you working today, Dad?"

"No, I'm not, bud. In fact, I thought we all might go fishing today. What do you think?"

A slight flicker of something passes over Michael's face. A hint of reluctance perhaps, but then he swallows and smiles. "Does that mean no school today?"

"Sure does."

"All right!" the boy says, hopping down and running upstairs. "Mom! Mom! Dad's home and he said I don't have to go to school today!"

Cringing, he shares a look with Al. The older man raises his eyebrows. "That's not gonna go well, partner."

"Tell me about it."

They eat and chat some more until Kim comes down the back stairs with Michael in tow. She's dressed in a set of purple scrubs and a pair of white sneakers. Her hair is pulled back into a tight ponytail and her face is none too pleased. Still, she plays the part and crosses over to him, giving Derek a kiss on the cheek and a hug. "Welcome home," she says flatly.

"Thanks," he returns.

When they separate she can hardly contain her scowl. Al steps in immediately. "How about some breakfast before you head in, hun?"

"No, thank you, Al, I'm not hungry," she says while not breaking eye contact with her ex-husband. "So, you guys are going fishing today I heard?"

"Yeah, well, I thought it would be nice to. Since I've been away and all. A little time to catch up, you know?"

"Sounds great. Have fun," she says devoid of enthusiasm. Kim leans over and kisses Michael. "Be a good boy. Listen to your dad and Uncle Al." She turns to Derek, her eyes glaring. "I've got to get going. Want to walk me to the car?"

"Sure thing."

He follows her into the garage. No sooner has the door closed behind him than she whirls around. "You can't do that, Derek."

"Do what? Take my boy fishing?"

"No, interrupt his whole schedule just because you came back home. He needs his routines."

Derek feels the twinge inside of him. A precursor to his anger boiling up. Taking a deep breath, he attempts to put the cover back on. "I've been gone for six weeks, Kim. I missed my boy and want to take him fishing. He can skip one lousy day of school. Not like it's going to make a difference with that Common Core crap anyway."

"Yes, Derek, it is. He's behind. In all his classes, not just math. His teacher tells me he's having a hard time adjusting, and that he barely socializes. They're even talking about getting him services if he doesn't start to show improvement."

Derek swallows as his stubbornness kicks in. "So he's a little behind. I was a late bloomer myself. He'll snap out of it. And besides, some time outdoors might do him some good. One day certainly won't make a difference at school, but it could out there."

Shaking her head, Kim grinds her teeth against her own frustration. "Not everything can be solved by whittling sticks and starting fires with leaves, Derek."

"Is that what you think I do?"

Looking at her watch with a huff, she eyes him again. "I know it's not. It's just that you're not the one dealing with it, Derek, I am. He cries himself to sleep. Wets the bed. Wakes up screaming and soaked through with sweat. I have to deal with all of that, not you. And just when I think I'm getting him settled you come back and disrupt it all."

"I'm his father, Kim," Derek growls, "not a disruption."

"Okay, bad choice of words. But you need to understand that life is very different when you're not around. You can't keep coming in and out and expect to just call the shots when you do. Our son needs stability right now. More than anything."

Derek feels himself at the tipping point. The spot where he would fall over the edge and go off in a tirade. Then the image of the kids getting loaded into the FBI vans and trucks comes back to him. How much had he disrupted their lives? How many of them would be lost to years of neglect in the system? To untold amounts of therapy. How many would grow up looking for revenge? The cycle perpetuates itself, unless it gets broken somewhere along the line.

The realization walks him back from the edge. He exhales and his features soften. "All right, Kim. You're right. I'm sorry. I should have discussed it with you first."

She practically does a double take. "All right . . . thank you." Kim glances at her watch again. "I have to get going or I'll be late for shift change."

"Okay."

After she climbs into her car, Derek raises the garage door for her. Before she can pull out he knocks on her window. Kim lowers it. "I know this isn't the best situation, Kim. I never asked for them to put us in the same house together. Just somewhere that I could be close to you both. They screwed us over with this arrangement, but it's no excuse. I'll try to do better."

Kim sighs. "You are doing better. And I know this wasn't your fault. That you're doing what's right for our protection. Just try to remember that while you're protecting us, we need you to be there for us, as well."

"I will. Things are wrapping up. This should all be behind us soon."

"Glad to hear it," she returns with a weak smile. "We can talk more tonight when I get home."

"Sounds good."

As Kim pulls out of the driveway Michael ducks his head in through the door to the house. "Dad! Should I ask Pop if he wants to come too?"

"Sure, Mike," Derek replies with a smile. "Some fresh air would do the old man some good."

After getting ready the four men jump into Al's Chevy Suburban and head southeast toward the Geist Reservoir. Following Fall Creek Road just north of the body of water, Derek points out a clearing with a tributary stream. A stand of woodlands separates the clearing from the reservoir itself. "That looks like the perfect place."

Pulling over, Derek, Michael, and his father head down to the stream while Al stays by the back of the vehicle. Unbeknownst to both Michael and his dad, a pair of M4s with collapsible stocks sit in the rear compartment, ready to be deployed at a moment's notice should anyone make an attempt. For his part Derek wears his trusted Sig Sauer .40 caliber in a concealed carry holster at the base of his spine.

The day is perfect. The sun shines down on them while birds chirp and sing. His father, all decked out in waders, a gear vest, and a boonie hat lined with flies and hooks, seems a different person in the environment he thrived in as a younger man. Derek watches as his dad, a bastard to him most of his life, lovingly instructs Michael on how to lash his fly to his line, and then walks him through the syncopated rhythm of casting. The man even jokes and teases Michael, eliciting no shortage of laughter from them both.

The three generations of Harringtons fish side by side along the tributary, enjoying the morning. Appreciating nature. Derek smiles more than a few times, finding some of the peace he so desperately searches for. Being in the field on a mission acts counter to his need. There can be no peace when your life's on the line, and you may be forced to take other lives as a consequence. Yet here and now, with his father and son, he knows it's the closest he will ever get.

Two hours after first setting up, none of them have gotten a bite. "This stream is run dry, boys," his father says. "Let's head through those woods and find one closer to the lake."

"Good call, Dad. Mikey, pack up your gear. We're gonna head farther in." His father takes off, already wading his way across the stream. Derek starts to follow but when he doesn't hear footfalls behind him he spins around. Michael is frozen on the shoreline, his face gone pale. "Dad, hold up!" Derek calls. The old man stops in the water and shouts back.

"What's the matter? Hurry your ass up!"

Derek moves to his son and takes a knee before him. The boy's eyes are transfixed on the wood line. He stands locked in place, yet his whole body trembles. "What is it, buddy? The trees?" Michael looks at him, his eyes wide as saucers, and nods vigorously. "It's okay, pal. It's just some woods. We'll be through them in no time."

"Hurry up, boy!" he hears his father yell behind them. The man's voice is tinged with the edge Derek is so familiar with from growing up. *Oh no, not now.* He had hoped that the time fishing would spare them from any of his father's episodes.

"Just a second, Dad," Derek calls back. He rubs

Michael's shoulders. "We'll be okay, bud, I promise. I'll be right there with you. Every step of the way."

"It's just a little way. Get that pansy moving, boy! I always knew he'd take after you!"

Michael hears the words and tears up. He presses his hands to his eyes as urine spreads across his groin. Derek sees the moment. Hears his father's condemnation, both out loud and in his head from decades ago. Had this been him back then, reacting this way, his father would have dragged him through the mud into those woods, slapping him upside the head the entire time while commanding him to stop crying and humiliating him for pissing his pants.

But he doesn't have to be his father. He swore he never would be, on the very first day he held Michael in his arms. And now confronted with the same moment, Derek recognizes it for what it is. He doesn't let his anger rise. He realizes he can break the cycle.

And so he does.

Standing, he turns and shouts back. "Shut your mouth and get in the car, Dad. We're leaving." The man stands stunned and then slowly starts walking back to their side of the riverbank. Derek leans down and takes his son in his arms. "It's all right, buddy. We're not going in there, okay? We'll just head home and try another time, all right?"

Michael breaks down further. "I'm sorry, Daddy, I want to be strong like you. But I'm scared."

Derek feels himself shudder. "You're the strongest boy I know, Mikey. Now come on. Let's go home and get you cleaned up."

Back at the house Derek gets them both settled down and taking naps. Later on he has to explain to Kim what happened. To her credit, she holds back from voicing "I told you so," even if her eyes still have a hint of it. Maureen comes over around six and they all have dinner together. Afterward the women retire to the couch while Al heads back across the street.

"How about a cigar?" he says as he leaves.

"Go ahead. We're here," Kim offers.

The two men head to Al's backyard. Derek gets a fire going while Al grabs two rocks glasses with ice molds and a pair of Macanudos. The men sit and sip, smoking and watching the flames in silence. Al is the first to break it.

"It got bad out there, huh? When they grabbed Mikey?"

Derek sighs, ashing his cigar into the fire. "I've been in more than a few scrapes in my time, same as you. That was the scariest thing I've ever been through. Can you imagine it? Having your family in the middle of a firefight with you?"

"Well, actually, son, I can because I have."

Looking at the man a moment, Derek smiles. "Yeah, I suppose you two have, haven't you?"

"It's the price we pay, unfortunately. The residuals we come away with. But it's not right that your boy had to be subjected to it. We signed up for it. He was pulled in before his time."

"He was, and I'm afraid he's scarred for life now because of it." Derek upends his bourbon, as much to get rid of the sour taste in his mouth as to banish the thought.

"Listen, Derek," Al says, leaning forward. "I know we're not privy to the details, but Maureen and I lived the life. We know what you're doing is important. Yes, she does, even if she doesn't let on. So we know the stakes. What you're having to carry. You can't let what happened back in New York distract you. Your boy will be fine. We'll see to it. All of us. But you stay focused on the mission. If you don't, you won't ever be able to come back here and truly be at peace. You've got to see this thing through, whatever it may be."

Derek pours more bourbon for Al before refilling his own. "You're a good man, Al. Both of you are good people. We're lucky to have you."

"You know enough of our backstory. You kids are like the family we never got to have. So believe me when I say that I feel the heartstrings being pulled same as you when I see Mikey struggling. But it'll be okay. You'll see. You two care about him too much to let him falter."

Another deep sigh. "I just want this to be over, Al. To make sure they're out of harm's way for good."

"Derek, if there's anyone that I think can do just that, it's you. Keep your head on a swivel and double tap whatever gets in your way. And above all else, stay safe out there. Your family needs you."

The younger man nods and the two are content to sit in silence. Derek ruminates on the words as his cigar burns toward its label. Autumn's Tithe is on the run. He just needs that last knockout punch, and he can be done with them forever.

6

Jolting up, Sarah rips her pistol out from under the camp pillow on her cot. Echoes of her name still reverberating in the fog that exists between asleep and awake, she searches vacantly about. There's barely any light to see by, just a sliver of midnight blue in the total black. A shroud of apprehension lies draped over her mind.

Aware solely that she is alive and awake, Sarah wrestles the panic of not knowing where she is. She reaches out with her free hand. Trying to touch something, anything, in the darkness. At the same time she twitches her Glock toward the slightest sound. Slowly, the noises begin to register. A croaking bullfrog. Crickets. The wind rattling tree branches. Her free hand brushes up against something. Canvas. Her tent. She's in her tent.

"Easy, Sarah," a soothing voice says from beyond the sliver. She jerks her pistol back in that direction. "Easy now. It's Phyllis."

Touch and sound work in concert to lift the shroud.

As her sight adjusts to the dark she can make out the grounds of the camp through the sliver. Phyllis had pulled her tent flap back and was calling her name while standing off to the side. Her people knew the risks of trying to shake her out of her sleep. Hell, of waking her at all. No one wanted to be on the receiving end of a pistol whip, or worse, a bullet to the chest.

Fully recognizing where she is, Sarah groans as she lowers her sidearm to the cot. Swinging her legs over the side, the woman sits up and presses her hands to her face. After rubbing her eyes and shaking out her hair she croaks, "What time is it?"

"A little after four a.m.," Phyllis replies.

The early morning hour startles Sarah further. "What is it? What happened?"

"Nothing, Sarah. At least nothing we know of yet, anyway. We got a message. They want you to go secure and contact them right away."

Remembering now that Phyllis was working as the runner in the comms shack overnight, Sarah acknowledges the woman and sends her back to her post. Rubbing her arms against the early morning mountain air, she quickly dons her cargo pants and hiking shoes before digging the encrypted satellite phone out of her backpack. Another wave of chill assaults her as Sarah steps out of the tent. Within a few moments the device is powered on and dialing.

"Good morning, sunshine," Daniel's voice says through the line. "Did I wake you?"

"You know you did," Sarah replies. "What do you want?"

"Call it OPSEC. That's the term you Top Secret

types like to throw around, isn't it? Fewer ears to eavesdrop this early in the morning."

"Is it time to move then?" Sarah asks.

"You're not out of the doghouse yet. Maybe after some other things pan out. In the interim, I've got a job I need you to handle. Well, not you per se. The Copperhead. You can certainly help your cause by not fucking this up, m'kay?"

Daniel outlines the task. Sarah listens while the machinations in her head work out the logistics. There should be time for both. "I can make that happen, so long as you realize I'll need to have him report to the camp directly afterward. There's not enough time to have him return here, and that means he won't be available to us once he's done with your bit."

"You want to roll the dice with that decision, you go ahead. Not like your plan is approved yet anyway. This is the immediate concern." Sarah can envision the man shrugging on the other end of the line. "Be grateful for the scraps you're still getting instead of eyeing what's on the table."

Suppressing a mouthful of profanity, Sarah growls in response. "Anything else that I need to be aware of?"

"That's all. Have a *lovely* day," Daniel says as he disconnects the call.

Muttering the curses she choked back under her breath, Sarah goes through the process of wiping the call log and shutting down the phone. Once done, she grabs her flashlight from the tent and starts toward the tree line to find the sniper.

■　■　■　■　■

Despite being only thirty or so minutes from Grissom Joint Air Reserve Base, Jacob Leach drives his aging Ford F-150 pickup into the Pleasant Valley Mobile

Home Park well after sundown. The truck's tires crunch over the pebbles strewn across the road as he lazily turns the wheel and circles around to the west side of the grounds. Pulling up in front of his double-wide trailer, Leach throws the vehicle into park. Killing the engine, the man exhales before getting out of the cab. Another drill weekend finished.

Leach pulls his multicam uniform blouse down to smooth out the garment, an action that is as much reflexive as spitting out the accumulated saliva from the pack of Skoal Wintergreen in his lower lip. The man snorts a hefty wad of phlegm into his mouth to mix with the tobacco juice concoction and then expels it onto the fledgling grass at his feet. Leach cracks his back and then heads to the tailgate to retrieve his duffel. Stains from the oil and other lubricants he's constantly wiping on his coveralls seep through the exterior of the bag.

Blue-white light flashes from a window of the trailer next door, the rhythm syncopated to the volume of the reruns Lucille is blasting as loud as her TV will allow. Across the way on the east side of the park he can hear Darren and Janice arguing again, and that fucking stray dog with the incessant hoarse bark is back on the grounds somewhere. Silhouettes cross back and forth in front of his own windows, the voices of his wife and kids adding to the din of the park. Even though it's a Sunday night, a radio accompanied by raucous laughter and drunken banter acts as a backdrop to all the other noise. From the sound of it the participants have no intention of letting up soon. Leach contemplates joining them.

Goddamn Sergeant, keeping us this late. His unit had no shortage of work to complete even though they are a Reserve detachment, and Leach's ranking NCO had made a point to accomplish as much of it as possible while he had the majority of them together. The Sergeant was obviously trying to earn promotion points by having the highest equipment readiness rating in the company, but it was being derived off of Leach's and others' efforts. Well, that rating could be used to his advantage also. Leach's work over the weekend combined with the readiness percentages all but assured that Mercury Red 4 would be next in line for any training missions.

As it was, he'd barely have time to get any sleep before having to be up. His job at Greco's Junk Removal down in Logansport started early for neighborhood trash runs before shifting over to contracted jobs, and then his buddy Dillon had texted asking him to lend a hand in the afternoon at McCluskey's garage with a bunch of engine and transmission work that had piled up. In no place to turn down the money he had agreed, but that had been six hours ago, when he was alert and energized off of his second energy drink of the day. *Tomorrow is going to be a grind, and it will only be Monday.*

Stepping inside, Leach drops his duffel bag by the door. He can hear his wife and boys arguing in their bedroom. His youngest, Isabella, looks up from her coloring book on the floor and sprints to him. "Daddy!" she calls out while leaping into his arms.

"Oof," he responds as his back gives a twinge. Still, Leach smiles and squeezes her in return. "Hey there, baby girl. Have a good weekend?"

"Billy keeps stealing my crayons and melting them with Momma's lighter."

"Well, dang," Leach replies while setting her down. "I'll have to set that boy straight then. Now, can you be Daddy's helper and get him one of his special cans from the fridge?"

"Okay, Daddy!" Isabella says before running off. In the interim Leach takes off his blouse and throws it over the arm of the couch before collapsing into the cushions. The familiar waft of something stale kicks into the air as he does so. His daughter comes back from the kitchen and hands him his PBR before returning to her coloring. He's barely popped the beer open and taken his first sip when Bernice comes into the living room.

"About time you showed up," she says, planting her hands on her hips. When they had met she was all of five foot two, a hundred and ten pounds with the metabolism of a seventeen-year-old. Only a year ahead of her, he had proposed right on the parade field after graduating basic training, and they'd married a few months later once she graduated high school. But that was five years, four kids, and forty pounds ago. Not that he was any better. His paunch was growing faster than his hairline was receding. "Where the hell have you been? The kids have been driving me crazy."

"Goddamn, Bernice, I just walked in the door. Can't you even give me two seconds?"

"I ain't got two seconds to give. You gonna answer me or what?"

Leach slurps his beer, appreciating the warmth that spreads when it hits his belly. He burps before responding. "Sergeant Keavers kept us late. The birds needed a lot of work."

Arching an eyebrow, Bernice runs her tongue over

her teeth before the action finishes in a click. "You forget how fucking phones work then?"

"Lay off, all right? It's been a rough few days."

His wife shakes her head as if snapping awake. Incredulous, she starts ticking points off on her fingers. "A rough few days? Let me tell you about a rough few days. While you was off playing soldier boy, the toilet sprung a leak again on Friday night, and I woke up to the second coming of Noah's flood in here. Okay? Slaton has been throwing up all weekend, and Wyatt fell over and busted his tooth this afternoon. I had to beg Maria to watch the other three and have my brother pick us up to bring him to the dentist, which by the way is going to cost us eight hundred dollars that we don't have. On top of that . . ."

Nodding occasionally, Leach tunes his better half out as she continues her diatribe. Normally the news of both the plumbing and dental issues would be enough to set him off, but the job he had performed for his contact over the weekend should be enough to take care of both and still have a little left over. He could get his buddy Randy to do the toilet on credit and pay him back in a few weeks when he had the cash in hand, and they could dodge and delay the dentist for a while.

Miraculously, her rant and his beer run out at the same time. Crushing the can, he gets up with another groan for his back and heads into the kitchen to retrieve a second. Bernice follows him in, her brief respite now complete. She begins peppering him with questions about what he was going to do to address the issues she just listed.

"Damn woman, leave me be," Leach replies while

cracking open his replacement can. "Can't I have a few minutes' peace without your hollering?" Before she can respond the sound of a bottle cap popping and jangling on the surface of wherever it lands fills the space in the kitchen. Furrowing his eyebrows, he digs into his pocket to retrieve his phone and look at the text message.

Delivered. Check your mailbox.

A broad smile stretches across his face. Leach's contact had said payment would be fast, but he didn't think it would be here already. He'd barely been home thirty minutes. Always a sucker for the way his dimples cave in when he smiles, Bernice's demeanor immediately shifts in response. "What, Jacob? What is it?"

He holds up his phone and waves it back and forth. "Don't I always tell you I'll take care of us?" Stuffing the cell back in his pocket, Leach upends his beer before heading out the front. Bernice bangs through after him, hopping down the stairs. The screen door rattles as it settles back in the frame.

"Whatchu gone and done now?" she asks as he makes his way down the driveway.

"You don't need to know the particulars," Leach responds as he rounds the front of the mailbox and faces her. "I got an opportunity and I took it. Didn't think the money would be here so fast but it is."

As he pulls the mailbox door open and bends down to reach inside, Bernice asks, "When were you gonna tell me about this money?"

Leach doesn't feel anything so he looks into the space. When he doesn't see anything either he chalks it up to the dark and reaches farther in, figuring the package is at the back of the box. A mosquito flies into the bug zapper hanging over the porch and crackles momentarily. Leach stands back up, his face puzzled as he scratches behind his ear.

"What's the matter?"

"Weird. The text I got said to check the mail—"

Bernice flinches as something wet hits her across her face and chest. She watches in disbelief as her husband's body, now headless, crumples to the side in an unnatural heap. Her hearing dwindled to a bare murmur, the report of the rifle doesn't even register. The woman's eyes cloud with tunnel vision. Propelled forward by some far-off need to confirm that what she is witnessing is reality, Bernice moves down the driveway on shaky legs, each step taking concerted effort to do so. She stops when she reaches his body.

Looking down first at his lifeless corpse, she then notices the spatter across her tank top. Bernice wipes at the wetness on her face, her palm coming away red and drenched in her husband's blood. She wipes again with her other hand and stares at the two, comparing them side by side as if to confirm that everything she is seeing is actually there. When all of the information finally registers, Bernice begins to scream.

Something slams into her chest and sends her stumbling backward until she crashes against the tailgate of Jacob's truck. Her screams cut short, Bernice's mouth works open and closed as she gasps for air. The woman slides down the back of the truck, leaving a bloody streak in her wake before landing in a seated position. A wet slap is followed nearly instantaneously by a metallic *thunk* as a second shot passes through her skull and punches into the body of the vehicle.

The dog with the hoarse bark continues to do so. Lucille's television resonates with the opening theme to the next episode. Isabella stands in the doorway, another mosquito falling victim to the irresistible blue light drawing it in.

"Mommy? Daddy?"

7

After six days on top of one another with more exchanges of the same between himself, Kim, his dad, and Maureen, Derek decides it's best that he return to his cover routine. Having placed a call to Drysdale the night before to have the team report in the morning, Derek springs out of bed at four thirty a.m. and is out on the roads by five. While a lot of those he served with hated it, he always took well to running. After so many years the miles and paced endurance are ingrained into his muscle memory.

Derek jogs the streets around his subdivision, working his way farther from the house with each successive lap. The cool morning air betrays what the day's afternoon will be like if the weathermen are correct. Squirrels and chipmunks scatter at the early morning interruption of sneakers slapping pavement. Hitting Cumberland Road, he bangs a left for another half mile before finding the entrance to wooded trails.

The Marine loses himself under a canopy that is alive with songbirds. His nature-induced cardiovascular meditation is the best of both worlds: necessary physical conditioning combined with respite from a lifetime of accumulated emotional baggage. Amongst the trees he can just be. Out here he finds some semblance of peace. Small and momentary as it may be, Derek is grateful for it.

Even with how often he's gone, Derek has put in enough time over the last year to know these trails by memory. He lets his mind go. His heart pumps. His feet push off of fallen limbs and plow through leftover puddles.

After a few minutes more he crests a small rise and runs into a tiny cemetery, long since forgotten by all in town save for generational kin and the Fishers Historical Society. The grave markers date back to the Indian Wars, the Civil War, and the earliest settlers of the town. Going to the corner, Derek finds the overturned bucket that he stashed here. Righting it, he scoops up the bottle of bleach, a scrub brush, and the small set of chisels he left underneath. Diluting the bleach with some nearby puddle water, he sets about his latest headstone as part of a one-man mission to restore the historical site.

Having scrubbed the stone and re-etched some of the words, Derek replaces everything and runs back home. He glides into the garage and then pops through the interior door to the house like clockwork at six thirty a.m. From there it's a shower, getting dressed, and a cup of coffee before he is kissing Michael and out the door an hour later.

Wearing slacks, boots, and a button-down shirt with a fleece vest over it, Derek waves to the neighbors as he climbs back into his unassuming sedan. Pulling out of the development, he hops onto Interstate 69 headed south for the roughly forty-minute drive down to the office in Indianapolis. With the Ellis Anders Corporation headquartered in the city, it was easy to establish the team's cover.

Through cooperation with the corporate giant, the Bureau secured a small building on the sprawling E. A. Technology Center campus in the West Indianapolis section of the city. As a result of a hefty contracted lease agreement, the building was adapted to specifications necessary for the team's training and anonymity, with access rights and no questions asked negotiated as part of the agreement. Arranged through several intermediaries and shell companies, the FBI set up an LLC front that, for anyone looking, appeared to be a service-disabled veteran-owned machinery inspection and maintenance firm with a subcontract for mechanical support.

The sheer size of the campus, number of employees and contractors coming in and out every day, and the secure perimeter made it easy for the team to get lost in the routine mix of Ellis Anders business. Moreover, the corporation owned a private recreation area to the south of West Raymond Street bordered by the White River. Also within a secure perimeter and containing multiple lakes and acres of forest, Derek and the QRF-E were able to get outdoors to practice maneuvers and survival techniques in a real-world environment.

Posing as a Senior QA/QC Equipment Specialist, he and the other team members fit well into the company's veteran subcontracting initiatives, adding further credibility to the fabricated identity of the front. At the same time, the cover title gave Derek a plausible story for his constant travel and absenteeism. The team's time in the field was easily explained away by a need to conduct another round of inspections, maintenance, or both at the company's various locations.

The QRF-E had to take a crash course in pharmaceutical production and the requisite machinery processing, but it was no different than the covers Derek had to establish for his collection teams during his Marine Corps HUMINT and counterintelligence days. The extraction team learned more than enough to cover themselves through casual conversation, and Derek taught them how to redirect discussions should they come up against someone truly in the know.

After swiping into their building near the southern edge of the facility footprint, he passes through a small office area adorned with desks and computers. The room behind that is set up with work benches, machinery in various stages of disassembly, spare parts, and a wide array of tools and diagnostic equipment. The back wall of the workshop holds another door, one that requires an additional swipe of his access card, an eight-digit code, and a retinal scan by a device hidden behind an electrical panel.

A series of clicks is followed by a loud unlatching. Stepping through the door into the back two-thirds of the converted building, Derek finds the extraction team already on the section of open floor that's covered with foam wrestling mats. Changing quickly in the adjoining locker room, his day begins in earnest.

The team starts with physical training. First calisthenics to get the blood pumping and then combatives. Each member takes a turn leading the classes during the five-day week based on their different disciplines. Drysdale instructs them in Krav Maga. Ortega teaches boxing, while Ortiz shows them jiujitsu and police-level disarming techniques during her sessions. Gerbowski brings it all together with his wrestling and MMA, while Derek contributes his knowledge of Marine Corps martial arts and edged weapon fighting.

After PT the team breaks up to shower and change. Each wears their nondescript civilian attire should they have to quickly move into the workshop or office if someone comes by the building. They eat breakfast and then transition into target practice in another section of the building set up as a soundproofed indoor range with an accompanying shoothouse. The team progresses through their primary, secondary, and sidearm weapons before switching off to do the same with other team members' armament, thus building redundancy and familiarity of all weaponry across the entire group. They squeeze off hundreds and hundreds of rounds for both accuracy and live fire, practicing any extraction scenarios that either Drysdale or Derek can come up with.

After lunch instruction picks up again according to each member's specific focus. One day Ortiz goes over field medicine techniques. The next day Ortega will cover new technology and equipment utilization. Drysdale and Derek combine to work them through team SOPs, while Derek and Gerbowski combine on intelligence gathering and investigations. They spend time going over any new intel reports or threat assessments that the Bureau's analysts have derived and war-game their next possible courses of action. When not reviewing the latest information, they study the intricacies of pharmaceutical machinery to further support their covers.

Late in the afternoon the group staggers their departures from the campus and reconvenes in the recreational area. Derek finishes each day with survival instruction. He shows the group everything he knows. From fire production and shelter improvisation, to wild edibles, trapping, and water purification. The three younger team members, used to working their law enforcement positions in urban environments, soak up the wilderness training like sponges. Even Gerbowski, who is well versed from his hunting experience, is mesmerized by the depth and breadth of Derek's knowledge.

For the instructor it's all about redundancy. Should Autumn's Tithe continue to have additional camps, or should other militias crop up in the remote places of the continent, Derek knows that extra capacity will be needed. That, and he doesn't plan on doing this much longer. He hopes that the passing of his skill set will eventually enable each member to act as the reconnaissance element for their own extraction teams. Instead of one unit there would be four spread out across the country for a better response. Once Derek was free of Tithe he could help stand up other teams if necessary. He just hopes the need never gets to that point.

Beyond that there is the unspoken piece. The one that all soldiers know and acknowledge, but rarely give voice to lest it should come to pass. They all know that if Derek is killed or captured, one of them will have to take over where he left off. In this, they devote themselves to learning all that they can, with none so dedicated as the instructor himself in setting them up for success.

With classes done, the group disbands and melds into the rest of the city traffic for their various commutes home. Again staggering their departures, each day they leave at a different time so as to avoid establishing any patterns as part of their countersurveillance measures. In the morning they'll pick back up where they left off, conducting the same routines of training and assessment to maintain the highest level of operational readiness. All the while waiting for the next piece of the Autumn Tithe's puzzle to fall into place.

* * * * *

Two weeks after returning to the training regimen at the facility, the phones for Gerbowski and the Double O's blare alive at 3:48 a.m., the jarring alarm overriding any silent or do not disturb function thanks to a specially installed application. The only way to dismiss the noise is by opening up the accompanying text message:

ALERT. ALERT. ALERT. Immediate assembly. Kokomo Municipal Airport. Aircraft Ownership Solutions office. NLT 0500. Acknowledge.

Each send an "acknowledged" text message in response. The roughly hour drive north on Route 31 from Indianapolis sends the trio scrambling. Throwing on utilitarian clothing of cargo pants and hiking shirts, they affix their sidearms and scoop up go-bags pre-positioned at their front doors. Given the early hour and open roads they push their vehicles beyond the typical speed limits in order to gain some time.

Turning off County Road E 400 N, the trio arrives within minutes of one another, each circling the area until finding the one-story office building nestled near the center of the airport and closest to the runways. A blacked-out Suburban and a few other vehicles are parked in front and pale yellow light shines through the windows facing the airstrip. Gerbowski and Ortiz shrug at each other as they make their way to the office door. Inside they find Ortega already present, leaning on a desk with his arms folded, his bleary eyes looking out from under the brim of his ball cap.

The office is small with two desks facing one another to the left and right of the door. File cabinets line the walls. The back left of the space has a small table with four chairs arranged around it. In the opposite corner is a kitchenette and single bathroom. Radio equipment, maps, and laptops are arranged on the tabletop. Piled against the wall near the bathroom are their individual kit bags, chest rigs, and weapons.

Rob and Jason sit at the table in front of their laptops, muttering softly to one another while sipping from large cups of coffee. Chief Drysdale and Derek bisect the space between them and the team, standing in their field camouflage. "Morning, ladies," Drysdale begins before nodding over his left shoulder. "Ground your go-bags then suit up. Mission brief in ten."

As Derek and Drysdale retreat to the kitchenette for their own mugs of morning caffeine, the three team members move over to their gear. Ortiz heads into the bathroom to change while Ortega and Gerbowski strip down and don their uniforms in the common area. Once dressed they gather around the table. Derek gives a nod to Jason, who picks up the hand mic attached to the radio and keys up. "Mercury Red 4, this is Grizzly 6. Start your approach."

"Roger, Grizzly 6," the radio crackles back. "Inbound time now."

Putting the hand mic down, Jason gives Drysdale the thumbs-up. The Chief turns back to the team members and orients them to the maps on the table. "Today's exercise is a recovery and extract of Slingshot with three team members, simulating one of us going down due to injury, KIA, etcetera. The three of you will be inserted here, north of the Slocum State Forest recreation area on the east side of Mississinewa Lake. Upon completing insertion you're to establish a patrol base and await instruction for the exercise to begin. Slingshot will then be inserted south of your position in the vicinity of Slocum cemetery, here—" the Chief says while stabbing a finger at a topographical map. "Your mission is the successful evasion of opposing forces and any civilian presence in the area, recovery of Slingshot, and then secure movement to this clearing for extraction by the helo."

Derek chimes in. "After my fast rope, Chief will be inserted between your group and me in an unknown location. He's acting as the OPFOR in this exercise and will work to either intercept you, me, or all of us if and when we've linked up. Your primary objective is my recovery while evading OPFOR, but if you should become compromised, then your secondary objective is actions on contact. While Chief and I will both be playing our respective roles during the field problem, we're also acting as observers throughout."

"You're being evaluated on your mission planning, execution, and achievement of the objectives," Drysdale picks back up, "as well as your response to any variables or contingencies that arise during the simulation. Grizzly 6 will serve as the command element for the exercise, and will provide you with any additional instructions or information you require during your planning phase. Scepter 5 is here evaluating the overall exercise as well as providing coordination with higher. As you heard, the chopper is already inbound. You have between now and your insertion to complete all mission planning, outfitting, and pre-combat checks."

Silence fills the void after the Chief is done speaking. The junior team members stare at their leadership. After a moment Derek shakes his wrist out from under the cuff of his sleeve and holds his watch up. "Clock's ticking."

The three spring into action, quickly digging into cargo pockets to produce waterproof notebooks and pens. They hunch over the map, Gerbowski pulling out a protractor and affixing it to grid squares, going through the necessary computations to establish their line of travel while adjusting for magnetic declination. Working in concert, they evaluate the terrain through a map reconnaissance and begin to formulate their plans.

"So we push southwest from the LZ to this point here," Gerbowski says. "That'll gain us some elevation and give us high ground to work with. Then we can pivot and move along a south, southeast azimuth. That should allow us to hug the shoreline while still remaining inland enough that we can't be observed from the water."

"And puts us on roughly a direct course to the cemetery," Ortiz adds.

"Exactly," Gerbowski agrees. "What's your take, B? You're the best we have with a compass when we're on the ground."

Ortega scratches his head before leaning in closer and squinting. "Yeah, I concur. I don't like the look of all these clearings and access trails along the east side of the AO. Even without running into civilians or OPFOR, we'd need to cross too many linear danger areas, and that'll add time to our movement. I think the shoreline is the way to go, but just to play devil's advocate, these contour lines are tight in some places. We could end up being slowed down by terrain and elevation there too."

"So we move in a file as much as need be," Ortiz offers. "Better to get us through the dense stuff while keeping tabs on each other. If it opens up we can shift to a modified diamond for extra security."

Ortega nods and smiles at his de facto older sister. "Sand People always ride single file to hide their numbers."

Rolling her eyes, Ortiz slaps him upside the head. "Enough with the *Star Wars*, pendejo. Focus."

"At least it wasn't a prequel reference," Gerbowski jokes. "Okay, being down one we need to realign some things, so how about Brian, you stay on point and act as our primary navigator. Angie, you pull rear security but act as backup to Brian's nav. I'll handle comms with higher and actions on contact should we need them. You two good with that?"

"Good," Ortiz replies.

"Good to go," Ortega says.

"All right," Gerbowski adds while looking at his watch. "That helo is probably only a few more minutes out. B, you've got the most gear to inspect. You get started on that now. We may need your drone for the actual recovery. Once you're done, start looking over our gear to give us a little help."

"I'm on it," Ortega replies. He wheels around and heads over to the wall where their equipment is piled up.

Gerbowski turns to Ortiz. "I'm going to tie in with Grizzly and get our comms plan worked out. You want to double-check my work on these grids and headings, and then help Brian when you're done?"

Ortega smiles. "You got it."

Derek and Drysdale lean back against the kitchenette counter sipping on their coffees as they watch the three break off from one another to tackle the various tasks needed simultaneously. After Gerbowski and Ortiz have finished their items they consolidate on Ortega, where Gerbowski shares the communications information on primary and alternate frequencies for themselves, the aviation unit, and higher command. Having copied the information down, the trio goes through hurried inspections of their gear before donning their chest rigs and slinging their weapons. They're in the process of conducting communication checks with their radios and applying their camouflage face paint when the rotors of the helicopter are heard.

Gerbowski slaps Ortiz on the shoulder. "That's our ride. Let's do this!"

"Roger that!" she replies.

As Ortega hefts his M249 and heads for the door, the other junior members following him out, Derek and Drysdale pour out the remainder of their coffee and toss their cups into the sink before putting on their own gear. While the main focus was on evaluating their subordinates, the senior members were using the exercise for their own practice as well. Unspoken though it may be, they each understood that the scenario set them up for their own cat-and-mouse match against one another, on top of the challenge of avoiding any civilian detection as well. You always train as you fight.

Outside the office the sky's deep blue of predawn is melting away from the fiery oranges of another morning's start. Derek and Drysdale jog out to a grassy patch between the two runways where the other members of the QRF-E are already on a knee awaiting the incoming aircraft. The rotor blades increase in volume and in short order a UH-60 Black Hawk comes into view. The bird banks over the airfield and turns perpendicular to the team before the pilot brings it into a hover and lowers the helicopter to the ground.

As soon as the wheels have touched down the door to the cabin slides open. Gerbowski taps Ortega on the shoulder and points at the chopper. The team gets to their feet and jogs forward while remaining crouched to avoid the dip in the rotor blades. Within seconds they are all strapped in, putting on headsets for communication inside the helicopter during the flight. The aircraft's crew chief pulls the door shut and the Black Hawk lifts back off, heading northeast to the training area.

8

The pilots push the speed of the aircraft as if in response to an actual extraction. The reality of the mission against Autumn's Tithe and the decision to use Derek as a solo operative to infiltrate their camps brought with it a bevy of risks. At any moment he could be discovered by the enemy and have to evade them. Caught in a firefight. Wounded. Injured. Sick.

All contingencies that they try to anticipate and war-game for, crafting their SOPs to meet each challenge and subsequent wrinkles head-on. It was a calculated gamble, trading the stealth and knowledge of a single individual for the added security and greater chance of being discovered. The course of action was one that Derek himself had lobbied for and ultimately won the approval of.

Which made conducting these training exercises as close to reality all the more imperative. The helicopter shudders with the increased speed, the passengers inside the cabin feeling the vibrations through the metal brackets of their seats. The open terrain and farmland of rural Indiana rockets by underneath the helo, the fields awash with early morning sunlight making the grain and alfalfa appear to be ablaze.

The trio sit on one bench, hunched over their maps going through their plan again to make the most of their time while also putting any last-minute adjustments in place. Derek and Drysdale sit opposite them. To ensure help with the authenticity of the scenario, the Chief's headset is dialed in to the Black Hawk's crew so that he can't hear the team's discussion. Derek listens to the junior members, observing, cataloging, and analyzing their strategy and coordination amongst one another. Drysdale gets the word from the pilots in his ear and taps Derek on his leg. The man holds up two fingers and then goes back to looking out the window.

Leaning forward in his seat, Derek speaks into his headset microphone, the metallic amplification of his voice slightly muted by the high-pitched whine of the aircraft and the wash of the rotor blades in the background. "Two minutes."

"Roger that, two minutes out," Gerbowski echoes.

Derek waves the three to move in closer to him and then looks the group in the eyes each in turn. "Remember what we've rehearsed. Stealth and security are always a factor, but you're being evaluated on speed as well. If the call for extract ever goes out, survivability could be measured in a handful of minutes. Every second counts."

The three nod in affirmation. "Don't worry, boss, we got you," Ortega says.

Nodding in response, Derek says, "Don't forget, you're not to proceed from your patrol base until all elements are in place. Once Chief and I are on the ground, Grizzly 6 will synchronize everyone's time and start the exercise. From then on you're on your own." Drysdale taps him on the leg again, this time holding up three fingers. "Thirty seconds. Stand by!"

The trio remove their headsets, twist the restraint releases, and disconnect their seat belts. Ortiz and Gerbowski move to the left door while Ortega moves to the right, each of them pulling on a pair of thick padded gloves designed to preserve their hands from the friction of the fast rope maneuver. Outside the door the reflected early morning sunshine sparkles off the surface of Mississinewa Lake. As quickly as it is there it is gone, replaced by the dense forest of the training area of operations.

As the pilots flare the Black Hawk to rapidly decrease the speed, members of the crew move to their respective cabin doors. The helicopter settles into a hover and then lowers in altitude even farther. In a flash the dimly lit cabin is bathed in sunlight as the cabin doors are thrown open. The roar of the rotors overhead is now nearly deafening without the doors shut and their headsets on. Hot air washes over the team, carrying with it the scent of expended fuel, churned-up foliage, and morning dew. A grittiness of fine dust and other particles kicked up by the hover pinch as they bounce off the trio's exposed skin, and force an unpleasant accumulation in their ears, noses, and mouths.

The Black Hawk's crew members release the thick rappelling ropes out the doors, watching until they are uncoiled and straight. Giving the thumbs-up, the Double O's each take a seat and grab onto the ropes with their gloves while pinching the ropes between their boots. A short jolt from their hips lifts them up and out of the helicopter and sends them rapidly sliding down the length of the ropes. Within seconds each disappears into the canopy of the forest below them. Gerbowski follows suit once he sees Ortiz go under the tree cover. As soon as all three are on the deck Gerbowski radios an all clear to the crew, who engage the chopper's auto belay insertion system and retract the thick ropes back into the aircraft.

On the forest floor Gerbowski dips his head to avoid the dirt and dust being kicked up and rotates to get eyes on his teammates, cradling his rifle at the low ready in the process. Already the Double O's have moved off a short distance and taken up positions to his left and right. They lie prone behind naturally occurring cover and concealment, Ortiz behind a large rock formation and Ortega amongst a stand of thick trees, no doubt already working to designate their overlapping fields of fire and determine necessary ranges in their sectors.

As the bird overhead begins to drift off, Gerbowski starts toward them, scanning the terrain for an acceptable emplacement to close the perimeter of their patrol base. He's only gone a few steps when above the canopy a loud noise can be heard over the wash of the rotor blades, followed by an immense *clang*, the sound of metal snapping in a way it was never intended to. The man twists his head to the treetops, searching for the chopper through the cover.

"What the fuck was that?" Ortega says into the closed frequency intercom the trio shares. He and Ortiz are instantly on their feet, all three knowing full well that the sound isn't normal.

Rather than answering, Gerbowski starts moving to the sound of the Black Hawk. The Double O's trail after him and all three come to a stop when a break in the trees allows them to get eyes on the helicopter. Gerbowski turns the dial on his push-to-talk button housing to the shared aviation frequency and keys up. "Mercury Red 4, this is Pegasus—"

In a blast that sends all three to the ground for cover, the right engine blows apart in a brilliant ball of flame that sends fiery debris streaking in every direction like the fragments of a meteor that has broken up in the Earth's atmosphere. Thick black smoke bellows from the destroyed engine and begins wafting through the crew compartment. The QRF-E members on the ground watch helplessly as the aircraft's tail starts swinging to the left, only then to overcompensate and swing wildly to the right, all while drifting over the treetops trailing smoke behind it. The Black Hawk rapidly changes direction and heads for the lake.

The junior team members take off running after the bird. Gerbowski shifts to the all-channels frequency and keys up as he runs, leaping over fallen limbs and crashing through branches. "Flash! Flash! Flash!" his adrenaline-enhanced voice calls into his mouthpiece. "Pegasus 4. Real-world emergency. I say again, real-world emergency. Mercury Red 4 is going down. Need immediate emergency response and water rescue assets deployed to the vicinity of my location, time now!"

Inside the Black Hawk the pilot wrestles with all his strength against the increasingly unresponsive stick and collective, trying to gain some elevation to clear the taller treetops and buy them extra time. He presses with all his might against the foot pedals to keep the aircraft stable while angling toward the lake. Alarms blare in the cockpit and a multitude of warning indicator lights flash on the console in front of both aviators.

The copilot switches the engine power control lever to the off position and then pulls the engine emergency off T-handle all the while calling into his radio, "Mayday, mayday, mayday! Mercury Red 4, we've got an engine on fire! I say again, Mercury Red 4 has single engine failure and we're currently on fire!"

"Hit the bottles!" the pilot screams at his counterpart.

Throwing the main fire extinguisher switch, the copilot waits for the rush of the retardant to be released. When it doesn't come he flips the switch again. The result the same, he yells back into his mouthpiece. "Main isn't responding! Going to reserve!" The copilot throws the reserve fire extinguisher switch but nothing happens. Frantically flipping the switch over and over he screams, "Malfunction! I've got nothing from either bottle!"

"Crew evac!" the pilot screams into the aircraft's intercom. "We gotta ditch! Get ready to jump!"

The initial blast and resulting jolt had snapped Derek's head back so violently into the frame of his seat that he momentarily blacked out. The sounds of multiple layers of radio traffic shouting over one another in his headset brings him back, followed by immediate coughing from smoke inhalation. Head still swimming from the hit and his vision clouded, Derek works himself free from the safety restraints and ducks his head out the open cabin door, desperately pulling in much-needed oxygen. He notices the Black Hawk passing over the lake's beach and heading out to open water before turning back inside.

Through the columns of dark smoke he sees the Chief on the opposite side of the cabin helping a crew member toward the door. His skin stained from the emissions and sweating profusely, Drysdale appears none the worse for wear otherwise. Derek braces himself against the fuselage as he works his way over to his friend, fighting against both the imbalance from his head and the rocking of the increasingly destabilized helicopter. When they are close enough the Chief yells in his ear. "We gotta jump! Check the other guy!"

Spinning back around, Derek lowers himself to his belly and crawls toward the crew chief's position, flames readily visible through the hole in the roof of the bird. Derek finds the man lying on the deck, the left side of his body charred and smoking, large sections of jagged metal puncturing his body in the neck, shoulder, and upper back. The crew chief's helmet visor having shattered in the blast, Derek sees the all too familiar stare of vacant eyes. Still, he works his fingers under the man's jawline and presses into the flesh. His hand coming away slick with dark blood is the final confirmation to the absence of a pulse.

When he gets back to the opposite door, the Chief has managed to get the crew member into a seated position with his legs hanging out of the aircraft. The smoke whips around them as the Black Hawk bucks and lurches, limping toward its inevitable demise. Derek shakes his head and Drysdale leans back in. "This guy is fucked in the water, you gotta stay with him. You good?"

Blinking a few times, Derek wipes at his eyes and then gives the thumbs-up. "Good to go."

A single nod is the Chief's reply. "I'm going for the cockpit. Bail out once we're low enough and get him clear. Don't wait for me." Derek doesn't have the chance to respond before Drysdale is headed back into the smoke-filled cabin. Instead he engages the quick releases on his chest rig and shrugs out of the equipment and then helps the crew member to do the same with his vest.

As Drysdale works to climb toward the cockpit, the copilot crawls halfway over the center instrument panel that divides the space between the two aviators. "Crew evac! Everyone out! We gotta ditch!"

"What about you two?" Drysdale screams back.

"I'll bail from up here and he'll try to get some distance before ditching! Go!"

The Chief doesn't wait. Tears and snot streaming from his eyes and nose, Drysdale works his way back to the cabin door, shoving his head out the opening so that he can breathe. Below them the water ripples outward in hundreds of cascading waves. He grabs onto the crew member's and Derek's shoulders and leans his head in between them both. "Ready! Go!" he screams at the top of his lungs and then shoves the two men out of the aircraft. Taking a deep breath, the Chief jumps a moment later, pinching his legs tightly together and crossing his arms over his chest, trying to enter the water as vertically as possible.

Breaking through the tree line, Gerbowski and the Double O's rush down to the beach only to witness the Black Hawk writhing through the air as it heads out over the lake. They turn south and run along the shore, panting as their boots splash in the water. When the helicopter settles into a hover Gerbowski pulls up short, Ortiz and Ortega almost barreling into him as a result. Two people exit from the side of the aircraft facing them, followed by a third a moment later. On the opposite side of the bird another individual drops from the helo and enters the lake. The chopper's nose dips slightly before it continues farther south. Gerbowski gulps in air as he searches about. To the northwest a stretch of the shoreline juts into the lake.

"You two get to that peninsula," he yells while pointing at the landmass. "Angie, you set up a casualty collection point and pop smoke for the rescue teams. Take over comms and call in any nine lines that you need to. Brian, get in the water and find Derek. I'm going for the pilot."

"I'm the better swimmer, let me go for the pilot," Ortega counters.

Shaking his head, Gerbowski puts a hand on the younger man's shoulder. "That's exactly why you're going for Derek. Secure our principal. That's the mission. Now go!" he says, shoving off and sprinting in the opposite direction.

The man runs as fast as his legs will carry him. In what becomes simultaneously a positive and a detriment, the Black Hawk begins to arc toward his section of the shore where the terrain inclines up a rocky abutment. Gerbowski angles back into the tree line and then races up the slope. Vision now obstructed, the sound of the helicopter in its death throes echoes over the water. Secondary blasts ring out while the remaining engine stalls. The volume of the rotors drops, and Gerbowski knows this is the end.

Reaching the top of the slope, he drops his weapon and shrugs out of his pack. The quick releases on his chest rig come next, and as it falls away Gerbowski rips his survival knife from its sheath. Breaking back out through the trees onto a small cliff twenty feet above the surface, he sees the Black Hawk streaking across his vision from right to left. The man is just able to cut his leg holster free and drop the knife before the chopper slams into the water.

The flames hiss and the greasy, black smoke is swallowed up as the fuselage rolls over itself, splashes back down, lists to the left, and disappears under the water. Gerbowski crouches down, steadying himself as best he can, taking in deep breaths while his limbs tremble. The rotor blades slam into the water and shatter, fragments flying in every direction in a rain of debris. When he believes that the rotors no longer pose a threat, he takes a three-step leap and dives off the cliff headfirst.

The lake is frigid. Instantly saturated, he feels the weight of his uniform and boots working to pull him under. Just beneath the surface the water shimmers with streaks of sunlight, but the remains of the Black Hawk are rapidly drifting into the dark. Gerbowski follows the path of the air bubbles heading upward in escape, swimming in the opposite direction to reach the helicopter before it gets beyond his reach. Having had almost no time to catch his breath from the run along the shore, he already feels his air waning. Pushing himself, Gerbowski closes the distance and grabs onto the pilot's doorframe, the window punched out in the crash.

A sudden jolt knocks him free from the fuselage and Gerbowski drifts a few feet up. As clouds of sediment erupt around the helicopter he realizes that they have sunk to the lake bottom. Before it can be completely lost in the churned-up dust Gerbowski makes a few more strokes to get back to the doorframe. He wrenches the door open with a single pull with both his arms, surprising himself in the process.

Ducking into the cockpit, Gerbowski finds the pilot motionless, the man's arms suspended in the water, chin tucked to his chest. Blood streaks from his nose, mouth, and other cuts on his face only to dissipate a moment later. Gerbowski twists the release on the pilot's harness, freeing him from his restraints. Putting a hand under each arm, he heaves the pilot free from the wreckage. Shifting his grip and securing the man with his left arm across the pilot's chest, Gerbowski aims for the surface and begins pulling with his free limb.

The shimmer of the sunlight is so far away. As he strains against the weight of the pilot's body and his waterlogged clothes, his lungs burn from both the effort and the lack of oxygen. How long had it been? A minute? Two? More?

He feels himself tiring. Slipping backward a little after each pull. His strokes aren't coming fast enough to keep the upward momentum going. The pilot's weight is an anchor. The surface is closer now but still so far away. Gerbowski's eyes begin to cloud at the edges. He fights to keep his mouth clamped shut.

Gerbowski squeezes his eyes shut as tight as his mouth. The thought of his coach in high school pops into his head. The man was always spurring him on. Always encouraging him to push just a little bit harder. One more lap. One more repetition. Hold out just a little longer and the clock will sound.

He pulls and pulls and pulls again. And just when he thinks he is about to black out he sends up a prayer with what is surely his last stroke, and then he breaks the surface. Thrashing around, his chest heaves as he takes deep breaths, while still frantically trying to keep himself afloat. After several seconds of this, he reaches under the surface and pulls the pilot's head above water.

"Over there!" a voice calls out. Gerbowski turns toward the sound. He catches sight of a column of orange smoke before his eyes settle on the shoreline. Two Indiana Conservation Officers stand on the beach just to the right of the ledge he leapt off of. One officer whips her hat off and drops her duty belt as she charges into the lake, breaking into a breaststroke toward him as soon as she hits the deeper water. Behind the officer her partner speaks into a radio before dropping his gear and swimming out in the same fashion.

The officer reaches Gerbowski and helps him tow the pilot to her partner. The man takes hold of the pilot and swims him back into shore while she gets an arm around Gerbowski and aids him in swimming the rest of the way. Once in shallow water she leaves him coughing and panting to run over and assist her partner in CPR.

Gerbowski flops onto his back. The wake of the water returns to gently lapping at the shore, the crash and rescue no longer disturbing it. As the other Conservation Officer counts out the repetitions of his chest compressions, sirens from other units draw closer. Gerbowski can hear the rotors of another helicopter approaching in the distance just as the pilot regurgitates the water he ingested. The two officers roll the man onto his side to help him expel the fluid. As the vomiting turns to coughing, the pilot is finally able to croak out that he's okay.

Gerbowski closes his eyes and lets the sun and a smile warm his face.

9

It's good to see the team in better spirits, Derek thinks as he watches the hugs and back slapping occur before him. Despite it only being a few days since the helicopter accident, that kind of an event somehow seemed to simultaneously elongate time while also shaving years off your life. Tragic as it was to lose the Mercury Red 4 crew chief, it had been a miracle that everyone else had escaped the catastrophic engine failure relatively unscathed.

Sure, Derek had had his bell rung pretty good and suffered a lingering headache for a day after, but the doctor who checked him out said the injury barely qualified as a concussion. He and Drysdale had managed to help the aviators get to shore, an action that was made immensely easier when Ortega reached them. That boy was a fish.

Angie had called in the reinforcements while the water rescues were underway. Really the only one who needed any kind of treatment was Gerbowski, but the same doctor that had attended to Derek assured him that he was only being kept for observation on account of his passing out on the shore after pulling the pilot to safety. The man was patient and courteous to the hospital staff, but insistent that he never actually passed out, merely closed his eyes.

Given all that had happened, after attending the funeral for the crew chief Derek and Drysdale gave the entire team another two days off before having everyone report to the Indianapolis facility to pick up their training regimen. Seeing the group smiling and trash talking over the events of the crash lifts Derek's spirits. The team was already cohesive, but now they were becoming family. They had experienced and survived a life-threatening, real-world event together, something that could pay dividends down the road should they find themselves in another scrape. But more than that, they had worked in concert and acted decisively. The team's actions had saved lives.

That's why it's no surprise to him when the door to the training area opens and SAC Liu steps inside, followed by Jason and Rob. The senior agent beams with a smile but something about the rest of his demeanor seems off to Derek. A rigidity and almost resignation in the eyes and body language that doesn't mesh with the grin.

"Good morning, team!" Liu bellows into the cavernous space. "I knew I had the best the Bureau had to offer when I took charge of this operation, and boy oh boy did you prove it the other day!" He offers more praise and congratulations to each of the three junior members as he shakes their hands. Gerbowski and the Double O's smile politely and return Liu's compliments with the decorum befitting agents addressing their commander. "Please, have a seat. All of you."

While the three agents comply with the invitation, Liu crosses over to Derek and Drysdale. "Chief. Chief," he says, shaking their hands in turn.

Derek and Drysdale echo their subordinates, each shaking hands and giving a small smirk in response. "Good to see you, sir," Derek responds.

"Thanks for coming, sir," Drysdale adds.

"Of course, of course. Think nothing of it," Liu says with a wave of his hand. "You know I couldn't pass up on this opportunity." When the two operators don't offer anything further, Liu smiles weakly again. "Well, let's get started, shall we? Chief Drysdale, will you join us please?"

The SAC makes his way to the head of the table where he remains standing as he addresses the four that are seated. "I know that you have classes to get to, and I have a feeling this group isn't one for long-winded speeches, so I'll keep this short." He clears his throat before continuing. "It goes without saying that the actions you each undertook the other day were ones of selflessness and courage. Without your quick thinking and decisive action the loss of life could have been much greater. You all exemplified the virtues the Bureau strives to uphold, and as such, it is my great honor to award each of you the FBI's Shield of Bravery."

Momentarily surprised, the group looks at each other in disbelief. Standing behind them, Derek breaks into a cheer and starts clapping. Rob and Jason do the same, and Liu's disconnected smile returns as he joins in a moment later. After the applause dies down,

Rob reads their citations in turn. Each member of the QRF-E stands when their name is read off and accepts the medal from the SAC while Jason takes photos on his cell phone. When the ceremony is complete they all sit back down.

"Again, congratulations on your exemplary actions. Obviously given the nature of this team, these awards and photos cannot be made public until such time that operations have ceased and the records are deemed unclassified," Liu says.

There it is, Derek says to himself as the SAC goes on. *He's miffed he's not getting a chance to show this off.*

"Needless to say, the Bureau recognizes you for your incredible acts of heroism. The citations and awards will be added to your personnel files and of course incorporated into any future considerations for promotions and assignments. Again, after this operation has concluded." When no reply comes other than nods of affirmation, the man gives one final smile. "Well, I won't take any more time away from your training, and we have to catch a flight back to D.C. anyway. Congratulations again, team. You deserve this."

The four stand up and rounds of handshakes and thank-yous are exchanged amongst the group. Rob shakes Derek's hand and pulls him into a bro hug, speaking low in his ear. "Wish you would've let us pin one of these on you too."

"They're pinned on the ones who deserve it. Besides, I don't really work for you fuckers, remember?"

Rob laughs and Jason repeats his sentiment while speaking to Derek before Liu, already standing by the exit, calls them over. After the doors have closed and they are certain the SAC has left, Derek and Drysdale turn to the group. "All right. Let's get back to work," the Chief says.

* * * * *

The Howl at the Moon bar is at less than half its capacity that night. The still sizable crowd is the perfect mix for the team. Large and loud enough for them to blend in and speak freely while not being crushed by the throngs of partygoers. As the group's music aficionado, Ortiz had picked the place due to their eclectic live acts, and had picked this night in particular because of the local Latin pop band playing their sets of vibrant salsa and reggaeton. The place is jumping, the drinks are strong and flowing freely, and the team is in high spirits.

"So then . . . so then," Chief Drysdale says, barely able to complete the story through his premature laughter, "EOD is giving us the countdown over the net. Mind you, we've got the house cordoned off so the civilians can't get near it, but they don't know what's coming and the street traffic is still continuing behind us."

"Oh no, what did you guys do?" Ortiz askes after a hefty sip of her margarita.

"Not me, it was the disposal guys," the Chief offers while laughing. "So here it comes, right? The countdown is happening. One minute. Thirty seconds. At that moment a donkey cart with a grown man and like a thirteen-year-old kid is passing by. The kid wants to see what's going on so he stands up on the bench."

Derek smiles, sipping on his beer and awaiting the punchline. The thought of another nearly thirteen-year-old on the other side of the world flashes into his mind. The eyes are there. The flames. He chugs a few more gulps and forces the imagery back down to where it came from. Tonight is a night for celebrating his team. He won't allow his shit to ruin that.

"Then *boom*!" Drysdale yells out, slapping his hand on the table and causing the glasses and bottles to rattle together. "House goes sky high in a cloud of dust. Then this donkey, this broken-down, mangy-looking animal that's probably a week away from death's doorstep just . . . takes . . . off! I mean it is flying! Fucking blast scared the thing so bad that it turned into Seabiscuit!"

Now everyone around the table is laughing. As the Chief goes on, Ortega has to struggle to keep his beer in his mouth. "The kid tumbles backward head over ass into the back of the cart and then again out onto the street. At the same time the guy up front is trying to pull on the reins with one hand while holding onto the bench for dear life. I swear to you, he looks like he's straight outta *Ben-Hur* for a minute, and then the cart hits this bump. Now it's his turn to go ass up. Dude is flying through the air."

The whole team is in hysterics but Drysdale doesn't stop even though tears are running down his cheeks and he's laughing nearly every other word. "But the guy . . . the guy doesn't let go of the reins! So now he hits the ground, gets dragged for a bit, and then finally lets go, which sends him tumbling into a street vendor's stall and knocking over all the merchandise. Those people start screaming and yelling while the kid goes sprinting by chasing after the cart!"

Ortega finally manages to swallow down his swig and bursts out laughing. "Wait, what happened to the donkey?"

"Hell if I know! Probably still running!" Drysdale replies, setting off a resurgent bout of laughter.

In the aftermath of the story Ortega announces that he's heading to the restroom only to use it as justification for ordering a round of tequila shots. "I told you we weren't gonna keep up with that bourbon shit if I had anything to do with it!"

The group tosses back the liquor. The band starts a new song, their fastest one yet. "Come on, baby bro," Ortiz says. "I need to work off some of this before I drive, and I don't have the time to teach these fools how to dance."

The Double O's head off to the dance floor and immediately fall into rhythm with the music. A moment later the Chief pulls his vibrating cell phone out of his pocket and answers. "Hang on, baby, let me get outside first," he says as he walks off.

Gerbowski waits until his team leader is gone and then takes a rather long pull of his drink. Derek eyes the man. "You okay, Gerbs?"

The man shrugs. "No worse than anyone else I suppose."

"You sure? You look like you've got something on your mind."

Eyeing where Drysdale just walked out, and then to the dance floor, Gerbowski turns his attention back to Derek. "Things were close. The other day. Closer than they ever were for me."

Derek nods and leans in. "They were, and it's perfectly acceptable to feel however it is you're feeling right now. I've been there, so I get it. There's no right or wrong way to process it. Just ride out the wave and take what comes at you. But I'll tell you this much, don't dwell on it. You can recognize what happened, but don't linger. The sooner you realize that, the sooner you'll stop letting things eat away at you."

"Damn, boss," Gerbowski replies, "I didn't realize Marines could be that insightful."

"Yeah, well, I guess all that therapy is starting to pay off." They both laugh. Derek eyes the man and then decides now is as good a time as any. "I don't want to discount what Angie and Brian did the other day, not in the slightest. The Chief either. But the truth of the matter is that without you doing what you did, things would've turned out very, very different."

Cocking an eyebrow, the man regards him for a moment. "Not sure I follow you, boss."

"Aaron, you were setting yourself apart long before we ever got on that chopper. From the get-go you took charge of the exercise and showed true leadership. You didn't bark orders at the Double O's, you worked with them and incorporated them into the plan. You asked for their advice. You listened to their feedback. You established yourself as the one calling the shots but did it in such a way that they didn't feel belittled or jaded. To the contrary, they bought into you taking charge because you valued their contributions."

Derek takes another swig before continuing on. "It was even more apparent once we did the after-action review. You acted decisively. You didn't hesitate when the engine blew. You recognized the situation and designated your team members to the appropriate action based on their strengths. I don't even need to go into the disregard you showed for your own safety when you went into the drink after the pilot. You're all deserving of that award the SAC gave you, but in my eyes you're deserving of more than just that."

"Man, Derek, I don't know what to say," Gerbowski replies. "I mean, I just did what anyone else would."

"Not anyone else, Aaron," he returns with a shake of his head. "You displayed real ability, and how humble you are only solidifies my decision. This is Drysdale's team, but there will be others. I'm recommending you for command of your own team once the Bureau stands the next one up."

Gerbowski smiles. A genuine, warm smile as the realization that his actions, and the recognition of them in response, finally dawns on him. "That's . . . that's incredible. All the more so coming from you, Derek."

"Whatchu smiling at A-A-Ron?" Drysdale says as he slides into the seat between Derek and Gerbowski. The man looks over at Derek. "You told him, I'm guessing?"

"Just finished," Derek replies with a smile.

The Chief turns back to Gerbowski. "He's got a better way with words than I do, Gerbs, but you should know that I feel the same. You deserve to be the next man up. We're going to start having you take charge when and where we can to prep you further."

In light of the news, Gerbowski's smile fades rather than increasing. Derek reads into the response right away. "Something else bothering you?"

First glancing once again at the Double O's, Gerbowski leans in closer. "I didn't want to say anything in front of the entire team. It could be nothing, so I didn't want to raise my concerns unnecessarily."

Furrowing his eyebrows, Drysdale tilts his head. "What are you getting at, Gerbs?"

"Look, it's no secret that Autumn's Tithe isn't operating in a vacuum. We know there are people funneling them money and material. We also know that there are very real connections to the group from within our own government. Hell, our own agency. Sarah confirms that much. We just don't know how far that reach extends."

"I think I see where you're headed with this," Derek says, leaning back in his chair.

"You'll have to indulge my ass then," the Chief replies. "Lay it all out for me."

"What if those connections have been able to pinpoint our team? Not the members, I trust us implicitly. But who's to say other elements couldn't be compromised? People and units called on to support our mission. What if it was known that we were doing an exercise the other day? What if that training accident wasn't an accident at all?"

The latest song fills the void left by their silence. Gerbowski sets his drink aside and digs his cell phone out of his pocket. He punches a few buttons and then flips the phone around for the other men to see. His screen displays a headline from a local newspaper in the area about a couple that was killed. "Like I said, I didn't want to start raising concerns unnecessarily, but the crash left a nagging feeling that something wasn't right, so I started to do a little digging.

"Husband and wife shot dead in their driveway. Only three gunshot wounds between them both, including two headshots. The husband? An Army Reservist. Guess what unit he was assigned to? The very same aviation unit that took us out. Guess who performed the maintenance on Mercury Red 4?"

"Jesus," Drysdale says.

"You talk to the local P.D.?" Derek asks.

Gerbowski grimaces as he puts away his phone. "I did. They're short on leads. Told me the caliber was a .300 Win Mag. Based on that and the low light at the time, they're thinking this might be some kind of hunting accident."

"Someone took him out. Had him sabotage the engine and then shut him up," the Chief says flatly, giving voice to what they are all thinking.

"If that's the case, and our training schedule was compromised, then we've got a big fucking problem on our hands. Who knows how far we've been infiltrated?" Gerbowski says with a shrug.

"We need to take this to Jason and Rob," Drysdale returns.

"Yeah, but can we trust them?"

"Those two we can," Derek replies. "Sarah was their undercover. They've been chasing this since the beginning, trying to make it right after their failings in New York. I don't see them being a part of this. That's way too elaborate of a scheme. It doesn't serve a purpose to either of them."

"Okay. So what's the next move? Do we pull them in?"

Nodding, Derek looks at them both. "Yes, and fast. If what you've turned up so far is true, then we need to intercede on the local P.D.'s behalf and seize whatever evidence we can from this Reservist. He may be the missing link between Autumn's Tithe and the government collaborator."

Their faces are solemn, the heady effects of the booze fading by the second. "I'm gonna go make a call," Derek says.

"I'm gonna hit the head," Gerbowski replies.

"I'm gonna grab us another round. I need a beer and you bastards do too. I'm not drinking alone after hearing this shit," the Chief adds.

10

The customary three raps on a door to announce himself is an action Rob can't stop himself from doing, no matter how many years he's been out. The SAC, nestled inside his office at Quantico, calls out in response, "You may enter."

Looking quickly at his partner, Rob opens the door and crosses the threshold, Jason following him in. They both carry several file folders in addition to their tablets. Liu, sitting behind his desk, glances briefly at the duo before turning back to his monitors. "What's the latest on the interviews?" he asks.

By now the junior agents had figured out that if they wanted to sit they needed to do so of their own accord rather than waiting to be invited. "Nothing new on that front, sir. The ones we suspect are the most heavily involved in operations are sticking to their guns. They've either lawyered up or are staying silent. The ones that do talk appear to be part of the whole Marshal message."

"Some of them even think he's going to be resurrected and free them. He twisted these people up pretty good," Jason adds.

"Uh-huh," the SAC replies. The man shifts from the computer, his finger hovering over an open three-ring binder on his desktop. Several other binders just as thick are stacked off to the side, clinging precariously to the little bit of real estate they still have. Liu finds his place in the binder and then twists to his keyboard to continue typing. "Well, if there's nothing new, why are you here instead of working on them further?"

Suppressing a grimace, Rob starts opening one of the folders he's holding. "Nothing new on the West Virginia camp, sir, but we've derived some interesting—"

Liu suddenly throws his hands up and faces Rob. "Incredible. Agent Jackson, are you aware of just how lacking our investigation is in the appropriate protocol? It's a wonder we're able to get anything done at all."

Briefly sharing a look of puzzlement with his partner, Rob turns back to the ranking agent. "Sir, that approach was by design. The need to stay fluid and ahead of any possible insider threats to the operation."

The SAC emits a condescending grunt. "Tell me, what good is an operation such as this if we can't secure convictions? My predecessor may have preferred to do things fast and loose, but I prefer to do things in accordance with the rule of law." Picking up his pen, Liu hurriedly scrawls something on a legal pad before slapping the implement back down and returning to his keyboard. "Go on with what you were saying."

"We've received new information that we think

warrants our attention. Gerbowski took the initiative and put together enough—"

"Wait. Isn't he the cage fighter? That's your source?"

"Sir . . . Aaron had a stellar reputation as an investigator before switching over to the tactical side," Jason replies.

Staring at Jason for a few moments, Liu then breaks his gaze to go back to his monitors. He starts typing again. "Very well. Continue."

Jason looks off to the corner of the ceiling, no doubt biting his tongue. Rob only hopes the man can keep his trademark snark in check for the remainder of the meeting. Even so, better to accelerate things while he's able to. "Long story short, sir, the information was enough for us to take a closer look into a member of the Army Reserve unit responsible for maintenance on the Black Hawk that carried the team. Turns out he and his wife were shot and killed outside their home two days before the helo accident."

The typing stops. Liu spins in his chair to face them. "Coincidence or connection?"

"Definitely the latter, sir," Rob goes on. "Maintenance logs at the unit show that this Corporal, Jacob Leach, worked directly on the chopper. It also appears that he may have doctored other aircraft logs so that Mercury Red 4 would be tasked with the flight. We're fairly certain that once the wreckage has been recovered we'll find evidence of tampering with the engine. Based on this, Agent Tatum coordinated through the local jurisdiction and had a search warrant executed at the Leach residence. The deceased's cell phone and laptop were clean, but the P.D. found an external hard drive as well."

"The drive was filled mostly with downloaded

porn files riddled with viruses," Jason says, "which we think was meant to throw the casual observer off. Our tech guys downstairs discovered a series of hidden folders that were encrypted using fairly sophisticated methods. We checked. Leach was a career wrench turner. Worked as a mechanic in practically every job he ever held. Nothing in his background suggests that he would have the knowledge to encrypt those files himself."

Leaning back in his chair, the SAC folds his hands over his chest. "All right, agents, you have my attention."

"While they were sophisticated, they weren't anything our guys couldn't handle," Jason says as he opens one of his file folders. "Once they got past the encryption they found all sorts of incendiary material. Pamphlets and writings from hate and extremist groups. Downloaded discussions from Discord chat rooms centered on revolution and the coming of the next American civil war. We were able to identify one of his many usernames being linked to several militias looking to recruit service members and veterans."

"On the surface this sounds promising," Liu begins, "but I still don't hear anything that rises above circumstantial. Just because he was a dissident does not mean he's involved with Autumn's Tithe. He could have been radicalized by any of the groups he was in contact with and decided to simply sabotage the Black Hawk of his own volition. There's nothing here that conclusively shows he knew who was going to be on the helo that day."

"Exactly our thoughts, sir," Rob says while pulling a piece of paper from a different file. He scoots forward in his chair and hands it across the desk.

"However, the drive did have a number of locations on it. They're not the remote areas Tithe is used to operating from, but when cross-referenced with some of the materials, we believe that these sites could be part of a support network. Places that act as waypoints for moving recruits, weapons, and supplies. We want to pull on this thread. If we hit these locations, maybe we can turn up something that connects the dots."

The SAC spends long moments reading over the findings. "Very well," Liu says. "Get the team spun up."

There's a momentary pause as Jason clears his throat. "With respect, sir, we're proposing an alternate course of action for these locations."

Squinting at Jason, Liu replies. "Are these sites associated or not?"

"We believe they are."

"Well, if they are then we send in the team."

"Sir, on the surface they definitely seem to be Autumn Tithe's M.O.," Rob chimes in.

"An abandoned church. An old rail yard. A closed-down feed and farm store. Virginia, Kentucky, Tennessee. I'd say they more than fit the pattern, Agent Jackson."

"Normally I'd agree, sir, but these don't quite meet the same profile. They're derelict but they're still in rural, even somewhat suburban areas. The locations come up in online threads as occasional meeting places for the groups Leach was in contact with. None of that gels with Tithe. We only learn of their additional camps through perpetrators directly apprehended at previous ones. Autumn Tithe's locations are so isolated that we can't even recon them unless we send in Derek. These other sites I can pull up for you on Google Maps right now."

"Then just what is it you're proposing here?" the SAC responds.

"Like Rob said earlier, sir," Jason replies, "we think this is a possible support network, or at least a collection of like-minded groups that may have crossed paths or had dealings with one another. We want to roll them up and see what intel can be gained."

"We'll use local police and sheriff departments for the boots on the ground action," Rob adds on. "Generate a separate premise for the support request on each location. Then coordinate the raids to take place simultaneously. Since it'll only be us coordinating the ops, and given the geographic separation, the departments won't know they're all executing at the same time. This way we don't give the locations a chance to warn each other if they do happen to be part of a network, and we insulate the anonymity of our ongoing op with Derek. Even a mole inside the Bureau would only see this as separate actions against hate groups, if they learned about the raids at all."

More moments go by as Liu regards them both. Their cards laid out on the table, Rob and Jason can only wait for his response. Finally, the man speaks. "All right, gentlemen, we'll do it your way. I'm still new to this mission and as such you both are more intimately familiar with Tithe than I am at present. So I'm going to grant you a little latitude. Put together the operational plan and set up a meeting to brief the details before I give the final go-ahead. I want this done quickly and quietly, agents. Are we clear?"

"Roger that, sir," Rob says. "We'll get started right away."

"Very well," the SAC replies while turning back to his monitors. The duo stands up and heads for the door. Just before they are about to exit, Liu calls out to them. "And gentlemen, one more thing."

"What's that, sir?" Jason asks for them both.

"I only want you on this, Agent Tatum. You can help him coordinate efforts on your own time, Agent Jackson, but for now I'm going to need your assistance on this project here."

"Understood, sir," Rob replies while trying to keep his voice from sounding too deflated. Once they're outside in the hallway and have gone a short distance, Jason can't hold his laughter in any longer. Rob shoves him against the wall. "Yeah, yeah, smartass. Let's go. We've got work to do."

■   ■   ■   ■   ■

Back in the day the abandoned Mt. Carmel church sitting on Route 624 in Craig County, Virginia, probably looked like something out of a Rockwell painting. The entrance and tall steeple sit near the road while the rest of the building stretches back to the nearby wood line, the entire property surrounded by a wrought-iron fence. Jason can imagine the freshly painted white church welcoming local families in their Sunday best week after week.

Looking through his spotting scope, the reality of the building's current state stands in stark contrast to the idyllic Americana landscape that would have been captured by the artist. The paint is faded, large sections having flaked off ages ago. The exterior is worn from years of neglect. Stained, moldy, and weatherbeaten. What appears to be the original clapboard shutters are closed over many of the windows, those missing some of their slats reminiscent of gaps in a set of teeth. Sheets of plywood sit over the openings where the shutters no longer hang, but even at this distance Jason can see spots where the coverings have been knocked aside to reveal the darkness within. The wrought-iron fence now sits rusted and forgotten.

The pastureland directly across the street from the church and the accompanying homestead set back a considerable distance from the road is the perfect observation point. With the cooperation of the landowner and under the guise of an exterminator coming to fumigate the dilapidated barn on the property, Jason and a small surveillance and communications team had inserted the day before. After a few hours the van departed, but Jason and his two technicians remained behind.

To anyone watching it would have appeared innocuous, but no one was watching. The sleepy farm and cattle community surrounding the church limited the potential for prying eyes to be in the vicinity, and even if they were, the distances between properties would negate any curiosity. Sitting atop the foothills of the Blue Ridge Mountains and just a stone's throw away from the border with West Virginia, it was assessed that out of the three locations on Leach's external hard drive, the church would be the most likely to provide any new leads. As such, Jason had made it his primary location while coordinating with the others and Quantico from inside the barn.

He checks his watch and then looks through the scope again. Still quiet. Not even a chipmunk stirring on the property. Pulling his gaze away, Jason repeats the look at his watch after realizing he never made note of the time at first glance. It's 7:53 a.m. At eight o'clock a tactical team from the Virginia State Police accompanied by units from the Craig County Sheriff's Department would hit the church and secure the scene before he would make his way down the driveway to conduct a site exploitation.

Jason claps the man sitting at a folding table next to him on the shoulder. "Give me a final comms check, Terry," he says. The technician complies, radioing to Quantico command center, who then relays the message out to the other states. Similar law enforcement units in northern Kentucky and eastern Tennessee check in. After getting the thumbs-up, Jason takes over the communication directly. "All right, everyone, stand by. We go in five," he says into his hand mic.

The accompanying affirmations are overridden by a squelch, immediately followed by the static delivery of a Virginia drawl. "Yeah, Bureau, this is Virginia State SWAT. We need to delay about five or ten mikes. Our convoy encountered a washout in the road. We're detouring now, but will need the extra time to get back onto 624."

"Son of a bitch," Jason growls to no one in particular. "Fucking local cops." He gathers himself before keying up again. "Roger that, Virginia. Break. All units stand by for my go. I say again, do not proceed on the zero eight time hack."

Moments ticking by feel like an eternity. The logical part of his brain tells Jason that the delay will more than likely amount to nothing. The place appears deserted and they hadn't seen a car go by in a half hour. Another few minutes isn't going to mean the unraveling of the whole mission. The key component is the three raids being synchronized, and he still retains the ability to make that happen.

The other part of his brain, the one that spent many

an occasion in Professor Murphy's Law class, knows that this is exactly how shit gets twisted. Something as innocuous as a few extra minutes could be the butterfly wings flapping that results in a typhoon. Jason takes a deep breath to calm his nerves and shakes out his limbs as they wait.

Looking at his watch yet again, his head snaps up at the sudden sound of squealing tires on the road. Jason watches as a coyote-tan Lenco BearCat armored vehicle comes screeching to a halt in front of the church. "For crying out . . . first they're late, then they're unannounced."

As he raises the hand mic to his mouth, six Virginia State Police tactical team members, three on either side of the vehicle, clad in olive drab jumpsuits and gear, hop off the running boards and charge toward the opening in the gate. As they do so the doors on the BearCat open and other officers dressed the same spill out, bringing their weapons up as they form a perimeter. Two Chevy Suburbans pull to a halt east and west of the church. Additional tactical team members rush toward the building, looking to complete the encirclement and secure the rear of the church.

"All units, this is—"

The church explodes, a cataclysmic fireball bursting from inside out that immediately flings the primary team backward from the shockwave and sends the perimeter teams sprawling to the ground. The windows on the homestead blow out from the pressure of the blast. Jason and the technicians flinch and instinctively duck down behind the walls of the barn. As the pillar of flame shoots skyward it curls in on itself, transforming into thick, black smoke. A moment later the shattered debris of the building, wooden splinters engulfed like a thousand torches, rains down all over the pasture land and surrounding woods.

Jason peeks back over the window ledge in the barn, taking in the scene. Seemingly hundreds of fires are scattered about. Most of the tactical team members that had formed the perimeter crawl their way back from the flaming remnants of the church. Some writhe on the ground, impaled by shrapnel sent flying by the explosion.

Members of the breaching team lie up against the fence, while two have been thrown clear over it. One team member runs around frantically slapping at his left arm set ablaze, until two of his comrades tackle him to the ground and start trying to smother the flames.

For a few moments he is frozen by the carnage, but then the situational awareness snaps into place. "Abort! Abort! All units hold! I say again, hold! Do not breach the targets!" The command is echoed through the radio and relayed to the other states. "Get EMS and fire in here," he says quietly to the technician. Out on the road, patrol units from the sheriff's department come racing onto the scene.

. . . . .

When Daniel gets on the line he sounds dejected. "Your plan that we talked about. How far along are you?"

"As far as I'm able to take it at this point," Sarah replies. "Where are you on the material?"

"The order is being processed. Get yourself out to Arizona for retrieval. She wants you to handle it personally. The details of the meet will be coming shortly. You've been given the green light."

The sudden authorization when it seemed as though

her usefulness was all but severed just a few weeks ago leaves her intuition clamoring for more. "Why the sudden go-ahead? Has something developed?"

His frustration and exhaustion come through the line, with no shortage of arrogant attitude heaped on top. "Let's just say other avenues didn't pan out."

Not so easy in the operational world, is it, you stupid ass? Grinning, Sarah replies, "Roger that. You have a replacement for me for my long-range asset? I'm going to need the cover and you retasked my other one."

"Yes, I remember. We're activating one from the talent pool out West. He'll meet you there. File is being sent to your phone shortly." Daniel abruptly hangs up. Sarah smirks as she heads to tell the others of her upcoming departure.

11

The level of obliviousness in the airport is obnoxious. As if society wasn't self-centered enough already. The elevation of everyday inconsideration while walking through the terminals and boarding planes always accentuated the ongoing narcissism of America for her.

Sarah hides her disgust with sips of coffee and eyes that could land her at the World Series of Poker. The arrivals and departures board switches the flight she's monitoring from ON TIME to ARRIVED. She gets up and moves to the baggage carousel, leaning against a support post to watch the personnel coming from the plane.

Picking him out instantly, Sarah is pretty certain he does the same with her. His sudden flinch her way, small as it may have been, would have given her the advantage at a table. Save for the swagger, Sarah sees the man's composition for what he really is underneath. Carries everything in his left to keep his gun hand free. Or was it the need to salute? Perhaps both.

Muscular build that slims into a tight waist, with cargo pants tucked into a solid pair of boots.

Even after he grabs his bag and starts to walk over she can see the hours of drill and ceremony being barely held back by his post-military persona. When he's close enough Sarah pushes up from the post she's leaning on. "You Dwight?" she asks.

The man holds her gaze a moment, his as even as hers, and then sets his bags down in front of her. She watches the subtle shifts in his bearing. He nonchalantly takes a step back from the luggage, clearing his feet from any potential entanglement. At the same time he makes a show of cracking his neck to one side before looking in the opposite direction while scratching the back of his head. Sarah can't help her smirk as she realizes he's checking the location of the exits.

"Never met anyone named Dwight before." He glances at her with a side eye and then hesitates before adding, "I was supposed to meet Reggie."

"Reggie couldn't make it tonight. Bad weather and all. He sent me instead."

Turning to face her fully, the man looks her up and down, spending a little longer on her hips and thighs than she cares for. "And who are you to him then?"

"I'm his granddaughter. The one who lives in Sedona, obviously. Who else would I be?"

Another hesitation but it's shorter than the last, banished by the man flashing a million-dollar smile of perfectly straight, perfectly white teeth, the predetermined tradecraft responses satisfying his wariness. "Just making certain." The man licks his lips and gives a short inclination of his head. "How you doing?"

"Seriously?" Sarah replies, rolling her eyes. "Grab

your shit and let's get going. We've got a decent drive ahead of us, and I need to make sure everything is in place well beforehand."

Shrugging and grabbing his gear, he starts to follow her through the terminal. "Whatever you say, boss, but let's squash that Dwight shit right now, okay? You can call me Deep."

The two make their way toward the exit. "Why the hell do you call yourself Deep? Or don't I want to know?"

He chuckles. "Because of my distance, baby. On and off the range. If you're feeling it later maybe I can set up a demonstration. You know what I mean?"

"Won't be any feeling going on, Deep," Sarah replies over her shoulder without breaking stride. "This thing goes south though, you might get to show me."

"All right, I see how it is," Deep says with another laugh. "All business. I can respect that. Still, keep it in the back of your mind for when the job is done," Deep adds as they cross into the rental car garage.

"There's a whole lot more to do before we can say that we're done," Sarah says.

A few minutes later they're exiting the Yuma International Airport and heading east on Interstate 8. Sarah is content to conduct the drive in silence, but after a few minutes Deep gets antsy. "I didn't expect to get the call so soon. I thought everything was still happening on the East Coast. Something transpire that I should be aware of?"

"Plans changed," is all she offers back. "That reminds me, let me see your phone." Deep fishes it out of a pocket and hands it over. Sarah rolls down the driver's side window and throws it out of the car. At eighty-five miles per hour the device may as well be made of crystal. The phone shatters as soon as it hits the road.

"Yo! What the fuck was that?"

"Calm down," Sarah replies while lifting open the cover to the center console. She pulls out a burner phone and hands it to him. "Operational security. In case you were being tracked."

"I know about OPSEC, lady. We just did your whole alternate verification routine in the airport, didn't we? And there's no way I was being tracked. Do you have any idea how many fillies' numbers you just cost me?"

Sarah spares him a sideward glance with furrowed eyebrows. "Come on now. With a name like Deep you're telling me you can't replenish them in a snap?"

"Shit. Of course I can. Point is I shouldn't have to."

"You can get a new phone with your old number when you get back. We're paying you enough."

"If you think that's coming out of my cut you're crazy. If we even get that far. As it is, this gig is already off to a fucked-up start. Don't pull any shit like that again, especially when it comes to my gear. You understand? Trust me, lady, I'm not the one you want to be—"

As he rants on Sarah takes her foot off the gas and lets the car decelerate as she feigns listening to the tirade. When the car has dropped more than half its speed she slams on the brakes, the car pitching forward before rocking back on its chassis. Not expecting the sudden stop, Deep lurches toward the dashboard only to have his seat belt catch and rip him back into his seat. Sarah throws the car in park, not even bothering to pull off to the side of the road. She twists to face him, her face devoid of emotion.

"All right, let's get a few things straight. I get you're new to us. So I'm willing to cut you a little slack here."

"You're gonna cut me slack? Lady, you just threw my fucking phone—"

"Enough of that shit. It's done." Their eyes remain locked, neither willing to tear their gaze away. "We picked you because your service record is impeccable and your skills are beyond compare. The confirmed kills both while in and as a contractor speak for themselves. I know that you're good at what you do, but it's a fact that you were briefed about being placed under my command and what's expected with that, no questions asked. Am I wrong?"

To his credit, Deep doesn't let his expression betray him. The man's bobbing Adam's apple as he swallows does, however. "Nah."

"Nah? Nah what?"

The man exhales forcefully through his nose before replying. "No, ma'am, you're not wrong."

Sarah presses on. "I know all about your cushy private school upbringing and how you pissed away six years at Albion because Daddy kept cutting checks no matter what. The same Daddy who later absconded with his client's money, left you and your mother destitute when the lawyers came looking for blood, and ultimately forced your hand to join the military so you wouldn't starve after her suicide."

The conjuring of distant recollections and the seriousness of her tone causes Deep to shift in his seat and face forward. Sarah doesn't wait for the man to reply. "You're a soldier, a highly qualified one, but still just boots on the ground. While you're with me you're going to fall in like everyone else, which includes going along with whatever methods I choose to employ to keep this group secure. Above and beyond throwing your phone out the window, if that's what it takes, and you'll do so without threats or insubordination. Got it?"

A low rumble emits from Deep's throat as he grinds his teeth. "Yes, ma'am. Got it."

"Good. Make sure you remember it. You do that and we'll get along splendidly, and then you'll get paid. Trust me, if you were looking for a path back to the wealth you were so accustomed to, you've come to the right place."

Sarah stares at him another few moments before turning back to put the car in gear and press her foot on the gas, bringing the car back up to speed. Deep looks out his window, watching the desert roll by.

"What's the op?" he says after a while, the edge conspicuously absent from his voice.

"For now, reconnaissance and overwatch. You're going to let me know what I'm dealing with, and then you're going to watch our backs."

"Easy enough. And later?"

Sarah looks at him again, a hint of a smile on her lips that comes nowhere near touching her eyes. "Later we're gonna give a bunch of people a really bad bloody nose."

Deep nods his head and rubs his hands together. "That's what I wanted to hear. It's about time."

They drive on in relative silence. A few miles west of Wellton, Sarah leaves the highway and connects to the service road running parallel to it. She turns onto S Ave 25E, also known as El Camino Del Diablo the farther south they go. The road bisects open desert, with mountain ranges bracketing them on their left and right.

The sun begins to dip, the sky a rolling twist of purples and orange. About halfway between the interstate and the Mexico border Sarah slows the car to a stop and pulls over. A Nissan Pathfinder sits parked on the side of the road ahead of them. A man steps out of the SUV wearing jeans, a bomber jacket, aviator sunglasses, and an Arizona Diamondbacks ball cap. His right hand rests by the back of his hip until he sees Sarah get out of the rental. Deep steps out next, which garners a passing if not gauging nod from the other driver.

"Kyle, Deep. Deep, Kyle," Sarah says as they draw close to one another.

Kyle looks over at Deep again. "Deep? That's what you're going with?"

"Yeah, Kyle sounds about right for you too. You look like the Maverick and Goose collection straight outta L.L.Bean."

Sarah catches herself before fully laughing and points at the trunk of the Pathfinder. "Show him, Kyle."

The man opens the tailgate and then undoes the clip closures to a hardened rifle case. Deep walks up on an M2010 Enhanced Sniper Rifle complete with magnified optics and a starlight attachment for the scope.

"Will this do?" Sarah asks.

"Chamber?"

"It's a .300 Win Mag," Kyle replies.

"Smaller than I'm used to. I'm a Barrett man, but I can make this work."

"Well, if all goes according to plan you'll have your Barrett by the end of the night."

Deep spins to look at them, doing a double take. "Whoa. Hold up. Tonight? Like before the clock strikes twelve and shit?"

"At eleven, actually. We're gonna ride you out to the hills in a little bit. Let you pick your hide. You need to make sure that you do a countersniper sweep up there before you set up a permanent position," Sarah replies.

"I've got an MP5 and a day pack for you too. Rations, water, radio, ammo," Kyle adds.

Steepling his hands over his nose and mouth, Deep hesitates for several moments before speaking again. "Just so we're clear," he begins after dropping his hands. "You two want me to do a night overwatch, countersniper surveillance without any prior reconnaissance while using an untested rifle?"

Her voice increasingly annoyed, Sarah glares at the man. "Unfortunately this is how the timeline worked out. You want to play in the big leagues? This is what it takes. I don't have time to debate it with you. We just had this conversation a little while ago."

"Yeah, and back then I thought this group was legit, but this is a bunch of amateur-hour bullshit. I signed on for serious work and the money that comes with it. This is some Tom Berenger, Billy Zane concoction."

Sarah takes a step forward. "No one is more serious than me, and therefore none of the people I have with me are sandbagging it. You accepted both the job and the mission, and you're being compensated accordingly. Now it's your turn to deliver." Her hand goes to her back hip. Kyle goes a step further, actually drawing his pistol and holding it by his side.

"I bet if I ask, Kyle will attest to not seeing a car come through here for hours now. That right, Kyle?" she calls over her shoulder without moving her eyes from Deep's face.

"Might be even longer. A couple of days actually."

Sarah smirks. "You just got off a flight. I know you don't have anything on you, and I didn't give you a chance to get anything out of your checked bags. You want to continue on, you can make a lot of money while we fuck up Uncle Sam for what he did to us. But make no mistake, Deep, you've been warned twice now. There won't be a third. Question or argue with me again and I'll put two in your brain and the world will forget you ever existed by morning."

The three stare at each other for long moments before Deep flashes his smile. "Damn." He looks at Kyle. "She's a badass, huh?"

"You have no idea."

"All right," Deep says, holding his palms up. "I'm in. Okay? Hell, I've worked with less before. But even then the equipment was up to snuff. I can't watch your backs without zeroing this thing."

Sarah shrugs. "Do it now. Kyle will put out a marker."

"What? Here?"

"I told you no one comes down this road. If anyone hears the shots at all they'll just think you're killing coyotes."

Deep takes in the surrounding landscape. "All right. If that's how you want it."

"You've got a five-round magazine. If you're as good as you're supposed to be, that should be two rounds too many."

Lifting the rifle out of the case, Deep smiles again. "Watch me go to work."

After three rounds he and Kyle find Sarah leaning against the hood of the rental, her arms folded across her chest. "Good to go?"

"All set," Deep replies.

"Outstanding. Secure the rifle and get in the Pathfinder. You two follow me."

■ ■ ■ ■

Turning up the collar on her fleece, Sarah suppresses the shiver emanating from the desert cold. Up ahead three pairs of headlights crawl toward them. Kyle flashes the lights on the Pathfinder once to orient the oncoming vehicles to their position but then moves off to the side. He clutches a Mossberg 500 combat shotgun attached to a tri-point sling angled across his body. Not exactly the easiest weapon to maneuver if you're standing behind a car door for cover.

For Sarah's part she stands on the passenger side of the SUV, hands in her pockets against the cold but her sidearm exposed. The exchange had been arranged through her contact, but international arms dealers typically didn't accept AMEX, so that meant cash. Cash means greed. Greed means betrayal.

"Overwatch, we've got incoming. You tracking this?" she says through her Bluetooth earpiece. They had left her rental car at the release point where Deep went up into the hills above them.

"I've got eyes on. Although you two could've gotten me a spot with a little more elevation. This anthill I'm on isn't much to work with."

A muscle in Sarah's jaw pulses. "Lock that shit up. We're a go."

The response comes back from Deep clear, level, and without hesitation. "Roger that."

The first vehicle is a standard U-Haul box truck that pulls to a stop about fifty feet to Sarah's right. A Ford F-250 pulls up next to it, directly across from their Pathfinder. The third vehicle is a Chevy Suburban that parks off to their left, but it does so at an angle so that its front bumper lines up with the pickup's passenger-side headlight. When the men get out of their vehicles they stay within the wedge-shaped space between the Suburban and the truck.

Three men stand in the wedge, obviously armed but with the headlights, distance, and vehicles blocking their vision it's hard to tell with what. Another man stands in the flatbed of the pickup clutching an AK-47. The driver of the Ford and the passenger of the U-Haul walk forward toward Sarah while the driver of the box truck contentedly leans against the fender and lights a cigar.

"The box truck is blocking my line of sight," Deep says into her ear. "Stall them while I reposition."

"Move your ass," Sarah says through clenched teeth. "We're completely outgunned here."

As she starts forward to meet the men she notices the one on her left has sagging jowls with pockmarked skin. Even in the dark a sheen of grease covering his forehead reflects the headlights. The same light accentuates the streaks of slicked-back hair on the man to the right. His skin is smooth and he sports a pencil-thin mustache. The trio stops ten feet from each other. The man on the left looks her up and down.

"You don't look like a Dolores," he says with a thick Mexican accent.

Thinking of the time she needs to buy Deep, Sarah

engages the man with the opening he provided. "What, in your estimation, does a Dolores look like? Just out of curiosity."

"You know. Fat ass and saggy boobs. Curly hair pushing a vacuum around and shit."

"Well, sorry to disappoint you. If it's any consolation, you look exactly like a Felix."

"Oh yeah? Como es Felix?"

"You know. A porky grease monkey that drinks shitty tequila and eats too many tortillas."

The man blinks twice. A moment later, he doubles over laughing. Sarah shifts her eyes ever so quickly to the right. While Slick has a smirk on his lips his eyes never leave hers.

She looks back at Felix and nods over her right shoulder. "You get everything on the list?"

"Fuckin' hell of a time doing so, especially the goddamn launchers, but yeah, it's all there. Even on short notice Felix always comes through, although I find it funny I'm selling most of your own shit back to you. Speaking of which . . ." He holds out a hand rubbing his thumb against his other fingers.

"Money after we've done the inventory."

"Sure, sure," Felix says, holding up his palms. "Your benefactor is one of my biggest customers. I would never cross them, but please, look all you want."

"Set," Deep says over the net. "Adjusting my range now."

She looks over to the man on the right. "And you are . . . ?"

"My name is Aran Villalobos," he says, placing a hand over his heart and bowing slightly. "I'm pleased to make your acquaintance."

"My friends work through a shared business

connection," Felix offers. "Given the items in your order, I requested their assistance and they graciously agreed to provide it. This is my gift to you. On top of the equipment, no additional charge. I trust that information will make it back to your contacts."

"We don't work with outsiders," Sarah curtly replies. "Keep your present."

Felix laughs and Aran's smile broadens. They share an all-encompassing glance dripping with the misogynistic perception that the woman before them is clueless. The squat man turns back to her. "Aran here was part of the Unidad de Operaciones Tácticas Especiales for many years. Even worked some, let's just say . . . special . . . assignments directly for el Presidente Carvajal."

"These guys at the trucks look all tensed up," Deep's voice says into their earpieces. "Stay alert, they're nervous about something."

Unable to reply verbally lest she reveal that they had an off-site asset in play, Sarah quickly thumbs the push-to-talk switch on her Bluetooth transmitter in her pocket and releases it. The short squelch of the radio in the trio's ears serves as an acknowledgement of Deep's statement.

"President Carvajal," Sarah says flatly, trying to gauge the activity of the silhouettes behind the two men. "You're a long way from Venezuela. What sort of special assignments are we talking about?"

Aran chuckles and looks at the ground before replying, childlike in his feigned humility. "My brother, Cesar," he says while gesturing to the U-Haul driver smoking the cigar, "is a former officer in the Dirección General de Inteligencia Militar. Our expertise is in guerilla warfare. Insurgencies, in particular."

Nodding, Sarah throws a look at Felix before turning back to the man. "So what, you've done operations with ELN? FARC? Both?" she asks, using the acronyms for two antigovernment militia groups active in Colombia. Hugo Chavez had openly welcomed members of the groups to train and operate in Venezuela. Carvajal, while much less public about his endorsement, didn't do anything to stop the rebels working in his backyard either.

"Amongst others."

"I see," Sarah says. Behind her the silhouettes begin to shuffle about, putting space between themselves.

"They're taking up positions," Deep confirms. "Keep them talking for a few more seconds while I finish dialing in. And be ready. I think it's about to jump off."

Prickles come up the back of her neck, a heat quickly spreading through her body that she hopes doesn't reach her face. Sarah gives another click in response while suppressing the urge to swallow. "Be that as it may, and as generous as your offer is, gentlemen, I'm not entirely convinced that you should be tagging along."

Grins and jovial demeanor quickly begin to evaporate into grimaces and annoyance. "I assure you, this is an arrangement in your best interest, Dolores," Felix says, the sarcasm heavy on the use of her code name.

"We share mutual interests," Aran adds, "and my brother and I have a particular skill set pertaining to helicopters."

Sarah tilts her head while her eyebrows perk up. "So . . . y'all have experience in this sort of thing? What was it, Iraq and Afghanistan then?"

"Syria actually."

She nods approvingly. With the ongoing civil war in Syria, and Russia's ties to both that country and Venezuela, the concept of associated insurgent cells getting real-world operating experience wasn't a far stretch of the imagination. Groups had been using the War on Terror battlefields in the Middle East as a proving ground for their tactics since the U.S. first landed in Kandahar.

"Fuck. It's going down," Deep crackles over the net. "I've got to engage if you're gonna have a chance. It's now or never."

Sarah's gaze drifts back and forth between the two men, her eyes finally settling on Felix. The man smiles broadly, a devious pride touching his eyes. She does her best to smile back. Her heart pounds in her chest while she tries to stay upright on shaky legs. "Well, all right then. Let's get this inventory done so we can all be on our way."

The two men turn toward the rear of the U-Haul, sharing an eye roll as they do so. Sarah waits until they take a few steps before keying up and muttering, "Now," into the radio.

The man standing in the flatbed shoulders his rifle and begins to raise his barrel at Sarah when he's suddenly launched out of the back of the truck. The report from the round that turned his torso to jelly echoes over them a moment later. Felix and Aran freeze where they stand, watching as the gunman falls to the earth in a heap.

Sarah draws her Glock 9mm and fires a round into each of their backs. Then, wheeling around, she heads for the cover of the Pathfinder. Cesar, now choking from inhaled cigar smoke as a result of witnessing his brother being gunned down, scrambles to get a pistol out from his waistband. Sarah double taps the man in the chest and puts one in his forehead for good measure before diving down behind the front right wheel well of the SUV.

Across from Kyle the three remaining men raise their weapons at the same time he swings his shotgun up. Kyle fires and pumps from left to right, expending his entire tube magazine in an attempt to keep the gunmen's heads down while giving him a chance to retreat back to the Pathfinder for cover as well. One of his bursts of double-ought blasts through both the passenger and driver windows of the Suburban, catching an adversary with a face full of glass and buckshot. It ruins the man's day.

The two men left in the space between the Chevy and Ford hesitate before attempting a hasty plan. One armed with a machine pistol raises it over the hood of the Ford without looking and depresses the trigger, letting loose with an entire magazine of covering fire. The other man, also armed with an AK-47, pops up and leans his rifle across the hood of the Suburban. Sighting in on the Pathfinder, he begins to depress the trigger when his head ceases to exist.

"You've got one tango left," Deep says before the gunman's body has even hit the ground. "I don't have a clear shot. Try to flush him out."

Sarah looks to Kyle, the both of them now behind the Nissan. She points to herself and then holds her hand out flat and horizontal, moving it left and right. Kyle gives a nod while shoving new shells into his weapon. He pumps the Mossberg and then mouths the word, "Go."

As Sarah pops up and starts firing, Kyle wheels

around the backside of the Pathfinder. Crouched low and using the covering fire to his advantage, he crosses the distance to the rear of the Suburban. He waits until Sarah stops engaging and the remaining man starts to return fire before swinging around the back end of the Chevy. Kyle's first shot turns the man's forearm into a pink cloud in the night sky. His second sends the man to his grave. Kyle crouches back down and freezes, the echo of the momentary gunfight dissipating in the cold night air. The entire shootout took less than a minute to transpire.

"Overwatch, give me a scan," Sarah's voice crackles over the radio.

"Wait one." Another thirty seconds go by before the reply comes into their earpieces. "All clear. No targets in the area. We're good."

"Roger that," Sarah says while reloading her pistol with a fresh magazine. "Hold your position and call out any new contacts. We'll come back to you when we're done here. Be ready to move."

"Standing by."

Kyle pops up from behind the Suburban. "Jesus Christ, Sarah! What the fuck just happened?"

Standing, holstering, and heading to the U-Haul, she barks back at him. "Now's not the time. We've gotta move. Get over here and help me."

They find the keys to the U-Haul and the padlock securing the liftgate on Cesar's corpse. When they throw open the door Kyle lets out a long whistle. The box truck is stacked with crates and hard cases. A large, square box sits in the back right corner. To their immediate left are four elongated rectangular boxes stacked atop one another.

Sarah climbs in and spends a minute counting the boxes, checking the number with the inventory in her head. She pulls a tactical folding knife out of her pocket and flips it open. Kneeling, Sarah quickly pries up the lid on the large, square crate just enough to peek inside. Rows of MP7 submachine guns sit inside of it. Standing, she stomps on the lid once to nail it back into place.

Sarah climbs out, pulling the strap to the liftgate with her as she jumps down. She secures the lock and hands the key over to Kyle. "No time to check them all. On the off chance someone heard those shots I want to be long gone before anyone shows up to investigate."

"What about that whole, 'just someone shooting coyotes' thing you said to Deep?"

"Snap out of it, man," Sarah replies. "There's a big difference between a couple of one-off cracks of a rifle and a fucking gunfight. I don't care how isolated we are out here, we can't take any chances."

"Sarah, this isn't good. You have any idea how bad this is going to be for us?"

She did, more so than Kyle did anyway. International arms dealers didn't exactly grow on trees, and having one trusted enough to be connected to their network suddenly eliminated would certainly cause its fair share of repercussions. "Nothing we can do about that at the moment. Besides, they were the ones that drew down on us. What were we supposed to do, let them kill us?" She turns and starts heading for the SUV.

"You're certain about that?" he says, following her. "I don't know about you but all I could see were shadows with their headlights shining the way that they were. Everything about their imminent attack came from Deep." Sarah stops short and spins around. "All I'm saying is what do we really know about this guy other than what's contained in a file folder?"

Sarah holds his gaze for a few seconds. "Noted, but right now we've got to go. Give me the keys to the Pathfinder. We can sort this out later." Even though she's a foot shorter, her command presence makes it seem like she's towering over him. Kyle frowns but does as he's told.

The SUV and the U-Haul proceed back north to where Deep was let out and the rental car parked. The sniper is waiting for them in some nearby brush and approaches once he sees that they're not compromised. "Well, that was something else, wasn't it?"

"You're certain that it was a double cross?" Kyle blurts out.

Furrowing his eyebrows, Deep cants his head slightly to one side. "What? You think I get off blasting fools just because I'm a sniper or something? There was a threat. I called it out and we neutralized it. End of story, Top Gun."

"That had better be the case. The fallout from this is not going to go over well."

"It is what it is," Sarah interjects. "Nothing we can do about it now, and we still have a mission to get underway. At least we're coming away with the weapons we needed. We'll deal with the rest if and when it comes up. Deep, help Kyle transfer the MP7s into the trunk of the rental. I'll grab the rest of our stuff from the Pathfinder. It's too shot up to travel in without being noticed."

Deep gives a shrug of his shoulders. "Whatever you say."

While Kyle and Deep move the crate with the submachine guns as directed, Sarah strips the license plates and VIN number placard from the bullet-riddled Pathfinder. After she tosses the plates and placard into the trunk of the rental she turns around and faces them.

"Drive slow. No bullshit between you two, got it? You're driving in a U-Haul. It's not the most inconspicuous of vehicles. Stop at red lights. Use your turn signal. Go straight through to Kentucky but under no circumstances can you get pulled over and searched. We lose these weapons and we're done. The cause is crushed. It's last stand time, got it?"

Kyle nods. "Roger. We'll make it happen."

"Good," she says with a curt nod of her own. "I've already sent Kellen ahead to start his preparations at the site. Remember what I told you about him. Take command when you get there. Once I've set the rest in motion I'll contact you." Sarah goes to turn away but then stops, doing a double take at the look on Kyle's face. "You good?"

Kyle lets out a deep breath, still coming down from the adrenaline of the gunfight. "I got it."

Another nod. "Okay then."

As Kyle makes his way to the driver's side of the U-Haul, Sarah crosses to the Pathfinder. Flipping open her knife again she slices the driver's seat and shreds some of the foam contained inside. Producing a lighter, she sets fire to the material that quickly catches and engulfs the rest of the fabric. The flames spreading throughout the interior of the car, she turns back to head for the rental. Sarah stops short, seeing Deep staring at her with furrowed eyebrows. "DNA. Now get going."

The man climbs into the cab with Kyle. Pulling onto the road a moment later, the two vehicles leave the burning carcass of the SUV flaming in the dark of midnight.

12

"Okay, great. Thanks, Captain, I appreciate you reaching out to us. If he says anything else in the interim, you've got my cell." Hanging up, Rob slumps back in his chair, closes his eyes, and rubs his temples with his fingers by making slow circles on his skin. After a minute or two he lets his arms drop to rest on his chair before eyeing the clock in the lower right hand corner of his computer. It's 7:27 p.m.

Why does this shit always jump off right when I'm about to leave?

Groaning, Rob sits up and pulls the desk phone from its cradle. He punches the preprogrammed button for the SAC's office and waits for it to dial. Liu picks up on the second ring. "Yes, Agent Jackson?"

The rustling of papers in the background lets Rob know that he's on speakerphone. "Sir, I just finished a call with a captain from the Bureau of Prisons that—"

"The B.O.P.? Can't this wait until morning, Jackson?"

"Possibly, but you'll want to hear this."

Making no attempt to hide the annoyance in his

voice, the senior agent replies, "Make it quick. What did the good captain have to say?"

"It's about one of the detainees from the West Virginia operation. The guy is waiving his right to counsel and requesting a meeting with us. He says he has information regarding Autumn Tithe's last camp."

There's a frenzied clatter on the other end of Rob's line as Liu picks up the receiver. "Who? What else did the captain say?"

"Guy's name is Pat Graelish. The captain said that normally he would have gone through one of the AUSAs assigned to the penitentiary, but apparently the information is time sensitive and he didn't want it getting lost in the mix."

"What penitentiary is this guy being held in? How quickly can we get there?"

The SAC's last question is all the indicator Rob needs to know that he's not going home anytime soon. Especially given what he's about to relate. "That's just the thing, sir. Graelish was sent to USP Lee but the guy has late-stage leukemia. They weren't equipped to handle him there, so he was transferred to the UVA Medical Center."

Liu's voice is practically giddy when he speaks again. "That's fantastic! Charlottesville is only two hours from here. Finally! This is the lead that we've been waiting for. Get together whatever you need, Jackson. I want to be on the road in five minutes."

The order catches Rob off guard. "Sir . . . you're coming? You don't want Jason and me to handle this?"

"After the way you two handled the last lead? No, thank you, Agent Jackson. I don't need any more exploding churches on my watch. I don't even want to look at Tatum right now. We will go, and I will handle the interview personally."

Suppressing another groan at the thought of spending four hours round trip with the man in the same car, Rob replies, "Understood. I'll go grab the car and meet you out front."

"Call the Uniformed Division on the way. I want two of our officers stationed on this Graelish's door around the clock from now on. And then call the UVA police department and have them put men there until we can relieve them. Let's move, Agent Jackson."

In what ends up being one of life's little blessings, traffic has mostly cleared by the time they leave the academy grounds. The drive is smooth sailing, with Rob using the urgency of his boss combined with the speed of the vehicle to complete the drive in just over ninety minutes.

Waving credentials to anyone that might impede their progress, Liu and Rob quickly ascertain the detainee's location and head up to the corresponding floor. The elevator doors open to reveal a mix of federal, state, and local police and corrections officers standing in the hallway. They part ways for the agents as the two men head directly for the door. A man built like a tree trunk in the charcoal B.O.P. uniform stands just outside Graelish's room.

"Are you the one that called it in to your captain?" Liu asks.

"Yes, sir, that was me. C.O. Delacroix." He holds out a hand like a bear paw. Liu takes it and shakes vigorously.

"Well done. Is he awake?"

"Last I checked. Just a heads-up though, gentlemen.

This asshole is a giant racist. The cancer doesn't help either. He's prone to spewing all sorts of stuff."

Liu stands at the foot of a bed, the nearly skeletal remains of a man resting under the covers. Gangly arms draped to his sides, the right is hooked up to an IV. The left is so thin that Rob wonders what the point of the handcuff restraining him to the bed frame is.

"Mr. Graelish, I'm Special Agent in Charge—"

"Mr. Graelish is what the social workers called me. I hated that. You ain't a social worker, are you?"

Not a man used to being interrupted, Liu swallows down his indignation before continuing. "All right, sir, what would you like to be referred to as?"

"My friends call me Pat."

"Okay. Pat, I'm—"

"But you ain't my friend, are you, zipperhead?"

"You told the officer outside that you had information?" Rob interrupts.

Graelish doesn't even acknowledge the statement. He keeps his eyes fixed on Liu while he nods his head to the right. "You always let your field hands talk over their master like that?"

"You can drop the field hand shit right here and now," Rob replies, taking a step forward. The SAC puts an arm out across his chest to stop him.

"As I was saying, sir, I'm Special Agent in Charge Samuel Liu. I can assure you that Special Agent Jackson is by no means a field hand. I can also assure you that any continued racial bias on your part will end this interview immediately."

Graelish stares back before giving them a pain-laced grimace. "Okay, Sam, let's go with sir. Ain't been called that much in my life. Kinda has a nice ring to it."

"Very well. As Special Agent Jackson alluded to earlier, you said you had information on Autumn's Tithe?"

"I do."

"Specifically, the location of their other camps?"

"Ain't no other camps, plural. Not that I know of anyhow. Just the one left."

"I see. What concessions are you seeking?" Liu asks. Rob takes out a pad and pen.

"What concessions? I just want this madness to stop before someone else gets killed."

Liu chuckles, looking down at his shoes. He pauses before picking his eyes back up, his face as stern as ever. "Sir, you don't get to my position without having done this once or twice before. So please, if you don't mind, let's stop beating around the bush."

Rolling his head to the side, Graelish stares out the window for a few moments. He's still looking when he starts to speak again. "What I said is true. For one person in particular."

"You know someone in the camp?" Liu asks.

He nods. "I got a niece there. Only family that still talks to me. I don't need you fuckers blowing her to bits too."

"The only ones who were eliminated were the aggressors. Aggressors that were about to attack innocent people, may I remind you," Liu replies.

"Yeah, whatever. Assholes." Graelish mutters the last word before turning back to them. "Look I'm going to level with you two. I don't like you very much."

"There's a revelation," Rob says, earning a brief glance of reproach from the senior agent.

"Please continue, sir," Liu states, turning back to Graelish.

"What I was gonna say is that I like having the wool pulled over my eyes even less. We were fooled. I was fooled. Marshal convinced us to live and prepare not for a new society, but for his own petty revenge. People died for him. Good people that I knew. And for what? It was all bullshit!"

Graelish goes into a fit of coughing while his EKG monitor ticks upward and begins beeping more rapidly. Liu crosses over and hands him a cup of water from the bed stand. "Try not to get too excited, sir."

After calming down with a few deep breaths, gritting his teeth along the way, Graelish continues. "I'm dying. Obviously. When you're facing the end things start to clear up. I ain't about to go out as the butt end of someone else's cruel joke. I ain't no fool. And like I said, my niece Holly, she's mixed up in this too. You promise me you can get her out of there safely, and I'll tell you where they're at."

"We'll do everything we can," Liu says in his best attempt at a sympathetic voice.

"Not good enough," Graelish says with another cough. "I need to hear you say you promise. I'm the reason she's in this mess. Maybe if I can get her out, get her back to my brother, I can redeem a piece of this worthless life."

"Okay," the SAC replies. "I promise. I will use all of my assets to retrieve her safely. You have my word."

Graelish looks at them both several times, the long moment dragging by. Finally, he swallows and then croaks out, "Kentucky. In the southern part of the state near the border with Tennessee. The Daniel Boone National Forest. There's a horse ranch in there somewhere. Or it used to be one anyway. If you bring me a map I can show you the general region it's in. That's all I know."

"You're a good man, Mr. Graelish. This information is going to save lives," Liu says, patting the end of the bed as he already begins to head for the door.

"Yeah, whatever. Just get Holly out."

Out in the hallway Liu breaks into a purposeful stride, barking over his shoulder and wagging his finger as he weaves his way through nurses, doctors, and officers on the way to the elevator. So quick is the senior agent to take off that, after stuffing his pad in his back pocket, Rob has to jog a few steps to catch up. Even then he remains one step to the rear and to the left, military deference for a ranking officer.

"This is great! This is great! Call Tatum. Tell him to get the team spun up. I want everyone in on this right away."

Rob looks at his watch. It's almost eleven. "You mean tonight, sir?"

"You're goddamn right I mean tonight. That camp could be loading trucks as we speak. You want me to wait until morning? They might already have a VBIED out there."

Never mind the fact that if Tithe did, the likelihood of them catching it tonight was slim to none. Rob can only imagine Jason's response when he gets the call. Better to do that one separately. "Roger that, sir."

"And then have him alert that Neanderthal thug. I want him in the field as soon as possible."

"Sir . . ." Rob hesitates. "Derek and the extraction team have absorbed their fair share of body blows as of late."

Liu stops short so suddenly that Rob strides past him and has to double back. "So?" the senior man replies, indignant.

"So shouldn't we corroborate this information first before putting assets in play? Give them a little extra time for preparation?"

Looking him up and down, the man's face cringes with disdain and annoyance. Liu stares at Rob as if seeing him for the first time. "I'm not surprised that you've already forgotten, but the feed store in Kentucky was one of the locations on that aircraft mechanic's hard drive." Rob doesn't correct the man on the fact that the feed store was in Tennessee and the rail yard in Kentucky. "So obviously they need to have a camp in the area if they were able to boobytrap the store as well." Rob doesn't correct the SAC on his confirmation bias either.

"This isn't my first rodeo, Agent Jackson. Of course I'm going to corroborate the information further. That's why I'm pulling the team in right away. But I'm not wasting any time either. Graelish's information follows the geographical pattern we've seen established by this group, and the hard drive supports his declaration. I don't care if that troglodyte is inconvenienced. Work up a plausible sector and insert him at once." Liu starts walking down the hall again.

"Sir, Derek is an asset, but he's also a civilian. He may not realize it yet but he's gone above and beyond his initial agreement with us. He's the reason why we've got this group on the ropes. I think it's in our best interest to keep him cooperative."

The last earns him a sideward glance. Liu punches the button to the elevator. Rob can see the man's ears getting red. After a few moments the SAC sighs. "Very well," he says without looking back. "Give him a forty-eight-hour WARNO. But you, Agent Jackson, will spend every one of those hours corroborating the information and working up an operations order for this. Your precious Derek can have his days off, but at the end of that time frame he better be in the woods."

"Yes, sir," Rob replies flatly.

"You can drop me back at home on your way to the office. Call me if anything develops tonight."

"You're not coming in with us, sir?"

Liu's head snaps around as the elevator bell chimes. "Why would I do that when I have all of you?"

13

Pulling off the gravel road onto the property, the U-Haul tilts left and right as it bounces over the ruts present in the dirt tracks leading toward the stables and homestead. In the cargo area something topples over with a crash. Deep looks at Kyle and cringes, to which Kyle shrugs. *Nothing we can do about it now.*

Surprisingly the ride from Arizona had been efficient and uneventful. Deep's qualifications and experience meant an ability to stay awake for far greater durations than Kyle, as well as needing far less sleep to recover. The combined efforts of both men resulted in being on the road almost constantly as they traversed the country.

Deep had even lightened up enough to start talking on their second day together. Whether it was genuine or just to pass the time, Kyle was grateful for the conversation to help break up the monotony of the trip. Tuning the radio every so often to capture a radio station long enough for some songs was short-lived respite. When Deep's mention of the Detroit

Pistons opened the door to their shared love of the NBA, the two had a practically nonstop debate over drafts, players, teams, and championships the rest of the way.

Homestead drawing closer as Kyle eases his way up the track, the ranch is alive with the constant movement of beehive-like production. Adults and children alike move about the property completing the necessary tasks for their survival and salvation. A trio stand in the middle of the dirt road where it forks off to the various buildings dotting the ranch. The woman amongst them sees the box truck approaching and starts waving Kyle toward the stables. One of the men with her jogs to the building. He shouts for Kyle to back the vehicle into a spot next to the structure and then acts as a ground guide until the U-Haul is parked.

Climbing out the cab, Kyle first greets the man and introduces Deep before asking him to get a work party together to unload the contents. Turning back to the dirt road, Kyle and the sniper stride over to meet the woman. Dolores is a burly woman in her late fifties with muscled arms used to working farms all her life, a hawkish face, and a tangle of short salt-and-pepper curls. She wears a worn set of jeans with an equally worn denim vest over a dirt-stained T-shirt. Never one for any displays of affection, especially public ones, the woman shakes hands with Kyle, crushing his hand in her viselike grip.

"Good trip?" she says, leaning over to spit some of the tobacco juice accumulated from her plug of dip.

"Good enough," Kyle replies. As Dolores straightens she gives a short grunt in acknowledgement before looking Deep up and down. "This is Deep. Deep, meet Dolores." As the two shake hands, Kyle goes on. "Deep here is a long-range asset. Going to give us a real leg up in the things to come."

Spitting again first, Dolores says, "Just so long as you're not a fucking weirdo like the other one we got."

"Who's that? Pugh?" Kyle responds.

"Yup, that's him. I think the guy has got a few pieces missing from the board if you ask me."

Turning to Deep, Kyle points back to the U-Haul. "Why don't you go secure your Barrett? After you've got it, ask any of the others to show you where you can bunk. I'll tie you in with Kellen a little later."

Giving them both a look, Deep goes to move off. "Not a problem. Just keep in mind I'm gonna need to zero the thing properly, and then start doing recon around here." He looks at the surrounding hills and woods. "Could take a while. Wouldn't mind getting some chow beforehand either."

"Dinner is in a little bit. Supper at sundown. Listen for the bell for both," Dolores says.

"Roger that," Deep returns as he walks off.

When he's out of earshot Kyle looks back at the woman. "What's the deal with Kellen?"

"He showed up a few days ago, but with no warning. Just appeared all of a sudden coming out of the woods wearing that tree-covering thing. Couple of the kids saw him first and started screaming. Didn't affect him none. He just kept ambling on, rifle clutched in his hands."

"I mean, that's not the best way to announce yourself, I guess, but does it mean that he's crazy?"

"If that were the only thing, I'd say no," Dolores replies. "Except it wasn't the only thing. A couple of us drew down on him when we saw what spooked the kids. He just kept coming. When we finally got him to stop he just stood there. After a while he took off the hood, but then he just sorta... stared at us. Wouldn't respond to any of our questions. Was like a friggin' statue."

"All right," Kyle says. "What else?"

"When we finally get things sorted and he gives us the confirmation, the guy starts acting like he's the main attraction. Telling us all of the things we're doing wrong. Redirecting people on Sarah's authority. Said that we were here to support his part of the mission, nothing more. A few of us got into it with him, myself included. I finally ended up banishing him to the silo. He ranges out into the woods mostly but comes back after a few hours and starts stirring up the same shit again. But it's not like he's arguing because he's not getting his way."

"Not sure I follow."

Spitting again, Dolores looks off to the sky. "It's like... like we never had the previous conversations in the first place. I swear, if you talk to him you think you're speaking to someone with amnesia or Alzheimer's. Guy is putting everyone on edge, and we got enough on our hands already, you know?"

Kyle nods. "I get it. He's at the silo now?"

"Last I checked."

"Okay. I'll go have a chat with him and set the record straight. From now on he only speaks to us. In the meantime continue with the preparations as Sarah directed. I'll link up with you later to get a status report on where we stand."

A nod and another spit. "Sounds good. Glad you're finally here, boss."

The two split off, Kyle heading toward the northeast section of the ranch where the silo stands. As he nears the doorway, long since bereft of its actual door, a sneaking suspicion causes him to pull his pistol from the concealed carry holster at the base of his spine and do a press check of the chamber. Seeing the sliver of brass, Kyle stuffs the weapon and his hands into his jacket pockets before stepping inside.

The dilapidated structure stinks of mold and decay, both from the wood of the silo and whatever contents it once held. Holes and broken sections span the height of the vertical tunnel. The intermittent light mixed with the dusty remnants in the air throw strange shadows across the interior. High above pigeons flap their wings before exiting out of the opening at the top.

A shuffle near the far side of the silo draws Kyle's attention. Although the man's face is mostly obscured by darkness, a beam of light cuts across his torso. Kellen sits on a camp stool with his back completely erect. Kyle can just make out the rifle laid across his lap, the man's hands resting gently atop it.

Not wanting to get any closer, Kyle speaks from where he stands. "Kellen, I'm Kyle." When no response comes back he presses on. "I understand there's been some trouble around camp since you arrived."

"The trouble is with them. They're leaderless."

"Well, see, Kellen," Kyle says as an edge creeps into his voice. "That's where you and I disagree. I've known Dolores since the beginning, and she's as capable as anyone I've ever met."

"I cannot complete my mission if they will not follow my orders."

"See, there you go again. This isn't your mission,

and you weren't sent here to give out orders. You're a piece of the puzzle, not the whole picture, understand?" Silence greets Kyle in response. "I know for a fact that Sarah sent you here to begin preparations for your role. I also know that she has had Dolores here running this camp for months now, and that I was given explicit orders to take command upon arrival and implement her plan. Not yours. Now, are we going to have a problem with that, or are you going to drop this Napoleon complex you've got going on?"

Giving the man a few moments to let the information sink in and a chance to respond, Kyle presses on when Kellen says nothing in return. "So here's what's going to happen. Another sniper arrived with me today. You two are going to link up, and starting first thing in the morning, you're going to recon the entire area surrounding this camp for the best vantage points and firing lanes. Then when you're done and I am sufficiently convinced of where you can be incorporated into Sarah's plan, the two of you are going to patrol and conduct observation posts until their arrival. If you have to come in at all, you speak to me or Dolores and no one else. Have I made myself clear?"

After a long minute there's a shuffling at the other end of the silo. Through the bands of light Kyle watches as the sniper stands to his full height. Clutching his rifle in his left hand, Kellen bends out of view and grabs something off the floor. Kyle pulls his pistol out of his pocket and leaves it down by his side.

The man straightens and walks directly at Kyle. He is just about to raise his weapon when Kellen diverts around him and heads to the doorway. Standing in the opening and backlit by the sunlight, the man's red hair radiates as he looks back over his shoulder. Kyle can see the sniper's ghillie suit in his right hand. "I'm starting south southeast and will work counterclockwise. Have him find me there."

Turning to his right Kellen heads off to the tree line. Kyle lets out the breath that he didn't realize he was holding.

■ ■ ■ ■

The eyes staring back at him are not his own.

They may be the same shape and color. They may have borne witness to the same events. But there is no mistaking that the eyes in his reflection belong to another man.

Gone is the husband and father. The son and caregiver. With each successive mile toward his release point the wall comes up. With every stroke of camouflage face paint put into place covering the pigment of his skin, so too does another brick fall into place.

It is the wall that separates the two. The obstruction that allows Derek to do what must be done. To step behind it means to sever himself from attachment. From emotion. Behind the wall there is only the mission, and missions require warriors. People ready to think and act while unencumbered by the trials and tribulations of civilian life. To make the hard choices for the greater good.

To kill.

Derek exhales at the last, just as his final streak of black covers the high shine area of his forehead. With it the transformation is complete. The man staring back at him now is a man detached. Closer to a bear than a human. At one with nature. A being powerful in its own right. That has no qualms killing for its own survival. Or to protect those it loves.

The van they're in bucks as it turns. The distinct sound of tires on gravel signals to the team in the back that they've left the hard ball road and are now driving into the woods. Sure enough, Drysdale, driving up front while dressed as a utility worker save for the silenced pistol tucked under his leg, comes over the net. "All elements this is Pegasus 6. Five mikes out from R.P. Stand by for insertion."

"Roger that, Pegasus," Jason's voice replies on the radio. "ISR overhead shows no signs of anything larger than a squirrel for three miles in all directions of the R.P. You're clear to insert."

"Gee, thanks, Dad," Derek says into the transmission network. The rest of the team chuckles in response.

The tail end of Jason's laugh comes through their earpieces as he keys up to reply. "Cute, Slingshot. Try not to catch any rounds in your fourth point of contact while you're out there."

"Roger that," Derek chirps back.

"Funny," Ortiz says over the closed frequency team intercom. " 'Clear to insert' is what I say to the men I take home after last call." This elicits another round of laughter, louder this time.

"Ortiz, you are absolutely one of a kind." Derek laughs.

"Just telling it like it is, mi amor. Besides, I wanted to leave you with a nice thought to keep you warm while you're out there."

"I feel a lengthy PowerPoint presentation focused on fraternization in our near future. Thanks for that, Ortiz," Gerbowski chimes in.

"All right, knock off the grab ass and cut the chatter. One mike out. Get ready," Drysdale says.

Like a Viking berserker of old, Derek enters the final moments of his preparation for battle. He focuses on the potential actions on contact to be taken if they meet opposition when the doors open while systematically and almost unconsciously checking his gear one last time. Boots laced. Fatigues buttoned up. Harnesses and holster strapped and secured. He rotates around and lets Ortiz slip his pack straps over his shoulders, the bag containing all his usual technology, rations, survival gear, spare ammunition, and grenades. Hefting his rifle, Derek pulls the charging handle back, putting a bullet in the chamber.

The team, dressed and painted the same in case they need to immediately scatter into the woods, rack their weapons as well. Gerbowski and Ortega rotate on their benches to face the rear of the van, each with a boot on a door, Ortega with a firm grip on the handle. Ortiz winks at Derek before moving closer to the rear of the van. She takes a knee in between the two men and cradles her weapon at the low ready. With their chest plates all square to the opening the trio effectively creates a bullet-stopping human blanket of sorts. The action, one intended to protect Derek at all costs as per the mission of the team, is still one that he reluctantly accepts.

When they first started creating team SOPs and drilling together, he had stated that it should be him in the center. Not because Ortiz is a woman, but because she's the team medic, and if she got hit they would be in a world of hurt, relying then on himself and cross-trained backups. Also citing his size as the reason for the place in the formation, Ortiz finally told him to pound sand but softened it afterward by saying he could buy her a drink whenever he wanted. Derek stopped protesting.

He's just taking a knee behind her when Drysdale comes back over the radio. "Pegasus 6 to all Pegasus elements, report redcon status." Each of the trio quickly keys up with their readiness condition.

"Pegasus 2, redcon one," replies Ortega.

"Pegasus 3, redcon one," replies Ortiz.

"Pegasus 4, redcon one," replies Gerbowski.

"Slingshot 6, redcon one," Derek says.

"Central, this is Pegasus 6, all Pegasus elements redcon one at this time. Ten seconds to R.P. Stand by."

"Roger that, Pegasus 6. Good luck, Slingshot." The van bucks again and then makes a wide sweeping arc. Braking, Drysdale throws the vehicle into reverse and slowly backs up before coming to a stop. "Open," he calls into the team intercom.

Ortega pulls the handle and then he and Gerbowski push off with their boots. As the doors swing open their weapons come up. The three team members scan a wood line full of pine trees and nearby picnic tables. The two on the outside look from far to near while Ortiz scans from near to far. All the while everyone listens, waiting for the sound of voices, cracking branches, or anything else that might denote an ambush. After a minute of observation Gerbowski keys up.

"Pegasus 6 this is Pegasus 4, we look clear."

"Roger that. Disperse," comes the reply order.

The two men hop out and swing their weapons ninety degrees, Gerbowski to the left and Ortega to the right. Ortiz leaps out next, keeping her belt-fed machine gun pointed straight ahead. Again they freeze for another thirty seconds before keying up.

"Move," Gerbowski commands.

Choreographed like the finest ballet, the group starts forward. Ortega stalks at a quicker pace, picking up the point man responsibilities to guide the team with his GPS. At the same time Derek steps from the van, spins to the right, and sweeps his weapon up to cover Ortega's vacated field of fire. As the young man passes Ortiz to take the lead, she slows and angles herself to the right until she links up with Derek. He then slides back to take the rear position of the diamond, all while the formation silently traverses the landscape.

The team moves with stealth, their eyes and ears attuned to the surroundings. Gerbowski takes control of the progression, using hand and arm signals to direct Ortega around fallen trees, boulders, and the like. The park is quiet this early in the morning, with only a few birds chirping through the fresh sunlight. Systematically Ortega's whisper comes over the intercom as they continue to move.

"Five hundred meters.

"One thousand.

"Fifteen hundred meters.

"Two clicks."

They go another thousand meters. Just after Ortega calls out the distance, Derek halts the group with a silent transmission over the intercom made possible by quickly keying and releasing his push-to-talk, followed immediately with a raised fist. He opens his fingers into a knifehand and spins it around his head. Derek then four finger points to a nearby saddle strewn with boulders, marking their rally point. Gerbowski nods and Ortega moves over to the terrain feature that will provide them with both cover and concealment.

Once there, the team again operates with the fluidity of seasoned veterans. Each spins to face a cardinal direction. Pointing outward, they close the formation so that their packs and boot heels are touching one another. The group then drops to a knee, giving them a tight 360 degrees of coverage. Derek whispers into the intercom while everyone stares at their section of the wood line.

"No signs of patrols, observation, or listening posts. We're still several clicks from the first target. Safe to say that if they were looking for us, it wouldn't be this far north. We'll release from here."

"Roger that," replies Gerbowski. Given their range he switches over to the radio. "Pegasus 6 this is Pegasus 4."

"Go for Six."

"R.P. time now. We're heading back."

"Roger over. Break. Central, Pegasus 6. Show Slingshot R.P. from the Pegasus element at this time. All team members are returning to the vehicle. Will signal when en route R.T.B."

"Copy, Pegasus 6. Break. Slingshot, we'll keep ISR on station for as long as we can. After that, let us know when you've reached the first target reference point."

"This is Slingshot. Roger, over."

"Central. Roger out."

Standing, the group gives him head nods and fist bumps before they separate and meld into the forest around them.

▪ ▪ ▪ ▪ ▪

"Central, Slingshot 6, over," Derek whispers into his headset microphone.

"Go ahead, Slingshot," comes the reply.

"I've got twenty-two hours on TRP eleven with no signs of activity. Location appears abandoned. Recommend eliminating and proceeding to next location, over."

The radio crackles in his ear before going dead with a long pause. Derek knows they're mulling it over the way bureaucrats whose job may be on the line with every decision tend to painstakingly do. After some extended moments the line comes back to life.

"Slingshot 6, Central. Roger, Target Reference Point eleven is a no go. Proceed to TRP twelve and begin recon, how copy?"

"Central, Slingshot 6. Good copy. Slingshot out."

The morning sun streaks through the trees overhead. Derek gathers his gear into his pack and begins his trek farther south. The hasty intelligence package that had been put together identified seventeen probable locations that needed reconnaissance, thirteen of which the drones couldn't provide, so thick was the tree cover overhead. The sites are comprised of just the kind of remote bases of operations that Autumn's Tithe is known for. Abandoned farms. Bankrupt lumber camps. Failed mines. A slew of horse barns used for both training and trail riding on the numerous paths crisscrossing the landscape. With the spring weather Derek had traded possibly running into a random deer hunter with potentially encountering a leisurely horseback ride winding its way through the forest. As such he always makes sure to give the stables a wide berth and checks the trails for fresh tracks before negotiating the terrain.

Each TRP corresponds to a ten-digit grid location on his GPS and backup map. Preloaded to correspond with the operations order, Derek can simply punch a button on his wrist-top computer or call in the TRP number, and an Intelligence, Surveillance, and Reconnaissance drone will be launched to scan the route to the location and the location itself. In this same vein, should he come into contact upon reaching a site, the Pegasus extraction team and air support elements can be dispatched to provide reinforcements in a matter of minutes.

Even those sites that had open air space over them or showed presence through thermals required further investigation. After the site exploitations of previous camps, they learned that Tithe would often keep caches of weapons and explosives away from the main buildings so as to avoid any prying eyes of a random game warden or Department of Environmental Conservation officer doing an inspection. ISR could let him know what he was walking into, but it was Derck that had to get eyes on in order to determine whether or not a particular TRP was the one they were looking for.

Holstering his binoculars and slinging his pack onto his shoulders, Derek then punches TRP twelve into the computer. Instantly a route highlights its way through the woods. He knows that with the coordinates entered, the ISR drone is already on its way to scan for him before his arrival. Double-checking with his map and compass, Derek determines the easiest terrain that matches with his heading. Taking a sip of water from his integrated reservoir and clutching his rifle, he begins his trek farther south yet again.

For close to three weeks in the field now he had

kept the same rhythm as he worked his way from site to site. It was slow, deliberate work to traverse the swath of dense forest between State Highway 1756 to the west and U.S. Highway 27 to the east. Derek had to rule out each location as quickly as possible, lest Autumn's Tithe proceed with their plans before he could discover their camp. The group's reliance on courier messaging and limited electronic communications had worked against them in that the coordination for operations took longer than they would if technology was their primary method. To date, Derek and the FBI had benefited from the built-in delays, but that in no way meant they could take their time.

While having to act quickly, he also needed to move with stealth. Tithe already employed listening and observation posts at the perimeter of their camps, but if Sarah had learned any lessons from New York and the subsequent locations, it was that patrols would be needed as well. Derek had to ensure that he made it to each site undercover and without detection, otherwise the entire op could be jeopardized.

Quick and quiet was the key. To do this he set a moderate and steady pace through the wilderness. Taking great care to periodically stop and observe the closer he was to a TRP, Derek risked a little more noise to travel at speed when he was well between them.

With three to four hours left of sunlight, Derek would begin scouting for a campsite for the night, making note of any rabbit tracks or trails in the area. In order to not leave any trace of his presence, he always selected naturally occurring shelters like caves or fallen trees. Then it was only a matter of finding shorn branches to throw up a hasty lean-to.

The routine was simple. The same mantra he taught his students, just applied tactically. No cut branches or lashings that could be tracked, but a shelter that could still provide concealment, both from the elements and the enemy overnight. If far enough from a TRP, Derek would set out wire snares on the trails and pump water through a Katadyn filter from a stream or river, both occurring in abundance in the hills of Kentucky. Instead of open fires for warmth, he used a state-of-the-art lightweight bivy sack, essentially a camouflage astronaut blanket turned sleeping bag. Any game caught was cooked on a field stove, otherwise he subsisted off hiker meals and beef jerky rations from his pack. Should his supplies dwindle enough, he could make his way to predetermined drop points where a drone would deliver more food, ammo, or medical supplies if need be. Once camp was set up it was simply a matter of putting out a solar panel to charge his batteries with the remaining beams of sunlight.

At night he would activate his electronic beacon marking his position for the ISR, so that he could be watched over with the unmanned aircraft's FLIR heat-sensing cameras while getting some sleep. Sleep came easily enough. Much easier than back in society, strange as it may sound.

The woods are where he finds solace. His sanctuary from the intrusive thoughts. Here there's no need to drown them out. To silence them with booze. Here he has the orchestra of nature. Songbirds chirping in the day are his flutes and piccolos. Owls at night his clarinets. The skittering of squirrels up trees the snare drums. The rustling leaves a high hat cymbal. A distant peal of thunder serves as a timpani drum. The buzz of mosquitoes the strings of violins. The crickets keeping time as the conductor.

All of this combines to ease Derek back. Not all the way. He can never fully release the alter ego, not in the field where he needs to be ready to meet a threat instantly. But it does take him away from the threshold. Just enough to let the tension drain from his muscles. For his nose to drink in the clean air and the smell of fresh pine. For his mind to relax, to slip around the wall and take a peek.

In those moments before sleep grabs him he thinks of Michael. Kim is there too, his longing to make things right with her ever present. Occasionally he remembers the happy moments with his father. But for the most part, Derek's thoughts are of his boy.

Of protecting him. Raising him right. Caring for and loving and spending time with him. Soon. So soon. Once this mission is over Autumn's Tithe will have been eradicated, and he can finally focus on what's most important: getting back to his family and picking up the pieces.

14

Twenty-three days after entering the woods of Kentucky, Derek approaches TRP twelve from the north. The morning sun shines brightly. He had been moving since before dawn, his early start giving him an acute sense of his surroundings, as the birds and critters hadn't risen yet. Now that the sun is up, he can see his objective clearly ahead.

At a thousand meters out he slows practically to a standstill. Every step is deliberately chosen. Every tree is a part of his cover. Every sound is as silent as possible.

A steep hill covered in trees and rocky outcroppings rises in front of him. Derek knows from his map and the intel brief that this is the key terrain feature marking the target reference point. On the other side of the hill will be the Saddle Oaks horse ranch. Lowering himself to the ground and lying prone, Derek searches out a suitable position. Seeing a tangle of brush fifty meters off to his right, he cradles his rifle across his chest and begins to painstakingly low-crawl.

Inch by inch Derek slides across the forest floor. He

moves, a foot or so at a time, and then stops. Waiting. Watching. Listening. Looking for any sign of the enemy. Any sign that they have detected his approach.

It takes well over an hour to reach the brambles. With the same deliberate action, Derek slowly removes his pack. Holding his rifle in front of him with his right hand, and his pack by the carry handle in his left hand behind him, Derek shimmies and slides his way into and under the brush. Once sufficiently in the concealment, he keys up his radio.

"Central, this is Slingshot. LP, OP established just north of TRP twelve. Marking GPS and initiating surveillance now."

After a moment the response crackles back in his ear. "Roger, Slingshot. Listening post and observation post established. Waiting on your signal." Derek punches the requisite entry into his wrist-top computer. A blue dot emerges on his GPS map with rings emanating from it every ten seconds. "We've got you, Slingshot. Strong signal. Proceed."

He waits. One hour. Two. Ants and other insects crawl over him. Down his sleeves. Across his gloves. Derek blinks away rivulets of sweat streaking into his eyes, refusing to move unless absolutely necessary. Confident in the coverage of the brush, he rocks onto his side ever so slowly and relieves himself before sliding back down into the prone position.

He radios in the passing of each hour so that they can adequately chronical the time and analyze any patterns in patrol lengths. Except no patrols come. Derek glasses the ridgeline at the top of the hill extending east and west from him in an attempt to locate any crow's nests like the ones that were employed at the other camps. Nothing. He's beginning to think he has another abandoned location, another victim fallen to the Kentucky economy, when a truck engine turns over.

Derek marks the time and calls it in, straining now to listen further. After the vehicle drives off he can just make out voices. Two men calling to each other. A woman's shrill laugh. Perhaps children playing. At just before 8 a.m. it resembles the sounds of a site coming alive, although most functioning farms and ranches would have been well underway already.

"Central, Slingshot 6. No signs of any patrols or OPs. Confirmed there are people present at the TRP. I'm moving in for a closer look."

"Slingshot, Grizzly 6," comes Jason's voice. "Copy. Proceed with caution."

Low-crawling out from under the brush, he dons his pack again and moves as quickly and quietly as he can to the base of the hill. Ducking behind a thick oak, he glasses the ridgeline above with his rifle's optic one more time before picking out the best route to ascend the steep hill. Derek spies a naturally occurring set of relatively feasible switchbacks and makes for them.

Like it is with all his other movements this close to a target, Derek ascends with a blend of stealth and speed as he works his way up in elevation. He takes only a few breaks, crouching low under a rock ledge or behind another tree wide enough to hide behind. Here he'll catch his breath, gulp some water, and glass one more time before picking his next formation out and making for it.

At the top of the hill the land flattens out. Just to his south, directly ahead of him, Derek can see breaks through the trees. Thinking that must be the clearing where the horse ranch is located, he begins low-crawling again, this time toward the open air. Edging over to his right, Derek finds a rocky outcropping jutting between the roots of two tangled oaks to either side of it. He moves to the spot, wedging himself into the tight space. Derek smiles as his intuition proves correct. He has a clear line of sight to the ranch below.

As steep as the proceeding side of the ridge was, the southern face of it is practically a sheer cliff. The ridgeline continues off to his right, curling around to the west and then running south. Off to his left he can see where the land slopes down to the clearing below. While trees are scarce on the cliff face, a thick wood line of oaks and pines surrounds the ranch on three sides, with only the south laid bare.

Below Derek, two structures sit to either side of his position. On the right is an open-sided pavilion with a corrugated, peaked roof. Various pieces of aged and rusted-out farm equipment sit underneath it. To his left is a farmhouse, dilapidated and weathered. Where the roof doesn't sag it lacks in shingles, and where it doesn't lack in shingles it's covered with moss and decay.

Adjacent and to the left of the farmhouse is a three-story grain silo. Pockets of the sides are missing and the sliding door at the top of the structure sits open. To the left of the silo are a pair of stables running parallel with the eastern edge of the property. Like the farmhouse, the stables show signs of disrepair. A number of the stalls are missing the top halves of their doors, and the red and white paint is faded and flaking. A pair of men come out of the farthest stable, one of them producing a pack of cigarettes that they both begin smoking.

A horizontal two-post wooden fence marks the

eastern property line and runs behind the stables from north to south, where it links up with the same type of fence running east to west and marking the southern edge of the acreage. The east-west fence runs parallel to a gravel road, not a hard ball but not a dirt track either. It's the latter that leads through the property from the access road.

Twisted like a crooked trident, one branch breaks east toward the stables. The middle branch runs mostly straight north from the road to the homestead, while the west branch leads to a circular corral on its south side before bending north to the pavilion. The corral is constructed of the same fencing as the rest of the property, save for it having three horizontal posts compared to the two everywhere else. Four children run around inside of it playing tag.

Derek takes in the scene, slowly panning his rifle around to look more closely at each building. It's on his second pass that he notices something he missed. Tucked behind the southernmost stable is the front end of the unmistakable orange, white, and green paint combination of a U-Haul truck.

At that moment an engine revs and a pickup comes into view from the wood line at the far southeast of Derek's vantage point. A screen door slams and a moment later three men enter into view. They're each wearing sidearms, and the middle man has an AK-47 slung across his back.

The pickup truck pulls into the space between the two stables. The driver gets out and lowers the tailgate. Derek's heart sinks. The flatbed is laden with white sacks. The armed men link up with those smoking and start offloading the cargo, bringing them into the southern stable through an open stall door.

He checks his wrist-top computer to make sure his GPS is still transmitting. Derek swallows before keying up. "Grizzly 6, you still receiving my location?"

"Affirmative, Slingshot. You got something?"

"Roger that. Mark my grid and start the ISR right away. I've got eyes on."

Derek knows the scramble he just caused on the other end. He uses the pause to let down the tripod on his rifle and to power on the video transmitter function of his optic. Derek gingerly slips off his pack and sets it up next to him, preparing to settle in for what could be several hours if not days of observation. He reaches into the appropriate compartment and removes his grenades, securing them on empty gear loops by their spoons. Should he need to scramble from his hide in a hurry, he would want the added capacity close at hand.

"Slingshot, this is Grizzly. Can you say again?"

"TRP twelve is our location. Start ISR and prepare to receive video feed from my location."

"Roger," comes Jason's excited voice. Another hole on his promotion belt has just been punched.

"And Grizzly?"

"Go ahead, Slingshot."

"Get a move on with mission planning. We're running out of time."

- - - - -

Eleven hours later, the conference room in Quantico is filled with a bevy of agents, analysts, and other support personnel. The most senior of them sit at the elongated oval table, while the assistants and other essential contributors line the walls, ready to present any information that falls within the parameters of their expertise. Carafes of coffee and Styrofoam cups are as plentiful on the table as the maps, still photos, targeting packages, and satellite images.

The group is weary and strung out on caffeine. At the snap of the SAC's fingers their day had turned from a pedestrian nine-to-five to a blistering flurry of analysis and planning. Operating with speed and alacrity to coordinate all the necessary requirements, Liu insisted on being presented a full mission brief before any of the proposed elements were moved into place. As it stood, the men and women in the room would be working long into the night once they received the senior agent's approval.

The chatter is rambling and forced. Intel and operations were two different sides of the same coin. Offensive and defensive players on the same football team. Yes, they all wore the same uniform, but their roles were vastly different. The groups rarely mixed well together under normal circumstances. The intel analysts begrudging the field agents for their brawn-over-brain tendencies. The agents, especially HRT, scowling at the keyboard warrior's lack of experience out in the streets.

Drysdale watches the scene unfold via video conferencing, his image and that of some others displayed on a monitor facing the head of the table. In the hangar behind him his team sits in a loose semicircle, close enough to hear the proceedings but far enough away not to be seen by the camera. The team leader wants them present for the briefing despite the SAC's predisposition toward junior personnel in the room.

When Liu enters with his aide in tow the banter doesn't immediately break off. He stops dead in his tracks, his disgust plastered across his face in a condescending sneer. "Excuse me. Time is of the essence here, people. Let's cut out the chitchat."

No shortage of eye rolls ricochet around the room as the SAC settles into his seat and his secretary spreads the mission brief materials in front of him. "Now, perhaps we can get on with this briefing," Liu says while his secretary sits in the chair against the wall behind him. "Lord knows it took you all long enough to put it together."

He leans forward and puts his elbows on the table, interlocking his fingers. "Ladies and gentlemen, the situation is this. At approximately zero nine hundred hours today our infiltration asset in the field located and identified another camp. Our intelligence leads us to believe that this is the last bastion of Autumn's Tithe. Once again, we have gained the advantage on them, but time is short. If our asset is correct, the group is within hours of attempting an attack."

He lets the statement settle a while longer, making eye contact with each of those at the table before continuing on. "That attack will not occur on my watch. Make no mistake, there will not be a repeat of the failure at the church. It's fitting that it was once a house of worship, because it was a miracle that no one on those teams were killed," Liu says with a sideward glance at Jason and Rob. "But there isn't going to be some far-fetched cover story about a natural gas leak or some other bullshit no one believes, because this is going to go down my way. By the numbers, with audacity and aggression. We are going in hard and fast and hitting them with a knockout blow. Have I made myself clear?"

Several murmured responses in the affirmative

populate the space while head nods abound. "Very well then. The mission is to conduct an interdicting raid that will detain, dismantle, and ultimately destroy Autumn's Tithe once and for all. I cannot stress enough to all of you in this room the importance of speed and efficacy in this endeavor. Seizing this last known camp will not only deny the enemy of their objective—an objective, ladies and gentlemen, that is to take innocent lives—but it may finally provide us with the necessary information we need to complete our investigation as to who in our own government is funding and supplying this group." Again he pauses. After long moments the SAC turns to his left. "Intelligence, let's start with you."

A lean man in his late forties with horn-rimmed glasses and chestnut hair begins speaking. "Sir, ISR as well—"

"Please stand while you're briefing me, Donaldson."

The senior analyst flushes but complies with the order. "As I was saying, sir, since the alert by our field asset we have allocated ISR drones and satellite coverage to gain both imagery and an estimation of the group's disposition. The asset's live feed from his weapon's optic has also added to this information, allowing us to cross-reference what was discovered from our surveillance over the last few hours."

"What can you tell me about the site itself?"

Donaldson picks up a controller and points it at the monitor. The screen changes from those on remote access to an overhead image of the camp. "It's called Saddle Oaks horse ranch. Historical deeds and tax records show that the site was originally founded as a prospective coal mine in the thirties, but switched over to horse breeding and sales. Several factors led to the ranch's eventual bankruptcy twenty-plus years ago. From there it was foreclosure and eventually abandonment. Between its circumstances and remote location, the site fits the profile as one that Marshal would have targeted for acquisition."

"All right," Liu replies. "What is HRT facing here?"

Donaldson nods and begins using his laser pointer. "The camp sits in a horseshoe clearing that only allows for one approach along the road to the south. The terrain to the north and west is dominated by the steep ridgeline and oak trees. A thick stand of oaks along with a bog hampers any possible approach from the east."

"Not ideal, but it will have to do. Weather?"

Donaldson defers to one of the analysts sitting behind him. The young woman stands up, following her superior's lead. "Before morning nautical twilight is zero six three seven hours, sir. Temperature will range between fifty-two and sixty-three degrees. We can expect partly cloudy skies and no precipitation, although there is a sixty percent chance of scattered showers in the afternoon."

Liu lifting his hand is the only acknowledgement he gives to the woman. The SAC inclines his chin toward Donaldson. The analyst flushes and looks at the carpet as she takes her seat.

"Sir, the optical footage provided from the field asset along with these satellite images," he says while the screen changes, "show at least twenty-eight adults. Sixteen men and twelve women. There are also a dozen children on the site. We've observed various small arms, typically AK-47s and AR-style rifles. There is also at least one rifle that would qualify as a long-range sniper weapon. We've no indication of crew serve weapons or other munitions at the camp. This, along with the drastically decreasing amount of these types of firearms we've seized from the previous camps, suggests that their supply chain has been disrupted. It is likely that long rifles and pistols are their only armament. The absence of vehicles, save for this pickup and the U-Haul we believe they rented or stole to perpetrate their bombing, supports this theory. Previous sites planned on utilizing caravans for their attacks, plus several other vehicles and ATVs to act as logistical support in and around their properties. We believe that the lack of weaponry and transport corroborates the information received from Mr. Graelish that this is in all likelihood Autumn Tithe's last camp."

The SAC nods once. "Very good, Donaldson." The man sits while Liu shifts his gaze to the right side of the table. "Commander Herschel, the floor is yours."

The HRT commander stands, albeit more slowly than his predecessor. Tall and broad in the shoulders, he wears his gray hair in a close-cropped high and tight. Dressed in an olive drab flight suit, the man is as picturesque of a life in military operations and law enforcement as one can get. He chews on a piece of peppermint gum as he speaks, turning to the monitor to present his portion of the briefing.

"Sir, the enemy's probable course of action is to have guards posted in the stables here with a rotating shift. This is to keep close watch on the stacks of fertilizer and likely other bomb-making materials. We can expect at least one guard at the top of the silo, more than likely their qualified sniper, with a possible second gunner. That would provide them with three hundred and sixty degrees of observation. The bulk of their force will be here, in the homestead. The optic footage has captured the shift changes observed to this point as well as the women, children, and men all returning to the farmhouse for meals and sleep rotations. If this is truly their last camp, we can expect any heavy opposition to come primarily from this building as the adults will be armed and will look to defend the children."

Liu folds his arms across his chest. With his left hand he covers his mouth. His eyebrows furrow in deep consideration. After a few moments the SAC speaks. "We'll concentrate our air power on the homestead. Neutralize it from the start. Then support with our ground teams."

Herschel nods, ignoring the statement in favor of letting the SAC think his idea is an original one. "Roger that, sir. Two Apache gunships will provide air superiority while two Black Hawks drop teams of HRT to storm the main building. We're looking to achieve surprise and shock effect, catching them at breakfast.

"As the birds come on-site our MRAPs loaded with SWAT teams will approach from the east along the southern road. Vehicle One will head straight for the homestead. Vehicles Two and Three will follow the eastern branch of the track, with Two hitting the silo and Three hitting the stables. Vehicle Four, containing the extraction team, will break left along the western track and secure the equipment overhang. This will put them in position to recover the field asset once we have cleared the site."

"What do we have in the way of local support?"

The commander grimaces but quickly suppresses the gesture. "We're standing by to alert U.S. Marshal detachments in the area. They'll be used to assist with escort to the site to help expedite our travel, and then provide roadblocks to the west and east. We have the numbers to town, county, and state police departments, but out of an abundance of caution we won't notify them until we're about to go in. Again, we can't risk any of the local jurisdictions being on the take like we experienced in upstate New York."

"Good. Good. A solid plan, Commander. How long until you depart?"

"The MRAPs are being prepared as we speak and my teams are gearing up. It's roughly five and a half hours to the staging area where we'll pick up the extraction team, then another forty-five to sixty minutes to the site. I estimate our time on target to be just after eight a.m. It's not ideal but we'll have to brief the teams en route. Time is not on our side with this one."

"No, it is not. Let's wrap up then so we can get you on the road. Agent Jackson."

Rob stands up and clears his throat. "Sir, in terms of service and support, the commander has already highlighted the local police departments. On top of that we will be contacting fire and EMS when the raid begins to get their assets on-site. Local hospitals will be contacted and alerted of a possible mass casualty event. Blood banks will be put on standby as well. We will have CPS lined up and ready to take possession of the children once the site has been secured. The West Virginia National Guard is providing air support out of Bluefield. We have the ISR on station and a Predator armed with two Hellfires will be in the air at the time of the raid."

Liu looks past Rob to Jason seated next to him. "Agent Tatum, Command and Signal if you will."

Like a Whac-A-Mole game at the arcade, one lowers while the other rises. Jason waves for the screen to change. A list of frequencies appears on the monitor. "Sir, you will be in overall command of the operation. After that, chain of command follows to Commander Herschel, then Agent Jackson, then myself. We will be present in a command vehicle at the federal marshal's checkpoint while Commander Herschel will go in with the mounted units. Upon entering the property, all assault units will be linked to Slingshot's direct feed so that he can provide any overwatch intelligence as the raid unfolds. HRT will have their own closed frequency, monitored through the command vehicle, on top of Slingshot's channel. Finally, each individual team and vehicle will have their own intercoms to speak person to person."

Liu shifts his gaze to the monitor. "Chief Drysdale, I assume your extraction team is ready."

"Roger that, sir. Pre-combat checks are complete and I will conduct a final pre-combat inspection after the briefing. We'll be standing by to link up with the vehicles."

"See that you are," Liu quips. The senior agent looks around the room once again. "All right, ladies and gentlemen. Excellent work. You've prepared well, but now it's time to see this through. Do what you do, but do it to the best of your ability. At zero eight hundred we end Autumn Tithe's threat to this country. We are a go. Thank you all." Liu abruptly pushes back from the table and heads out of the room trailed by his aide before anyone can ask any questions.

Commander Herschel receives a text on his cell phone. Upon looking at it his eyebrows raise. He mutters thanks to a few of the agents and analysts in the room as he makes his way over to the monitor. Standing in front of it, he dials the number attached to the text message. Drysdale answers on the other side of the call.

"Skipper, what the hell is going on with this? We just got eyes on this morning and we're going in already?"

Looking over his shoulder first, Herschel replies, "I get it, partner, but Liu is pressing on the timeline. It's your boy in the field that said it looks like they're getting ready to move. If we can take them without launching another missile up their asses then I'm all for it."

"All right, but what's with this zero eight shit? We got NODs, let's use them. Hell, we can insert to the south and walk up on them before they know what's happening. This shock and awe stuff is the same exact plan we used the last time."

"You're preaching to the choir, Chief. Between you and me there's a rumor going around that his aide was researching the regional news outlets."

Drysdale cocks his head to one side. "That son of a . . . this a fucking dog and pony show, Skipper?"

Herschel nods. "Choppers and MRAPs in broad daylight make for better headlines than teams sneaking in bin Laden style."

The team leader shakes his head. "Ain't right, Skipper."

"I agree with you." The commander looks around the room, noticing that it is mostly empty. "Look, the intel is solid despite the little we have. It's mostly women, children, and old men in there with small arms. They all seem to eat breakfast together from seven to eight, just like the other camps. We'll hit them hard and fast and roll them up before they've finished their grits. This is what we do. Get your team ready, and let's take them down once and for all."

Letting out a deep breath, Drysdale nods. "Roger that, Skipper. We'll be ready."

"Good man. See you in a few hours."

15

After strapping into the restraining harness in his pilot's seat of an AH-64 Apache gunship, 1st Lieutenant Harold Spriggs, Harry to the rest of the officer corps of the 150th Aviation Regiment, pulls out his preflight checklist bound in a cargo pocket–sized spiral notebook. He works through bullet after bullet, page after page, ensuring that his helicopter's systems are online and working properly.

Avionics, check. Target Acquisition and Designation System, check. Countermeasures, check. He gives a passing review of the Pilot Night Vision System, ensuring that it is fully functional but quickly moving on to other components. Today's mission is a daylight escort, and between his fuel range and the early morning sunshine they wouldn't have need for the nighttime optics.

Conversely, Spriggs tells his gunner, Chief Warrant Officer Two Thomas Kineis, to pay particular attention to the Ground Fire Acquisition System. The specialized thermographic camera and sensors work in concert to identify targets based on muzzle flashes coming from the surface, which according to last night's briefing, would be the only fire they anticipate taking during the mission.

Next to him in the motor pool they appropriated, two UH-60 Black Hawk helicopters engage their engines. Spriggs looks up to see the rotor blades slowly spinning to life. A moment later he fires up his own. The twin General Electric turboshaft engines thrum and howl with a high-pitched whine as the nearly two-thousand-horsepower machines warm up, the energy like thoroughbreds locked in their starting gates. Stamping and jostling against the metal confines. Waiting to be freed in an explosion of muscle and speed.

This is why he became a pilot. Why he loved to fly. To be a man of the skies, a part of ensuring air superiority for the safety of those on the ground. This is what his service was meant to be.

Charlie company's role was to provide command and control, air assault, and air movement missions as required by their higher chain. That's why when the opportunity came up to serve as escort and aerial support to an FBI mission, Spriggs jumped at the chance. Not only would it get him more time behind the stick instead of a desk, it would almost surely result in some sort of joint command accolade. The added bullet on his Officer Evaluation Report would surely jump him up above his peers in the Guard. Hell, it would probably give him a leg up on the active duty pilots. How many of them got the chance to fly for the Bureau?

Those weeks, as it turned out, were nothing but boredom. Normally based out of the Wheeling County airport, Spriggs's unit is only a stone's throw from Pittsburgh, where there is at least some sense of nightlife and excitement. Instead he and his wingman had been pushed down south to their staging area at the West Virginia National Guard station in Bluefield where the excitement was considerably less. Being on twenty-four-hour standby seemed exhilarating at first, but being tied to the seat of his Apache, figuratively and literally at times, did little for a bachelor with officer pay to burn.

So too was the prospect of being tied to a mission that was all cloak-and-dagger in nature. The FBI team was friendly and talkative except for anything involving their operational parameters. All Spriggs knew was that someone way up the food chain wanted the FBI ready to go at a moment's notice, and with plenty of firepower to back them up. Spriggs couldn't say as to what would require his services, but the fact that his Apache had been outfitted solely with Hydra 70 rockets instead of the typical mix of those and Hellfire missiles suggested that wherever they were going, they would be getting up close and personal.

Then the call finally came through. Late in the night first the WARNO was issued, then an hour or two later the full operations order. Although early to rise to get preflight out of the way, they would be conducting a daylight air escort for two UH-60 Black Hawks carrying the FBI Hostage Rescue Team, and providing cover for four MRAP armored vehicles filled with FBI SWAT. For whatever reason the team that had been on-site with them these last few weeks wasn't going to be in the choppers. Instead they had been designated to one of the trucks.

After checking his Integrated Helmet and Display Sighting System, Spriggs keys up and calls over the radio to his wingman. "Rattler Red 4 this is Rattler Red 1, how copy, over?"

"Rattler Red 1, this is Red 4, good copy over." Spriggs then listens as CW4 Walter Rycheck addresses mission command. Although he technically outranked the man, Spriggs had been in diapers when Rycheck first started flying Apaches. His expertise and lifetime behind the stick made it so that he would be taking lead on the escort. "Scepter 5, this is Rattler Red 4," he says over the hum of the blades. "Rattler element is standing by."

"Roger, Rattler," comes Rob's reply. "Bring your birds to redcon one. Dust off in five mikes."

Spriggs throttles up, the multiple blades overhead and behind increasing to such a speed that they appear to blend into one. The beating of the air resonates with the reverberations felt in the cockpit. In front and below him, Kineis pops two pieces of Dentyne Ice gum into his mouth, per his customary preflight superstition.

The lieutenant watches as armed men clad in woodland multicam uniforms and decked head to toe in tactical gear come pouring out of the National Guard building. The gaggle quickly forms into lines, each one streaking to their respective assigned vehicle whether it be a Black Hawk or an MRAP. For whatever reason the scene reminds Spriggs of an anthill.

As the armored trucks pull out of the motor pool the signal comes to the helicopters standing by. "All airborne elements, this is Scepter 5. You are clear to proceed. Dust-off time now with escort of vehicles to the target site."

"Scepter 5, Rattler Red 4. Roger. We're inbound." A moment later Rycheck comes over the platoon net. "Red 1, Red 4. Let's do it."

"Roger, Red 4." As the sun rises further, the purple

giving way to the orange and blue of early morning, Lieutenant Spriggs gently pulls up on his collective. The Apache lifts off the ground and into the air. The officer looks out his left window, watching as the two Black Hawks do the same and beyond them, Rycheck's gunship. Once all four birds are airborne, Spriggs depresses his pedals and angles the joystick. The Apache rotates toward the west. Nosing the bird down, the gunship takes off after the trucks.

* * * * *

In Kellen Pugh's mind there is a fundamental process to what he does. Lying prone on his perch, covered in his ghillie suit so that he seamlessly blends into the wilderness, the sniper exists in a meditative state. It allows his body to relax. To be at rest while his mind remains alert just enough to take in all that occurs around him. The shift in the air. The buzz of the insects. The calls and laughter of the camp members down below. And now, just at the fringe of human hearing, the beating of rotors off to the south.

A wry smile creases his face and is banished a moment later. Now is not the time for joy. Now it is time to work. He shifts ever so slightly, pumping blood back into his limbs. Regulating his breathing. Speaking at full volume, he calls to Deep. "Rotors."

The other sniper is positioned in the prone position just below Kellen and to his left on the western ridgeline. Although trees still sprout around their position, the rocky outcropping gives both men a clear vantage point of the horse ranch below. From their view the stables sit directly across from them to the east, while the farmhouse and silo lie to the north on their left. Like Kellen, Deep is covered in a ghillie suit matching the terrain. A sleeve of the same material is slipped over the elongated barrel of his Barrett .50-caliber rifle. "I hear them too. It's showtime."

It had been over three weeks since they were paired up. Three weeks of patrolling. Setting up static listening and observation posts for days at a time. It stretched both men's endurance, Deep especially, but in the end their training prevailed. Six days earlier they finished their last patrol, again coming up with no sign of the enemy, but deciding along with Kyle on the ground that a raid must be imminent. They meticulously made their way to their perch and lay in wait for four days now. Not a tremendously long stretch by any means for Kellen, even if it came on the heels of the several preceding weeks.

The Copperhead presses his thumb switch, engaging the open channel to camp leadership on their radios. "Helos inbound. Everyone to their positions."

In the clearing down below a flurry of activity suddenly seizes the camp. People begin scrambling to the stables, silo, and farmhouse. Weapons are unslung. Children are gathered and ferried into the homestead, their cries quickly silenced. Several men and women point their M4s and AK-47s at the sky, searching for the helicopters that can now be clearly heard as they make their way to one of the three buildings to which they're assigned.

Through the organized chaos, Kyle asserts calm while giving direction, aligning the plan with the opening moments. Ensuring that everyone is where they need to be. As the last few stragglers rush to their positions the man turns and sprints for the farmhouse.

On the western ridge, Kellen shifts his M24 to the north, sights, and squeezes off a round. Before the echo of the report can bounce off the rocky wall of the ridge, Kyle's head explodes into a fragmented amalgamation of brain matter and pink mist. His body careens to the ground, his right leg still twitching.

For good measure Kellen swings back to the east and puts a round through Dolores's left eye as she stares in disbelief at Kyle's fallen body. Her corpse crumples like a sack of manure dropped to the floor. He keys up the radio again.

"All stations, get down!" he calls into the net with uncharacteristic emotion in his voice. "There's enemy snipers in the southern wood line. Kyle is dead. Hold your positions while we conduct a countersniper sweep."

"What the fuck are you doing, Pugh?" Deep says off of the radio, incredulous.

"Change in plans," the Copperhead replies, his voice now back to its devoid tone. "I'm taking command."

"You're what?"

"Just follow my lead and do as I say. Be ready to let loose."

The last grabs Deep's attention and shifts his apprehension to the back of his mind for the moment. "All right then. Let's do this thing," he says while racking his bolt and chambering a round.

Pugh goes back onto the radio. "All positions stand by. We haven't located their snipers yet, but helicopters are inbound and will arrive any second. I will call out the engagement from my vantage point. Stay calm. Remember your jobs and do what we've practiced."

As the acknowledgements hurriedly come back from the three buildings, Kellen pulls in a deep breath. Letting it out, he allows the smile to briefly return. Putting his eyes on the southern horizon, the sniper opens his bolt and replaces his two expended rounds.

. . .

When the first shot rings out Derek's eyes are on the camp. He sees the spray of pink just over the farmhouse roof on the main dirt track leading to it, but he can't tell who was hit. Derek scans the clearing with his rifle's optic, searching for the shooter when the second shot rings out. This time he catches sight of a woman going down by the stable buildings, the back of her head blown out and her brains showering the ground. From the direction of the spray and how her body falls he immediately shifts his scan to the right. A plume of white smoke dissipates above the western ridge.

Keying up, Derek speaks quickly into his radio. "Grizzly 6, this is Slingshot. Any snipers on-site?"

"Say again your last, Slingshot?" Jason replies.

"Snipers, Grizzly. Are there any Bureau snipers at the target location?"

In the pause that emits after his question the roar of the approaching helicopters increases. Derek looks over his rifle to see the four birds bearing down on the ranch. He picks up his scan again, this time frantically searching along the western ridge.

"Uh, negative, Slingshot," comes the confused reply. "Only Bureau element on-site is yourself. Incursion is one minute out. SITREP?"

The hair on the back of his neck stands up. *Something isn't right.* "Two in the camp just went down from shots fired from the western ridge. Someone is taking them out." Derek scans the ridgeline and then back to the clearing, which is now empty save for the bodies. "Abort!" he suddenly calls onto the open channel.

"Say again? Slingshot, can you confirm?"

"Abort damn it! There's a sniper emplacement somewhere on the western ridge!"

"All elements this is Scepter 6! Disregard that order!" Liu's voice says, overriding Derek. The choppers continue racing toward the site. "We are thirty seconds away from execution. Rattler Red 4, pay attention to the western ridge as you come on-site. Reports of a possible sniper emplacement in that area."

The whine of the engines and rotors mixes with the static of the reply transmission. "Roger, Scepter 6, wilco," the pilot replies.

Derek looks up, the helicopters now clearing the southern wood line, racing over the ranch, and flaring their bellies to come to a rapid halt. As the gunships and transports level out they reorient themselves. One Apache sits to Derek's far left, covering the farmhouse with its M230E1 30mm chain gun. The two Black Hawks also face the homestead, spaced with about fifty yards between them. The final Apache on Derek's far right is oriented on the farmhouse, but begins turning to face and scan the western ridge.

As the ropes drop out of the sides of the two transport aircraft, four MRAPs come racing into view from the east along the southern road. They make a right turn onto the property, now heading north. Each vehicle breaks off from the one in front of them so that they all come online as they race to cover the distance to their assigned respective buildings.

Too late, Derek thinks.

. . . . .

The helicopters flare and then level out off to Kellen's left. His wry smile turns into a full grin. "Mine group, go," he calmly broadcasts over their net.

Farther to the north, about halfway between the sniper's position and where the ridgeline bends to run east to west, a moss-covered wooden lid is freed from the vegetation holding it in place and slid to the side. A man climbs out wearing a woodland camouflage poncho, the hood up, his face obscured by a death's head bandana with grinning skeleton teeth. Another poncho sits tucked into his belt, falling over his legs like a makeshift skirt. Reaching back down into the mine shaft, he grabs the hand of the man behind him and hoists his fire team partner out from the depths below. Dressed in the same fashion, the second man reaches into the shaft and produces a Stinger missile launcher. The shoulder-fired surface-to-air munition is an elongated five-foot tube, affixed with a trigger system and an open rectangle of metal fans denoting the Identification Friend or Foe targeting module on the front end.

A second weapon is produced, and then the two men retreat some fifty feet away from the mine shaft opening. As they do so, four more men wearing the same ponchos climb out of the shaft. Two of them carry belt-fed M249 Squad Automatic Rifles, while the other two carry M4s with M203 grenade launchers attached under the barrels. They quickly sprint off to the south into the trees of the ridgeline, not waiting for the two men with the missile launchers. Those men shoulder their weapons and point them toward an opening in the tree canopy above.

"Stinger team set."

"Fire," comes Kellen's reply.

The men squeeze their triggers. The missiles streak into the air with a rush, leaving a cloud of white smoke by the men and tails of the same coursing through the sky. No sooner have they launched their fire-and-forget weapons than the two men drop the Stingers. Unslinging their assault rifles, they take off after their comrades rushing along the ridge to the south.

The missiles clear the tree line and rise into the blue sky above it. The infrared sensors on both warheads activate, fixating on the heat produced from the helicopter engines below. Immediately they twist and spiral down until they streak toward their targets with precision and speed. Watching from inside the command vehicle, the feed from the ISR drone captures the launch from high above, everyone inside suddenly more alert than they were a moment ago. "Whoa, what was that?" Jason calls out.

"Where'd that come from?" Rob exclaims at almost the same time.

A second later Liu leans over both their chairs to look at the monitors. "What's happening?"

In the cockpits of all four choppers the missile alarms go off. "What the hell?" Rycheck calls out, but decades of flight training already has the CW4 moving. "Scramble! Countermeasures!" he screams into the radio. The pilot slams on his joystick and pulls up on his collective, attempting to bank his aircraft away from the missile. The Black Hawk on his right initially moves as well, but with men mid-rope on their descent to the deck and the proximity of all the helicopters to one another, the pilot manages only to shift his chopper slightly.

At Rycheck's command all four birds release their countermeasures, sending a bevy of glowing white flares showering into the sky. The Stinger missiles' ultraviolet sensors activate, allowing the munitions to further fixate on the radiation produced by the aircraft's engines and ignore the IR heat of the flares. Fired in such close confines and with little room to maneuver, even Rycheck's attempt at evasion proves futile. A Stinger slams into his fuselage, blowing it apart with a concussive explosion that splits the Apache in half. The top rotors continue to circulate, sending the aircraft into a fiery spin. The gunship careens off to the west before quickly succumbing to its wound and crashing into the wood line. Another more massive fireball emits from the wreckage.

The westernmost Black Hawk shifts to its left into the minimal space vacated by the downed Apache, but the second Stinger explodes upon impact with the helicopter's port side engine. A chain reaction detonates the starboard engine as well as the fuel tanks. The entire Black Hawk erupts, sending fragments of the aircraft and the men on the ropes raining from the sky. The fuselage drops to the ground in front of the overhang protecting the ranch equipment.

The doors at the top of the silo open. Two men shouldering rocket-propelled grenades sight in on the remaining two helicopters. "RPG!" Lieutenant Spriggs screams into his radio. He pulls hard on his collective and banks his gunship up and over the Black Hawk next to him just as one of the men fires. The grenade streaks under the belly of the Apache and detonates in the ground in front of the homestead, sending up a geyser of dark dirt.

The pilot of the Black Hawk helicopter hits his left pedal, shifting the aircraft away from the silo. The move similarly avoids the second RPG round that is fired, which explodes near the corral. The men on the ropes hang on for dear life as they suddenly swing back and forth with the movement.

Kellen smiles. "Now, Deep."

"About time," the man replies. With a flick of the safety Deep squeezes off five shots in quick succession, a metal ping accompanying each of the elongated rounds as they eject from the weapons system. All five shots tear through the port-side engine of the remaining Black Hawk, which bursts into flame and belches out a dark cloud of black smoke. Deep shifts his sight picture to the right and fires again and again, this time with a steadier rhythm. The .50-caliber rounds punch fist-sized holes through the tail section. The last round impacts the tail rotor blades, shattering it, and sending the Black Hawk into an uncontrolled spin. The sniper ejects the empty box magazine and quickly reloads as the only untouched helicopter, the Apache, roars up and over the ridgeline heading south.

At the same time Deep works his rounds through the fuselage of the Black Hawk, Kellen sights in on the four men already on the ropes. Just to inflict the most amount of agony that he can, the Copperhead shoots them in the gut.

His first shot impacts in such a way that it contorts the HRT member and twists the man around his rope, halting his descent. Kellen shifts his aim to the far side of the helicopter and fires again, this time his round launching the man clear off and to the ground with a thud. Sighting back on the near ropes, he watches as the FBI member attempts to climb back up and into the cabin of the aircraft. Kellen puts a bullet into the base of his spine. The man lets go of his rope and sails to the deck, landing in a heap with such force that it cracks his tactical helmet on a rock. He spits up blood as he impacts.

The fourth man is nearly to the ground when Kellen sights on him, but the helicopter is now spinning so erratically that the HRT member is clinging to the rope with all that he has. Finally realizing the bird is about to crash, the man lets go and slams into the deck tumbling end over end. He rights himself, jumping up to his feet and untangling the sling to his rifle just in time for the Copperhead to put a round through his open mouth. The chopper careens out of control, spinning wildly until it crashes into the section of property fence where east meets south. Yet another massive fireball erupts into the sky.

Kellen's grin is a permanent fixture. As he chambers another round the sniper turns his attention to the vehicles that are now breaking off to the different buildings on the property. The man keys up his radio. "All positions. Open fire."

■ ■ ■ ■ ■

Commander Herschel, sitting up front in the lead vehicle, watches as the two helicopters on his left explode in midair. While the flaming wreckage is still falling to the earth, the Black Hawk on his right wheels out of control and out of view, trailing a thick plume of black smoke. The remaining Apache arcs and speeds overhead to the west, traveling out of view just as the sound of the second Black Hawk exploding carries over the clearing. The radio blares to life with hysteria.

"Holy shit!"

"Two, no, three birds down!"

"What the fuck!? What the fuck!?"

"What's happening up there?"

"Let's get the hell out of here!"

Commander Herschel manages to slice through the sudden onset of the fog of war and move his hand mic to his mouth. "Flash! Flash! Flash! All Mammoth elements, this is Mammoth 6. Accelerate and press to targets. Go!" The commander slaps his driver on the shoulder with the back of his hand. "Get us to that house!" he yells, and then pulls on his gunner's pant leg. "Put some fire on that silo!"

Just as his gunner starts to squeeze off rounds, the lower half of the Dutch door at the front of the homestead swings open. A .50-caliber machine gun begins its thumping percussion as the heavy weapon slings rounds at the lead vehicle. At the same time, the windows to the right and left of the door shatter as twin M240 machine guns let loose with a torrent of 7.62 belt-fed death.

Herschel ducks down behind the dashboard as the heavier rounds slam into the engine compartment of his MRAP. The two streams of 7.62 fire pelt the bulletproof windshield, shattering it under the hailstorm of bullets. The rounds continue through the cabin, taking the driver in the chest, neck, and face while others slice across the gunner's abdomen, cutting him in half. Herschel squeezes into the floor space as best as he can while the rounds decimate his crew and bathe him in their blood.

To the right of the lead vehicle, which is now stalling out due to the withering fire, Mammoth 2 breaks for the silo. The gunner in the MRAP aims for the opening at the top, firing with his turret-mounted M240. Two RPG rounds come streaking down in reply. The first slams into the front passenger tire, the second into the engine, both detonating and halting the progress of the vehicle. The gunner is thrown about like a pinball inside his turret, finally dropping back into the crew cab, eardrums ruptured and bleeding. Dazed and more than likely concussed, he climbs back up to man his weapon. Having reloaded their launcher, one of the assailants lets loose with another RPG. This time the round explodes on the roof of the MRAP, taking the top portion of the gunner's body with it, his right hand and forearm still gripping the M240.

Behind Mammoth 2, Mammoths 3 and 4 break right and left respectively to reach their targets. As Mammoth 3 races toward the stables the ground erupts in front of them. The IED disables the engine while lifting the front end. Immediately following the first blast, a daisy chain of claymore mines and other IEDs lining the southern edge of the path go off. The force of the explosions, combined with the front end of the vehicle already being lifted, topples the MRAP over onto its side. As soon as the vehicle crashes, men and women jump up from behind the bottom portions of the Dutch doors denoting the separate horse stalls. They open fire with their M4s and AK-47s, sending a barrage of bullets at the front windshield and exposed underbelly of the vehicle.

Mammoth 4 races to the equipment overhang, trying to get out of the blistering fire that is enveloping the entire site. From the ridgeline to their west, .50-caliber rounds begin raining down upon them. The gunner opens up, spraying wildly at the trees and hills above, hoping beyond hope that the return fire might help to keep the head down of the sniper up above.

Fires rage from the burning helicopters. The smell

of fuel and gunpowder fills the air. The radio is frantic with calls for assistance, clouded by Scepter 6 relentlessly calling for a status update. The transmissions get washed out by the continuous gunfire of heavy and fully automatic weapons. From the silo, RPG rounds continue to be launched at the three disabled trucks, impacting in an attempt to break through the armor and destroy the men in the troop compartments. "All stations," Herschel calls out. "All stations sound off. SITREP!"

"Mammoth 3, we're flipped over and pinned down!"

"Mammoth 2, our engine is destroyed. Taking heavy fire from the silo and homestead."

"This is 4, at the overhang but taking sniper fire. We can't deploy!"

The commander quickly realizes that he has been rendered combat ineffective. Pinned in his vehicle, unable to see the ground as it is, with so much confusion and chaos, only one action comes to mind. "Slingshot 6, this is Mammoth 6. I need your eyes. Assume command and tell us how to neutralize the attack."

"What? No! I am still in command, Mammoth—" comes Liu's voice.

"Shut the fuck up! We're getting killed down here! Slingshot 6, do you copy? It's yours to call!"

. . . . .

The carnage below is on par with the worst he's ever seen. The enemy has prepared a sophisticated, L-shaped ambush using all types of munitions and tactics, and now the FBI is caught in the crossfire. All Derek can do is watch until the transmissions come over.

"Slingshot 6, do you copy? It's yours to call!"

The command shakes him free of his disbelief. "Roger, Mammoth. I've got it. Break. Saber 1, you read me?"

Far off in a trailer in Arizona, the Predator pilot responds. "Slingshot 6, roger over. Standing by."

"Excellent, you're cleared in hot. Put a Hellfire into the western ridgeline."

"Uh, we don't have a target, Slingshot."

"Goddammit, there's a sniper position up there somewhere. Launch one and let's at least put their heads down."

"Roger, Slingshot, inbound time now."

"Roger, over. Break. Which Apache is still with us?"

The whirring of the rotor blades comes through the radio. After a brief hesitation the pilot transmits. "Slingshot 6, this is Rattler Red 1."

"Okay, Rattler, what's your position?"

"South of the access road, holding here."

Derek can hear the tremor in the man's voice. He doesn't blame him. Seeing three of your compatriots shot down within moments of one another would be enough to shake any pilot. "All right, Rattler, listen to me. You're the key here. Everyone is pinned down and taking fire. A few more minutes and they're all dead. We need you to level the playing field. Got it?"

He can almost envision the man letting out a deep breath. "Roger, Slingshot. Tell me what you need."

"Hold there until you see the blast from the Hellfire, then give me a strafing run along the western ridgeline. Hit it with your cannon and rockets, then turn your attention to that silo, understood?"

"Roger, Slingshot. Lining up for my run now."

"Great, break. Mammoth 4, prepare to deploy Pegasus into the wood line to the west. The harassing fire may not catch that sniper. They need to neutralize him. All other teams prepare to dismount and engage the target buildings. I want you to lay down suppressive fire on the farmhouse and stables." A series of affirmatives comes through over the radio. "The sniper is key. If we don't get him the dismounts will get picked off. Everyone stand by. We go on the Hellfire. Saber 1, bring it!"

■ ■ ■ ■ ■

He laughs over the net, not caring for the lack of discipline it shows. The scene down below is one of pure beauty. A symphony of death and dismemberment. His own personal concerto of which he is the maestro. Kellen can't help himself. Such orchestration is worthy of the highest accolades.

Yet while it is reaching its crescendo, his piece is not finished yet. There are still long bars that must be played out, and his conducting is not complete. The machine guns and RPGs hammer the MRAP vehicles, attempting to bust through the bulletproof windshields and armor. The Copperhead gets ahold of himself, his face returning to the placid mask he always wears as he sights in on the rear doors of the transports.

At some point they will have to come out of the troop compartments. At some point they will have to try and engage. They cannot sit there accepting such punishment much longer. When they do, Kellen and Deep will be ready. They'll pick them off one by beautiful one, each a percussionist note bringing his opus closer to the finale.

"Pugh, are we clear to move the kids through the mine?" comes a voice from inside the homestead.

"We've got them pinned down. Now's as good a time as any," comes another.

"Negative," Kellen curtly replies. "Hold them in the farmhouse until further notice. The sniper that got Kyle and Dolores is still out there. Wait until we've neutralized him first."

"Yeah, but the shaft—"

The transmission gets overridden first by a high-speed *whoosh* followed by an earth-trembling explosion. A massive column of flame and black smoke shoots up and curls into the air above the western ridge. Pugh and Deep instinctively cover their heads and the optics to their weapons. The blast wave washes over them, carrying suffocating heat intermixed with loose debris from the forest floor. Sticks and soil rain down upon them.

They're just lifting their heads when the ridgeline erupts in a series of smaller explosions, each preceded by a scything through the air. The geysers of dirt and tree limbs continue to be flung about as the rockets from the Apache march their way from south to north along the rocky formation. In between the detonations, bullets from the 30mm chain gun mounted to the front of the aircraft pulverize the wood line.

Although they have to remain under cover from the raining shrapnel, the missile and the helicopter's attack occurs behind their position. After it passes overhead and the air clears, Kellen picks his scan back up, intent on putting a bullet into the brain of the chopper's pilot. He tracks the aircraft as it circles to the north, coming around to hover while facing south.

The Apache drifts from left to right. Kellen is about to put a shot through the canopy when the chopper disappears behind the silo. A moment later the *thump thump thump thump thump* of the chain gun pierces the air. The top portion of the silo blows apart like a strong wind hitting burnt leaves. For good measure the gunner of the Apache launches two rockets into the base of the silo. Flames fly up through the interior and explode out of the vacated space created by the gunship's cannon. A moment later the entire structure collapses in on itself and comes crashing to the ground in a great cloud of dust and fire.

The Apache roars over the field, again attacking the western ridgeline in a strafing run with rockets and chain gun fire before it breaks off to the south to make its turn. This time when Kellen lifts his head he can see that the teams of FBI SWAT have emerged from their vehicles. The fourth truck has pulled into the space between the first and the third, forming a loose triangle that the teams now use as cover to engage both the stables and the farmhouse simultaneously.

Kellen is about to start firing again when he hears a hail of gunfire much closer to his position on the ridge. He recalls that he never saw a team leave from the back of the fourth vehicle. He climbs to his knees and scoops up his rifle. "I'm relocating to support the bunker," he calls out to Deep. "Keep engaging the SWAT in the middle of the field."

The report of Deep's Barrett is the only response Kellen receives.

. . . . .

Even with the firefight raging in the clearing behind them, Drysdale moves the extraction team with deliberate steadiness. *Slow is smooth, smooth is fast,* Ortiz says to herself, drilling the mantra into her mind to help steady her nerves. She had been in scrapes before. Plenty of times in Afghanistan. More recently a few officer-involved shootings back when she was with the

Miami PD. But those especially were limited engagements. Usually over in a matter of a few seconds. A few shots fired. Even during her tour in support of OEF she never experienced a sustained hornet's nest of hot lead flying through the air like they are now.

Shaking her mind free, Ortiz catches the signal from her team leader to bound forward. She and Drysdale do so, rushing ten meters to the next pair of trees that can cover them. Once set, they scan the forest with their weapons while Gerbowski and Ortega rush past their position in order to take up their own overwatch. Using this bounding maneuver, the former SEAL works his team up the side of the hill toward where the Barrett continues to fire.

She shoulders her snub nose M249 and scans the hill they are ascending. Off to her right, Gerbowski and Ortega begin their next rush. A single shot is fired, much closer and different from the louder cracks of the Barrett up above them. In a puff of pink mist, Gerbowski's head ceases to be.

One moment he was a man. A friend. Still alive and running to the rescue of his comrades in arms. Now . . . nothing. An empty vessel. Gerbowski's body sags backward until the corpse is lying on the ground. It slides a few feet back down the slope before coming to a stop.

Ortega drops to the prone position and begins firing, laying down a blanket of 5.56 rounds at the hillside. Likewise, off to her left, Drysdale screams from behind his tree. "Motherfuckers!"

The team leader lets his 40mm grenade loose from the M203 launcher affixed to his rifle. The shell explodes near the top of the hill, sending up a column of dirt and shattered stone. As Drysdale empties the magazine of his rifle a single shot comes in reply. The bullet rips through the SEAL's abdomen and severs his spine, instantly paralyzing the man from the waist down.

Jumping up, Ortiz screams as she dives behind Drysdale's tree. With all the strength she can muster, she drags the sizable man back behind the cover of the large oak. A round skits off the edge of the tree, the bark scraping against her face. The pain it produces sears like a bare-legged slide across pavement. Ortiz circles around the other side and squeezes off a blast of her belt-fed weapon before turning back to her team leader. Shrugging off her pack, she begins digging through it for blood-clotting bandages. Next to her and slumped against the tree, Drysdale is going into shock, his face already turning an ashy shade of gray. That's when the hillside erupts.

From off to her right and up the hill, assault rifles and at least one belt-fed machine gun fire at them from a black gap near a rock formation. She counts at least four different muzzle flashes, possibly even five. The earth and trees around her begin to ripple with bullets. Ortega, seeing the direction of their fire, sights in on the gap and empties his cartridge drum at it. The brief respite his return fire achieves allows Ortiz to pack Drysdale's entry wound with the clotting bandages. She takes up her weapon and rolls to her right, firing at the gap to cover Ortega and give him a chance to reload. As she does so a single shot ricochets off the tree next to her, narrowly missing her head.

"Pegasus 6, Mammoth 6. We're getting hammered by that Barrett. SITREP, over!"

Ortiz keys up, her voice calm and collected despite

how frantic she feels. "Pegasus 4 is dead. Pegasus 6 is hit and bleeding bad. Pegasus 2 and I are pinned down. There is a bunker in a rock formation at the top of the ridge keeping us from reaching the sniper."

"Pegasus 3," comes Derek's voice over the radio. "Can you or Pegasus 2 mark the bunker with smoke? We can get the chopper in there to hit it."

"I can try, but we're danger close. It's only fifty, maybe seventy-five yards from our position." There's a momentary pause on the radio, one that helps to deepen her intense fear.

"Pegasus 3, that bunker is at the top of the ridgeline?" Derek asks.

"Roger," Ortiz replies, "with three large boulders surrounding it."

"Keep up your suppressing fire. I'm coming to you!"

. . . . .

A pillar of black smoke towers off to his left as Derek jumps to his feet and heads west away from it, following the ridgeline as quickly as his pace and the terrain will allow him. Between the thick tree cover and his camouflage pattern, he silently hopes that the sniper won't be able to draw a bead on him. Hopping over logs and splashing through puddles, he calls over the net as he moves. "Mammoth 6, Slingshot 6. I had to relocate and no longer have eyes on. Need you to reassume command."

"Slingshot . . . Slingshot, this is Mammoth 4. Mammoth 6 is down. He got hit trying to maneuver toward us."

Damn it. "Roger that, break. Rattler Red 1, you still on station?" Derek says as he continues to run.

The whir of the rotor blades can barely hide the

warble in the pilot's voice. "Copy, Slingshot. South of the access road and awaiting instructions for our next attack."

"Red 1, need you to reenter the kill zone and press your attack. Our men are pinned down and you are the only one who can turn this thing around. You understand?"

"Slingshot, won't they be danger close as well?"

"Rattler, this is Mammoth 4. We're getting slaughtered down here. The only way out of this is if you get us out."

Derek understands the hesitation, but he also knows the repercussions of not acting. "It's my call, Red 1. Attack danger close. All Mammoth elements take cover as best you can." In his mind's eye, he can almost see the pilot taking a deep breath.

"Roger, Slingshot. Mammoth elements hang tight, we're inbound now."

The response comes just as Derek rounds the bend in the ridge, now heading south toward his extraction team. "Pegasus 3, I'm almost to you. Need you to mark the bunker."

Ortiz's frantic voice comes back in reply. In the background the rip of Ortega's M249 can be heard. "I'm working on Pegasus 6. If I stop he might bleed out."

- - - - -

Upon hearing the transmission, Drysdale's eyes open. He blinks a few times and then cradles his rifle to his chest. "Slingshot, this is Pegasus 6. I gotchu." With that the big man slumps over to his left, using his upper body to get himself into the prone position behind the root system of the tree. He sights in and then fires from his forward trigger, launching a 40mm grenade.

The round hits on the left side of the bunker, blowing a body clear out of it. The corpse slams into the logs that comprise the top of the shelter, effectively ripping the roof off of it.

* * * * *

The geyser of dirt and flame that rises into the sky sends a clear indication to Derek as to where the bunker is.

Sprinting the next hundred yards, he crashes through branches and barrels through briars. He reaches a thick pine and stoops underneath. Taking a knee, Derek can see the top of the bunker now open below him and to the right. A charred and broken body lays nearby, while five men dressed identically in woodland camo ponchos exchange gunfire with Ortega and Drysdale down below. Ortiz works on the team leader's back, but the tree and roots that they are behind are barely enough to cover them both.

Ripping his frag grenade free, Derek pops off the safety clip before pulling the pin and heaving the munition at the bunker. Taking another second to ensure none of the Pegasus team members are in his sightline, Derek flips his selector switch to fully automatic. Depressing the trigger, he begins raking his rifle back and forth at the exposed enemy below. The grenade explodes nearby, showering the assailants with dirt and debris. In an instant thirty rounds are gone and he is dropping his magazine, slapping in another, and slamming the bolt release with his left hand to chamber the round.

This time when he sights in he can see one man slumped forward, but the other four have turned toward him. As Derek fires in an attempt to keep their heads down, they key in on his muzzle flashes and return fire. Needles and branches begin to rain down upon him as the automatic fire closes in. Magazine empty again, he pulls the pin on the flashbang grenade and hurls it from around his cover, hoping the blast might serve to disorient them, or at the very least make the men flinch long enough for Derek to reload and get back into the fight. It goes off like a thunderclap trapped inside a tunnel.

■ ■ ■ ■ ■

Down below, Ortega sees his chance. With Ortiz and Drysdale out of the fight for all intents, and a fresh drum loaded into his weapon, he jumps to his feet and charges the hill. His boot breaking through a rotted log is just enough of a downward slip to avoid the single shot that whistles past his head. Unable to contend with the sniper at the moment, Ortega continues his frenzied charge, now firing from the shoulder as he nears the bunker.

As he comes upon the four men, Ortega goes from apprentice to master painter. His SAW the brush. His targets the canvas. He paints them all, one after the other, with equal parts bullets and blood. The remaining men in the bunker are shred to pieces under the onslaught of the fully automatic weapon.

Ortega stops firing when the last man falls. He continues his sprint and dives the final yard, landing hard in the bunker and rolling over just as another sniper round smacks into the logs that make up the front wall. Righting himself into the prone position, he quickly opens the bipod from its storage space under the foregrip, cups his left hand over the top of the stock, presses his cheek to his hand, and lets loose with the remainder of his drum. A steady stream of bullets rip through the surrounding woods to the south, an attempt to keep the sniper's head down.

When the drum runs dry he discards the weapon and unslings his M4 from his back. As he does so Derek is suddenly there next to him, opening fire and covering Ortega while he readies his weapon. The two men shoot through another magazine each before dropping down. Derek quickly grabs a body and stacks it up on the southern facing edge of the bunker. Ortega helps him with the second body, which they pile on top of the first. Then both men sag down, chests heaving, their lungs pulling in the tendrils of carbon gun smoke drifting up from their breeches and muzzles. They listen for sniper fire but all that can be heard is the continued gunfight down below at the ranch.

A moment later the explosions resume.

* * * * *

"Roger, Slingshot. Mammoth elements hang tight, we're inbound now." Then Spriggs says to his gunner, "All right, Tom, we're going in and we're going in fast. Strafing runs only. Maybe that'll be enough to keep their heads down while we avoid that Barrett. Cannon until I say otherwise. You with me?"

"I'm with you," affirms the gunner. "Let's get some."

Spriggs throttles up and noses the aircraft down, gaining speed and flying it nap-of-the-earth. Banking it hard to the right, the Apache soars over the treetops on the western ridge before aligning with the stables. As the bird rockets across the open field, Spriggs can see the FBI teams pinned down below him. Peeking out from behind the edges of the disabled and overturned MRAPs, they exchange gunfire furiously with the two buildings, doing their best to remain out of the line of sight of the large-caliber sniper rifle.

Kineis squeezes the trigger on his joystick. The chopping sound of the chain gun echoes over the battlefield as the cannon fires, ripping a line in the soil just ahead of the building and then cutting through it. Planks of wood shatter and splinter while roof tiles rip from the structure. Spriggs banks hard again to his right, increasing his speed to stay ahead of the Barrett. Swinging around, the pilot orients the gunship so that it is facing north and aligned with the homestead.

Again Spriggs noses the chopper down, racing it over the top of the raging battle below. While the .50-caliber machine gun continues to thump its cartridges forward, the M240s angle upward. Twin streams of bullets streak at the aircraft, forcing Spriggs to work his cyclic and collective in concert in order to evade the gunfire. As soon as they have cleared the men pinned in the center of the field, Kineis opens fire, the rounds piercing and ripping through the homestead.

This time Spriggs banks left, wheels the aircraft around to the west, and then lines it up with the stables a second time. He brings the helicopter to a brief hover behind the western ridgeline to do a battle damage assessment. The result is negligible. The FBI teams still receive fire from the buildings. As if to confirm the BDA, Spriggs's radio suddenly crackles to life.

"Rattler Red 1, we're getting hammered down here! We're not going to last much longer! We need an immediate re-attack!"

Spriggs knows what has to be done even before the request is finished being made. "Tom, we're going back in. Prepare to hit both targets with the rockets."

"Roger that."

"Mammoth 4, re-attack is inbound. Take what cover you can. We're hitting them hard."

Spriggs punches the throttle. The twin engines launch the aircraft forward. As it clears the trees again and flies over the teams, Kineis locks his aperture onto the stables. Squeezing the trigger, he fires four Hydra 70mm rockets. As Spriggs pulls up to halt their advance, the rockets impact, exploding in a rush of fire and death. The initial blast ignites a secondary explosion that sends flaming wood and debris flying across the battlefield. A massive cloud of dirt and black smoke kicks into the air.

The pilot wastes no time. Hitting his pedals, Spriggs rotates his tail rotor so that the gunship faces to the north. Both rotor blades work in concert to curl the smoke into spirals down and away from the aircraft. While the men below become obscured by the cloud of dust, the Apache becomes the sole focus of the homestead. Again the M240s open up but the attack is short-lived. Kineis depresses his trigger again, sending a salvo at the farmhouse. Another four rockets blow it to pieces. The blast wave shatters trees, sending wood and debris showering onto the already littered field. As the wreckage settles, dozens of scattered fires burn across the ranch while the remains of the two buildings are engulfed in raging infernos.

Spriggs moves his aircraft off the northwest and orients it facing south, an attempt to still provide cover and avoid the Barrett sniper. As the helicopter hovers the radio comes back to life.

"All elements! All elements! This is Scepter 6! SITREP goddamnit. What the fuck is happening up there?"

It takes a few moments but the reply slowly comes from the different sections. "Mammoth 4. Targets neutralized. We're no longer taking fire, but that sniper might still be out there." The man pants in between transmissions. "We've got multiple casualties and KIA, plus the site is covered in flames. Get EMS and the fire department in here now."

"Once the scene is fully secure. Pegasus team, what's your status?"

"We've got men that aren't going to make it unless you get in here now!" Mammoth 4 screams.

Derek interjects. "Scepter 6, Slingshot 6. Pegasus has two down, one wounded and one KIA. We're no longer receiving sniper fire. They must have withdrawn."

"We don't know that for sure, Slingshot. They could be lying in wait for us to bring in our resources and provide them with more targets."

Derek can hardly hold back his temper. "Just get in here and tend to those wounded. I'm in pursuit of the snipers."

. . . . .

Derek turns to find Ortega crouched over one of the enemy combatants. He pulls back on the man's poncho, revealing a green, intricately woven mesh sewn into the lining. The same is found on the poncho draped over the man's legs like a skirt. "What do you make of this, boss?" he says.

Derek wipes a hand over his face, his sweat smearing the camouflage paint and dirt accumulated from weeks in the field. He grabs the poncho and looks at it himself. "Some kind of adaptive camo maybe? But if so, why is it on the inside?"

"I dunno. Between these and the missiles they used

to take down those choppers, pretty sophisticated shit for a bunch of backwaters. What the hell happened here, Derek?"

"I couldn't tell you. Not now anyway. Right now you have to get Drysdale to the medics, and I'm going after those snipers."

"Let me come with you," the younger man says. "I can grab Ortiz's spare drum. Help you even up the odds."

"Drysdale is your priority. I need you to keep watch over them, and I can't wait until you get back. Even now we're burning precious seconds. If I have any chance of catching those snipers before they've bugged out I have to get on their trail now."

Ortega nods. "All right. Just be careful out there, boss."

Derek slaps the man on the shoulder. "Make sure that once Chief is safe you tell site exploitation to get up to this bunker. These ponchos are a piece of the puzzle. In fact . . ." He starts to strip the body armor and kit off of one of the Tithe members. Ortega follows suit, helping remove the man's web belt, and then assisting in pulling off the top poncho. He turns around so that Derek can stuff the garment into his pack. The older man slaps the younger on the shoulder once his ruck has been zippered back up. "Let's move."

The two step out of the bunker and slide down the hill, making use of the terrain to expedite their rush to Ortiz. When they get to her she wipes her upper lip with the back of her hand. It leaves a streak of the team leader's blood on her face. A strand of hair has come loose from her ponytail under her helmet. It sticks to her sweat-laden forehead. She shakes her head back and forth, looking directly at Derek. "I've staunched the bleeding for now, but he's in a bad way. Probably going to start again if we try to move him."

"No other choice," Derek replies. "He's got to get to the medics as quickly as possible." He kneels down in front of the wounded man, cupping his face with his right hand. "Look at me, Chief. You stay alive, you hear me? No one gave you an order to fall out, understand?"

Drysdale forces a slight smile. "Fucking Marines always thinking they can boss everyone around." He coughs and then spits out a wad of bloody phlegm. "This ain't shit. I'll be back to normal by tomorrow."

Ortega and Derek share a gaze, one that conveys the man will be anything but normal tomorrow. If he even reaches tomorrow. "Let's get him up."

Shifting behind the man, Derek lifts him up from under his armpits while the Double O's get in next to Drysdale on either side. They slide one arm behind his back and grab onto each other while holding him under the knees with their other arms. Hoisting him in a seated position the two start to hurriedly move down the hill the rest of the way toward the clearing.

Keying up, Derek radios in. "Grizzly 6, Slingshot 6. Pegasus 2 and 3 are on their way back to the ranch with Pegasus 6 in tow. Need immediate MEDEVAC. He's lost a lot of blood, over."

The reply comes in amplified but under control. "Roger, Slingshot. We've got ambulances inbound, time now," Jason's voice says, coming back through the radio. "We're almost at the scene. I'll make sure Pegasus gets out okay."

"Roger that," Derek replies. "Is that Predator still armed and on station?"

"Affirmative. One more Hellfire."

"Good, retask it to key in on my GPS and follow me for as long as it can. If I get the chance I'll blast those bastards to hell."

"Roger, Slingshot 6, wilco. Grizzly out."

Derek sprints over to Gerbowski's body, doing the best he can to avoid looking at the pulverized mass that was recently the man's skull. First he exchanges his empty magazines for full ones from Aaron's kit, then pulls out two ten-round box magazines for the man's H-S Precision sniper rifle. Derek unfastens the olive drab rifle with a telescopic sight from the man's pack and checks the chamber to see that the weapon is loaded. Seeing that it is, he slings his M38 across his back, clutches the sniper rifle to his chest, and sprints back up the hill.

* * * * *

SAC Samuel Liu stands in the middle of the ranch grounds, watching his future literally go up in smoke. Around him is complete and utter chaos. Fires burn everywhere. The homestead and stables. The downed choppers. Patches of debris and the vehicles. Black smoke envelops everything, at times obscuring the sky above and the ground below. When that happens, the field is an eerie place. Glowing a violent, flickering orange and filled with screams. Screams of pain. Of dying.

Amidst it all Liu walks, aimlessly, watching the wounded loaded into ambulances and squad cars from the local PD. Firefighters trying to combat the raging fires from what is left of the buildings. Grown men, some of the most hardened and battle tested this country has ever produced, crying over the corpse of a fallen brother. Or clasped in the teary embrace of a fellow member. Reporters scurry about trying to get the first responders to divulge what happened, their ambitions for being the first to get the story out overriding what the men and women have just gone through.

Despite all this, the sweat coursing down his back isn't for the lost. It's for what he is about to lose. All Liu can see is his dreams of one day being Director vanishing into the air with the black smoke.

The man's stomach turns over and his legs begin to shake. Wobbling, he falls to his knees and then a moment later doubles over. He vomits onto the green grass, now beginning to turn gray from the falling ash. Anyone watching might believe it is for the situation.

"Sir," Agent Jackson says from behind him, "ISR picked up movement to the northwest. I sent a mixed team of marshals and SWAT to check it out. There was a mine shaft there. A few of the people that were in the house were using it to escape."

Liu looks up at the man, a dribble of vomit still hanging from his lip. "There . . . were survivors?"

Shaking his head, Rob grimaces. "Only a few, sir. It's bad. Most of them were holed up in there. A lot of women and children amongst the group." Liu's head sinks again. "There's more, sir. At the entrance to the shaft we found discarded Stinger missile tubes. That's how they brought down the first two birds. We think the Barrett took down the third."

Such a disaster. A failure. But not mine. The plan was sound. This was a failure of intelligence. Liu's head snaps up. "Where is that Neanderthal? I want his ass here immediately! This is all his doing!"

"Derek? Sir, he's not here."

"Not here?" the SAC's face begins to grow red.

"What in the hell do you mean he's not here? Get him in front . . . of . . . me . . . now!"

"Sir, he's in pursuit of the snipers. He's fairly certain they're retrograding and he can track them down."

"Fairly certain? Fairly certain? Like he was about what we were facing here today? I've had it with this son of a bitch! I'll have him crucified for this by the end of the day. Now, you get him here, Agent Jackson, or it's your ass!" Standing up and brushing himself off, Liu storms back toward the access road where the command vehicle is parked.

16

The top of the western ridge reveals two firing positions. Derek had spotted them from below as he ascended. Two ledges, one above the other. Upon arriving at them his suspicions were confirmed. Spent brass littered the flat rock formations, and the vantage point gave clear access to the ranch and the airspace above it. The .50-caliber and .308 shell casings tell him that there were two snipers here at one point. That and the fact that the Barrett was still firing at the field when Gerbowski was killed. In ghillie suits and nestled in with the vegetation, they would have been unobservable to the naked eye.

The real riddle is why the ISR drone didn't pick them up, or the team in the bunker for that matter. Their heat signatures should have been spotted easily by the FLIR camera on board. Perhaps the strange mesh Derek and Ortega had found lining the ponchos of the men in the bunker had something to do with it? If that were true, it wasn't far off to think that the sniper's ghillie suits had it as well.

Derek falls back on his woodland skill set. Broken branches and two distinct boot prints in the soil confirm the direction of their travel. Shouldering Gerbowski's long-range rifle, Derek begins his hunt.

He sticks to the edge of the trail so as to not leave tracks of his own. Wherever he can step on a rock he does so, or on moss to soften his step. All the while the survival instructor reads the signs of the woods. It's no different than tracking a hare or a squirrel. These men are his prey. His rifle the tool to take them down. If he can, he will bring them in alive so that they can face justice for what they have done this day. If not, then either he or they will meet their maker.

The men ahead of him are moving fast. Trained snipers though they may be, they are clearly exchanging stealth for expediency. More than likely they're assuming no one would be in pursuit given the chaos back at the ranch. It works to Derek's advantage in that their trail isn't hard to follow. On the other hand, he has to pick up his own pace to match that of the snipers, something that decreases his own stealth. That said, if he can just find the right vantage he may be able to sight in on them and take one if not both out from afar.

Derek's heart races and sweat pours down his body and into his eyes. His mind is a jumble. Everything from the pursuit at hand to how the events unfolded to the lives lost. The lives he himself took as well. It occurs to him now, on the trail and away from any support that his own life is precariously on the line. He tracks not one but two trained snipers. While Derek has experience with long-shot weaponry, he was never the best with them. Pitted up against these odds is a serious detriment.

Derek's thoughts go to Michael. Of leaving him without a father. Of Kim having to explain why he is no longer there. Why he always chose to be elsewhere instead of with his boy. Not for the first time Derek makes a silent promise, that if he should escape with his hide still intact he will spend more time with his son. With his family. That he will forgo the field that keeps pulling him away. Make no mistake, there is a part of him that relishes the thrill of the hunt. But how many chances does he have left? How many firefights will he make it out of? He feels like a cat on its ninth life.

He just hopes that this time he can keep his promise.

. . . . .

Deep hands the Barrett up to Kellen. After the man takes it, Deep scales the rock wall in front of him. Coming up on top of it, the man doubles over, putting his hands on his knees. He pushes back the hood of his ghillie suit. Steam rises from his skull while sweat pours off his face. When he doesn't take his rifle back immediately after Kellen holds it out to him, the Copperhead sets it down on the ground. Unslinging his M24, the taller of the two begins to walk off again. When Deep doesn't follow, Kellen turns back. "We have to keep moving."

"Calm down, man. There's no one coming after us. We fucked them up back there and lost them in the aftermath."

"Perhaps. Even so we have to get back and report what happened. Sarah will need to know. Soon this entire region will be covered with law enforcement assets. If we're not out of the woods and on the road when that happens . . ."

Pinching his ghillie suit and holding out some of the

fabric, Deep looks at the other man. "What? We can't hide from all that with this on? Worked pretty well back there."

Kellen doesn't respond. He just stares. Like always. Staring. Computing. Freezing. Deep is about to ream him out when there's a crash in the brush behind them. Instinctively they both drop into the prone position. Deep quickly reorients his Barrett to face north. Kellen glasses the wilderness through his optic, looking for further signs of movement. When he doesn't see any he turns back to his fellow sniper and sends him a hand signal. *Move south.*

Shaking his head, Deep whispers back, "Fuck that. We've got the high ground. Let's add to our tally." Kellen repeats the hand signal more emphatically, but Deep simply spits in reply. "You go then. I'll take this bastard out. I need another kill anyway."

Grimacing, Kellen turns away and glasses once again. When he turns back he sends a series of hand signals. *Ten minutes. You, base of fire. I'll flank west.*

Deep nods and shoulders his rifle. The Copperhead turns to his left and begins to slither off, low-crawling through the brush to find a better vantage point.

■   ■   ■   ■   ■

The log Derek steps on suddenly gives way under his weight. He manages to catch himself but the log goes crashing down the side of the hill he is on. Quickly maneuvering behind some brush and dropping into the prone position, he lies perfectly still, searching the woods ahead of him for any movement. More importantly, he listens. Being able to see at any real distance is negated by the dense forest. A few hundred yards at best. But sound can give away a position as easily as sight.

Stupid, Derek berates himself. *Rookie fucking mistake. Watch where you're going.*

He waits for another few minutes of relative silence before painstakingly low-crawling out from under the brush. Again the expert woodsman waits and listens. When he is sure there is no movement up ahead, Derek stands and continues his stalk along the men's trail. Rounding a bend in the terrain, he's faced with a rocky saddle leading up to a short wall of boulders about three hundred yards away. The slightest tick of motion causes him to pull back against a broad oak.

Derek pulls out his binoculars and inches toward the edge of the tree. He scans from west to east, finding nothing, then back east to west. Just when he is about to start his scan back in the other direction another flicker catches his eye. This time it's unmistakable. The sole of a desert-tan boot.

Throwing the cord to his binos around his neck, Derek edges around the tree and aligns his optic with where he saw the boot. He begins to scan to his right, looking through the trees and underbrush.

There!

A ghillie suit. Derek approximates where the torso will be, hoping to hit the man in the armpit to avoid any possible side plate protection. He flicks off the safety but his sight picture is too unsteady. Derek drops to a kneeling firing position, both to steady his aim and better align his scope with the path his target is taking over the terrain.

Just as he drops, the space where his head was a moment ago explodes in a shower of shredded bark and splintered wood. Derek pulls back his rifle and flattens against the tree as more rounds impact it, clearly coming from the .50-caliber weapon. Under the hail of gunfire, Derek drops his sniper rifle and pulls his M38 out from behind him. The .50 continues to pound the tree, the man operating it trying to accomplish with volume what he could not with precision. Derek reaches his assault rifle around the oak and fires blindly, hoping that the return salvo of rounds will at least give the sniper cause to temporarily halt his attack.

The action works. The .50-cal stops firing. However, the second sniper squeezes off a round somewhere from the west. The single shot strikes Derek's rifle where the upper receiver meets the barrel and severs the weapon in half. Pulling it back around, Derek curses while he unhooks the destroyed firearm from his person and tosses it aside. Taking up the sniper rifle, he steadies his breathing and flattens himself into the prone position as best he can.

Two rounds slap into the tree, the second coming just after the report from the first has dissipated. The sniper duo's way of letting him know that they have his position sighted in. *Smug assholes.* Derek weighs his options. For the moment he is safe behind the ancient oak, its thick trunk his saving grace, but that won't last long. One or both of them will maneuver to get a better shot. He keys up and whispers into his mic.

"Saber 1, Slingshot 6. You still on station?"

The radio crackles back. "Roger, Slingshot, although we're close to black on fuel. We'll need to pull off site soon."

"Perfect. I need you for one more run. Do you have my GPS position?"

"Slingshot 6, where the hell are you?" Liu's voice interjects. "I want you back here now!"

"Scepter 6, stand down. I'm engaged with the snipers."

The radio crackles back. "Say again, Slingshot? Did you just tell me to stand down?" Liu's voice is incredulous.

Derek emits a low growl as he replies. "I say again, I'm engaged with the snipers. They've got me pinned. I need Saber 1 to take them out."

An inordinately long pause plays out given the circumstances. Derek is just about to key up again when Liu replies. "Your request is denied. We're not about to launch a Hellfire indiscriminately into the woods."

"I didn't request anything. Break. Saber 1, calculate for two hundred and seventy-five meters south of my position."

"Negative, Saber 1. You are not authorized to fire. Slingshot, break contact and return to TRP 12 immediately," Liu counters.

Another shot slaps into the tree. Derek can feel his face getting flush as his anger boils up. "How do you propose I do that if I'm pinned down, you moron? At least get that Apache overhead and launch a few more of those rockets to cover me."

"You don't get it, do you, Slingshot?" Liu shouts into the mic. "This whole thing is fucked! The op is over. It's done! We're grounded! There is nothing available to retrieve you. I send in more birds or men to get you and they might end up KIA as well."

"Scepter," Derek says. "You can't just leave me out here."

"I really don't give a damn about you, Slingshot. You wanted to play Lone Ranger. Now you're on your own. Scepter 6 out."

Motherfucker! Derek's mind races. Not only does he have zero chance of taking out the snipers with the Hellfire now, but he also has no idea how he's going to get out from under the crossfire he's stuck in. He searches about the terrain, looking for anything that he can use to help gain an advantage.

There. Twenty yards to the west a small depression is surrounded by several large boulders. If he can get to it he'll have a makeshift foxhole to operate from, but getting to it is the problem.

A quick peek around the trunk of the tree causes another .50-caliber round to slam into it, but the glance is enough. In the rock-strewn space between himself and the ledge the snipers are on is all manner of broken branches, downed trees, and dried-out brush. Derek unhooks his smoke grenade and pulls the pin but keeps the spoon tight against the cylinder. Drawing his sidearm, he fires several shots into the air before heaving the smoke grenade toward the ledge.

Two shots return, both impacting the oak close to his head. A moment after the reports have dissipated the pop comes from the smoke grenade. Derek waits, taking the tactical pause necessary for the orange smoke to waft out of the cylinder and hopefully mask the sniper's line of sight. In those few moments he takes deep breaths, steadying himself physically while he prepares mentally for his next move.

A whoosh of larger flame igniting brings a smile to his face. Crackles and popping soon turn to roaring as the flames quickly spread. The smell of burning wood fills the air as black smoke begins to rise and mix with that of the orange cloud already present. Derek does a combat reload and exchanges the magazine in his pistol for a full one.

Another peek, this one without gunfire, shows a fire spreading in the rocky space. The orange-and-black smoke obscures the better part of the ledge. Now is his chance. Grabbing the sniper rifle in his left hand, Derek bursts out from behind the tree firing his pistol while he runs for the natural foxhole. Shots ring out after him from the .50-caliber.

One round shatters a nearby stone, the shrapnel hitting Derek in his right foot. The impact forces him to call out and trip over his feet. Derek crashes against a boulder and tumbles to the ground. He keeps his momentum going by continuing to roll even though he loses his grip on both weapons. Finally coming to rest on his back in the makeshift foxhole, Derek looks up at the sky.

Well . . . shit.

. . . . .

"Yeah, boy! What's up now, huh?" Deep yells over the sound of the fire. "That's how I roll, baby!" In his ear the radio comes alive.

"Lock it up! You're giving away your position!" comes Kellen's voice.

"Whatever, bro. I got his ass. He's got nothing left for us."

"Are you certain?" Kellen replies. "Can you confirm the kill?"

"What did I just say? If I said I got his ass then—"

"Boy, you two can't hit shit, can you?" the Marine yells back at them. "You sure killed the hell out of that tree though. Nice work. I know Boy Scouts that shoot better than you fucks."

"Why that little . . ." Deep fires his Barrett, the round impacting one of the large rocks near the depression the man ran toward. After that he sights in on the man's handgun and puts a bullet through it, and then does the same with the sniper rifle. Deep goes to fire again into the rocks but his weapon clicks empty when he squeezes the trigger. Quickly ejecting the magazine, he goes to his kit to produce another, only to find that all of his pouches are empty. "Shit," he mutters to himself. Reaching behind his back, he pulls the snub-nose MP5 that Kyle gave him around to his front. "Copperhead, I'm out."

"Damn it! Why did you waste so many rounds?" Kellen's response crackles through the radio.

"Relax. I took out his weapons and got him pinned down. Besides, it's not like we're getting anywhere fast with me hauling that thing through the woods. This'll be quicker. Cover me while I get to his hole and smoke his ass."

"No!" Kellen replies, his voice emphatic. "I have no shot. The boulders are covering him."

"Then relocate to my position and cover me from here," Deep returns as he starts to stand up.

"We don't have the time for this."

"Would you rather tell the boss that we had him and let him go? Now move your ass. I'm going down."

Kellen is incensed. "Wait! Wait until I'm in position!"

"You better hurry then. I'm through playing games with this asshole."

Deep moves back to the edge of the rock wall, sliding down it gingerly. As he does so, Kellen gets up from his position and begins sprinting back over the top of the wall to the east to take up Deep's former spot. Below them the fire continues to spread.

* * * * *

The sound of metal on metal is heard outside his makeshift foxhole just over the report of the large-caliber rifle. Derek lifts his head for a split second to see the smoking remains of what once was his firearms. *Time to go to plan B.*

Except he has no idea what plan B is.

A weapon. I need a weapon. Something ranged that I can strike from a distance with. Think, Derek, think!

Time is running out. He searches about his person. He has his slingshot but without the element of surprise it'll be hard to get off an effective shot. Plus the farther the ball bearing flies the less accurate and effective it will be. At this range it's not even a consideration. Derek still has his knife, but that would require closing the distance with them. Something he's certain he can't do without getting shot by one or both. Crashing up above forces Derek to lift his head once more. Over the licking tongues of flame he can see the back of a ghillie suit slipping down the face of the rocks.

They're relocating. One to cover while the other comes for him. He has moments. Moments to come up with something. Unfastening his survival kit from his MOLLE gear, Derek unzips it open and searches through. He finds his fishing tackle and pauses. *This could work.*

Grabbing the line, Derek quickly pulls a length from the spool and severs it from the rest with the cord cutter integrated into his StatGear survival knife's sheath. Next, he takes the incendiary white phosphorous grenade and his pouch of fishhooks and begins lashing them together, taking care not to overlap the munition's spoon. A burst of automatic weapon fire replaces the sound of the burning trees for an instant, the rounds ricocheting off of the rocks. Derek sinks down farther, wrapping the line around and around the cylinder. As he ties the knot off, another burst of automatic gunfire ripples across his cover, raining chips and fragments of stone down on top of him.

Pulling the pin, Derek squeezes the grenade to keep the spoon in place, knowing full well that he has one chance at this. His attacker repeatedly depresses their trigger, sending short bursts into the rocks. The weapon falling silent, Derek hears a spent magazine clatter to the rock-strewn ground a moment later.

As his assailant reloads, Derek cooks off the grenade, letting the spoon fly free and start the internal fuse. After a second he pops up, locates the sniper, and heaves the cylinder toward him before dropping back to the ground and covering his head.

The brilliant flash is outdone only by its searing heat. In an instant the fourteen-hundred-plus-degree explosion sends out hundreds of streaks of glowing metal fragments in all directions, both from the body of the grenade and the fishhooks strapped to it, while at the center of the detonation a white cloud emits, instantly sucking the oxygen out of the air. The man drops his MP5 and begins to scream as the fragments slip under his skin as easily as an acetylene torch cutting through an ice cube. Trails of steam and smoke rise from no less than a dozen wounds. Frantically clawing at his face, he tries desperately to remove a section of jagged fishhook embedded in his left eye.

Ripping his knife from its sheath, Derek rushes out from behind his cover. He crashes into the man, driving his blade so far into the sniper's midsection that it strikes bone. The two men go end over end, landing hard on the ground and rolling over one another. A shot rings out and Derek hears the whistle as it soars past, but then the two are obscured by the brush and trees.

Derek manages to roll on top of the sniper and blasts his fist into the man's left eye twice, further impaling the metal. A milky, white jelly spurts out with each punch, the sniper screaming further in hysterics. Grabbing hold of his knife, Derek twists it once and then pulls it free. Orienting himself quickly, he rushes off to the north, sprinting as fast as his legs will take him away from the second sniper and spreading flames.

· · · · ·

Kellen watches the two men go tumbling over. He fires at the tangle of both of them but the shot sails high. Before he can chamber another round they roll into the tree line and out of his view. Even over the fire he can hear the crashing of brush marking their struggle. Kellen waits, seeing who will emerge, if anyone.

After a few moments the struggle subsides and the sound of rustling moves away from him. Kellen gets behind his scope just in case his adversary acts with his balls instead of his brain. He tracks the wood line where the two disappeared but neither emerge from it. After a moment Deep's panicked voice echoes over the burning trees.

"Help me!" the man cries. "Help me! I'm fucking bleeding out!"

Kellen picks himself up and continues south. Within half a click Deep's cries are already lost to the woods.

17

Scents and sounds let Derek know that he is close to the ranch. Burning wood and vehicle fuel mix in the air with spent gunpowder and carbon dust. At the same time a light but steady rain begins to fall. The roar of the flames is met by the cries of the men furiously trying to quell them, grateful for the assistance of Mother Nature. There is still chaos but it is an organized chaos now.

Derek follows the sounds until he can see the smoke billowing over the treetops. From there it's only a few minutes more before he finds himself on the western ridgeline. Making his way through the rocky outcroppings and foliage, at times he slides small stretches for expediency. When he is finally on level ground he makes his way through the woods and emerges from the tree line near the corral.

The smaller fires have been put out, as well as those of the helicopters. The local fire department seems content to let the homestead and stable burn out on their own and work to clear the areas around each so that the nearby woods don't ignite. The absence of ambulances tells him that the wounded and dead have been removed. Despite this, a multitude of law enforcement vehicles of all makes, models, and jurisdictions litter the open field.

He gets as far as the corral fence and then has to stop and lean against it. So much devastation. So much death. How did Autumn's Tithe manage such a sophisticated, well-equipped attack if they were on the ropes?

Because they weren't on the ropes. They were using the rope-a-dope and we fell for it.

And just like George Foreman they got knocked out. Derek can't help the overwhelming feeling of guilt. Was it his lack of perception that caused this? He had done his reconnaissance diligently and never observed the advanced weaponry the group had employed. Nor the hidden bunker and sniper hides. Could it be that Tithe was just that well prepared that they were able to defeat all of the government assets brought to bear?

Even if that is the case, Derek succumbs to the weight falling on his shoulders. Just like Iraq, blood is on his hands. Only this time the blood is that of his comrades. Men and women of the same ilk, the same brotherhood of operators. Yes, they all knew the risks. Yes, they all ventured forth in spite of them. Yet it was his job to make sure they knew what they were going into, and in that, the evidence of failure is all around him.

Jason spies him and comes jogging to the corral. He pulls a bottle of water from a cargo pocket and hands it over. Derek upends the bottle and drains it. He didn't realize how thirsty he was until the water hit his lips.

"Bad day," the man says.

"Yeah, you could say that," Derek replies.

"How you holding up? You hurt at all?"

"I took some shrapnel from a rock in the foot. Bloodied it up a bit, but it's not bad. Certainly not as bad as here."

"Yeah," Jason says flatly.

"How's Eric doing?"

His handler leans up against the fence next to Derek. "Well, the Chief is the chief. Tough bastard, you know? They say he's going to pull through."

"But?"

"But the prognosis isn't good. Paralyzed. From the waist down."

"Goddammit," Derek spits out. "What the hell happened here, Jason? How'd they get the drop on us?"

"Stinger missiles, my man. And infrared-defeating ponchos. That's what we found on the bodies up by the bunker. ISR couldn't see them and neither could you."

"Something stinks here. That's too big of a jump for this group. Where'd they get their hands on that kind of hardware?"

"That's the question everyone is asking. Apparently those ponchos aren't even a part of the U.S.'s arsenal. Still in the R and D phase for us. Which means—"

"That they were foreign supplied."

"Bingo," Jason says.

Derek lets out a deep breath. "One of their snipers is back to the southwest about a click and a half. Maybe more."

"Dead?"

"Should be by now. The way I left him he was bleeding like a sieve. It'll be easy to find him if he isn't dead already. Just follow the trail."

"I'll get some guys together."

"Make sure they tread lightly, okay?" Derek advises. "There's a second one out there still. I suspect he's bugging out but you never know. Could be some martyr shit that ends up costing us more lives."

"Got it." Jason gets up from the fence. "You gonna be all right?"

"Yeah. I need a minute is all."

"There he is! Get over here, you bastard!" Liu yells out from across the field.

"Looks like you're gonna be short on that minute, brother."

"No shit."

When the SAC realizes that Derek isn't making a move toward him, he breaks from the group he is with and strides across the battlefield. Rob walks with him in tow, his face a mask of pure disdain. Whether it's for Derek or his superior remains to be seen.

Getting within two feet of him, Liu stops and points a finger directly at Derek. "Well? What the fuck do you have to say for yourself?"

Derek looks at Jason and Rob in turn before turning back to their boss. "What the hell are you talking about?"

Liu's eyebrows skyrocket. "The hell am I talking about?" He gestures to the burning field. "This is a failure of intelligence, Harrington! Your intelligence!"

Before he can reply the junior agents come to his defense. "Sir, these guys were using some highly classified gear," Jason replies.

"Not to mention a network of hidden mine shafts to move about," Rob adds.

"They what?" Derek asks, looking at Rob. The man nods in affirmation.

"Don't make any excuses, men. If this Neanderthal knew how to do his job, we would have known about the enemy assets present here."

Derek is like a bottled-up furnace, the pressure building to unsafe levels. He stands up from the fence. "Tithe made a concerted effort to hide those assets from our surveillance. Assets that appear to include cutting-edge technology. They were lying in wait for us and caught us asleep at the wheel. Am I part of that? Sure, but don't try laying this all at my feet."

Liu's face goes placid, with a hint of a smirk on his lips. He walks forward and stands practically nose to nose with the taller man. "That's exactly what's going to happen, Harrington. I'll be damned if some second rate, has-been contractor is going to be the end of my career." He makes a show of trying to look around Derek. "Feel those grooves on your back, Derek? Those are from the tire treads once I throw you under the bus."

Derek looks at Rob and Jason before turning back to Liu. "You know what, Liu? Pound sand. Watch that you don't step in your own bullshit along the way." He turns toward Jason, shaking his head and walking away.

"You smartass little bitch," the SAC calls after him. "This. This whole thing here today. This is on you. The men in those choppers. Your friend Drysdale. All on you. You're an utter disgrace. How's it feel knowing that you're the cause of your friend having to shit in a bag the rest of his life? That it was you who killed these men today?"

Derek wheels around and jolts forward, but Jason and Rob spring at the same time. Jason grabs him around his waist while Rob hooks Derek's right arm coming up to punch the SAC square in the face. "Don't do it!" Rob yells out.

"No, let him go, men. Let him see how much more trouble he's in after hitting a superior federal officer," Liu goads Derek on.

"You fucking worthless piece of shit! Good men died today and you did nothing! Don't you dare hang this all on me!"

"Interesting choice of words, Harrington. Hang is exactly what you are going to do." The SAC looks at his subordinates, both still struggling to hold Derek back. "Get this sorry excuse out of my sight before I have him put in shackles." The man turns and walks away, his stride a little quicker than before.

"Chill, Derek," Jason calls out, straining against the strength of the man. "Damn it, chill! He's gone!"

"Calm down, man," Rob adds. "Calm the fuck down!"

After a few more moments Derek relents. The weight of the day's events finally catch up to him. He feels his adrenaline drain out. Exhausted, he leans back against the fencepost and then drops to the ground. The two agents crouch down next to him.

"You gotta be smarter than that, Derek. You hit that fool, good as it may feel, you'll be playing right into his hands," Rob says.

"The guy's a snake, bro. Don't play his game," Jason adds.

Derek lets out a long sigh. "What the hell are we gonna do, fellas?"

"You're gonna go home, Derek. That's the play right now," Rob replies. "Out of sight, out of mind. We'll debrief you via WebEx later on, and in the meantime

Jason and I will run as much interference for you as we can. Everyone knows this wasn't on you."

"You've earned the time and then some. Go and take a break, bro. We'll call you back if and when, you know?"

At that moment, home sounds like the best place he can possibly be. Rob stands and offers an outstretched palm, which Derek takes and gets hoisted up. He lets them know where the remainder of his gear is stashed, and then hooks up with a junior agent to drive him off the scene.

. . . . .

Brilliance. Sheer brilliance. That's how Daniel describes it to her over the secure satellite phone, just a few short hours after the ambush concluded. They had struck one for the underdog. Bloodied the nose of the Jolly Green Giant and laughed while he cowered and wept like the true bully that he is. That's all bullies really are. Make-believe giants that cry and piss their pants after you punch them square in the face and show them you're not afraid to do so. Sarah smiles while standing outside the ancient machinery. She beams after she relays the news to her small contingent still in the abandoned mining camp with her. They respond with a raucous cheer. Hugs and kisses abound.

That was the first call.

The second call comes later that night and is much different in tone. Daniel erupts over the line. Every profanity imaginable spills from his mouth as he berates her again and again. She can't even get a word in edgewise, so Sarah stands resolute, picking what information she can out of the man's tirade.

Eventually what she is able to decipher causes her to shake. The revelation is torturous. Her legs suddenly weak, Sarah has to sit down. She knew those families. Every man, woman, and child. There were two toddlers at Saddle Oaks. She had sent them there.

On top of it all, somehow the news outlets were on the scene before the paramedics were. Within minutes of arriving, coverage had gone viral, first spanning the U.S., then shortly thereafter, the world. It was publicity they didn't want. The group was supposed to remain in the shadows, not be broadcast around the globe.

"Do you have any idea of the shitstorm this is creating?" Daniel screams at her. "They're carrying children out in body bags on the fucking news! These are optics that we can't contend with. This exposure puts serious restraints on our future initiatives."

Somewhere far off and disconnected Sarah hears someone speaking. "Those sons of bitches. Those absolute bastards." It takes a moment for her to realize the words are coming from her.

"You find out what went wrong! You find out why those kids were still there and get back to me immediately, do you understand? Immediately!"

He speaks like a man who feels his own head on the chopping block. With this much heat she can't blame him. Attention to this degree could unravel everything, eventually catching him up in the tornado that would whisk them all to a federal supermax for the rest of their days.

Sarah finally gets him to settle down enough to assure him she will get to the bottom of what happened. Not that it really matters now. Dead is dead. The damage is done. They would be better off trying to strategize their next moves. Figuring out how to adapt to the situation instead of playing catch-up. But when the power wants answers, Sarah knows to give them.

Except she can't get any of her own. Punching in number after memorized number, she tries the handful of satellite phones at the ranch to no avail. After that, she rings the network of outlying safe houses, hoping that in all the carnage someone was able to escape to one.

Early in the morning of the day after the ambush it's apparent that the plan has come apart at the seams. Sarah can't get anyone on the line. Can't get any reports from her people downrange. Lives have been lost. Not combatants expecting to give their life for the cause. Early on from Marshal's days, it was clear that there were those who would sacrifice, and those who would sacrifice their lives.

Her plan never involved having the former still on the site at the time of their ambush. Yes, she wanted them there as close to the raid as possible to lull the Feds into a sense of false security, but Sarah had selected the ranch specifically for the tunnels and mine shafts that lay beneath it. They were supposed to have escaped well before the first agent set foot on the camp.

All those lives lost. The lives of families. Men, women, and children. *The kids. Oh my God, the kids.* How had they not gotten out in time? What had happened?

Sarah makes her way from the control room and outside to the camp proper. Frank and a few others see her approaching and stop what they're doing. "Break camp," she says upon reaching them. "Evac plan alpha. Start gathering up what gear we have left. I'll give you the details later."

Most of the group exchange glances but then go about following her orders, knowing full well not to languish or question her motives. Frank stays behind, waiting until the rest are out of earshot. "What's going on, Captain?" he asks, his voice still raspy from the injury sustained at the hands of Pugh.

"Something went wrong at the site. The Feds wiped out our entire camp. They may have prisoners. If they do, this place could be compromised. We have to be in the wind and fast."

"What about our next move? The migration west? All that recon? We just gonna give it up, Cap?"

Sarah sighs, looking over the measly collection of tents and hastily constructed plywood buildings. *Giving up all this.* As if it were the fortunes they all secretly longed for and felt they deserved. "Those plans are still viable. We just have to disperse and go to ground for a bit. When it's time to reconvene you'll know." She pauses, looking off into the distance. After a moment she shakes her head. "Better go help the others."

"Only a half dozen of us, boss, counting you. Gonna take us a few days to sort this all out and break it all down."

"I know. Work as quick as you can."

"You got it." The man ambles off to join the rest while Sarah retreats to her table in the control room.

The next thirty-six hours go by in a blur. Sarah continues trying to reach members of her group at the site and the safe houses to no avail. Beyond that, everything is a flurry of activity trying to sanitize the camp. Equipment being packed. Vehicles loaded. The makeshift buildings taken down, the lumber burned. Interspersed with the labor, Sarah goes to the control room to plan their next move. Without the proper evacuation from the ranch this operation had cost them dearly in terms of personnel. They would need to replenish their ranks quickly. The move out West would have to be sped up. The recruits there told to report in as soon as a new camp could be established. Deep might be able to help with that, if he's still alive.

Sarah is still in the control room when heavy feet pound through the facility, only to come to a stop before her door. The knock that follows is loud and hurried. "Captain, you're not gonna believe this," Frank calls from the other side, his voice straining against the limits of his throat.

She rips the door open. "What? What is it?"

"That maniac, Pugh. He's here. He made it back."

Pushing past him, she rushes out of the tipple. Kellen stands amongst the other four members of the camp still there. Just like weeks ago when he had shown up after his reconnaissance mission, the man wears his ghillie suit, the hood down with his trusted rifle slung over his shoulder. His face is worn and dirty. The quartet are asking for details about the ambush. Who made it out alive? Who was captured? For his part Kellen just stares straight ahead, emotionless and silent, in need of another reboot, it would seem.

As Sarah arrives the others fall silent. "You five finish getting the gear into the vans. We have to be out of here soon."

"Guy won't say shit to us, Cap," Andrew replies, a gruff former long-haul driver who'd had his rig repossessed.

"Leave it to me, Drew. Go about your business. I'll

find out everything." The group slowly departs with no love lost for the sniper. Frank glares at the man while Andrew spits on the ground before turning away. After they've left Sarah plants her hands on her hips. "I am going to find out everything, right?"

His gaze slowly drifts away from the departing members to meet her eyes. Kellen stares at her blankly. She is about to repeat herself when he opens his mouth and speaks. "Of course. I report to you. Not to them."

"Good. Now maybe you can fill me in as to what in the hell went wrong over there."

His eyebrows furrow. "What went wrong? I thought everything went off without a hitch."

Sarah blinks several times before shaking her head. "You can't be serious, Pugh. I haven't been able to get a single person from the ranch on the line. The reports that we have received said that everyone there has been killed or captured."

"Oh. That. Yeah, well . . ." The man trails off and returns to silence.

"Well what, goddammit! Why wasn't the camp evacuated prior to their assault? Do you have any idea what this has cost us?" Looking disinterested, Kellen turns and walks off. "Where the fuck are you going?"

"I need to sit. I'm tired." The man finds a tree stump and lowers himself down. He slowly unslings his rifle and lays it across his lap.

"Comfortable now?"

"Yes. Thank you."

Sarah feels the heat crawling up her neck. "You had better start talking."

The man sighs and looks off toward the tree line. "Truth be told, I don't know why it wasn't evacuated in time. Your man, Kyle. I kept reminding him that we needed to get everyone out, but he wouldn't budge. Said we needed to sell that the camp was benign for as long as possible. That we had no idea if Harrington was even on station."

"Kyle said that?" It goes along with her instructions, but Sarah trusted Kyle's judgment. He had to have known that they would be under surveillance. Could he have really estimated so badly?

Kellen shrugs. "Like I said, he held on too long. When we heard the rotor blades there wasn't anything anyone could do at that point. He ordered all the noncombatants to the basement. We barely had time to get to our positions. I'm surprised we pulled it off the way we did."

"Wait, so if they were all in the basement, how did they all get killed?"

His mouth compressing into a thin line, Kellen's disdain barely registers. It's the most emotion she's ever seen out of the man. "That's where your Derek came into play."

Sarah's anger continues to rise, but now it shifts away from the sniper. "Tell me what happened."

"The birds. We took down three of them and the fourth bugged out. We had neutralized their air power. The ground forces were getting chewed up. Then that Apache came roaring back in. Dumped its rockets right into the farmhouse. I can't say for certain, but he had to have called it back. Directed the fire. How else do you explain it? Everyone else was engaged. If he was in an overwatch like the last times . . ."

"Do you think he would have seen them taking cover in the house?"

Another shrug. "I don't see how he couldn't have.

The ranch was in a natural depression. High ground around it on nearly three sides. Plenty of vantage points. He had to have seen it."

Her teeth grinding, Sarah can barely contain herself. If Derek saw her people taking shelter in the farmhouse, that meant that he directed the helicopter's fire against it regardless. It fits perfectly. The man never showed anything but contempt for them, always looking down upon those in the group.

But now it was something more. Now it was revenge. Revenge for taking his family. For trying to murder them. Derek was sending her a message. Man, woman, or child, he was going to annihilate them all.

Well, messages can be sent in both directions.

"Andrew!" Sarah calls across the camp. The tall man spins to look at her. "What do we have here in terms of hardware?"

"Just our sidearms and that crate of HKs you brought back."

She turns back to the sniper. "Get yourself cleaned up and have something to eat. There's still some bread and woodchuck. We'll be moving out soon."

"Where to?"

"Our hides," she says, pulling out her satellite phone. When he just stares at her she adds, "Safe houses. Now go. I need to make a call." Sarah waits until Kellen has ambled off before hitting the button. The other line picks up and she tells the man to go secure.

After the requisite clicks and buzzes finish, Daniel asks, "What in the hell is it now? Have you relocated yet?"

"Working on it," she replies tersely. "Their point

man in all of this. Do you think you can find where they're stashing him and his family?"

"We've done that dance, remember? Besides, aren't you the one that said he would be off the books? All that tradecraft bullshit spooks like to hide behind."

"There has to be something we haven't tried yet," Sarah says. "Some other angle. This thing has caused an earthquake. Maybe it's shaken something loose. Leverage that."

A long pause emanates from Daniel's end of the line. Sarah knows he's still there; she can hear his heavy breathing. When he finally speaks again his voice is teetering on the edge of self-containment. "Rumor has it that the president is going to order a special commission to be impaneled as early as this evening. It'll be touted publicly to save face, but word is that the actual proceedings will be private. Testimony and evidence reviewed in SCIFs. TS/SCI clearances or above. It's a stretch but given the broad reach of these inquiries, new information may come to light. I'll tell you this though, she won't be happy with having to clean up your mess." The man's words drip with indignation.

"I don't give a shit," Sarah counters, her patience having run out. "We don't put an end to this operation, we could all go down. Do whatever you have to do, but get me an address."

"And what do you plan on doing with it once you have it?"

"You want to stop getting bit by the same snake, you cut off its head."

Daniel lets out a long sigh. "Excuse me, I don't speak backwoods redneck."

She knows he's being obstinate, but Sarah doesn't care. Let the message carry to his ass too. Let everyone know that she'll come for you if you cross her. "I'm going to kill that son of a bitch."

18

Pat Graelish is smiling.

Make no mistake, he is in pain. He grimaces more often than not, and has a continuous need to cough up wads of green phlegm. Yet today, he is smiling. His daily regimen, stretched on for weeks now, has finally borne fruit. As he flips through the news channels on the TV in his room he pauses when BREAKING NEWS banners flash on the screen. Normally he would switch over to Dhole, his preferred channel, but it being the middle of the day means that Brandy Baldinger is manning the desk for CNC, and damn it, Pat was always a sucker for tumble-down curls.

"Breaking news now out of Kentucky," the anchor begins. "CNC is learning that a federal law enforcement operation involving the FBI has gone terribly wrong. Developing reports suggest that an FBI raid on a former horse ranch has resulted in multiple fatalities. Details are still coming in, but initial reports are that Army National Guard helicopters carrying members of the FBI's elite Hostage Rescue Team were shot down during the operation. We're monitoring the story closely for you and will of course bring you more details as they are confirmed, but for now, again an FBI operation in Kentucky has failed and multiple fatalities are reported."

The other channels spout much of the same. Pat watches as tears of joy mix with tears of pain to streak down his face. In the next few hours overhead shots from news helicopters show a scene of disarray. Burning buildings spewing plumes of black smoke. Wreckage from the downed choppers and tactical vehicles. Debris and smaller fires scattered all over. Every inch of the ranch space is covered by ambulances, police cruisers, and law enforcement officers from the local, state, and federal level. Fire trucks pump water from a nearby well to try and bring the raging infernos to heel.

"New developments in the story we're following for you involving the FBI raid three days ago," Dhole News's Darren Briarett says into the camera. "Official numbers have just been released and we are sad to say they are not good. Sixty-four people have lost their lives, twelve of whom are children under the age of ten. In addition to these casualties, twenty-seven members of the FBI Hostage Rescue Team, FBI SWAT, and the Army National Guard have also lost their lives. This marks the highest loss of federal law enforcement lives in a single incident. Another seventeen have been wounded, along with five individuals that have been detained. This . . . this is just awful."

"Hard to believe that it's already been a week since that deadly FBI raid gone wrong," CBNMS's Jake Scarberia reports during his morning show. "Now we're learning through our sources that the botched operation was a raid on a domestic terrorist organization known as Autumn's Tithe. The group's name is apparently derived from their goal of bringing about the fall of the federal government through a series of violent attacks they refer to as tithes. The FBI raid that resulted in the deaths of ninety-one people was part of an ongoing, clandestine operation to dismantle the organization. However, it appears Autumn's Tithe was able to turn the tables on the FBI with what is now being described as a highly sophisticated ambush."

"New fallout this evening regarding the FBI operation that occurred two weeks ago," CNC's Allen Conroy states. "Unconfirmed reports regarding the group Autumn's Tithe suggests that the FBI was utilizing military assets such as drone missile strikes and Apache helicopters on the group's remote camps. If true, this raises some serious questions and concerns regarding the law enforcement agency's use of force domestically, as well as adding fuel to the already growing fire around the apparent lack of oversight within certain sectors of the Bureau. This amid new details coming out of the operation that the domestic terrorist group utilized powerful weaponry such as heat-seeking rocket launchers and state-of-the-art infrared defeating uniforms. If true, it begs the question, how did such a group get access to equipment reserved for our military?"

"Increasing pressure mounts on the administration to explain the actions of their Department of Justice, actions that led to the deaths of sixty-four civilians, including twelve children, and twenty-seven FBI members and Army National Guardsmen," Sam Herdsman delivers. "With the incident three weeks behind us now, it appears heads may be getting ready to roll. CBC has learned that the congressional inquiry ordered by the president to examine the events are turning up, quote, 'troubling details of overreach' and that the director of the FBI, the attorney general, and even the director of National Intelligence may be asked to resign or be terminated by the president."

"Breaking news for you today on last month's FBI raid gone wrong. This is 'Head Start.' I'm your host, John Broach. Let's get started. In a scathing rebuke, Senator McCullagh, chairwoman of the Senate Select Committee on Intelligence, issued a statement that highlighted the failings of the FBI and the attorney general in exercising their, and I quote, 'excessive and elevated use of force, tactics, and procedures that are suited for America's battlefields abroad, not in her own backyard.' The chairwoman's statement went on to address the 'gross and overbearing failure of leadership prior to and during the operation.' It can now be assumed that with the Senate's preliminary report published, along with this statement, that high-level resignations will be forthcoming, and an overall reshuffling of power will occur in the nation's top intelligence and law enforcement agencies. Senator McCullagh herself is considered the prime candidate for attorney general, should the current AG Clement resign."

"It's official," Caesar Shannon states as he begins his broadcast on Dhole News. "The nation's top law enforcement officer, Attorney General Anthony Clement, has submitted his resignation to the president amidst growing pressure calling on him to do so in light of the failed operation at the Saddle Oaks horse ranch. FBI Director Sellsbee is expected to follow suit in the coming days. Here's my take . . ."

Pat Graelish is crying.

The pain is too much, but the tears are not reserved for pain alone. They are for what he has accomplished. What he has managed to contribute from his meager life. That he could give this is enough. That he could witness the beginnings of the fall, a fall that he helped orchestrate, is everything. Pat Graelish is overjoyed and exhausted. He's seen enough. The man hits the power button to his TV and closes his eyes.

Pat Graelish never wakes up.

19

"News out of Capitol Hill tonight as the interim attorney general has been nominated," Weston Dwelley says, beginning his broadcast. "The Pennsylvania senator, Eleanor McCullagh, in a move that surprises no one, has been tasked by the president to fill the void left by AG Clement after the botched handling of his Department of Justice. Which of course culminated in the now infamous failed FBI mission at the Saddle-Oaks horse ranch eight weeks ago to the day.

"In what is a lightning-fast move for Washington, the president is clearly trying to right the ship of a DOJ that has been allowed to steer its own course for far too long. In appointing McCullagh, a nomination that is expected to be quickly ratified by both sides of the aisle, the president is putting a hard-nosed captain in charge of that ship, one who is expected to deliver on his promise of transparency and accountability within the department."

Derek's father starts coughing and rolls over. Derek

stands up and rubs the man's back, helping him to loosen the phlegm in his lungs so that he can spit it out into the bucket attached to the guardrail of his hospital bed. He had returned from the field after the battle only to find another one raging in his own home. Unfortunately for Derek and the rest of his family, this battle would have no chance at victory.

His father is dying.

In the final stages of hospice care, a hospital bed had been placed in the home's master bedroom. In between her shifts, Kim had been sleeping in his father's room, or more often than not, in bed with Michael. That was when she was able to sleep at all. Always the nurse, Derek would often find her tending to his father instead of taking care of herself. Just like when Michael was an infant, Derek had to force his ex-wife to take breaks for meals and sleep, such as he was doing now. With the two of them constantly rotating for his father, security had been left solely in the hands of Maureen and Al, each of them taking a twelve-hour shift in the house every day.

His father rolls back over, his chest heaving from the exertion. His eyelids are shut but his eyes flutter underneath them. Derek wonders what dreams or visions his old man is experiencing. What demons wreak havoc on an already plagued mind now that his consciousness was barely present to keep them abated. Or was it the opposite? Did his father now see angels beckoning him to come home? To welcome him and end his suffering? Was Derek's mother the sight Stanley Harrington now beheld, their hands outstretched toward one another but still just out of reach? He likes to believe it's the latter rather than the former.

Wiping at an eye with the back of his hand, Derek longs for a drink. When Kim wasn't there, hell, even when she was, the bottle became his go-to. Drinks at night by the firepit. Beers during the day while he worked in the garage or toiled around the house hanging this or fixing that. Sometimes the memories would come on so fast and so strong that a shot was necessary, whether it be three in the morning or three in the afternoon. The booze helped. It was a Band-Aid to his sucking chest wound. Derek knows that the pain and trauma go deeper than the bourbon can ever touch. He's just unwilling to dive down there. At least for right now.

The reliving of such things might be too much to bear, and he needs to stay present for his family. For the men and women that rely on him to do what he needs to do in the field. To stop this enemy that has shown a penchant for merciless and sophisticated killing. It may not have started as his fight, but for damn sure it was his now. He would see Autumn's Tithe taken down. Then he might find refuge.

But for now Derek needs that edge. He has to hold onto that bottled-up jumble of aggression and anger. How else can he do his job without it? What else is there to tap into in order to become what he needs to be to take this group down? Nothing. That's what.

His father's coughing brings him back from his thoughts. Even now the man refused to wear anything other than his olive drab sweat suit complete with the black eagle, globe, and anchor insignia on the chest. *Once a Marine, always a Marine. Semper Fi, Dad.*

Derek hates to admit it, but it pains him to see his father this way. This once great and powerful man, reduced to such frailty that his sweat suit hangs loose on him. Yes, he had been a bastard to Derek and his mom their entire lives, but how much of that had come from his own battle scars? How much of Korea had he brought back with him, in a time when talking about the horrors of war was taboo? No wonder his dad had taken to the bottle himself. No wonder he had his violent outbursts.

And while not excusing it, couldn't Derek now understand it? He never had and he never would put his hands on his wife or son, that much he would always hate his father for. But from his own experience Derek could draw the parallel. Know the source. That ... lessened things somewhat in the son's eyes while witnessing his father's final days.

For all his faults, he had also taught Derek valuable lessons. About tenacity. Fortitude. Perseverance in the face of adversity. How to hunt. How to fish. How to survive, not just in the wild, but in life. They were skill sets that Derek would pass on to his own son. Skill sets that he was grateful for. That made his father a figure to look up to in his eyes when he wasn't despising his conduct. Someone to care for in his later years. Yes, he was a bastard, but he was Derek's bastard.

"So just who is Senator McCullagh?" Dwelley continues on his program. "After graduating from the University of Pennsylvania Law School she joined the Air Force, serving first as an attorney and later as a judge in the Judge Advocate General corps. The senator retired as a full bird colonel after twenty years. Upon leaving the service in 1998 she began her career in politics, serving first as a representative from Pennsylvania's second district. The then-Representative

McCullagh cut her teeth as part of the House Committee on Veterans Affairs, where she quickly earned a reputation as a skillful and hard-nosed negotiator.

"After two terms in the House, McCullagh successfully defeated several key opponents for the seat left vacant by Senator Browback when he retired to run for governor in 2010. McCullagh's rise included seats on both the Senate Armed Services Committee and later the Senate Select Committee on Intelligence, which until just recently she served as chairwoman."

"Hey, there," Kim's voice says softly from the door.

Derek flinches from his father to look over at her. She leans against the doorframe, her arms folded across her breasts, her head tilted to rest on the wood. She looks tired but also beautiful. The light fixture from the hallway backlights her, and her hair looks like a wheat field with the sun shining on it. Still dressed in her aquamarine scrubs, she has a small smile on her face. "Hey, yourself. You're home early."

"Yeah, they ended up cutting the second shift. Guess it wasn't as busy as they expected it would be. You know hospitals and OT."

"Yup. Anything to avoid it."

She nods and then looks to his father. "How was he today?"

Derek takes a deep breath and lets it out. "Today. Well . . . today wasn't good. He's dying, but the man is so stubborn he refuses to let go. He fights through so much pain to stay here. I don't know why. I just want him to be at peace already."

"I know you do. When it's his time it'll be his time. Until then all you can do is try to make him as comfortable as possible."

"Yeah. You're right." Following her guidance,

Derek raises the sheets and blankets a little higher on the man.

"Tell you what. I was expecting to be up for the next few hours anyway. I'll sit with him. You go and get some sleep."

"What? No. You just got off a double. Well, a one and a half anyway. You're the one that should be getting rest."

She smiles and crosses over to him, putting a hand on his shoulder. "Doubles are nothing, and besides, if I went to bed now I'd just lie awake. Trust me, I'm okay. You go."

"Kim ... I ..."

"Derek. I know you haven't been sleeping. The crash and Kentucky and now your dad are spinning up all sorts of things for you. You don't have to talk about them to me, but that doesn't mean I can't see the signs. Go. Get some rest. If he wakes up or anything happens I'll have Maureen grab you."

As if on cue Derek yawns. He finally concedes, standing up and walking by her. As he does so he gives her hand a tight squeeze. Kim squeezes it back. Derek stops in the doorframe and turns around. Kim is gently stroking his father's few tufts of remaining hair. "Hey," he whispers. Her forehead furrowed, Kim looks up, wondering what else is needed. "We're lucky to have you."

She smiles. "Yeah, you are. Now go."

. . . . .

The darkness that envelops him is total and increasingly frigid. Derek tumbles head over heels, each revolution providing a momentary relief from the black. The spinning slows, the moments of visibility growing longer while the cold further penetrates his bones. As the revolutions halt altogether he is left staring straight up at the source of light holding back the dark. It's obscured and Derek's vision of the source shimmers. Instead of drawing closer he slips downward, the illumination shrinking away from him in the process.

Body shivering, his face and extremities are numb. His lungs burn in his chest, and Derek realizes that he can't breathe. As panic grips him a strange euphoria comes with it. The cold permeates his mind. His vision clouds at the edges.

Violent pounding and muted screams revitalize his alertness. Derek twists to his right, an action that feels like moving through quicksand. The interior of the Black Hawk is mangled. The steel twisted to create an unsolvable maze. The crew chief bangs against the window of the cabin door, hands working like pistons.

The man screams, the same muted scream heard before. When he does so bubbles escape from his mouth and float to the ceiling of the aircraft where they settle before bursting. As if sensing his presence, the crew chief turns slowly toward Derek. Half of the man's face has been ripped off, his exposed skull charred black and covered with blood that trails through the water with his movement. Jagged pieces of metal are embedded in his head, neck, and shoulder. The crew chief sees Derek and screams again, a cascade of muffled bubbles flowing from his mouth.

Panic overwhelms Derek, banishing the encroaching euphoria. All he feels now is fear. Fear and the cold. Derek thrashes about, trying desperately to find his way out of the helicopter's interior. Turning, he sees more bodies already limp and drifting listlessly. Drysdale and the other crew member. Ortiz and Ortega. Derek remembers that he can't breathe. He's so cold. When Drysdale's eyes flip open Derek screams, bubbles obscuring his vision for good.

Instead of the cold water rushing into his lungs Derek feels a deep burning. He chokes on heat, ash, and smoke. Still not able to breathe but now suffering from inhalation. Chilled to the bone a mere moment ago he is now enveloped in searing heat. All of his comrades are awake and animated. They cry out in agony as the flames swallow their bodies.

Fragments of the demolished Black Hawk frame pierce their bodies in multiple locations. Their existence is shattered when the twisted, burning wreckage hits the deck. Derek sees and hears it all while his own skin blisters and flakes away like charred paper. Trapped inside the mangled compartment, all he can do is add to the cacophony of screams as his body is consumed by the flames.

Except now instead of a burning helicopter he sees a burning tank. Feels the heat of the engine succumbing to the Molotov cocktail mixed with the oppressive summer temperatures of a sweltering Baghdad afternoon. The men inside the tracked vehicle scramble out of the hatches, their bodies bathed in fire. Their skin slakes off so that the bones underneath catches like tinder.

They line up on the street. Falling in. Dress right dress. Their eyes melt out of their sockets. Sections of skin and muscle evaporate as they stand at attention. Derek looks on in horror as the exposed bones of the crew members catch like the thousands of fires he's set in his lifetime. The tank commander renders a salute even as his mouth emits a death cry worthy of being a harbinger for the end of days. Lowering the salute, the commander points at something beyond Derek, skin falling off the extended finger in bubbling gobs of boiling tissue.

Twisting around he finds Gerbowski standing before him. The man smiles, his good-natured, country politeness seeping through the grin. Something draws Gerbowski's attention for a moment. As he looks off to the side his cauliflower ear is exposed. A fleeting notion passes through Derek's mind. A recognition for the countless hours of blood and sweat, dedication and perseverance the condition represents. Gerbowski turns back, his smile gone, his face a mask of fear.

Then his head disappears in a pink mist, pulverized with the effortless fragility of an egg dropped to the floor.

Derek is screaming as he spins, his rifle coming up to his shoulder. The Iraqi boy is there. In one hand an improvised wick stuffed into a bottleneck already ablaze. In the other, a recently fired AK-47, the barrel still smoking. The evil of fanaticism radiates from his eyes while maniacal laughter bursts from his mouth. Even after Derek puts him down the laughter continues.

Other snippets of scenes fill the void while Derek turns to find its source. A church exploding. Vehicles destroyed. Drysdale's vacant stare and ashen skin. Kelly bleeding out on a park bench. Gil standing before him with a knife to Kim's throat.

The laughter is pervasive. It saturates his skin with a feeling of vitriolic wrongdoing. As he turns the boy is there again, but with Marshal's face. Derek shoots the old man between the eyes yet the laughter doesn't stop. Another hurried spin.

No matter how many rounds he expends. How many enemies he puts down. There is always another. And then another. More people die. More loved ones are crushed. Each bullet sent toward a target is another family somewhere shattered forever.

Pain penetrates every fiber of his being. Mentally, physically, emotionally. Derek is on fire again. A strange sizzling comes from the flames until he realizes it's his tears hitting the blaze that envelops his body. His weapon empty, the laughter fills the vacancy left by the dissipated reports. All at once everywhere and nowhere at the same time. Derek falls to his knees in the litter-strewn Baghdad street and bellows to the sky as the fire finally swallows him whole.

Jolting awake, Derek sits upright and throws himself back against the headboard. He's vaguely aware of a pressure on his lower leg. His T-shirt is soaked through with sweat, his sheets cold and clammy from his perspiration. Derek frantically searches the darkened room. Soft cream paint mixes with that of the plywood walls in the improvised hooch, *Maxim* magazine pictures torn from the pages and stapled next to his cot. His gaze settles back on a woman standing at the foot of the bed. For a brief second his alarm spikes as the notion it is Sarah riffles through his mind. Derek clenches his fists, his body instinctively preparing for the fight to come even as the soft and soothing voice beckons him to the full realization of where and when he is.

Kim smiles weakly from the shadows. Instead of pressure on his leg a sense of reassurance replaces it.

Long ago she had learned to wake him from his nightmares by his feet so that she wouldn't be caught by a fist from his lashing out, or be pulled into a choke hold as had happened once before.

The heat from the flames is replaced by an intense shivering. A final frantic look around the room is met by her calming words. "It's okay. You're home. You're safe."

Her tired smile brings him back. When the realization of who she is, of where he is, finally comes to full fruition, Derek can't help breaking down.

Kim moves to her onetime husband, sitting in the bed next to him. Derek falls into her embrace and presses his face to her chest, her scrubs top absorbing his tears. He pulls her into him tight with his powerful arms. She gently rocks him back and forth the way she did with Michael when he was a baby. Wetness hits his forehead and streaks down his face and Derek realizes that it's her tears mixing with his own.

Her top rides up slightly from the embrace and their skin touches in the slightest of exposure, yet it is enough to send ribbons of electricity through them both. The soft feel of her touch conjures the images of her ivory body and memories of nights when they lay together in passionate entanglements of pure intimacy. The warmth of her, of what they once had, of what he longs for again in the future, is enough to slowly ease his shivering. Kim places gentle kisses on his forehead and runs her hand through his hair.

His breathing slows, and the vise grip he holds onto her with gradually relaxes. Derek feels the wave of exhaustion wash over and beckon him back to sleep.

Turning his head, he listens to the strong rhythm of her heart. He feels the steady rise and fall of her chest. Her own body releases the pent-up tension.

In moments they are both asleep.

20

In the morning Derek stumbles out of the downstairs guest room in a pair of shorts and a tank top. His head swirls and throbs from last night's combined intake and terrible sleep. Derek coughs his throat clear and rubs his bleary eyes. Blinking them open he finds Al at the island, the man's morning routine of fixing breakfast near completion as he plates stacks of pancakes.

"Well, good morning, sunshine," Al says, looking up from the task at hand. His voice is boisterous and jovial despite the early hour. "Get enough sleep?"

"Jesus, Al," Derek mutters. "You ever have an off switch?"

"If I do, it hasn't been found yet." He chuckles as he pours Derek a cup of coffee and sets it out in front of him on the breakfast bar. Derek finds a stool and leans over the cup, letting the smell of the roast dust out the cobwebs before taking a sip.

Today Al is dressed in a pair of golf shorts and a loose-fitting, light green polo. One look at the man and you'd say he spent his formative years on the fairway instead of the jungles of Vietnam and all the subsequent hellholes he found himself in. It's the kind of notion that Kim would get a kick out of if she knew the full extent of the older man's background.

Kim. Derek suddenly remembers that he had fallen asleep and never got back up to relieve her. "Shit, I gotta get upstairs. She's gonna have my head."

"Relax, Devil Dog. She's in bed," Al replies. "I came over a few hours early to spend some time with Maureen. When I did the rounds I found her there so I sent her off and stayed with him. He was sleeping as of a half hour ago. Have your coffee. He ain't going anywhere and we're both right here if anything goes down."

Derek takes a long pull from his mug. "Thank you again. Both of you. I know this goes beyond your scope of duty, my father and all."

"Say nothing more of it, my friend," the older man replies, putting a plate of breakfast in front of Derek. Al lifts his own mug off the nearby countertop. "Duty called and we answered. Nothing more to it than that."

Taking a pancake off the top of his stack, Derek curls it up and dips it in some syrup. One bite cuts it in half. "I'll give you this much," he says between chews, "for an Army puke you sure do know how to make a mean breakfast."

Chuckling, Al responds. "Do they even know how to cook in the Marines?"

"Nah. We just eat crayons and drink the blood of our enemies for nourishment."

Both men laugh. "Hey, listen. I was talking a bit with Kim last night. I know things have been even tougher on you lately than usual. First the field and now your dad. Why don't you come over tonight after my shift is done? Kim is off and Maureen will be here with them all. You and I can get a fire going and sip from the bottle a little bit. It's been a while since our last session."

"I really shouldn't. Kim has been putting in a lot of hours lately. And she hasn't taken kindly to the amount of drinking I've been doing."

"Don't worry about that. Maureen will cook a nice dinner while we have our fire and drinks. Then we can come back over and eat. All of us together. We won't get blasted."

"Where's the fun in that?"

Al smiles and chuckles again. Derek's first impulse is to refuse, but he admits to himself that he needs the chance to vent to someone who gets it after the last two months. "You know what, count me in."

From back inside his room Derek's cell phone starts to ring. Suppressing a groan, he reluctantly gets up from the counter, snagging another pancake in the process and munching it down as he crosses the living room. Once inside Derek flops back down onto the mattress, scoops the phone off of the charging cable, and looks at the home screen. It's Ortega.

"Hey, partner, what's up?" Derek answers as he swallows down the flapjack.

"Hey, boss, sorry if I woke you but this couldn't wait," the younger man replies.

"No worries, I was up anyway. Hit me with it."

"Ortiz and I are at the office. We just got word from higher that there's been a development. They want you in right away so that they can brief us."

Derek feels a knot pull tight in his stomach. He wonders what the hell Liu could possibly want to talk to them about. The man had been playing duck and cover his ass ever since the debacle in Kentucky, trying to salvage what was left of his career and hopefully be allowed to at least retire. From what Derek had heard, he'd shifted blame to everyone he possibly could, Derek primary amongst them. Even so, the official inquiry was turning up evidence to the contrary, and the man's entire career was now under the microscope. His well-earned reputation was being revealed as one who liked to turn a blind eye to the regs, so long as they furthered his advancement. It was not looking like things were going in Liu's favor.

Hence the reason for Derek's trepidation. What last-minute stunt was that asshole going to try now to save his own skin? "All right. Tell them I'm on my way in. I'll be there as soon as possible."

"Roger that, boss. See you then." Ortega hangs up.

Grabbing his pants off the floor and a polo from the dresser in the corner, Derek dresses quickly before heading back out to the kitchen. He explains the situation to Al and is in his car headed toward Indianapolis less than ten minutes after the call. After shutting off the engine, Derek heads to their building as quickly as he can. Since the ranch he had been keeping a low profile, spending most of his time at home. The last thing he needs now is to bump into one of the handful of passing acquaintances he had made in the parking lot. Exchanging small talk pleasantries while explaining his longer than usual absence is an exercise that Derek has a low tolerance for undertaking. Especially given the urgency of Ortega's message.

Stepping into their training space he finds his teammates sitting at the conference table set up just to the left of the door. The surface is adorned with Joint Worldwide Intelligence Communication System–encrypted laptops, the Department of Defense's secure intranet system that houses top secret and sensitive compartmentalized information. Additional computers that can access the department's SIPR and NIPR internet protocols, used for looking up secret and unclassified information respectively, also sit on the tabletop. A series of secure landline voice over internet protocol telephones that transmit through the three DoD classifications are also present. A large flatscreen monitor is affixed to the wall shared by the door.

The Double O's turn their heads as he walks in. Despite their smiles to the contrary, their faces are near perfect matches of strain and exhaustion. One look and Derek can tell he isn't the only one having a hard time with the aftermath of the battle. They both push their chairs back and stand up.

"How are you guys doing?" he says as he reaches the table. He and Ortega shake hands and then pull each other into a back-slapping bro hug. As soon as they let go Ortiz throws her arms around Derek's neck and pulls him in tight, resting her head against his chest. She holds on a little longer than usual.

"It's good to see you, Derek."

"Good to see you too, Angie," he says as they part. "What's this briefing all about?"

"We're about to find out," Ortega says as he wheels around and picks up the phone. "They told us to call when you got here. Wait one." Ortiz and Derek stand silent while he dials. After a moment the young man speaks into the receiver. "Yes, sir, we're all here. Roger that. Logging in now."

Hanging up the phone, Ortiz pulls the JWICS laptop closer and makes a few clicks of his mouse before typing in his username and password. As the video link boots up they all take seats, turning their attention to the flatscreen. When the picture from the camera on the other side of the feed comes through they see the inside of a nondescript office. There's a bit of a rustling, and then to Derek's surprise it's Rob's face, not Liu's, that pops into the picture. A moment later Jason comes into the frame, standing in the background.

"Hey, team. Derek. How are y'all doing?" Rob begins. His voice is somewhat subdued, and as soon as he's done speaking he looks off to his left. Derek recognizes signs of concern on the man's face.

"Rob. Jason. What's this all about?" Derek replies.

Rob looks off to the left again before turning back to the computer. As he does so Jason looks to the left. "We were in the SCIF less than an hour ago," he says, using the acronym for a sensitive compartmented information facility. "One of the detainees taken at Saddle Oaks finally broke and agreed to offer us something in exchange for a deal. We haven't even corroborated the information yet, let alone reported it up the chain, but we didn't want to keep this from you. You . . . deserve to know after what went down."

The trio on Derek's end exchange glances. "All right. Go ahead," Derek says.

Jason walks out of the frame while Rob watches him off to the left. After a moment Jason's voice comes back through the feed. "No one's out there. You're good to go."

Rob looks back. "Y'all remember the early word

we got from them? That one of our snipers was taking out members of Tithe before the assault even began?"

Derek nods "Sure do. I saw them go down myself."

"Right. From the spent brass on the emplacements you found, Derek, as well as being the only one onsite from our side at the time, we knew it couldn't have been us. The angles were all wrong for you to have made those shots yourself."

"Not to mention the fact that all the radio recordings and after-action reports from HRT and SWAT attest to taking sniper fire throughout the engagement," Jason adds. "So we know that they had snipers at their disposal even though they wouldn't admit it."

Rob continues. "Both Jason and I initially thought they were trying to spin what happened into some sort of justification. Like we fired first and all they were doing was defending themselves against the aggressor. Shit like that. Up to this point any statement that the shots didn't come from us have been met with dismissive disdain. Their mistrust of the government and mental conditioning won't consider anything to the contrary. They certainly won't entertain the idea that one of their own could have turned on them."

"Friggin' brainwashed," Ortiz says, her voice laced with annoyance.

"Yeah. Exactly."

"You said up to this point they wouldn't. So what changed?" Derek asks.

"In a word. Forensics," Jason replies from off camera again.

"We finally got back the autopsies and other reports," Rob jumps back in. "After reading them over we decided to take another run at one of the guys we assessed isn't as far gone as the rest. Approaches things with more logic and critical thinking than you typically see in a cult member. We dropped it all on him. Bullet trajectories confirming the origin of the shots. The caliber of the spent brass matching the wounds on the two killed at the outset. He initially tried to pass them off as fabrications but we could see by his demeanor that he was considering the science over our assertions. The bullet flight paths really seemed to resonate. This morning he asked to speak with us. After haggling a bit, he agreed to talk in exchange for a deal."

"I don't get it," Ortega chirps. "Why kill your own people, especially when you don't exactly have the advantage in numbers? It doesn't make any sense."

"We didn't think so either, but after hearing him out it adds up. One of the two that was killed at the outset was a man named Kyle Draubach. Apparently he was in command of the camp and the one overall in charge of conducting the ambush. When he was killed another member named Kellen Pugh took control of the fight from their side."

"All right. What's the connection?" Derek asks.

Jason pops back into the screen and leans in over Rob's shoulder. "I ran the guy. Ex-Army. Qualified sniper. He was discharged on a psychological. Guy had one too many questionable shoots during his time overseas. The big green machine finally had enough and chaptered him out. He goes off the radar after his time in until just recently when he resurfaces with Tithe. The man fits their profile to a tee. Military service. Cast adrift. The detainee told us he was sent there specifically by Sarah herself to give them an edge in the fight. Him and another sniper, Dwight Campbell. He matches up to the description of the one you tangled with, Derek. Has practically the same backstory as Pugh, except for the psychosis. We think he's more of a gun for hire."

"That guy Campbell," Derek interjects, "any sign of his body yet?"

Rob shakes his head. "No, nothing. Chances are he managed to get farther than we expected, and by the time our people got in the area and the choppers overhead he was dead and cold. If you wounded him as badly as you say you did, Chief, his body is more than likely lost to the woods."

"He would have to be," Derek affirms. "I practically gutted him."

"No doubt there, Chief," Jason says. "Don't worry. I'm still working with the local P.D. and arranging some more searches."

"That's good. Maybe a different set of vectors could turn up something."

"Before we get too far off topic," Ortiz interrupts, "can we get back to this guy Pugh? He took out their leader. Why?"

"Apparently there was no love lost between him and Kyle," Rob says, "but there's more to it than that. From what we've learned, Pugh altered their plan as the fight started. All of their noncombatants were supposed to sneak out of the farmhouse using the same tunnels that their crew with the Stingers did. From there they were to disappear into the woods to a rally point until whoever was left from the ambush could reunite with them. Except Pugh canceled all of that. He kept those people in the farmhouse. Told them to stay put, that our sniper was still targeting their personnel." There's a long pause as Rob lets the information sink in. "If that's the case . . ."

"Then Pugh intended for us to kill those people. He wanted women and children included amongst their dead," Derek says flatly. Ortiz swallows. Ortega stands up and puts his hands on his head, turning around and walking a few steps away from the table.

Nodding, Rob goes on. "That's what we're thinking at this point. Public outrage would only support their cause that much more. This is one psychotic bastard. He didn't give a shit about their lives. Just what their deaths could provide."

Long moments of silence hang over both sides of the transmission. "Listen, team," Jason says with an air of warning in his voice. "Like Rob said, we still need to corroborate this, but we're pretty sure we can get the rest of the dominos to fall now that the first one has. What we're not sure of is what's going to happen to the information once we do.

"Things here are pretty tense as you might imagine. A lot of people in powerful places are working real hard to sweep everything under the rug. There are those who think that the mere mention of those kids again, let alone the optic of finger-pointing the blame, will only throw fuel on the fire. It's not a far stretch to think they might impose a 'silence is best' approach," Jason finishes, using air quotes in the process.

"We shouldn't even be telling you this," Rob adds.

Ortiz clears her throat. "Why are you then?"

The men on the other side of the feed share a glance. "You need to know the truth," Rob goes on. "What happened out there. It wasn't your fault. Derek, especially you. We know you directed the Apache back into the fight. Those kids were never supposed to be in that house. These deaths, they're not on you."

Long moments stretch on. The silence lingers in the space of the open training area. Ortiz wipes tears from her eyes. Ortega sits back down and hangs his head between his legs. Derek grinds his teeth, the muscle in his jaw pulsing with the action. "No. No, they are not. But I know who they do belong to."

Derek clenches his fists. He feels the anger boiling up. A rage so punctuated that he can barely hold himself back. With effort, he manages to croak out his next words. "Jason. Rob. Get me everything you know about this Pugh."

21

The van skirts Indianapolis to the northeast on Interstate 69, exits on Route 37, and then takes a right onto East 131st Street. At Howe Road the vehicle makes a left, turning north, before making another left a few minutes later onto Meadow Lake Drive. Despite the GPS on her satellite phone marking the house near the center of the development, the van takes a circuitous drive around the perimeter streets. Slowly but surely it makes its way closer to their objective, the occupants of the front seats scanning the roads for any police patrols. Turning left from Brightwater onto Parkshore, the van makes it halfway down the street before parking across from the target house.

Inside the cargo area the other five members from the coal mine camp make their last-minute adjustments. Racking their pistols and stuffing them into holsters. Magazines get slapped into their Heckler & Koch MP7s, a boxier, more robust version of an Uzi 9mm. Some pull out the expandable shoulder stocks. Others fold down the integrated front post grip under the barrel. A couple do both. Sarah keeps the two adjustments in their collapsed position, preferring to have the weapon in machine pistol form. As one of the three that will be approaching the front door, she wants a low profile.

Across from her, Pugh gently strokes the barrel of his sniper rifle. He stares straight at her, his face more disconnected than usual. A slight tick flickers at the corner of his mouth, what appears to be a smile fighting to escape.

"Okay, one last time. Eric and Andrew head around the side to the back and cover any exits. Frank, Phyllis, and I go through the front door. Kellen covers the street and Rick keeps the van running. Call out any targets as we make our approach. Remember, they all die. Especially the kid. We're in and out in three minutes. Everyone sync to channel five." The group powers on their radios and adjusts to the right frequency. "Radio check."

They go around, sounding off into their throat mics and earpieces. The group charges their submachine guns. "Everyone ready? Move!"

Eric and Andrew throw open the doors to the van and take off across the street, ducking into the shadows on the left side of the house. Frank, Phyllis, and Sarah step out, adjusting their blue coveralls and reflective work vests. They wear white hard hats and clear ballistic safety glasses. Pugh takes a position in front of the car the van is parked behind, his head swiveling between opposite ends of the street before shouldering his rifle and scanning the second-story windows of the house. Rick steps out from the driver's seat and moves around to the passenger side, squatting down behind the engine block with his eyes on the house and his MP7 at the low ready. The trio approaching the front door hold their weapons down at their sides and slightly behind their backs.

At Sarah's signal Phyllis breaks off to the right, rushing across the lawn to stand in front of the garage. Overhead security flood lights flash to life. The woman quickly presses herself against the garage door and creeps to the corner of the house. Peering around it, she sees only trash cans. Phyllis looks back and shakes her head. Sarah motions her back to the front door. "All right, everyone. Here we go. On my mark."

"Wait one," Eric crackles into the radio. "We found a side door. I'm covering it now. Andrew is still working his way into position in the back."

"Hurry up, Drew, we're exposed out here."

"Almost to the back door," Andrew replies.

. . . . .

Al delivers the punchline and Derek can barely keep the whiskey between his lips. Swallowing it down, the younger man bursts out laughing. Al, laughing along with him, stands up and moves to the wood pile. Sitting on the table next to Al's, Derek's phone lights up with an email alert banner. He looks at the screen and sees that it's from Jason, the paper clip icon denoting an attachment, no doubt the files on Pugh that Derek requested earlier that morning.

Even with the probable confirmation that the sniper had orchestrated the deaths of the children at the ranch, a foul cloud had settled over the team after receiving the news. Derek had released everyone after a bit of venting discussion, letting the Double O's seek solace in their own way. For his part, Derek had returned home to spend the afternoon with Michael before heading across the street for the planned firepit session with Al.

Eyeing the clock, he notes that they still have time for another round before dinner would be ready. Not wanting to ruin his buzz and improved spirit, Derek locks the phone and sets it off to the side. He grabs Al's glass and heads back inside to refresh their ice molds.

In the few moments they are separated from their devices, neither Al nor Derek see the alerts pop up on their screens from the surveillance cameras above the garage and front doors. Before either has returned to their chairs, the screens have gone back to black.

. . . . .

Maureen absolutely loves this kitchen. From the large center island to the breakfast nook by the sliding doors leading out back, the array of pots and pans, and the glass-faced cabinets showing off Kim's fine taste in stemware. It has every possible utensil you could want or need. World-class appliances. Beautiful marble countertops. For someone who loved to cook, it was a godsend.

The prior owners of the home, whoever they were, obviously took pride in their kitchen above all else. She and Al lived directly across the street and their kitchen wasn't nearly as nice as this, not even by half.

As for the accouterments, that was all Kim. Maureen had to hand it to her. The woman worked hard and spent her money on things that would make her family all the more comfortable. She loved to cook nearly as much as Maureen did. In fact, were she not upstairs attending to Derek's father, she would probably be down here right now, helping Maureen prepare the evening meal.

The older woman just hopes that oaf Derek appreciates what he has with Kim, namely a second chance. Maureen had tried to stay in her lane, making sure not to pry or worse, add her feelings about the man into the mix. She wanted them to have as natural a chance of rekindling as they could, without outside opinions. And for the most part, Derek had managed not to step on his own johnson. Sure, the man was rough around the edges, and certainly possessed by that warrior ethos, placing mission above all, but in the pockets of time that he was home Maureen saw his dedication.

The man was trying. Trying hard to rid himself of his demons while he was adding to their ranks at the same time. Of that Maureen was certain. But he was also focusing. Putting an emphasis on Kim. Acquiescing to the needs of his boy, instead of barking orders and expecting the child to muster up like a recruit at the depot. She saw that after the fishing episode. How he had tended to his son instead of forcing him into something the boy clearly wasn't ready for.

And then there was Stanley. It wouldn't be much longer before the man was gone. Even now he was coughing up a lung in the hospital bed that had been delivered for his final days. Hospice caregivers had come and gone. The priest had come and gone. Yet the old codger kept trucking, refusing to give in to this mortal world. Maureen could see where Derek's tenacity came from.

And his ill temper.

Maureen sprinkles a little more salt over the vegetables sautéing in the pan on the front burner. As she does a motion sensor alert flashes across the screen of her phone. Maureen turns to look at it, noticing that it's an alert for the motion sensor over the garage, and brings up the corresponding surveillance camera. The driveway is empty.

Turning back to the stovetop, she flips her vegetables when another alert goes off, this time for the front door. A buzz works its way up the back of her neck, her intuition kicking in before her mind has. When Maureen punches up the surveillance feed on the iPad this time she sees three people, two women and a man standing on the front step. They're dressed in what appears to be utility worker garb. The trio looks around at the home, inspecting for . . . something.

Grabbing a dish towel and wiping her hands, she is about to turn to the front door when the floodlights in the backyard go off. Maureen freezes. She looks at the iPad. Out the back window. To the iPad again. Her intuition holds her in place, the sequence coming together quickly. The feeling of something being off.

That's when the back door begins to slide open.

. . . . .

Andrew and Eric run side by side across the street, darting for the shadows that obscure the left side of the house. As soon as they reach them Andrew spots the side door. He taps Eric on the shoulder and then points at the entranceway. Eric nods and creeps up next to the frame while Andrew continues on into the backyard.

Sarah's voice comes through their earpieces. "All right, everyone. Here we go. On my mark."

"Wait one," Eric crackles in response. "We found a side door. I'm covering it now. Andrew is still working his way into position in the back."

"Hurry up, Drew, we're exposed out here."

"Almost to the back door," Andrew replies.

As he rounds the corner, Andrew can see a deck outside of two sliding glass doors. Light spills from a window overhead. He presses closer to the house and starts to creep forward. A shape passes in front of the window, and Andrew just catches a glimpse of curly, gray hair. "There's an old lady in the kitchen. I can take her and then let the rest of you in."

"That's if no one else is downstairs," Sarah returns.

"Worth a shot, boss. What do you want me to do?"

The pause is slight, but it's still present. "Do it," she replies.

Andrew moves more gingerly, the hair on his forearms and the back of his neck standing up. His heart begins to race in his chest while sweat breaks out under his hard hat. The flood lights go off from an overhead motion sensor. Andrew crouches down and presses his back against the house. The shape crosses in front of the window again and then moves off a few moments later. Andrew picks up his stalk, edging ever closer to the double doors. He winces at the sound of the boards of the deck creaking under his weight.

Reaching out with a trembling hand, Andrew tests the handle. The door slides an inch. The man slings his submachine gun behind his back. Digging into a pocket and producing a folding Gerber knife, he pulls it open and keys up.

"Stand by," Andrew whispers as he slides the door farther.

. . . . .

Standing between the window and the stove, Maureen watches as a combat boot steps in through the back door. The next thing she notices is the knife. Scooping up the pan full of vegetables, she bats the knife to the side, the man's flesh searing as it meets the cast iron. The would-be attacker screams at the pain. Double clutching the pan, Maureen swings it back to her left, connecting with the side of the man's head.

If he screamed in pain before now he bellows in agony as half of the skin on his face comes away on the bottom of the pan. Smoking and bubbling, the attacker cradles his skull. Maureen throws a front kick into the man's chest, hitting something solid but sending him back out the door and crashing to the deck.

A shuddering bang sounds out against the front door. Maureen spins to face it, dropping the pan as her hand goes to the .380 kept in the holster at the base of her spine. Another bang but it is quickly overshadowed by the splintering of wood and shattering of glass as the side door explodes open from a burst of gunfire. Drawing her pistol, Maureen brings it up just as another man dressed like the first rushes into the kitchen holding what looks to be a type of Uzi. Raising her weapon to the side one-handed, Maureen fires five times in quick succession. The bullets slap into the man's chest and face, producing bursts of red. The dying man depresses his trigger, letting off a torrent of bullets, but the momentum of her shots rotates his body so that the automatic fire shreds through the wall.

A third bang at the front door, and it flies open, the dead bolt shearing away from the frame. A short, stocky man rushes into the hallway and immediately begins firing from the hip. Before she can bring her pistol to bear the man's bullets rip through a flower vase sitting on the breakfast nook table. Something slams into her stomach and Maureen is knocked onto her back.

All around her the nook erupts from gunfire. She crawls back against the furniture amidst the space being shredded apart, certain that there are at least two submachine guns firing at her. Pressing a hand to her bleeding stomach, Maureen reaches the pistol up and over the table and fires sight unseen, emptying her clip in the general direction of the front door.

Slide locked to the rear, she fumbles to get her only spare magazine from her holster with her free hand, now slick with her own blood. The two attackers from the front door stop to reload themselves. As the race to reload unfolds, a new burst of gunfire rakes across her right leg, punching a fresh hole through Maureen's calf. Instinctively she rolls to her left into the kitchen. The shots track her but are blocked as she rolls again to get behind the center island. In the scamper to avoid the gunshots, her magazine slips out of her hand and slides across the tiled floor.

In the brief respite that occurs as the third attacker reloads, Maureen can hear gunshots being exchanged outside amidst the screams of neighbors. Luckily, she doesn't hear Kim's screams amongst them. Not yet anyway. That's when the kitchen and the center island begin to fly apart as the gunmen open up with another salvo.

■   ■   ■   ■   ■

At the sound of the gunfire, Derek almost falls backward out of his chair. Both he and Al are up in a flash, but Derek stumbles, the shock and alcohol combining to make his legs shaky underneath him. Still, he recovers with a one-handed shove off the deck that rights him. In the second that it takes to do so Al barrels past, crashing through the screen door, not even bothering to open it. His feet pound down the hall toward the front of the house.

Right behind him through the screen, Derek is vaguely aware of his good fortune that the FBI placed them in this cookie-cutter subdevelopment. The layout of Al and Maureen's house is exactly the same as his, which means he knows exactly where the study is. More importantly, he knows that's where Al's gun cabinet is.

He finds Al strapping on a plate carrier laden with thirty-round magazines, the doors to the bottom section of the cabinet thrown wide open. Derek yanks open the upper glass doors and pulls out the first firearm he lays hands on. Coming away with it, Derek sees that he's grabbed a Remington 870 express pump action shotgun, one of the most tried and true firearms of American manufacturing. He's not surprised. In order to maintain their cover, Al's gun cabinet had been outfitted with rifles and shotguns that could easily be used for hunting purposes. A rack full of M4s with M203 grenade launchers attached might have raised eyebrows.

Since the standard operating procedure for firearms in their gun cabinets is to always have rounds chambered, Derek doesn't waste another second before taking off through the front door. He hears Al call after him, "Derek! Wait!" but he's already halfway across the lawn by the time the words register. In that same instance a man in blue coveralls, a reflective vest, and a hard hat crouched behind a white work van turns to face him. Derek sees the man's weapon coming around and shoulders his shotgun. With a flick of his thumb on the safety, Derek squeezes off a thunderous shell of 12-gauge supremacy.

The spread of double-aught buckshot slams into the man's left shoulder and bicep, throwing him against the front fender of the van in a massive, bloody smear. At such close proximity the shot pellets eviscerate the arm, leaving the lower half dangling. The man's face turns white with shock as blood cascades out of his shredded limb. Derek racks the forearm of the shotgun, ejecting a smoking shell and chambering another. Firing as the man slumps down toward the street, the spread takes off the top of his skull.

"Derek! Down!" he hears Al shout behind him. He drops to his stomach and covers his head as the snap of a bullet sails by. It's immediately answered by the rapid fire coming from Al behind him. The man stalks forward, a Ruger Mini-14 chambered in 5.56 belching rounds into a nearby sedan parked in front of the van.

"Sniper! Go! I got him covered!" Al yells as he changes out magazines in a flash.

Derek doesn't need any more instruction on top of what he just received. As Al picks up his suppressive fire again, Derek sprints across the street, listening to the sounds of shattering windows and bursting tires. The heavy *thunk* of rounds punching through the metal doors and impacting on the frame. At the same time he hears the automatic fire coming from inside his home.

Somewhere in the back of his mind and the bottom of his heart it registers. That this could be it. After all the trouble and extra precautions they took to protect his family, they could be getting slaughtered this very minute. That he had failed to do his duty to keep them safe. Again.

But at the same time there is the fight. The heightened senses overpowering his body. His subconscious mind acting in unison with his limbs, the years of drilled-in maneuvers practically acting on their own. His blood pounds in his ears while his heart pounds in his chest. He sucks in gulps of air while his legs tremble, yet they press on, under sure footing now that his adrenaline is compensating for the bourbon.

Derek pumps the shotgun again as he crosses the threshold into his home. There, at the end of the hallway that leads to the living area and kitchen, he sees a thin woman dressed the same as the man outside with her back to him. She fires a submachine gun from the shoulder in the direction of the kitchen. Stopping short and lining up the bead at the end of the ventilated rib barrel, Derek squeezes the trigger. The buckshot blasts the woman in the center of her spine and sends her careening across the room. She crumples into a heap against the far wall of the living room.

There's a break in the firing from inside the house although the fight still continues in the street, sirens now wailing in the distance as the local authorities rush to the scene. Derek chambers another shell as a woman rounds the corner on the landing at the top of the stairs.

Their eyes meet.

After so many months. All of the chase. The chess game they played against one another, there she is. Sarah doesn't give him one of her sarcastic smirks. No, her eyes burn with steely hatred, and her face is contorted into a grimace of pure rage. Double clutching what looks like an MP7 in her hands, she whips the weapon up while firing a burst. As the submachine gun belches, Derek dives to his left into the dining room, narrowly avoiding the spray of bullets that kick up splinters in the hardwood floors.

Regaining his feet, Derek moves to the entranceway to the dining room and leans out, angling his shotgun toward the landing at the top of the stairs. Instead of firing, however, he has to pull back in as a short, stocky man at the end of the first-floor hallway lets a burst rip from his MP7. The bullets pock the walls and punch holes through the wooden frame surrounding the front door. Another burst comes from up above, then a third from down the hall keeping him pinned.

"Come on, motherfucker!" the man screams as he fires short, staccato bursts down the hall. "You're dead! You're all fucking dead!"

Crouching down, Derek quickly leans out and levels his shotgun, letting another booming shot go in the hopes of taking the man across his groin. Not quick enough, the man ducks behind the corner of the wall as the shot sails by and hits the far living room wall. Sarah fires at him and Derek is again barely able to pull himself back before rounds rip through the drywall. He pumps his weapon, the smell of carbon and spent powder filling his nostrils.

Leaning against the wall, Derek takes a silent inventory of the rounds he's spent. When the realization comes to him he curses himself for having grabbed the firearm that he did. Even more so that he'd foolishly left his pistol at the house instead of keeping it with him while he was at Al's. Now it all came down to this. Two targets.

One shot left.

■　■　■　■　■

Maureen pushes out from behind the island and low-crawls across the kitchen. Her own blood seeping from her stomach and leg, her garments slick with it, helps her move as she pulls herself across the tile. Reaching out with bloody fingers, the retired operative grabs the magazine to her pistol from where it came to rest under the sink and rams it home. Amidst the continuous fire she lets the slide fly forward, chambering a round in the process, the noise lost in the cacophony of the battle zone.

Pushing off with the muzzle of her weapon, Maureen gets herself first to a crouch behind the island. Popping up to take a quick peek, she sees both of the assailants with their back to her. Maureen throws herself over the island. Propping up on both elbows.

The shorter man twists back into the living room. He reaches into his overalls for another magazine when his eyes catch sight of her. They go wide just as Maureen fires, putting a double tap into his sternum and throat. He is thrown back against the wall, his hands going to his neck as blood pours down the front of his body. She silences the gurgling with another round through his nose, blowing the back of his head out against the wall.

Immediately shifting her fire, Maureen sights in on the redheaded woman on the landing up above. The woman spins around, looking surprised to see that Maureen is still in the fight. The older woman opens up just as the redhead dives to her left, throwing herself to the floor in the direction of Kim's bedroom. Maureen tries to track and fire but her arms are growing weak. At the same time the woman rolls onto her side and wildly fires into the kitchen.

Maureen slumps back down as the rounds kick up

around her, sending shards of marble countertop and splintered wood into the air. She looks at the pistol in her hand, the slide once again locked to the rear. Derek's gun locker is in the closet in his bedroom. Across the living room. An entire floor plan's worth of open space with no cover.

Feeling weaker by the moment, she doesn't know if she can make it, but without any further ammunition she has no choice. Her principals, her adopted family, are in danger. As the firing stops overhead, Maureen pushes herself toward the far end of the island. If she can pull herself to her feet, maybe she can make a run for it before the redheaded woman reloads.

. . . . .

Derek hears the pistol fire coming from the kitchen and ducks out, seeing the man at the end of the hall being thrown against the wall. After another moment there is a loud, wet slap as a bullet finds his skull and snaps his head back. Derek pulls away from the fire up above, but then it abruptly cuts off and a loud thump sounds out overhead. There's an exchange of pistol and submachine gun fire and then both go quiet.

Derek darts out from the dining room and crosses the entranceway to the stairs. Racing up as fast as he can, he hears footfalls moving away from him toward his father's room, and then a slam against a door. A moment later Kim's voice carries through the house. "No! Leave us alone!"

Reaching the landing, Derek turns and finds Sarah plowing her shoulder into Kim's door, her MP7 held down in front of her. He goes to raise his shotgun but his adversary screams at him while whipping her submachine gun up first. "No way, Harrington! Drop the shit! Over the side or they're dead!"

"Derek! Help us!" Kim screams from inside the room. Barely covered by her frantic pleas are Michael's hysterical cries.

"All right, Sarah," he replies while holding up his left arm. A quick glance to his right shows Maureen peering at him from around the island. "All right, you win. Just don't hurt them, okay?" Derek heaves the shotgun with as much force as he can muster with one arm. It lands with a thud on the carpeting below, near the breakfast nook.

Sarah gives him a mischievous smirk. "You stupid bastard. You should have learned by now that I don't spare anyone. Your family is dead, Derek. I just want you to see it before you die yourself." She turns to the door and kicks it open. Kim and Michael scream.

Derek tries to rush forward but she quickly raises the weapon again to halt his progress. "Don't do it, Sarah! Please! I'm begging you!"

"Good, cowboy. I want you to beg. Do it some—"

"Shoot, Dad!" Derek screams as he throws himself onto the stairs.

From behind Sarah in the doorway to the master bedroom, the old man stands in his olive drab sweat suit. Frail and shaking, he is barely able to lift the antique over-under shotgun that normally hangs above his bed. But Stanley Harrington has always been a man of grit and determination. Of stubborn resolve and sheer focus. Dementia couldn't erase the training and combat that was ingrained into his very being. He squeezes the triggers and fires off both shells.

Not able to lift the firearm very high, the double dose of buckshot hits Sarah across her lower legs, blowing them apart. She pitches forward, screaming in agony. But still, the woman is set on her murderous path. Sarah props herself onto one elbow and fires a burst down the landing, the bullets ripping up through Stanley from his left hip to his right shoulder. The old man stumbles back and collapses onto his backside, slamming into a nightstand.

Next Sarah turns toward Kim's bedroom but Kim is flying through the doorway. She leaps onto the wounded woman, one hand grabbing the wrist that controls the MP7 while the other punches and claws with all of the fury of a mother whose young has been threatened. Sarah, writhing in pain from her legs, can do little to fight off the enraged woman. Kim twists her hand into Sarah's hair and repeatedly slams her head against the hardwood flooring, finally knocking her unconscious. Wrestling the gun away, Kim stands up and levels it at Sarah.

"No, Kim!" Derek screams as he gets back onto the landing. He rushes over to his ex-wife and grabs the weapon out of her shaking hands. He wraps his arms around her. "Are you okay? Are you okay?" he says over and over.

"What's happening? What's going on?" Kim replies, her whole body trembling. Her tears mix in with the sweat soaking the front of his T-shirt. Outside, sirens wail and the gunfire continues. Michael comes running out of his mother's room to join them. The boy cries hysterically, unable to form words.

"It's all right. The police are here now. It's almost over. Quick, follow me."

Derek moves toward his father's room, in the process spotting another man in overalls down below, standing just outside the sliding doors that lead out back. His face is a matted jumble of scorched flesh and blisters. The man grins and raises his MP7 to his shoulder.

"No!" Derek cries. He turns his back to the man and wraps his arms around his family, enveloping them with his massive frame.

Maureen rolls over onto her back, having crawled to the shotgun. With the attacker's focus on the landing above, he doesn't see the woman level the Remington 870 at him. She fires, the weapon bucking out of her grip and sending fresh pain through her wounds. The double-aught shot takes the man in his lower jaw. The attacker's eyes are still frozen in surprised agony when head and body tumble down separate from one another.

After the single shot, Derek looks back. The soles of the man's boots, toes pointing skyward, stare back at him. Maureen tosses the shotgun aside and slowly rolls onto her belly again. She begins crawling the last few feet to the couch. Bloody hands grasping the fabric, she starts pulling herself up to a seated position.

As the gunfire continues outside, Derek looks over his family. He pulls them down to the floor with him as the mantra of old priorities of work rattle through his brain. Establish security; address the wounded; redistribute ammo. He begins patting Sarah down, finding a tactical vest underneath her coveralls. Derek removes a pistol and a magazine for the submachine gun.

"What are you doing? Put a bullet in her and end this."

Derek shakes his head, his counterintelligence experience already making calculations. "We can't kill her. Quick, grab the sheet off your bed. Put tourniquets on her legs," he says while changing out the magazines on the MP7.

Kim looks at him with wet eyes, tears streaming down her face. Her lower lip quivers. "You want me to save her life? After she just tried to kill us? To kill Michael?"

"We need what she knows, Kim. This is far from over. Please. Hurry. I'm going to need your help with Dad."

Leaving her to tend to the woman, Derek races into the bedroom. His father lies slumped against the nightstand, blood soaking through his sweat suit. His breath comes out in ragged, irregular gasps. Derek kneels down and cradles the man in his arms. Stanley is thin and frail, a far cry from the powerful man he was in Derek's youth.

Three entry wounds stretch diagonally across his father's torso. One of them gurgles and produces bloody bubbles with every breath. Derek recognizes the sucking chest wound, and along with the other traumas sustained, that it is only a matter of time. Moments at best. He pulls the man closer to him.

Stanley's eyes flutter beneath his eyelids before popping open. They look around with a clarity Derek had not seen in them for several weeks now. Blinking, the father looks at his son and smiles. "Hey, lad. There's a good boy," he says, harkening back to the days when Derek was little. "You okay?"

"We're okay, Dad. Thank you. You saved their lives. And mine."

"Who, lad? Who?" His breathing becomes more irregular.

"Kim and Michael, Dad. You saved them."

"Michael," Stanley croaks out. "There's a good

boy." His eyes suddenly go wide. Stanley puts his liver-spotted hand on Derek's cheek. "You're . . . a good . . . man . . . son. Better . . . than me."

Tears fall from Derek's eyes. "Mom's waiting for you, Dad. Go to her. Be at peace now."

"Better . . . than . . . me." Stanley Harrington, Sergeant, United States Marine Corps, lets out one long, raspy breath that rattles through his broken body, and then his stare goes still.

Pulling his eyelids shut, Derek gently lays his father's body down on the floor. With the sirens and gunfight still raging outside, he knows that now is not the time to grieve. He kisses his father on the cheek and then picks up the weapons, running back out onto the landing. Kim is finishing up the makeshift dressings. Derek takes what remains of the torn bedsheets and quickly ties Sarah's hands behind her back. Next, he hands the pistol to Kim. "Dad's gone. Take this and lock yourself in his bedroom. Lie down on the floor. There's still bullets flying out there. Keep this gun trained on the door. Anyone tries to break in, you fire through it, understand?"

"Don't go, Daddy! Please!" Michael yells.

"I have to, buddy. Your Uncle Al is out there and he might be in trouble. But I'll be back. I promise." He looks Kim in the eyes again. "I promise." She nods and he leans forward, caressing her face with a bloody hand and quickly kissing her. He kisses Michael on top of the head. "Go. Now."

As Kim drags a crying Michael into the master bedroom with her, Derek rushes down the back set of stairs, past the broken side door, and crosses the kitchen. He finds Maureen slumped against the back of the sofa, her eyelids fluttering. Derek does a quick assessment of her injuries and then runs back into the kitchen, returning a moment later with several dish towels. He tears one in half and uses it to bind another over her leg wound. The woman suddenly jolts awake with pain as he packs the remaining towel into the bullet hole in her gut. Pale and bloody, she gives him a look of confusion. "The fuck are you doing here? Get outside and help Al."

"Can you hang on?"

Maureen inclines her head to the MP7. "Leave that one with me and grab one by the hall. I'll make sure no one doubles back and tries to get in this way." The woman winks at him and gives him a strained smile.

Smiling back, Derek puts the weapon in her lap, squeezes her hand, and kisses the top of her head. Rushing over to the squat man and pulling his submachine gun free from his lifeless grip. Derek finds the vest underneath the man's disguise and changes out the magazines. He grabs a spare and sticks it in his back pocket. Shouldering the weapon and holding it by the foregrip, Derek proceeds down the hall to the front door.

22

As Kellen's shot sails over a diving Derek, another man in a plate carrier opens up on the sniper, firing with the syncopated rhythm of a semi-automatic, but doing so with the reckless abandon of a man with an inexhaustible supply of ammunition. Kellen ducks down behind the sedan as the vehicle's windows and windshield shatter and pucker with spent rounds. He twists back into the street, putting himself by the front driver's side tire and chambers another bullet.

From behind the back of the van, Derek suddenly charges across the street toward the target house. Kellen tries to rotate and get his rifle up, but the man in the plate carrier suddenly appears from behind the van himself, his weapon already leveled. Kellen is barely able to get himself back in front of the sedan when the man opens up again. This time the tire that he was just seeking cover behind explodes with a rush of compressed air and burnt rubber.

Kellen raises his rifle over the hood of the car and squeezes off a round in the direction of his attacker. It feels wasteful, firing off a bullet without aiming first, but he has to make the ever-advancing man pause. The shot has its intended effect. Although it flies wide and impacts on the outside of a house down the street, the man halts his steady stalk forward. Instead he starts to inch closer to the van, squeezing off one or two rounds when he thinks he has an angle on Pugh.

The two shadow one another, Kellen moving between squatting in front of the engine block to rotating around to the passenger side, staying crouched the entire time so that he places his body behind the front tire. The man creeps out from around the front of the van to take two shots at him and then disappears back. Next he comes around the rear and takes a shot, the bullet shattering the passenger-side headlight and showering Kellen with glass.

The rate of fire slows, with the man seemingly content to keep Kellen pinned down at the front of the sedan instead of coming in for the kill. The sniper is trying to parcel out the strategy when he hears sirens in the distance. Realizing that the man is waiting until reinforcements can get to him, Kellen sets himself in motion. He times his adversary coming around the rear of the van back into the street and throws a shot his way just as the man begins to appear. The bullet ricochets off the side of the vehicle. His attacker dances back behind the van.

Kellen sees his moment. Dropping his bolt-action rifle, he sprints forward and jumps over the rear of the sedan, coming up on the passenger side of the van and crouching down by the front tire. He draws his pistol from his leg holster and waits patiently for his attacker to either come around his side of the vehicle, or take the bait he laid in the street.

His assailant chooses the latter. Opening fire rapidly, the man stalks toward the discarded weapon, more than likely thinking he had somehow separated it from Kellen and that the sniper was now incapacitated. Instead, as he walks by the front of the van, Kellen pops out from his hide. He fires three times in quick succession. Two rounds send up puffs of white dust as his bullets impact on SAPI plates, but the third hits the man high in his right shoulder, and Kellen's attacker pitches forward, hitting his head on the pavement.

The sniper moves cautiously in between the vehicles. Inside the house the sound of the massacre continues. The sirens grow louder with each passing second, but he still has time. All of his kills to this point had been at great distance. Kellen relished the faces in his scope. The look in his targets' eyes as they unknowingly breathed their last breaths. Spoke their last words.

Yet he never got to see what he truly wanted. The vacancy. The perpetual stare of the eyes, forever looking beyond as a result of the life that he had extinguished. The distance nullified bearing witness to the fruits of his labor. The caliber of his rifle did the same. Even if he could somehow walk up on his kills, there is no vacancy when staring into a pool of jelly.

Now there was an opportunity. Short though the window may be, Kellen knows he could never get this opportunity again. Walking over to the man lying prone in the street, Pugh thumbs back the hammer on his pistol. Kellen stands astride his unconscious attacker, grips his weapon in both hands, and aligns his sights on the spot where neck meets skull.

Just as he is about to depress the trigger, a police

cruiser rips around the corner and fishtails at the east end of the street. Pugh immediately raises his pistol and squeezes off shots into the windshield. The cruiser jerks to the left and then veers violently right, crashing into a parked car on the opposite side of the street. The sniper fires again, putting more rounds through the driver's side window.

As the passenger-side door opens up, Pugh sprints for his rifle and turns, holstering his sidearm in the process. Crouching in the space between the van and the bullet-riddled sedan, Kellen quickly reloads the bolt-action weapon from an elastic bandolier slid over the buttstock. As he does so the police officer who was in the passenger seat opens fire at him with his service pistol, but the shooting is frantic and not well placed. Rounds skirt around him but still the sniper leans calmly out from his improvised hide. He picks up his sight picture, regulates his breathing, and squeezes the trigger.

The bullet flies through the shattered driver's side window, across the cab, and into the officer's stomach, nearly folding the man in half in the process. Kellen racks the bolt on his rifle, grimacing as he does so. Gut-shooting someone always felt off to the sniper, unless it was his decision to have fun in doing so. True, it may lead to a kill eventually, but his was the ever-present quest for the pink mist. The headshot. The instant kill. Kellen had never settled for less than perfection, but under these circumstances he had to take what shots he could get. With the enemy so close there was no other choice but to put them down any way he could.

Two more police cruisers appear, this time approaching from the west. Kellen takes aim on one knee. His first shot takes the driver of the lead vehicle in the neck. The cruiser suddenly cuts to the right, so that the trailing car smashes into it. Bouncing the lead vehicle off of it, the trailing cruiser barrels forward.

Kellen fires his remaining two rounds into the driver of the quickly approaching car. The first strikes the female officer in the chest, the high-velocity round ripping through her bulletproof vest. The second takes off the top portion of her skull. Her foot having been on the brake, the officer's motor response to the sudden trauma is to press down. The vehicle comes to a screeching halt just a few houses down from the target home.

The officer in the passenger seat of the first vehicle exits with a Mossberg tactical shotgun and starts firing toward the van. Kellen hunkers down, reloading again and waiting for the shotgun to cease. When it does he leans back out into the street. His first round takes the officer in the knee. The second emits a wet slap as he gets a headshot on the fallen man.

More sirens wail at both ends of the street. Realizing that he is about to become seriously outgunned, Kellen drops the sniper rifle and rushes over to the man lying unconscious in the street. He rolls him over as the man emits a low moan. A shot snaps over the sniper's head and a second later another rips through the pavement next to him. Kellen quickly strips the Mini-14 from the man and grabs two spare magazines from his vest. As he rushes back to his cover, Kellen fires to the east, pouring suppressive rounds at the newly arrived officers.

Reaching the sedan, he quickly changes out magazines and then starts firing to the west to keep the heads down of the officers arriving there. Even with his suppressive fire, the quickly sighted shots occasionally finding a cop dodging from car to car, he knows it's only a matter of time before they completely close in. Kellen buys his fellow assailants extra moments with his barrage, but as the return fire intensifies, he knows that they need to exit the house in the next thirty seconds or they'll be trapped.

Changing out magazines for his last spare, Kellen catches a glance of someone in the doorframe at the target house. He immediately recognizes Derek's large build. The man levels a submachine gun at him. Pugh shoulders his Mini-14 and the two exchange bursts at one another. As Derek darts back inside Kellen knows it's time to go.

Kellen fires a few shots east and west to keep the cops' heads down then scoops up his sniper rifle and moves toward the still running van's driver's side. Rounds trail Kellen until one smacks into the action of the Remington and spins it from the sniper's hand. Kellen looks back at the shattered weapon lying on the pavement. Just as fast as the remorse is there it is equally pushed away. Kellen climbs into the driver's seat, throws the vehicle into gear, and peels out headed east.

* * * *

Derek's clip runs dry just short of cutting the sniper down, instead taking the long-range rifle out of his hands. Quickly dropping and changing magazines, he watches as Pugh climbs into the van and peels out. Al, shaking the cobwebs from his head, just barely realizes what is happening in time. The man rolls over and over to his left, narrowly avoiding the vehicle as it barrels down the street.

From inside the cover of his doorway, Derek sprays

the entire capacity of his magazine at the van but most of the rounds impact on the side of the vehicle and punch into the empty cargo area. Running dry again, Derek sprints to the side of the street where Al has come to rest against the curb. He finds the man plugging the hole in his right shoulder with his left thumb. Although obviously in pain, he seems to be better off than his wife.

"How bad?" Derek says upon reaching him.

"Straight through. Inside?"

"They killed Dad. Everyone else made it."

At the end of the street the van reaches the police vehicles. Pugh fires at the cruisers blocking the way and then drives around them, banging a left and heading into the heart of the development.

Derek looks back down at the man. "Al, Maureen's been hit. She's losing blood."

The man grimaces and then extends his free arm. "Help me up." Despite Al grunting in pain as he does so, Derek pulls the man to his feet. He takes a moment to steady himself and then looks him in the eye. "I'll take care of everything inside and call it in so the paramedics can get in here." Al's eyes go dark. The look of frustration and regret coming through at the same time. "You just get that bastard."

Handing the empty MP7 to Al, Derek sprints into the street to the nearest police cruiser. In the driver's seat he finds a female officer dead from a head wound. Lowering her to the ground as respectfully as time will allow, he climbs in and slams the door, throwing the car back into gear and taking off after the van. Derek pulls a tactical Mossberg 500 shotgun from its carrier position between the seats and puts the weapon across his lap. Reaching the end of the street, Derek whips the cruiser past the wounded and fallen officers, making a left and taking off after the van.

At first he can't see the other vehicle, but another left up ahead bears skid marks where the van slid into its turn. Derek cuts the wheel hard in that direction and then back the other way to compensate for his speed. Now racing up Meadowlake Drive he spots taillights in the distance. Derek guns the souped-up police package engine, the propulsion throwing him back in his seat.

Reaching the van, both vehicles turn left onto Plantana Boulevard. Derek takes to the left side of the street, racing up and alongside Kellen. He holds out the shotgun and fires through the passenger-side window, the shot punching a hole the size of a melon just behind the driver's side door. The sniper retaliates by jerking his wheel to the left. The two vehicles crunch as they collide with one another. Derek's cruiser ricochets from the hit and sideswipes a parked car before bouncing back, crunching into the van yet again.

Kellen's pistol appears out the driver's side window and the man starts firing down at the police car. A bullet rips into Derek's side, the blunt force accompanied by a searing burn as the metal tears through his body. Derek slams on his brakes, dropping back long enough to get out of the path of the gunfire and palm the wound. His hand comes away slick with bright red blood. Derek wipes it off on the front of his shirt and grabs his weapon again.

Gunning the engine to catch up, the two vehicles barrel down the road as it bends into a long straightaway. Racking the shotgun as he closes the distance, Derek fires at the left rear tire of the van. His shot goes high, a hole appearing in the panel just above it. He attempts the tire again but the van suddenly surges forward. The shot blows a section of the rear bumper off instead.

The sniper passes connecting side streets that would take them south but continues to head west along the straightaway. Still ahead of the cruiser, Kellen swerves the van back and forth to keep Derek at bay. Tires squeal and the smell of burnt rubber comes through the vents of the cruiser. Derek wipes sweat from his eyes and takes a few deep breaths, trying his hardest to regulate his breathing.

Have to stop him in the development. I can't let him get out onto the highway.

At Cypress Drive Kellen takes another left but then suddenly cuts his wheel all the way over in that direction and jumps the curb. The van slices into the neighborhood park between two massive oak trees. The vehicle's tires tear up the ground, throwing dual geysers of dirt and dust back at Derek. Flooring it as he jumps the curb, his car slips in the overturned earth. Derek follows the path of the dust and dirt trail, doing everything in his power to stay on Kellen's heels while also dodging in and out of trees.

The van and then the cruiser swerve to the right, both vehicles narrowly missing the community pool before smashing their way out of the park and back onto Cypress. Kellen cuts left and then a few moments later cuts right onto Brightwater Drive heading south. Derek follows and races up alongside the right side of the van. He jerks on his wheel and slams into the other vehicle. Kellen pushes back by pulling right on his wheel. The two vehicles grind against one another, throwing up sparks between them as they careen down the street.

Derek pulls the cruiser off the contact a bit, guns the engine, and then cuts back into the van again. This time the force of the hit makes it so that Kellen has no other choice but to turn left, back onto Parkshore Drive, and head toward Derek's home yet again. The van is confronted with a line of cop cars, their lights and sirens still spinning and wailing. With all of the officers already on scene either killed, wounded, or tending to the wounds of others, only two can produce their pistols and open fire.

Kellen slams on the brakes and throws his vehicle in reverse. Derek drives his cruiser up onto the front lawn of a house, throws the car into park, and hops out. Charging the shotgun, he shoulders his weapon and tracks the van. Kellen cuts the wheel as Derek fires, the shot ripping through the back doors. The sniper turns the wheel frantically in the other direction and puts the van back in drive.

Pugh begins to shoot out of his passenger-side window as the vehicle draws closer to his adversary. Derek drops into the prone position, the action sending a shockwave of pain out from his side considerable enough to override the adrenaline. Wincing, he manages to line up the bead on the end of the shotgun's barrel with the van's right rear tire. Stable and with a clear line of sight, Derek squeezes the trigger, his weapon bucking in response. The tire blows apart, shredded rubber spilling away in chunks with each subsequent revolution. The van lurches down the street, sparks and asphalt flying up as the tire gives way completely and the vehicle rides on its rim.

Racking his firearm as he pushes up from the ground, Derek climbs back into the cruiser and does a three-point turn. He accelerates quickly, both vehicles heading west. Kellen goes straight until he reaches Cumberland Road. Turning left and heading south, he leaves the development but Derek is quickly behind the van. This time when the lead vehicle swerves it does so out of a lack of control from riding on three wheels and a rim.

As the van passes the Hamilton Southeastern Schools district office, Derek races up along the right side so that the hood of his cruiser is even with the wheel showering sparks behind it. He cuts his wheel sharply to the left, putting the nose of the cruiser into the rear of the van in his best attempt at a police P.I.T. maneuver. The two vehicles lock together for a moment, inexplicably suspended as they grind against one another. Then the van spins out before pitching over its left-side tires and rolling several times across the pavement.

The cruiser surges forward as it separates from the van. Derek slams on the brakes but the vehicle is traveling too fast. It hops the curb, and the police cruiser crashes into a tree. The airbags deploy, knocking him for a loop.

. . . . .

Long moments go by as his head swirls and his vision clouds. He can hear the hissing of the vehicle's destroyed front, pieces clattering to the street as they finally break off from the rest of the cruiser. The seat creaks underneath his shifting weight.

As his mind begins to clear, Derek fights against the inflated balloon to get out of the vehicle as quickly as he can. Fearing a possible shot coming from Kellen, he drops to the pavement, the impact to his bullet wound making him cry out. Fragments of shattered glass spill out of the driver's seat with him and rain down onto the pavement before dancing away with a few bounces.

Suppressing a groan and gritting his teeth, Derek rolls onto his back. Staring at the sky, he does his best to catch his breath. Systematically he begins to take stock of his injuries. Despite being battered all over from the crash, nothing feels like it is broken. He gently probes the hole in his right side and then palms the wound, trying to gauge how much blood he's losing. Derek rocks slightly onto his left side and works his hand around to his lower back. The exit wound confirms that the bullet isn't still lodged in him. Tugging his T-shirt, Derek starts trying to force the fabric into the open holes.

As he does so the sound of a door being forced open comes from the wreck of the van. Derek searches the street by looking under the wrecked cruiser. A pair of boots hit the blacktop before Kellen crumples into view. The eyes of the two men meet. Suffering from his own cuts and bleeding, the sniper quickly pushes himself up to his hands and knees. Derek's focus on first aid recedes as he gets himself into a seated position. Reaching back into the cruiser, his hand finds the shotgun. Derek pulls himself up and leans over the hood, cradling his firearm as he tries to acquire his target. Locating the man as he dashes across the blacktop, Derek tracks the sniper and is about to pull the trigger when Kellen darts into a patch of woods.

23

They sprint through a misting rain, the clouds a promise of the volume to come. Derek's heart races. His adrenaline pumps through his limbs. His ears are attuned to the woods around him.

This time he is right on the sniper's heels. This time the terrain and trails are known to him. The land is in his favor. He loops around, coming up parallel to the old cemetery just as he sees Kellen entering it at a dead sprint. Shotgun to his shoulder, Derek tracks and fires just as the sniper disappears behind a tree. The bark explodes into a cloud of sawdust.

Two shots come back at him, hitting the tree next to Derek's head. He pumps his weapon, the empty shell looping to the ground as the rain begins to fall in earnest with it. Smoke tendrils curl up from the open chamber. A look into it reveals the absence of a shell sitting in the carousel, ready to be slammed forward.

Lifting his eyes he sees Kellen staring back at him from across the graveyard, as still and silent as the markers all around them. The slide locked to the rear on his weapon, he discards the handgun as if it were a finished corncob. Kellen's eyes remain fixed. Unwavering. As the rain comes down harder and begins to soak both men, Derek drops the shotgun at his feet.

The two start toward each other, walking between rows of centuries-old headstones. Derek assesses the man, his mind a constant evaluator, taking in all manner of information. Pugh's height and weight. The wiry frame with long limbs. While the data of his enemy registers, a plan of attack formulates in his mind. It takes all of his concentration to resist the tide of rage surging through his thoughts.

This man, who had left those women and children in the homestead. Who ordered them to stay there in the hopes of creating a catastrophe like the one that unfolded. The same man who then killed Gerbowski. Who paralyzed Drysdale. Who was part of the group that tried to kill his son. His wife. For the second time their lives had been put in danger by these terrorists. It's enough to send him into a frenzied barrage. To attack like the fabled Viking berserkers of old.

Instead, as they draw closer, Derek's calculations take hold. Kellen is a practiced killer, one possibly as steady and deadly away from his trigger as he is behind it. Rather than a tidal wave overcoming him, Derek feels the rush of hatred as if it were the pulse of water channeling through a hydroelectric dam. The turbines engage, spinning up with the extra rainfall.

Generating power.

His breathing steadies. His mind focuses, the pain of his injuries dropping into the background of his consciousness. His legs are limber and loose from the sprint through the woods, suddenly reenergized. Derek flexes his fingers into fists again and again, the water dripping from his knuckles. He suddenly dashes the last few feet, quickly closing the distance to Kellen in the hopes of catching the sniper by surprise. Derek adds to the maneuver by feinting a punch with his left and then delivering an over-the-top right.

The move works, his fist cracking Kellen in the left eye and spinning him halfway around. Despite the force behind Derek's punch, the sniper twists back, delivering a two-punch combo of his own with his right. An uppercut to the ribs and a hook to the jaw land in quick succession. The strikes are exacting, eliciting a sting and burn in both spots. The two dance back from one another. Although their eyes begin to swell, they stare each other down.

Now it's Kellen who presses, leading with a roundhouse kick with his right that Derek drops back from and a front kick with his left that Derek blocks. A straight jab and cross follow with Derek just getting his hands up in time to absorb most of the blows even though Kellen's knuckles still make an impact on his skull.

The sniper finds his range and starts making use of his long legs. Twice he crashes roundhouse kicks into Derek's left thigh. When Derek tries to advance, another right roundhouse is thrown. It slams into Derek's left side just as he is able to collapse his arm in to absorb the contact and protect his ribs. The sniper's shin bone sends a ripple of pain, followed by a numbing tingle through Derek's limb. Kellen adds a cross that cracks him just above the ear before spinning away from any possible counterattack.

Derek's head rings and his body reverberates with pain from where he's been hit. His mind computing all of the initial intake, a distinct style begins to fall into place. He realizes the longer, faster, and younger fighter is well trained in martial arts, most likely Muay Thai. Despite lacking the official confirmation, Derek's surmised conclusion immediately shifts to potential countermeasures. Before allowing the man to enter into another exchange, Derek rushes Kellen and latches onto him, looking to play to his physical strength and grappling ability.

Tying up with the man, Derek gets his left hand behind Kellen's neck and throws two short punches into the sniper's torso before curling his arm inward and landing his elbow flush on the man's jaw. Derek uses the momentum of the impact to twist into Kellen and toss him over his hip. The sniper goes head over heels, landing in the muddy ground and rolling into a headstone that topples over. The man springs up, his normally placid face locked in a sneer of pure savagery. The way a gray wolf might bare its teeth to a rival.

"Come on, you son of a bitch!" Derek calls over the rain, waving Kellen in with his hands.

The ensuing rush and onslaught of attacks is one that Derek is hard-pressed to fend off, with punches and kicks landing wherever the openings might allow. His concerted effort to protect the bullet wound in his side provides ample opportunity for his enemy to strike elsewhere. Derek tries again to tie up. To take the fight to close quarters. Kellen is ready for it. The sniper crashes an elbow of his own before interlacing his hands behind Derek's head. He begins sending knees into Derek's ribs.

The right-knee impact feels like a sledgehammer. Kellen's left knee lands near Derek's entry wound, eliciting an agonizing scream in response. When the right knee lands a second time, Derek feels the sharp pain of a snap and his breathing immediately gets shorter. Still, he manages to loop his arm under Kellen's raised leg and catch the man under his knee before Pugh can set it back down. At the same time he grabs Kellen by the throat and with a guttural yell, heaves the man through the air. The sniper crashes into another headstone, this time the ancient marker shattering upon impact.

Derek staggers back. Limping. Clutching his side. Doing everything he can to bring his breathing under control. Each inhale is fire. Each exhale is ragged.

The sniper pushes up from the ground, taking his time. He goes to a knee first, spits to the side, and then stands. Instead of the sneer, his placid mask has mostly returned, save for the hint of a smile on his lips. He knows the same as Derek.

The man comes forward, hands flashing up. He throws a series of three roundhouse kicks in quick succession. The left crashes into Derek's right arm. The right kick connects with Derek's damaged ribs, forcing out a cry that bends him to his left. The movement is enough to lower Derek's head to a level that Kellen's third kick cracks him in the skull.

The bigger man sails to the ground, crashing through a headstone and splintering it to pieces. Stars flash before his eyes. Derek shakes his head to ward off the threatening darkness. He feels the saturated ground soaking into his back. The rain pours down, hitting him in the face.

Move, riffles through his mind. *You. Have to. Move.*

Yet he can't. He's exhausted. He can barely breathe. He shivers against his drenched clothing. Derek watches as the man crosses to stand over him. Pugh bends down and draws a boot knife, his eyes momentarily diverted. In that same instant, Derek makes a last-ditch effort to keep fighting. He rolls over onto his right side in an attempt to get to his feet.

The pain of turning with broken ribs and a gunshot wound helps to snap him awake. There, at the edge of his outstretched hand, is a triangular shard of tombstone, elongated and jagged. As Kellen straightens, Derek grabs the stone and rolls back, thrusting the makeshift dagger into the inner thigh of the sniper and then ripping upward toward the groin.

Kellen jumps back, freeing himself from the impalement. The knife falls away as his hands clutch the gaping wound, the sniper's emotionless face alighting with shock. As he hurries away a thin stream of blood squirts between his fingers in synchronization with his rapid pulse. More blood cascades down his leg, covering his hands.

Derek rushes to his feet with a surge of adrenaline, dropping the shard in the process so that he can push off the ground. Kellen, so focused on his massive bleed, doesn't notice. Derek puts everything he has left in him into one final punch. His fist smashes directly into Kellen's nose. The sniper's head snaps back as the cartilage shatters, a spray of bloody fluid and water flying from his head in the process. As Pugh careens to the ground, he breaks another headstone in half. The man rolls over once onto his back, moaning lightly. Derek stumbles forward and drops on top of his bleeding adversary, pinning the sniper down with his knees.

"You left those women and kids in there to die," Derek says as he grabs the top half of the broken headstone. "You killed my friend. Came after my family." He raises the stone above his head. Kellen looks up and his eyes, perhaps for the first time in his life, betray him.

Fear.

"I'll see you in hell," Derek growls.

The headstone is brought down with such force that the sniper's blood flies into the air upon impact. Derek flinches as some of it lands on his face. Kellen's left leg twitches like a rattlesnake's tail before going still.

Derek lets the granite fall from his hands. He turns his face up to the sky, the rain washing over his bleeding and bruised body. After some time he flops onto his back next to the corpse. Shivering, exhausted, and too weak to stand, he lets the darkness start to close in. Before it overtakes him completely he thinks he sees beams of light slashing through the woods, and voices carrying over the storm.

24

Punching the power button on the remote tethered to his hospital bed, Derek tosses the instrument to the side and leans his head back against the pillow. The baseball game that was on the TV hanging up in the corner of his room winks out of existence. He had hoped that watching America's pastime might help take his mind off of things, even if only for a few hours. Hell, he would've taken a few minutes at this point, but it was proving impossible.

It seemed like every commercial break there was local news reporting updates on the firefight that had occurred in his home and neighborhood. Fishers is a quiet, tranquil community. The gunfight was still headline news three days later. The shootout even made national news for a time.

Derek had tired of seeing the anchors regurgitating the dribs and drabs of information that they had learned. Of seeing the BREAKING NEWS banner scrolling on the bottom of the screen. Of live shots of a field reporter speaking into the camera, the cover house the FBI had provided for his family acting as a backdrop.

Initially treated at the Indiana University Health Saxony Hospital in the immediate aftermath of the attack, the Bureau whisked Derek and his family away as soon as the doctors deemed him stable enough for travel. Placed in the hospital on the Grissom Air Force Reserve Base, Derek was kept under observation while Kim and Michael were placed in on-base housing. The secure perimeter put a halt to any possibility of reporters and photographers trying to get their exclusive with him.

She stopped bringing Michael by after the first night. The sight of his father, battered and bruised with all manner of tubes and machines hooked up to him, proved too much for the boy to handle, and rightfully so. A pit forms in his stomach and Derek groans every time he thinks of what his son has been through.

Derek shudders at the thought of how much damage has been done to his son. How traumatized he would be in the years to come. There would be countless iterations of therapy, no doubt. Derek wonders if Michael will ever feel safe anywhere, ever again.

With the thought comes the memory of what he and Kim had discussed yesterday. She had sat there at his bedside. Crying. Shaking. Knowing what she had to do but distraught over the fact that she had to do it. Barely able to get out the words, she had laid her head down on his mattress and let the sheets soak up her tears. Derek had stroked her hair gently, as he always had in their tender moments, and let his own tears fall unabated. She kissed him quickly on the lips not long after that and practically sprinted from the room, leaving Derek the rest of the night and all of today to contemplate.

A knock at the door picks his head up. Kim walks

into the room. She wears a pair of black yoga pants and a hoodie, her hair pulled back into a high ponytail. Kim gives him a warm smile but her eyes betray her. They're red and puffy, and it's clear that on top of her crying she has barely slept in the last three days.

"Hey you," she says.

"Hey," Derek replies, trying to force a smile of his own.

She jerks a thumb over her shoulder as she crosses to the chair next to his bed and sits down. "I just came from seeing Maureen and Al. Those two are too much."

"How are they doing?"

"They're incredible. Al is chomping at the bit to get discharged and Maureen, believe it or not, is practically right behind him. You would never know that the woman was on death's doorstep a few days ago."

Derek chuckles a bit. "They don't make them like they used to."

"Oh, for sure," Kim says, chuckling a bit herself. Both of their laughs fall flat. Eyes interlocking, Kim swallows before taking a deep breath. As she opens her mouth, Derek beats her to the punch.

"You're right, Kim. More than anything that you've been right about before. I'm going to do what you asked."

She looks a little stunned. As if prepared for a lengthy fight that she now realizes isn't going to happen. The defenses she prepared slowly begin to evaporate. "You are?"

"I have to." He raises a hand as she goes to respond. "It's not a matter of it being an ultimatum or anything like that. It's what's right. It's what's best for you. For the both of you."

Sniffling, the tears begin to streak down her face again. "The last thing I want to do is keep him from you. I know how much he means to you."

"He means everything," Derek replies, adding a moment later, "You both do."

"I know," Kim replies, lowering her head.

Taking her hand, Derek goes on. "Kim, look at me. Please." Her eyes meet his. "He's our son. We both know that either of us would trade our life for his. In this case, that's exactly what I have to do. I have to sacrifice a life with him, and with you, in order to keep you both safe.

"They've come after you twice. This group is merciless. Evil. They know that you're my weakness, and being near me puts you in even greater danger. " He swallows.

"So . . . you'll let us go then?" Kim asks, her lower lip trembling.

He nods slowly in response. They're both silent for a few moments. She squeezes Derek's hand and he squeezes it back. "You won't be going alone though. I know you'd fight tooth and nail to keep Michael safe, but this is my world, not yours. You're not in the intelligence business. You wouldn't last more than a week on your own, and quite frankly, I can't let you go if you insist on doing that."

Searching his eyes, Kim absorbs the words. She furrows her eyebrows, trying to figure out what he means while simultaneously being taken aback by his admission. "What do you have in mind then?" she asks.

"I spoke with some people today. Folks I know from my time in that have gone on to the private sector. Maureen and Al reached out to their own contacts. You're going to be set up with new covers. Get established in a new location. You're not going to stay in the U.S. From what we know, Autumn's Tithe doesn't have a reach beyond our borders, and you can have somewhat normal lives once you're in place. I don't know any of the details, so even if Tithe somehow manages to get ahold of me, you'll be secure.

"Everything is going to be done through multiple channels, with dead ends and double backs built in. All of the details will be segmented and compartmentalized. Most importantly, it'll be done outside of the agency networks. Whatever connections that group has inside the government will be neutralized. You'll be wiped from the grid. Gone without a trace. I should have done it at the outset of all this. I just didn't realize how much they have infiltrated our agencies. No one did."

"You can do that?"

Derek nods again. "I have done it. The wheels are already in motion. There will be people with you and watching over you for a bit. Ones that the three of us know and trust. Al and Maureen will join you once they are back on their feet."

"They're going to stay on with Michael and me?"

This time when Derek chuckles it's genuine. "I spoke at length with them this morning. You're not wrong about their vitality. I hope I have the motor that they both do when I reach that age. They wanted to re-up with the agency and help go after these bastards. On top of your lives being endangered, they both took getting shot really, really personally. With some effort I convinced them the best thing that they could do was stay with you two. That way I'll know you're safe and have the peace of mind I need to see this through. Their connections will wipe them clean as well."

"Derek . . . I don't know what to say."

His face grows grim again. "This won't be easy, Kim. You're going to have to alter your appearance. Nothing like surgery, don't worry about that, but things like your hairstyle. The color. How you dress. Michael too. You'll have to wear contacts to change the color of your eyes. You'll be remote, out in the countryside somewhere.

"The measures we're taking will help you live as close to a normal life as possible. Maybe let you get back to nursing at some point. Let Michael go to school and play sports. Have friends eventually. At the same time, I'm going to need you to train. Both you and Michael. You need to learn from Al and Maureen. By the time they're done, you two will be completely self-sufficient. You'll be safe, but you're also going to be prepared. I have to know that's the case if I'm going to let you go."

She wipes her eyes and swallows. Her face grows dark at the prospect of what he's laying out. "Derek, I get all of that for me, but he's a child."

"He is, but that time is short now. They did that to him. I want Michael to be a kid. To have a normal life. More than anything, I want that. Maybe he'll get to be for a bit longer, but at the same time he needs to be ready. You both do."

While she looks out the window, Derek is content to let the realization settle in. Life as they know it will never be the same. He watches her internalize what he has told her. Derek knows that she doesn't like it. Hates it actually.

A part of her probably hates him as well for putting them in this position in the first place. But she will always default back to Michael. To what is right for his protection. She might resent it for the rest of her days, but Kim would go along with Derek's plan. After a few moments she looks back at him. "What will you do?"

The anger wells up inside of him. A steady burn that continues to consume all the fuel it's been fed. His face grows red. The muscles in his jaw pulse as Derek grinds his teeth. Kim pulls back slightly at seeing the sudden transformation.

"I'm going to see this thing through to the bitter end. Before it was about going along with the FBI. Making sure that the conditions of our agreement were met. Yes, I wanted to stop them, but it was about justice. Now it's about revenge. Eradication. They have no idea what they've unleashed. What's coming for them."

She just stares at him. Her face is placid. Kim regards him, as if seeing him for the first time. In many ways that's the truth. He had worked his whole career and his time since retiring to keep this side of him walled away, but now there was no need to keep the animal caged any longer. Now was the time to let it out. "When does this all begin?"

He takes a deep breath to calm himself before continuing. "There are people at the house gathering some things for you two even as we speak. I've consulted with Jason and Rob. They're going to ensure a warm handoff between the agents assigned to your protection and my people. You'll be on the move by tonight."

The tears reappear. They fall with her acknowledging nod. "And you? Where will you go?"

"Sarah is still in her medically-induced coma from the blood loss. It'll probably take several weeks if not longer for her to recover and rehabilitate enough to travel. When the doctors give the go-ahead the FBI will be extraditing her back to New York to face indictment for what happened upstate last year. I'm going to be part of that escort, and then work with the FBI gathering the intelligence we need from her. She's the key. Sarah's knowledge can bring this entire network to the ground. Once we know what she knows, I'm going to tear them apart. Piece by piece."

Kim nods slowly. "All right."

They hold each other's stare for a long time, neither one willing to speak next. Eventually Derek works up the courage to do so. This is his mess, he should be the one to say it, not her. Besides, he had been preparing for this part all day. Walling up the emotions that might intervene brick by painful brick. Kim had only just learned of what was to come. It shouldn't be on her to pull the trigger.

"Kim . . ." he says quietly.

"Yes?"

"You have to go now. Please. Before I lose my resolve." His voice catches in his throat with the last few words.

She just stares, unable to move. Perhaps unwilling. He likes to think it might be the latter. Then she surprises him by springing out of the chair and throwing her arms around him. Kim buries her face into the crook of his neck as he wraps his arms around her back. They sob into one another. When he is able to find his words he whispers into her ear.

"I love you. I love Michael. Make sure he knows. Make sure that no matter what happens, he knows that I'm doing this for him. If I can find you two, if it's safe, I will. But if not, you keep your head down. You keep—"

She cuts him off by pressing her lips to his. They fold into the kiss, locked for a few short moments into what they once were. Derek experiences every ounce of love he feels for this woman. The electricity they felt on their first date. When he kissed her after they exchanged their vows. On the day that Michael was born. Through the wall he feels the twinge in his heart, and it's all that he can do to stop himself from begging her to stay. Or to let him come with her. But Derek knows. He knows that there can be no other way than this. Not until it's finished.

Kim must know it too. Must have accepted it, because she breaks off their connection and stares into his eyes. A moment later she wheels about and strides from the room without looking back. He can hear her crying down the length of the hall until she exits through the double doors leading out of the wing. Derek rests his head back against the pillow again.

Now he is truly alone. Truly separated from them. Now they will be safe. Now he can focus. Without impairment. Without distraction. Without concern.

Now it was time to hunt.

ACKNOWLEDGMENTS

The dream was always to get a book published. Just one. That's it. That's all I ever wanted, and I am exceptionally fortunate and grateful to live that dream. So you might imagine that when your agent tells you that they secured a two-book deal for you right out of the gate, you're absolutely floored by the dream doubling with a pen stroke. Such was the case for me, and I am indebted to my intrepid agent, Barbara Poelle, for making those dreams a reality.

During the process of writing this book, Barbara approached me with her plans to open her own literary agency, and very graciously and professionally presented me with my options moving forward. Without hesitation I told her that I was following her, such is my implicit trust in her. I feel privileged to have such a person in my corner for all the phases of this at times crazy industry, but it is especially rewarding to see someone who works so hard on behalf of her clients reaching her own new heights. Once again, huge congratulations to you, Barbara! I'm honored to be counted amongst the original cohort of authors signed with Word One Literary.

My other partner in crime in this endeavor is the exceptional Robert Davis, my editor. Once again, he has worked his magic, guiding the manuscript through revisions and rewrites in order to get the very best story onto the page. Between you and me, there was an entirely different construct to *The Infiltrator* when I first turned it in. Robert's expertise was on point, and helped me to realize what needed to stay, what needed to be tabled for a different book, and what I needed to add to get Derek and company up and above standard. With both Robert and Barbara I feel as though I've got a double-sided coin in my pocket. No matter how it lands, I come out a winner.

This is not to say that the contributions are any less for the multitude of people it takes to get a book into your hands. I have always said that I wanted and needed to go traditional, because quite frankly I'm not capable of handling everything necessary to bring a manuscript to life on my own. As such, I am tremendously grateful for the professionalism and precision that the Tor/Forge team brings to the table. In no particular order, thank you to Ariana Carpentieri, Ashley Spruill, Troix Jackson, Julia Bergen, Jeff LaSala, Heather Saunders, Jacqueline Huber-Rodriguez, Sara Robb, Peter Lutjen, Katy Robitzski, and Rafal Gibek.

Special shout-outs to Katy Robitzski, Emma Paige West, and Drew Killman on the Macmillan Audio side of the house, and the talented Jay Snyder for his tremendous presentation of Derek and company.

Much respect and admiration to my fellow members of the Poellean fearsome foursome (what we call ourselves), Nick Petrie, Bill Schweigart, and Don Bentley. These gentlemen are always available to impart their vast wisdom and encouragement on this rookie, and I am forever grateful for their mentorship and friendship. I continue to be in awe of the masterful storytelling that they produce.

There are a bevy of other authors across the spectrum that I also consider friends, mentors, partners in crime, etc. The list is expansive and I appreciate each and every one of you, but in particular thanks to Mark Greaney, Simon Gervais, Connor Sullivan, Joshua Hood, Brian Andrews and Jeff Wilson, Jeff Circle, Steve Stratton, A.M. Adair, and Jeff Clark. I'd like to especially thank Jack Stewart for helping me to achieve the authenticity I chase, in this context with the application of his close air support experience.

Special recognition goes out to the fellow members of my International Thriller Writers Debut Class of 2023, especially Lauren Nossett, Adam Sikes, I.S. Berry, Jon Payne, Michelle Cruz, and the incredible DEFCON5 duo of Dominique Richardson and Sorboni Bancrjee. I appreciate everyone's support, feel honored to be included amongst such talented authors, and look forward to seeing us all grow as authors together in the years to come.

The astounding beta readers that worked on this project deserve so much more than a few lines written here, as their unselfish donation of time and feedback worked to enhance the story to levels I couldn't see on my own. But beyond that, they are some of my most steadfast friends, and often their beta reader duties extend beyond critiquing a manuscript to also helping this author keep his motivation and sanity. First and foremost is my lifelong friend Manny Mosquera, whose depth of the thriller genre knows no bounds, and his lovely wife Chantal, who took a chance and dove into these stories reading *The Instructor* and then *The Infiltrator* back-to-back. Ms. Megan Hallquest, previously known as the Princess of Post-it notes, now forever to be known as the Queen of Quality Assurance. As always, thank you to Stacy Mallia, who has the astounding ability to provide either a kick in the ass or the sunshine necessary to dismiss my self-imposed woe-is-me clouds.

Large sections of the original draft of this novel were written while I was a patient receiving treatment in Veterans Affairs hospitals during the worst PTSD episode I have ever experienced. Quite literally, hitting rock bottom. As always, writing proved to be both an escape and a catharsis for me, but it was the exceptional work and care provided by the staff of the departments I progressed through that allowed me to offload burdens I had carried for far too long, and slowly but surely claw my way back to more of who I once was than I have ever felt since my treatment began.

The VA system rightfully deserves much of the criticism it receives, but within the walls of those clinics and hospitals are dedicated professionals working day in and day out to help heal wounds visible and invisible. I will never forget the kindness and professionalism shown to me during that time. To those nurses, doctors, case managers, counselors, and support staff—most notably those in the VA Northport hospital's Unit 22, and those in the VA Montrose hospital's Building 28 and Building 15CD—thank you. Without you I don't know if I would be here writing this today. You can never know how truly grateful I am for the second chance at life you helped me achieve.

ACKNOWLEDGMENTS

Thank you to my family, for whom that episode was a particularly trying time, and for whom I am forever thankful to have had your love and support in the years since. Being a part of a family as strong as ours is a blessing I hold dear. Thank you to MJ for all that you have done and continue to do for our girls. I see your hard work and dedication and appreciate it immensely.

Finally, to those two girls, not so little anymore. The joys of my life, Michaela and Charlotte, without whom my days would be meaningless. It is a privilege to be your father. To watch you both grow and succeed in all that you undertake. You have such intelligence, discipline, and talent that the world is yours for the taking. I firmly believe that you can achieve anything that you want in this life. You just have to be willing to put in the work and overcome the adversity. Do that, and your dreams will come true. I love you both, my beautiful daughters. Thank you for making my dream of being a dad come true.

TOR PUBLISHING GROUP

Your destination for all things genre

Visit **TorPublishingGroup.com** for a full catalog of our authors and titles. Plus, sign up for imprint newsletters for all the latest updates, including book recommendations for readers of all ages who love science fiction, fantasy, mystery, thriller, horror, romance, speculative fiction, humor, and contemporary fiction.